PAUL ROMAN MARTINEZ
PRESENTS

THE ADVENTURES OF THE 19XX
- BOOK ONE -

RISE OF THE BLACK FAUN

ALPHA 1933 EDITION

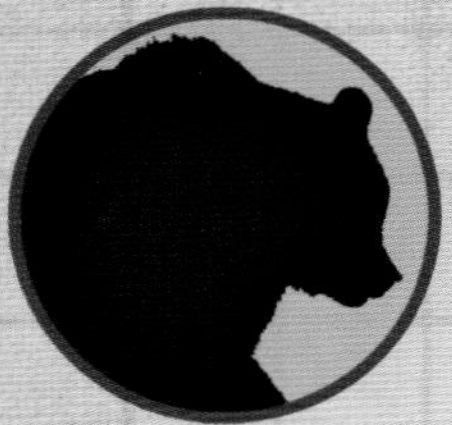

The Carpathian

THE LEGENDARY AIRSHIP THE 19XX CALLED HOME.

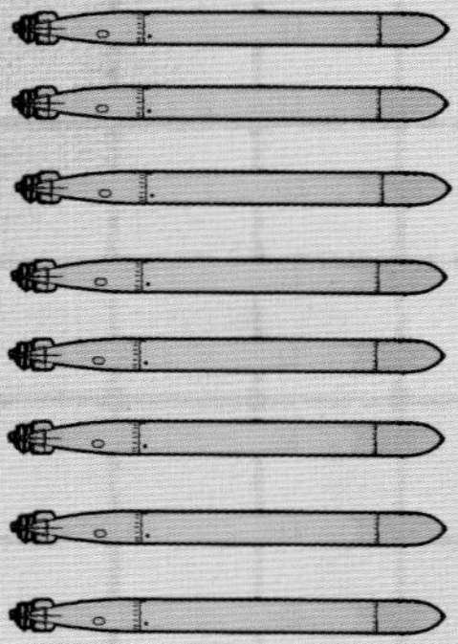

FACTS

Hydrogen/Helium Mixture

Weapons

Four hidden Bren Light machine guns
Two guns on observation deck–
2x Double Browning M2HB (Heavy Barrel)
Anti-submarine–up to 8 MK 15 torpedoes

Speed

8-1,050hp engines
Top speed of 95mph

Range

Over 30 hours of flying time

Length

810 ft

Up to 100 total passengers and crew

Technology

Long range radio
Electricity generating turbine
Long range visual communications
Communications and electrical systems designed by Nikola Tesla

Vehicles

Capable of carrying four small planes and several scouting balloons

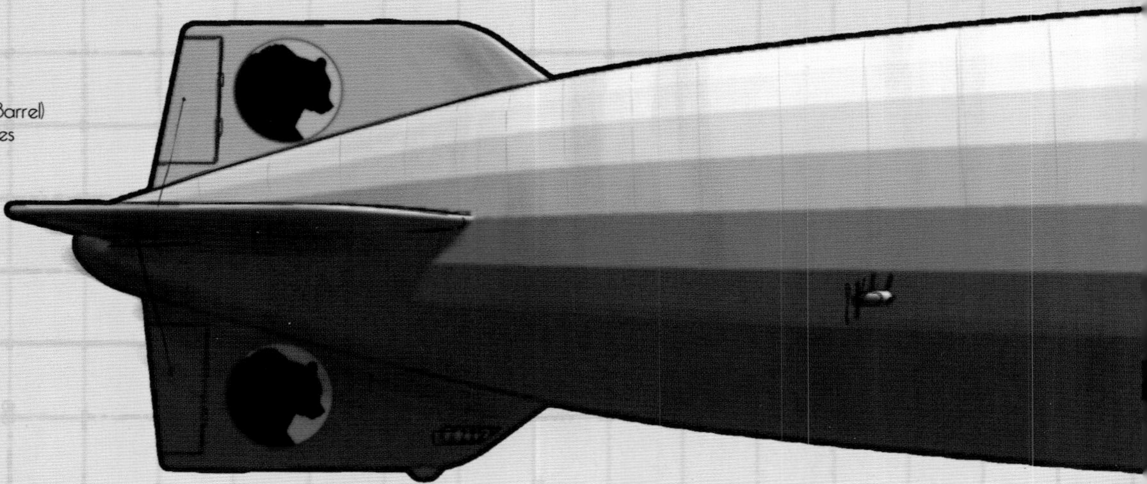

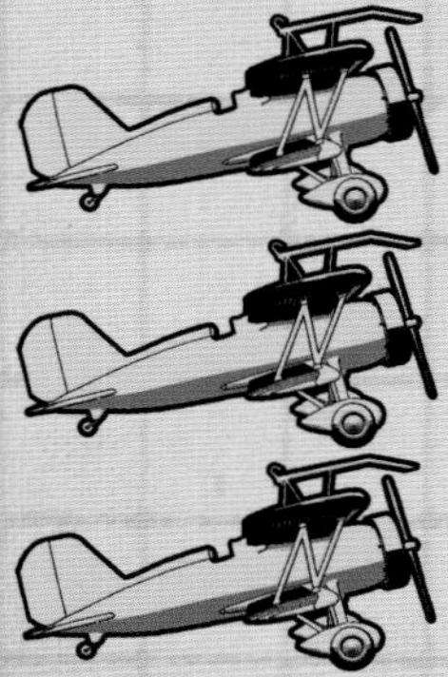

x4 Curtiss F9C-4 Sparrowhawks

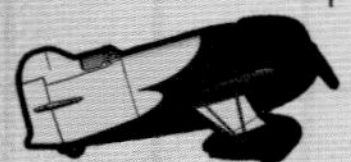

x1 Blue Bee pursuit plane

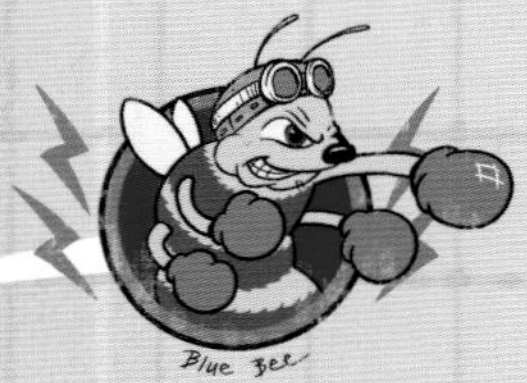
Blue Bee

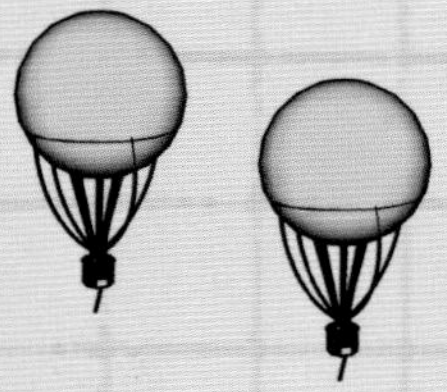

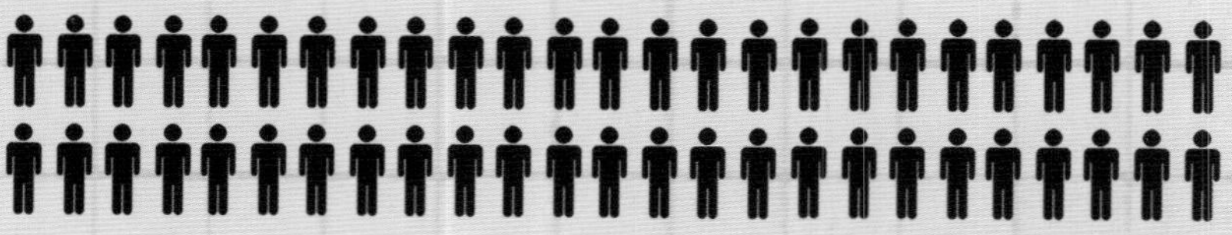

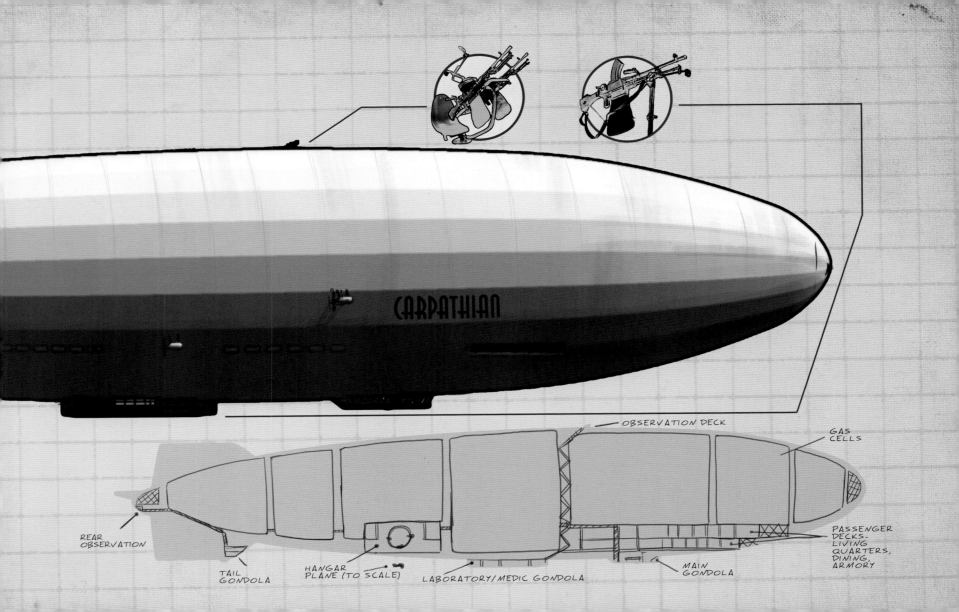

CARPATHIAN

OBSERVATION DECK

GAS CELLS

REAR OBSERVATION

TAIL GONDOLA

HANGAR PLANE (TO SCALE)

LABORATORY/MEDIC GONDOLA

MAIN GONDOLA

PASSENGER DECKS- LIVING QUARTERS, DINING, ARMORY

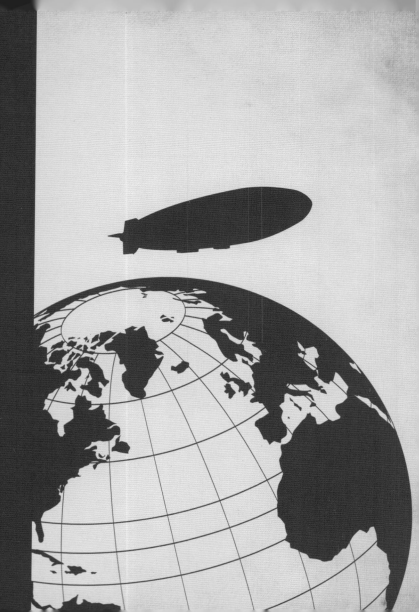

Welcome aboard! You are holding in your hands the first volume of *The Adventures of the 19XX*. This book was originally published in a small, experimental print run in 2011. The version seen here is once again self published. It contains the original pages plus new pages and reformatted artwork. My goal with the 19XX was to shine a light on aspects of the 1930s that are often overlooked in history classes. And as I started doing research for this project, I had more and more moments where I said to myself, "Wow, this was around in the '30s?!"

I read about buildings that today still look like they were created by visionaries. I read about aircraft that, if I hadn't seen pictures, I wouldn't have believed they ever flew. I read about genius inventors, obsessions with the occult, and watched a lot of excellent 1930s films.

I hope that you find a few of these things as interesting as I have.

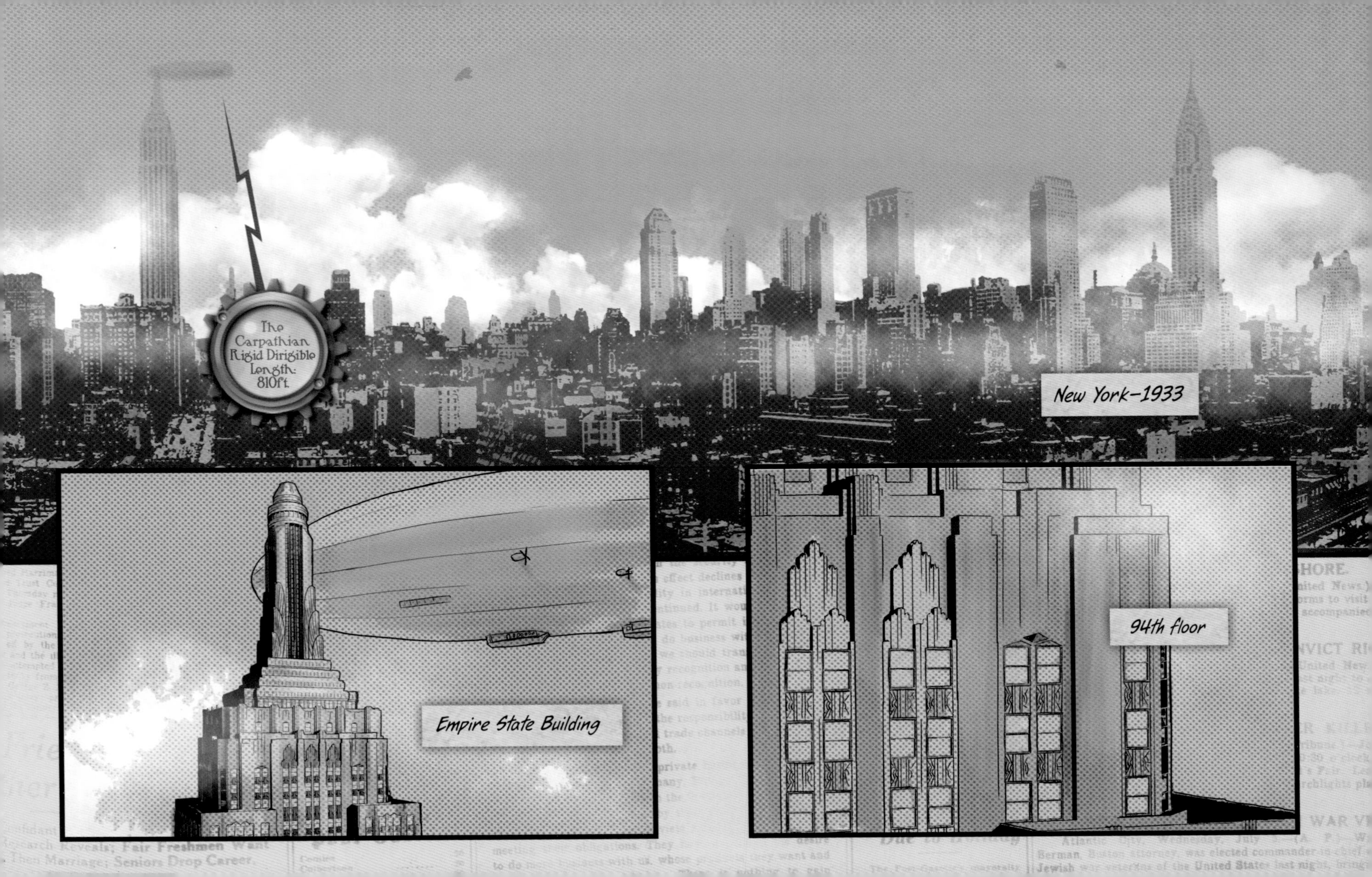
The Carpathian Rigid Dirigible Length: 810ft.
New York–1933
Empire State Building
94th floor

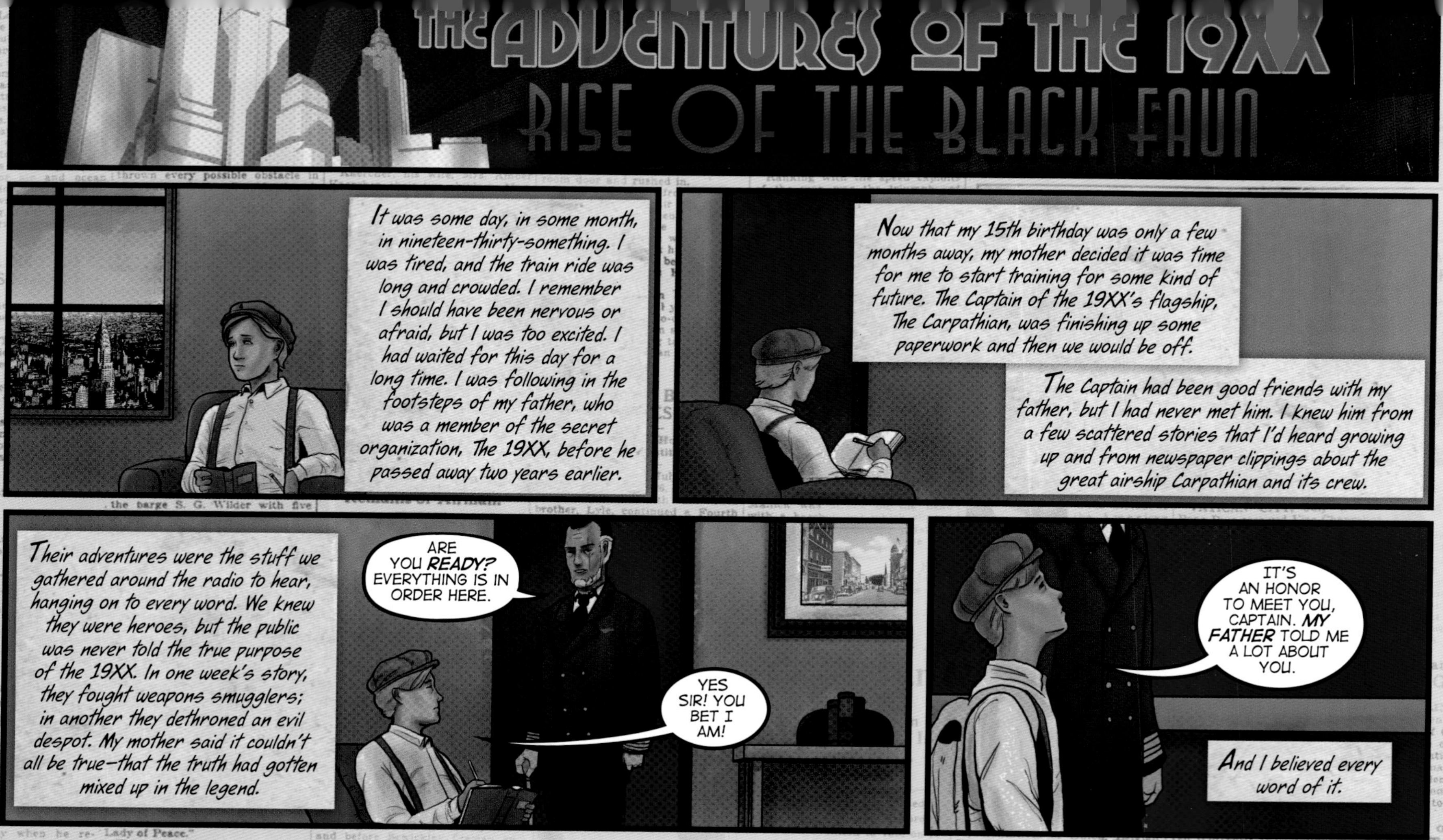
THE ADVENTURES OF THE 19XX
RISE OF THE BLACK FAUN
It was some day, in some month, in nineteen-thirty-something. I was tired, and the train ride was long and crowded. I remember I should have been nervous or afraid, but I was too excited. I had waited for this day for a long time. I was following in the footsteps of my father, who was a member of the secret organization, The 19XX, before he passed away two years earlier.
Now that my 15th birthday was only a few months away, my mother decided it was time for me to start training for some kind of future. The Captain of the 19XX's flagship, The Carpathian, was finishing up some paperwork and then we would be off.
The Captain had been good friends with my father, but I had never met him. I knew him from a few scattered stories that I'd heard growing up and from newspaper clippings about the great airship Carpathian and its crew.
Their adventures were the stuff we gathered around the radio to hear, hanging on to every word. We knew they were heroes, but the public was never told the true purpose of the 19XX. In one week's story, they fought weapons smugglers; in another they dethroned an evil despot. My mother said it couldn't all be true—that the truth had gotten mixed up in the legend.
ARE YOU READY? EVERYTHING IS IN ORDER HERE.
YES SIR! YOU BET I AM!
IT'S AN HONOR TO MEET YOU, CAPTAIN. MY FATHER TOLD ME A LOT ABOUT YOU.
And I believed every word of it.

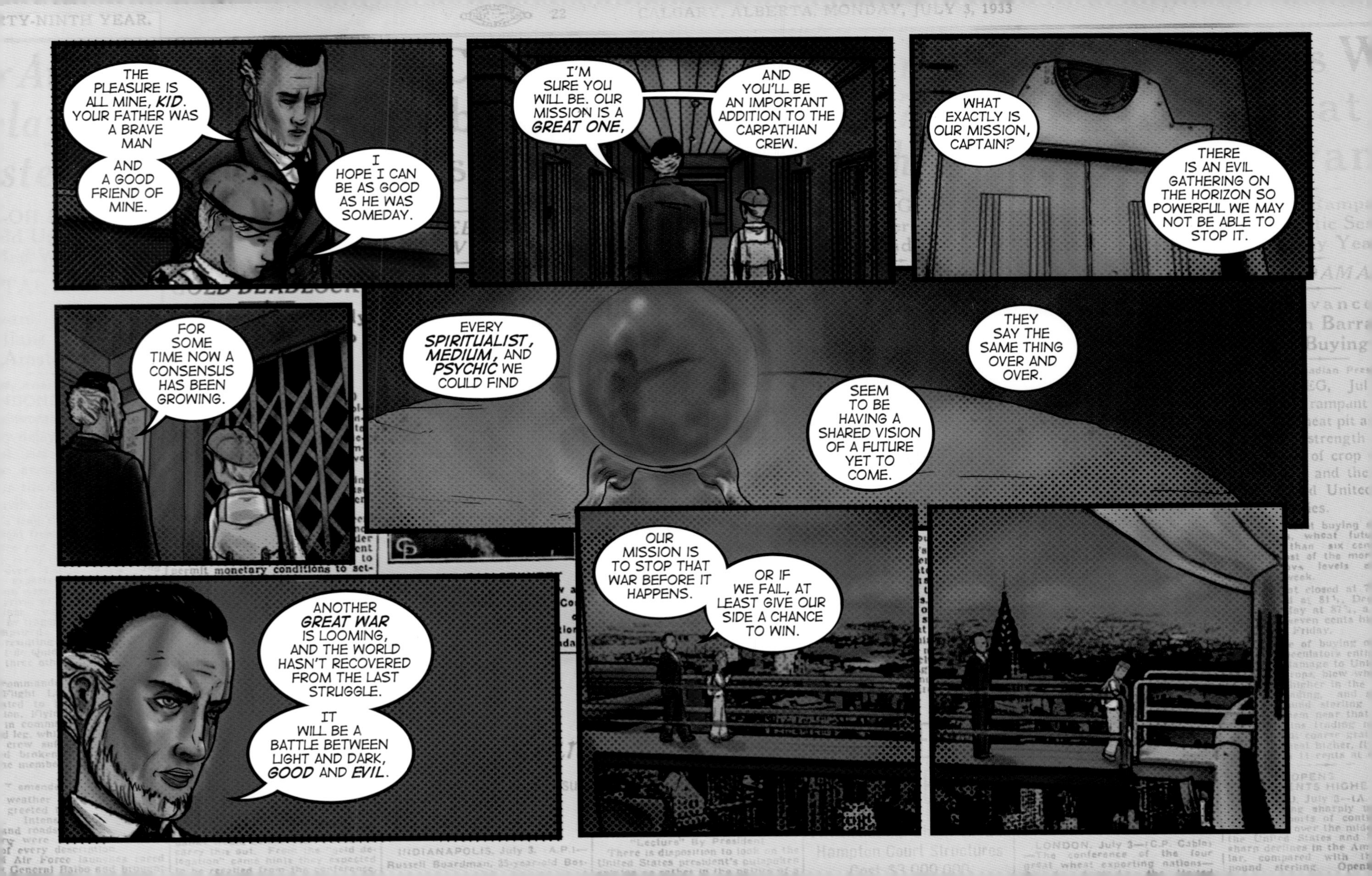
THE PLEASURE IS ALL MINE, KID. YOUR FATHER WAS A BRAVE MAN
AND A GOOD FRIEND OF MINE.
I HOPE I CAN BE AS GOOD AS HE WAS SOMEDAY.
I'M SURE YOU WILL BE. OUR MISSION IS A GREAT ONE,
AND YOU'LL BE AN IMPORTANT ADDITION TO THE CARPATHIAN CREW.
WHAT EXACTLY IS OUR MISSION, CAPTAIN?
THERE IS AN EVIL GATHERING ON THE HORIZON SO POWERFUL WE MAY NOT BE ABLE TO STOP IT.
FOR SOME TIME NOW A CONSENSUS HAS BEEN GROWING.
EVERY SPIRITUALIST, MEDIUM, AND PSYCHIC WE COULD FIND
THEY SAY THE SAME THING OVER AND OVER.
SEEM TO BE HAVING A SHARED VISION OF A FUTURE YET TO COME.
ANOTHER GREAT WAR IS LOOMING, AND THE WORLD HASN'T RECOVERED FROM THE LAST STRUGGLE.
IT WILL BE A BATTLE BETWEEN LIGHT AND DARK, GOOD AND EVIL.
OUR MISSION IS TO STOP THAT WAR BEFORE IT HAPPENS.
OR IF WE FAIL, AT LEAST GIVE OUR SIDE A CHANCE TO WIN.

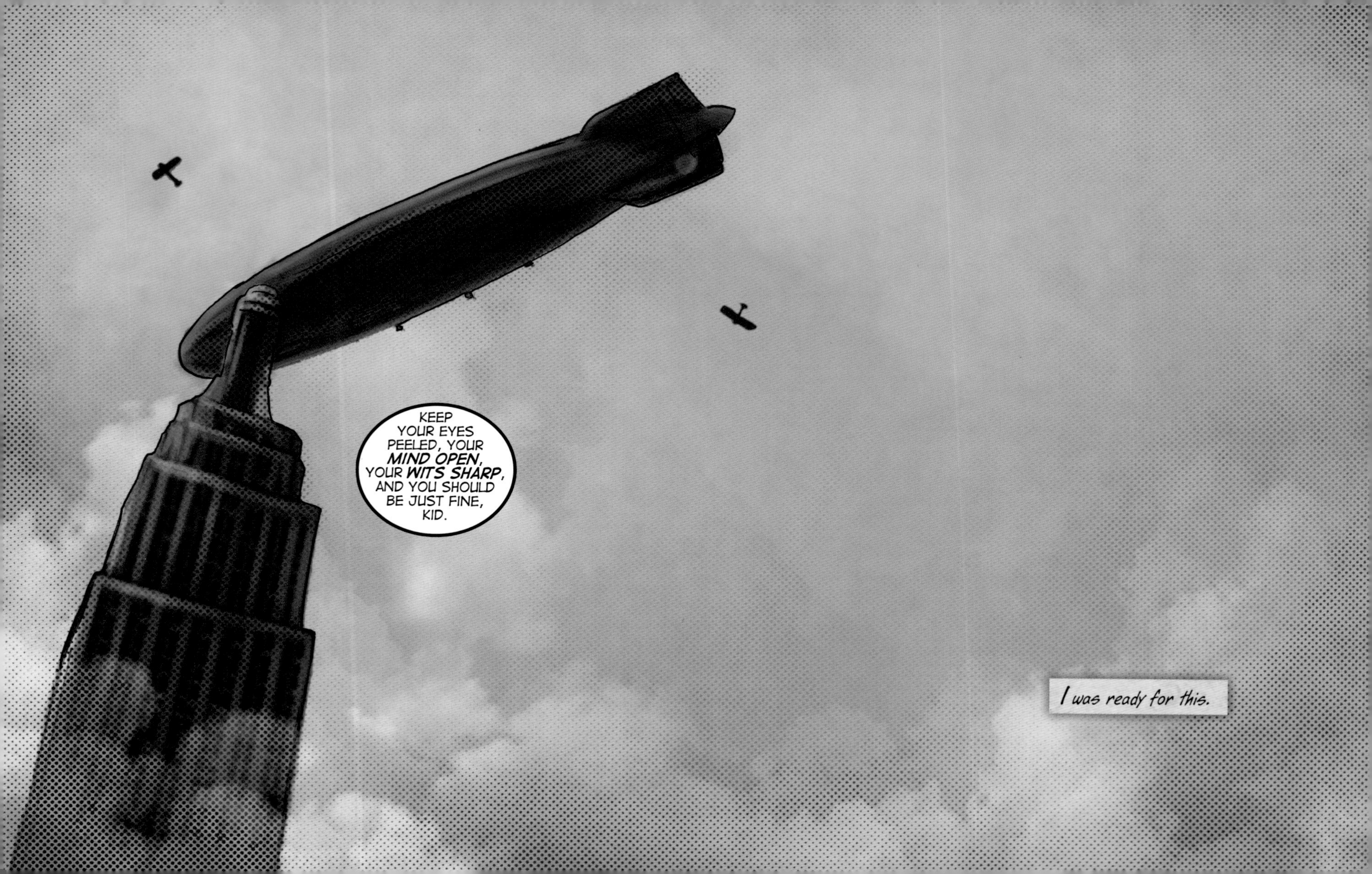
KEEP YOUR EYES PEELED, YOUR ***MIND OPEN***, YOUR ***WITS SHARP***, AND YOU SHOULD BE JUST FINE, KID.
I was ready for this.

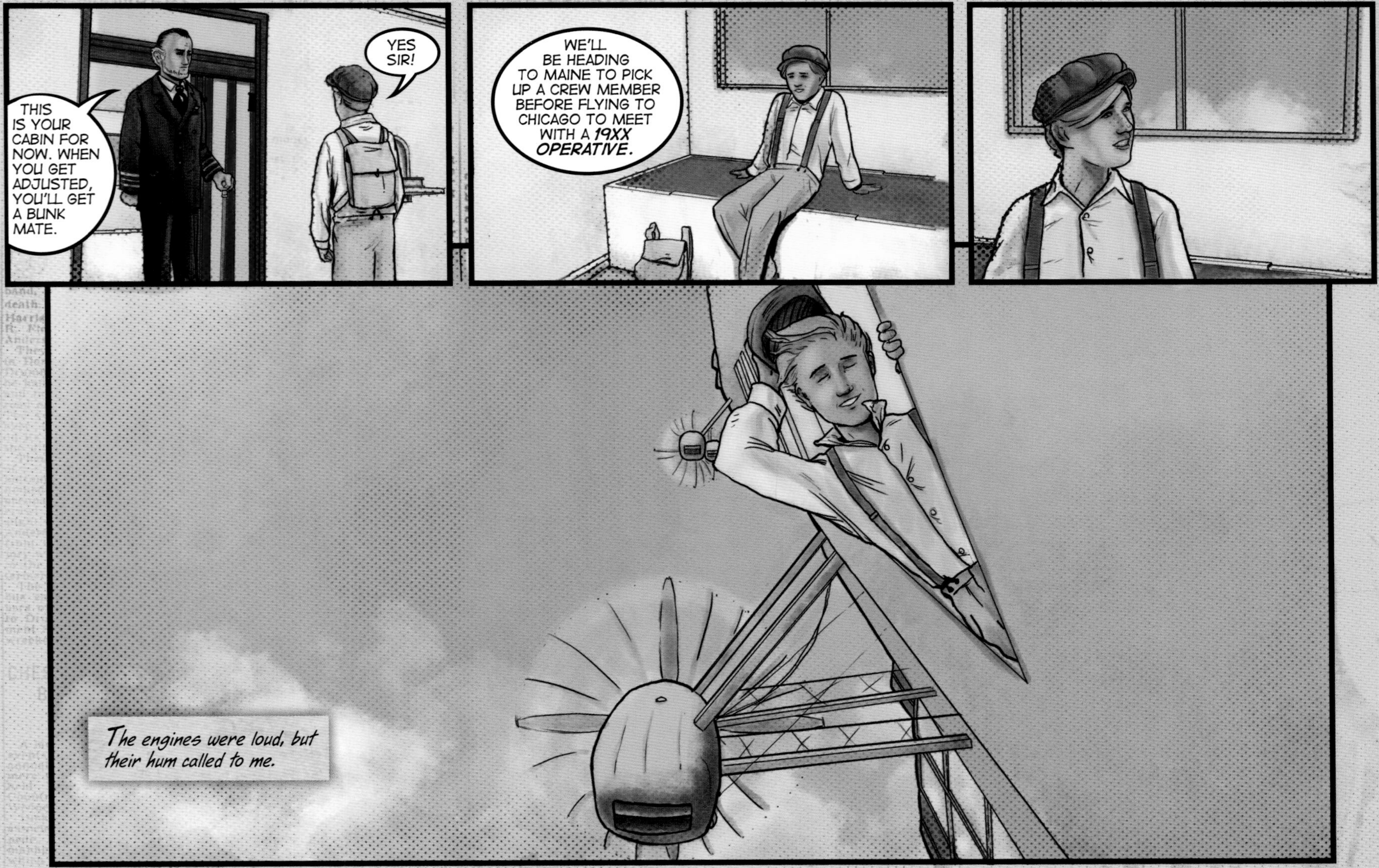
THIS IS YOUR CABIN FOR NOW. WHEN YOU GET ADJUSTED, YOU'LL GET A BUNK MATE.
YES SIR!
WE'LL BE HEADING TO MAINE TO PICK UP A CREW MEMBER BEFORE FLYING TO CHICAGO TO MEET WITH A *19XX OPERATIVE*.
The engines were loud, but their hum called to me.

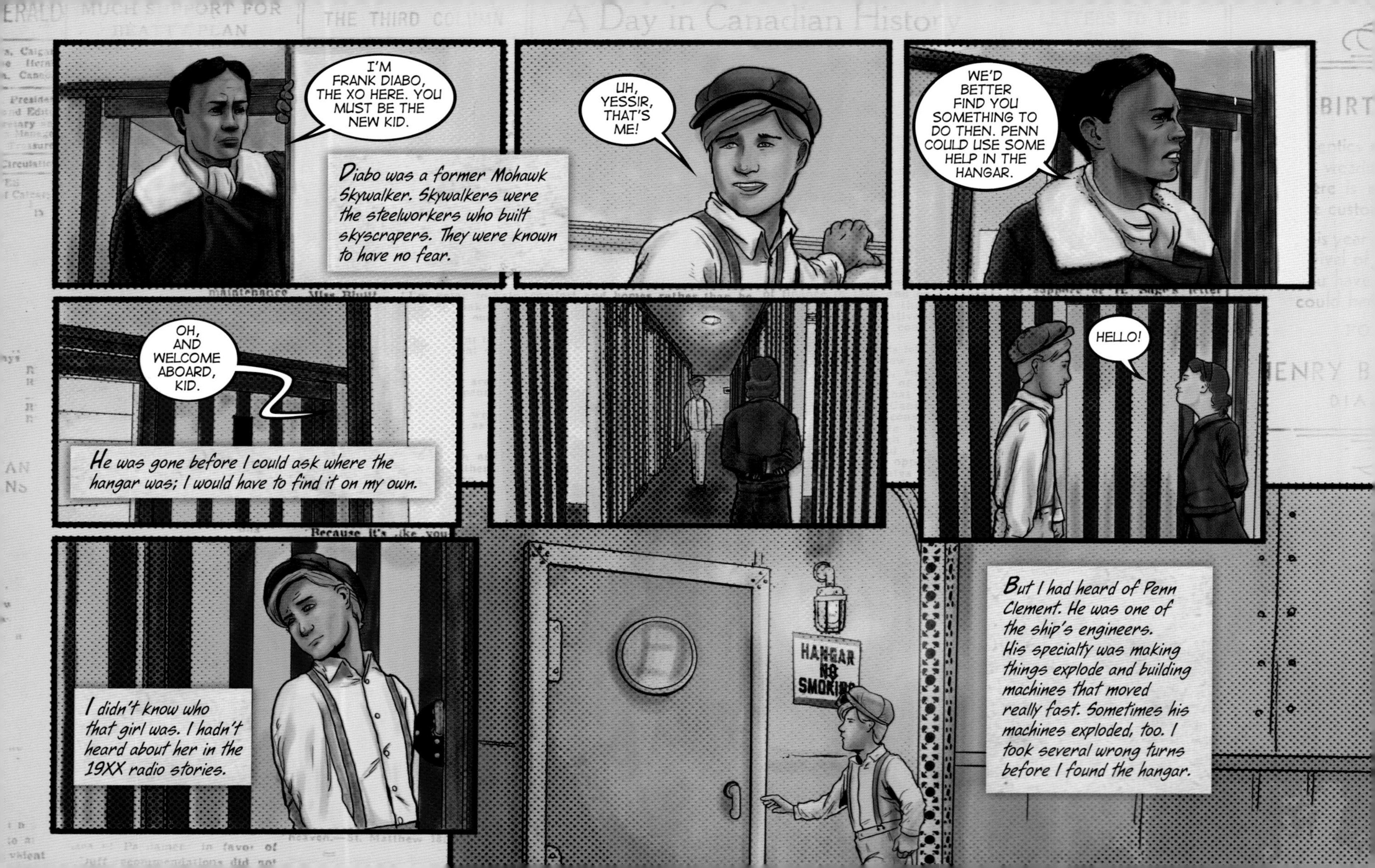
I'M FRANK DIABO, THE XO HERE. YOU MUST BE THE NEW KID.
Diabo was a former Mohawk Skywalker. Skywalkers were the steelworkers who built skyscrapers. They were known to have no fear.
UH, YESSIR, THAT'S ME!
WE'D BETTER FIND YOU SOMETHING TO DO THEN. PENN COULD USE SOME HELP IN THE HANGAR.
OH, AND WELCOME ABOARD, KID.
He was gone before I could ask where the hangar was; I would have to find it on my own.
HELLO!
I didn't know who that girl was. I hadn't heard about her in the 19XX radio stories.
HANGAR NO SMOKING
But I had heard of Penn Clement. He was one of the ship's engineers. His specialty was making things explode and building machines that moved really fast. Sometimes his machines exploded, too. I took several wrong turns before I found the hangar.

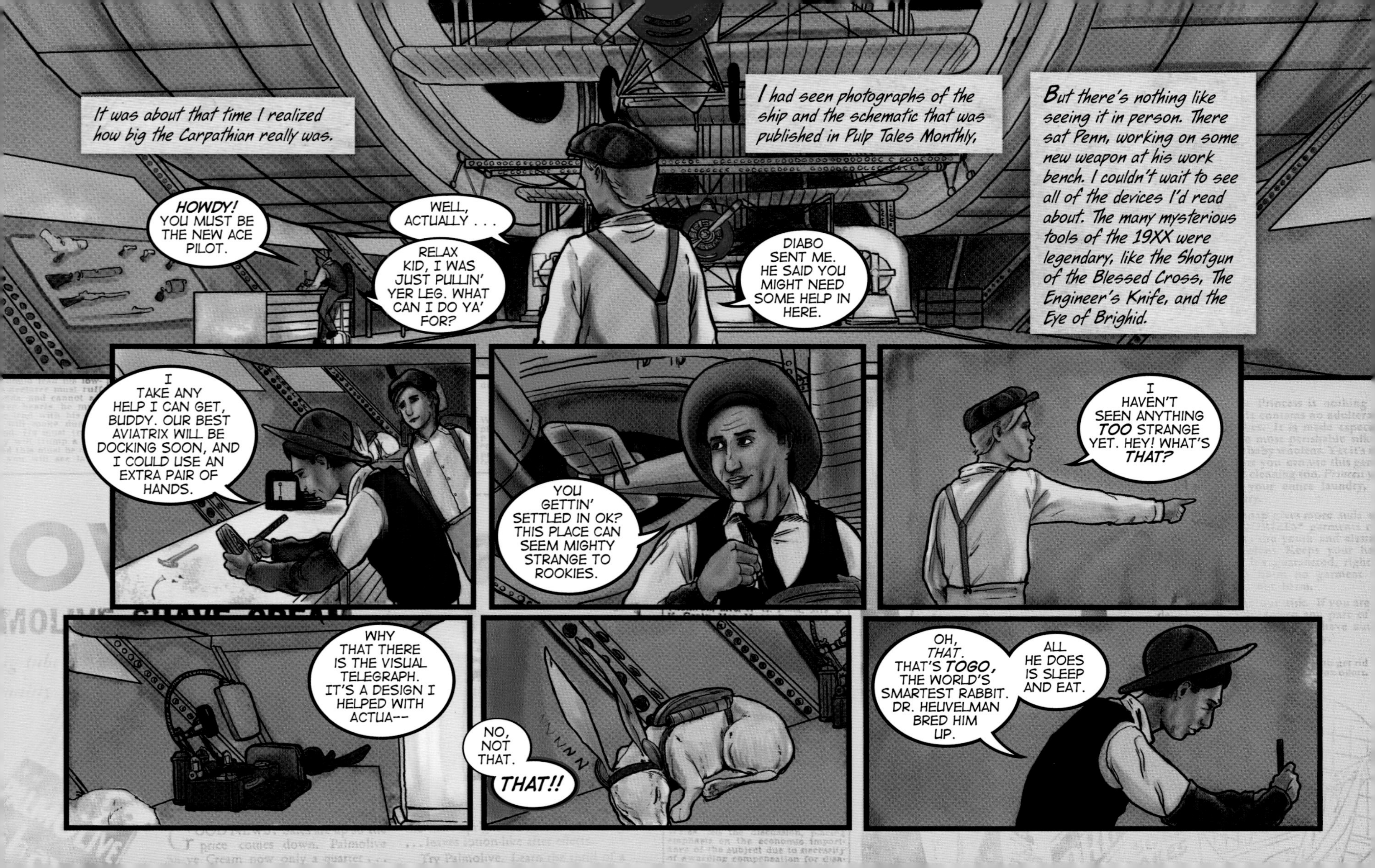

It was about that time I realized how big the Carpathian really was.
I had seen photographs of the ship and the schematic that was published in Pulp Tales Monthly,
But there's nothing like seeing it in person. There sat Penn, working on some new weapon at his work bench. I couldn't wait to see all of the devices I'd read about. The many mysterious tools of the 19XX were legendary, like the Shotgun of the Blessed Cross, The Engineer's Knife, and the Eye of Brighid.
HOWDY! YOU MUST BE THE NEW ACE PILOT.
WELL, ACTUALLY . . .
RELAX KID, I WAS JUST PULLIN' YER LEG. WHAT CAN I DO YA' FOR?
DIABO SENT ME. HE SAID YOU MIGHT NEED SOME HELP IN HERE.
I TAKE ANY HELP I CAN GET, BUDDY. OUR BEST AVIATRIX WILL BE DOCKING SOON, AND I COULD USE AN EXTRA PAIR OF HANDS.
YOU GETTIN' SETTLED IN OK? THIS PLACE CAN SEEM MIGHTY STRANGE TO ROOKIES.
I HAVEN'T SEEN ANYTHING TOO STRANGE YET. HEY! WHAT'S THAT?
WHY THAT THERE IS THE VISUAL TELEGRAPH. IT'S A DESIGN I HELPED WITH ACTUA--
NO, NOT THAT. THAT!!
NNNN
OH, THAT. THAT'S TOGO, THE WORLD'S SMARTEST RABBIT. DR. HEUVELMAN BRED HIM UP.
ALL HE DOES IS SLEEP AND EAT.

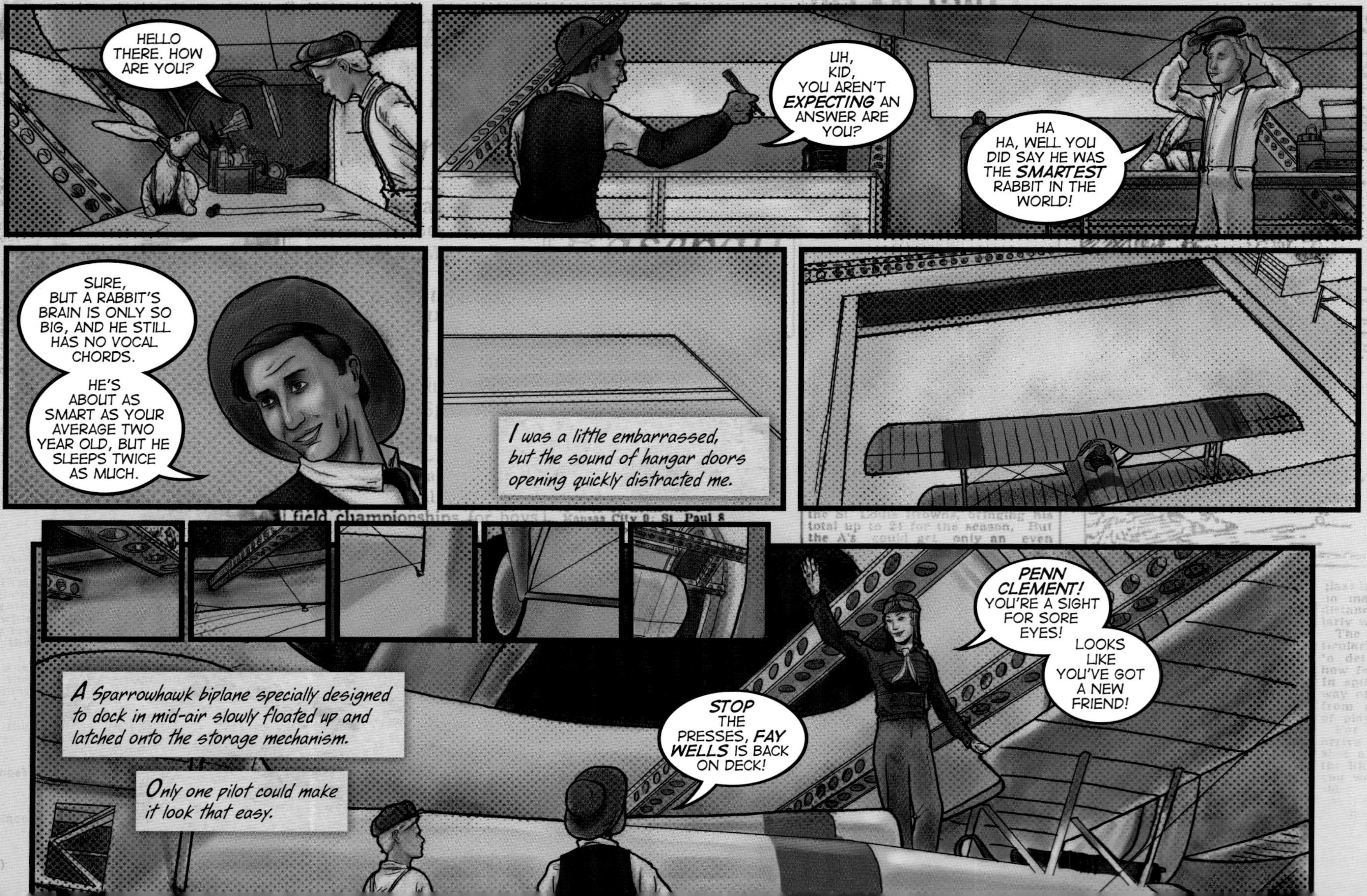
HELLO THERE. HOW ARE YOU?
UH, KID, YOU AREN'T *EXPECTING* AN ANSWER ARE YOU?
HA HA, WELL YOU DID SAY HE WAS THE *SMARTEST* RABBIT IN THE WORLD!
SURE, BUT A RABBIT'S BRAIN IS ONLY SO BIG, AND HE STILL HAS NO VOCAL CHORDS.
HE'S ABOUT AS SMART AS YOUR AVERAGE TWO YEAR OLD, BUT HE SLEEPS TWICE AS MUCH.
I was a little embarrassed, but the sound of hangar doors opening quickly distracted me.
A Sparrowhawk biplane specially designed to dock in mid-air slowly floated up and latched onto the storage mechanism.
Only one pilot could make it look that easy.
STOP THE PRESSES, *FAY WELLS* IS BACK ON DECK!
PENN CLEMENT! YOU'RE A SIGHT FOR SORE EYES!
LOOKS LIKE YOU'VE GOT A NEW FRIEND!

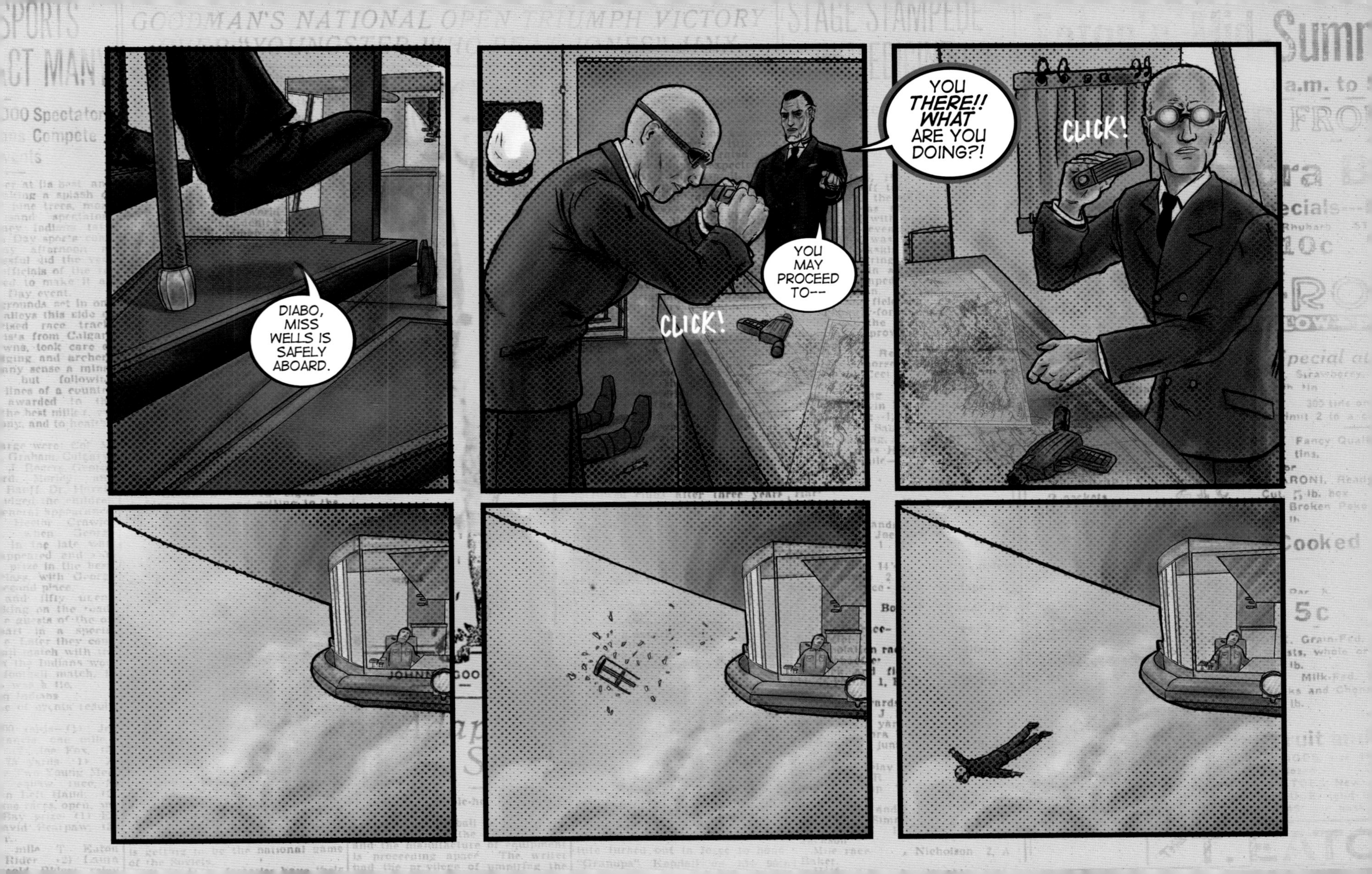
DIABO, MISS WELLS IS SAFELY ABOARD.
YOU MAY PROCEED TO--
CLICK!
YOU THERE!! WHAT ARE YOU DOING?!
CLICK!

MR. CLEMENT! WE'VE BEEN *BOARDED* BY A SPY!

HE JUST JUMPED FROM THE MAIN GONDOLA!

I NEED YOU ON THE GROUND, *NOW!!*

CAPTAIN, SHOULD WE GET FAY *BACK* IN THE AIR?

NO TIME! STRAP ON A PARACHUTE AND CATCH THAT SPY!

Penn looked like he had done this before.

He grabbed a small red bag,

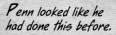

his parachute, and a radio.

Then he jumped.

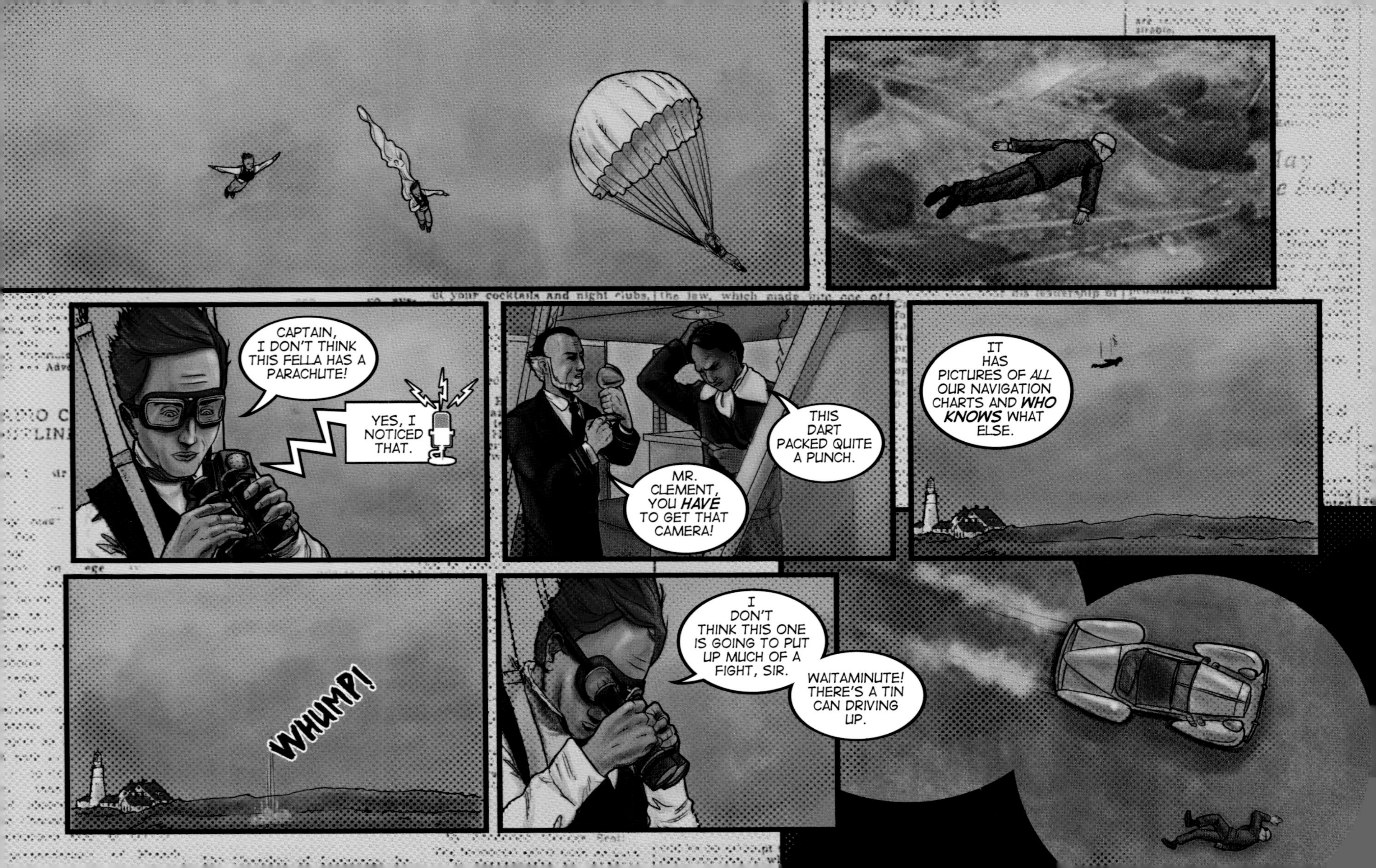
CAPTAIN, I DON'T THINK THIS FELLA HAS A PARACHUTE!
YES, I NOTICED THAT.
THIS DART PACKED QUITE A PUNCH.
MR. CLEMENT, YOU *HAVE* TO GET THAT CAMERA!
IT HAS PICTURES OF *ALL* OUR NAVIGATION CHARTS AND ***WHO KNOWS*** WHAT ELSE.
WHUMP!
I DON'T THINK THIS ONE IS GOING TO PUT UP MUCH OF A FIGHT, SIR.
WAITAMINUTE! THERE'S A TIN CAN DRIVING UP.

Auburn
Speedstor
150BHP
@4400RPM

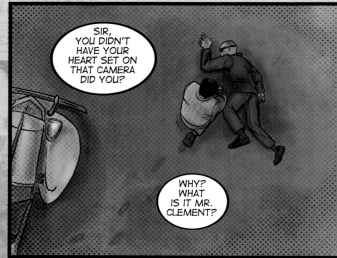

SIR, YOU DIDN'T HAVE YOUR HEART SET ON THAT CAMERA DID YOU?

WHY? WHAT IS IT MR. CLEMENT?

IT'S STERLING RISKIN, HE'S DOWN THERE!

HE'S USING HIS DEMONHAND ON THE BODY. *IT'S GONE!*

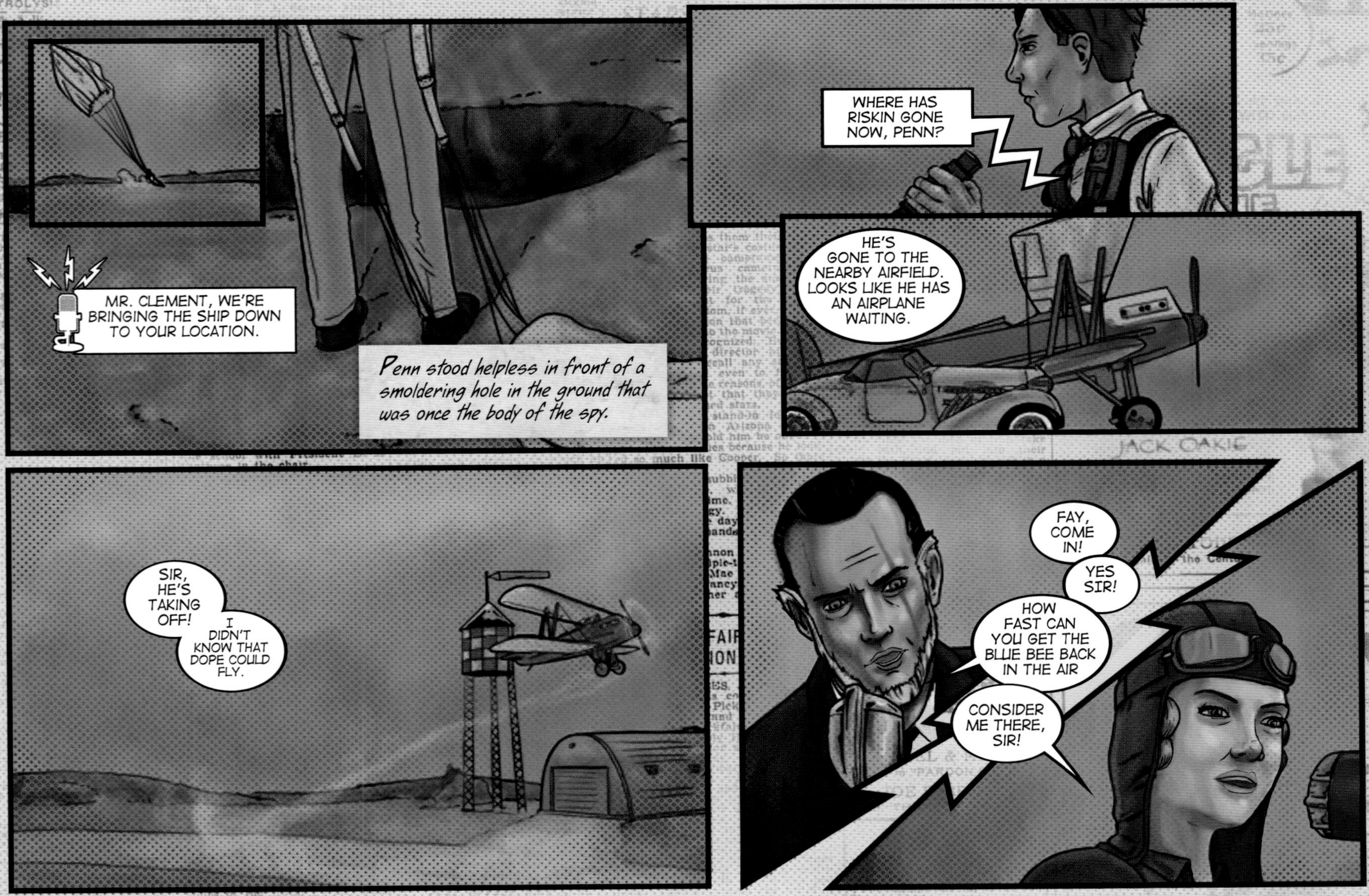
MR. CLEMENT, WE'RE BRINGING THE SHIP DOWN TO YOUR LOCATION.
Penn stood helpless in front of a smoldering hole in the ground that was once the body of the spy.
WHERE HAS RISKIN GONE NOW, PENN?
HE'S GONE TO THE NEARBY AIRFIELD. LOOKS LIKE HE HAS AN AIRPLANE WAITING.
SIR, HE'S TAKING OFF!
I DIDN'T KNOW THAT DOPE COULD FLY.
FAY, COME IN!
YES SIR!
HOW FAST CAN YOU GET THE BLUE BEE BACK IN THE AIR
CONSIDER ME THERE, SIR!

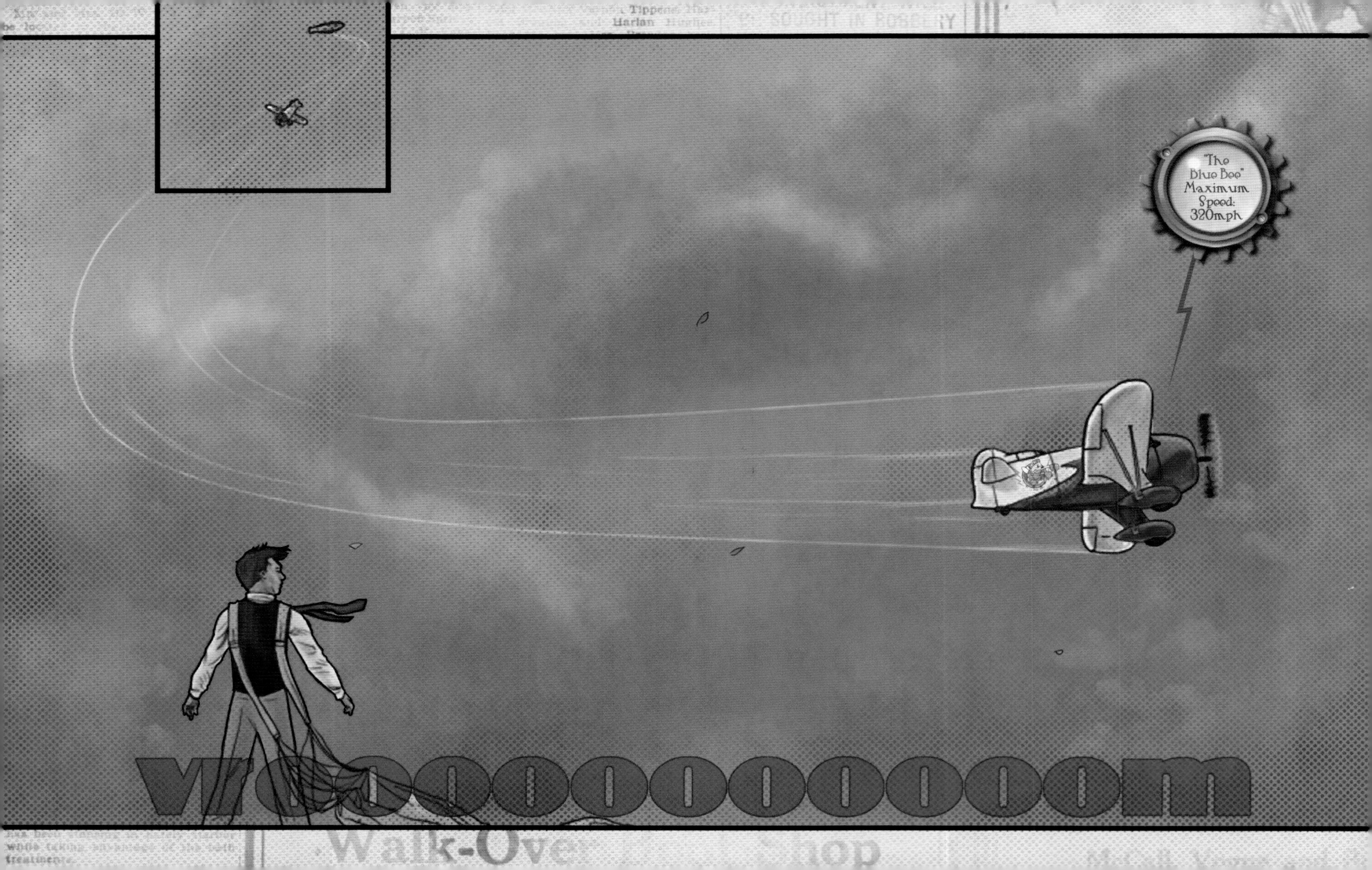
"The Blue Bee" Maximum Speed: 320mph
vrooooooooooom

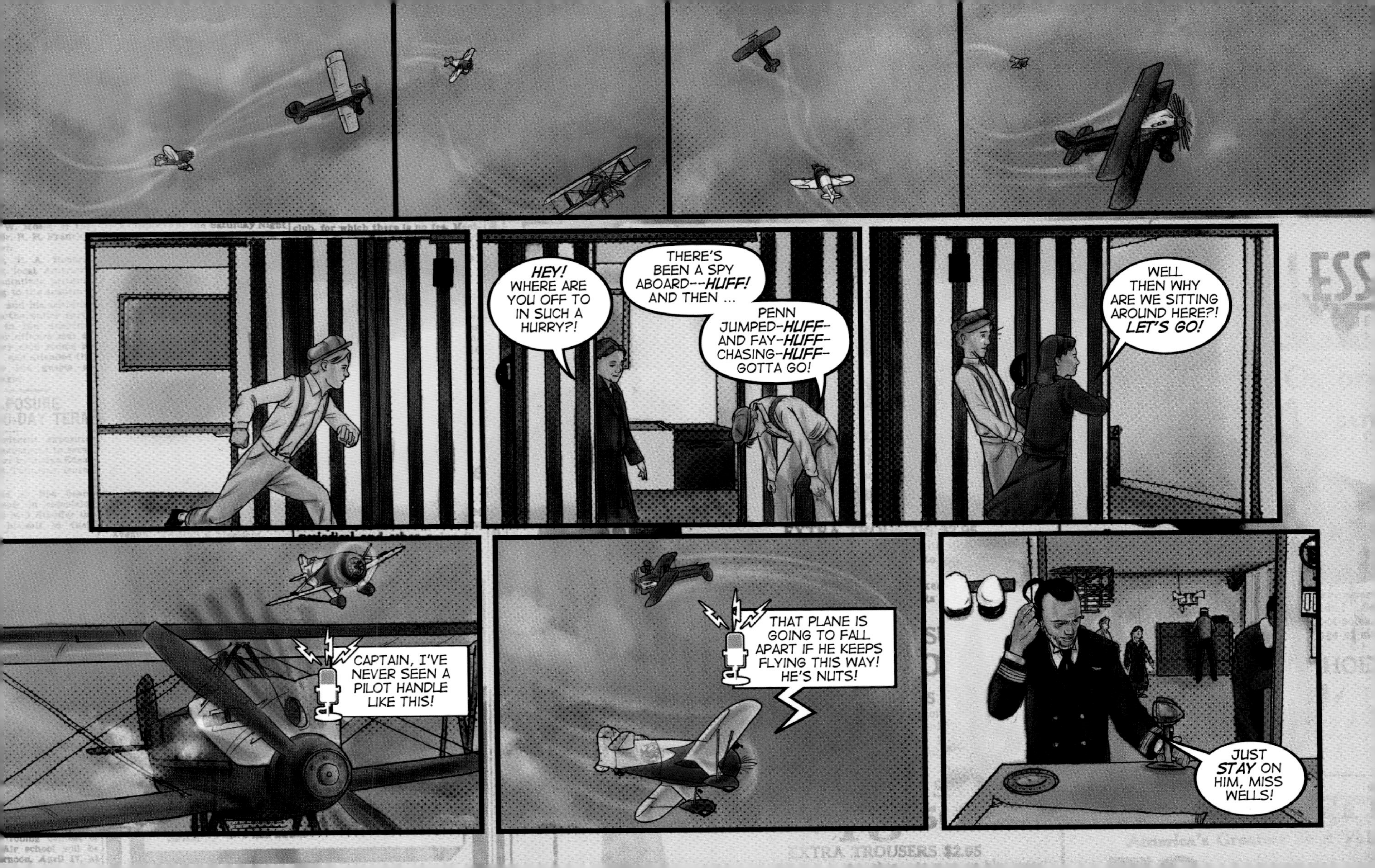

HEY! WHERE ARE YOU OFF TO IN SUCH A HURRY?!
THERE'S BEEN A SPY ABOARD--HUFF! AND THEN ...
PENN JUMPED-HUFF-AND FAY-HUFF-CHASING-HUFF-GOTTA GO!
WELL THEN WHY ARE WE SITTING AROUND HERE?! LET'S GO!
CAPTAIN, I'VE NEVER SEEN A PILOT HANDLE LIKE THIS!
THAT PLANE IS GOING TO FALL APART IF HE KEEPS FLYING THIS WAY! HE'S NUTS!
JUST STAY ON HIM, MISS WELLS!

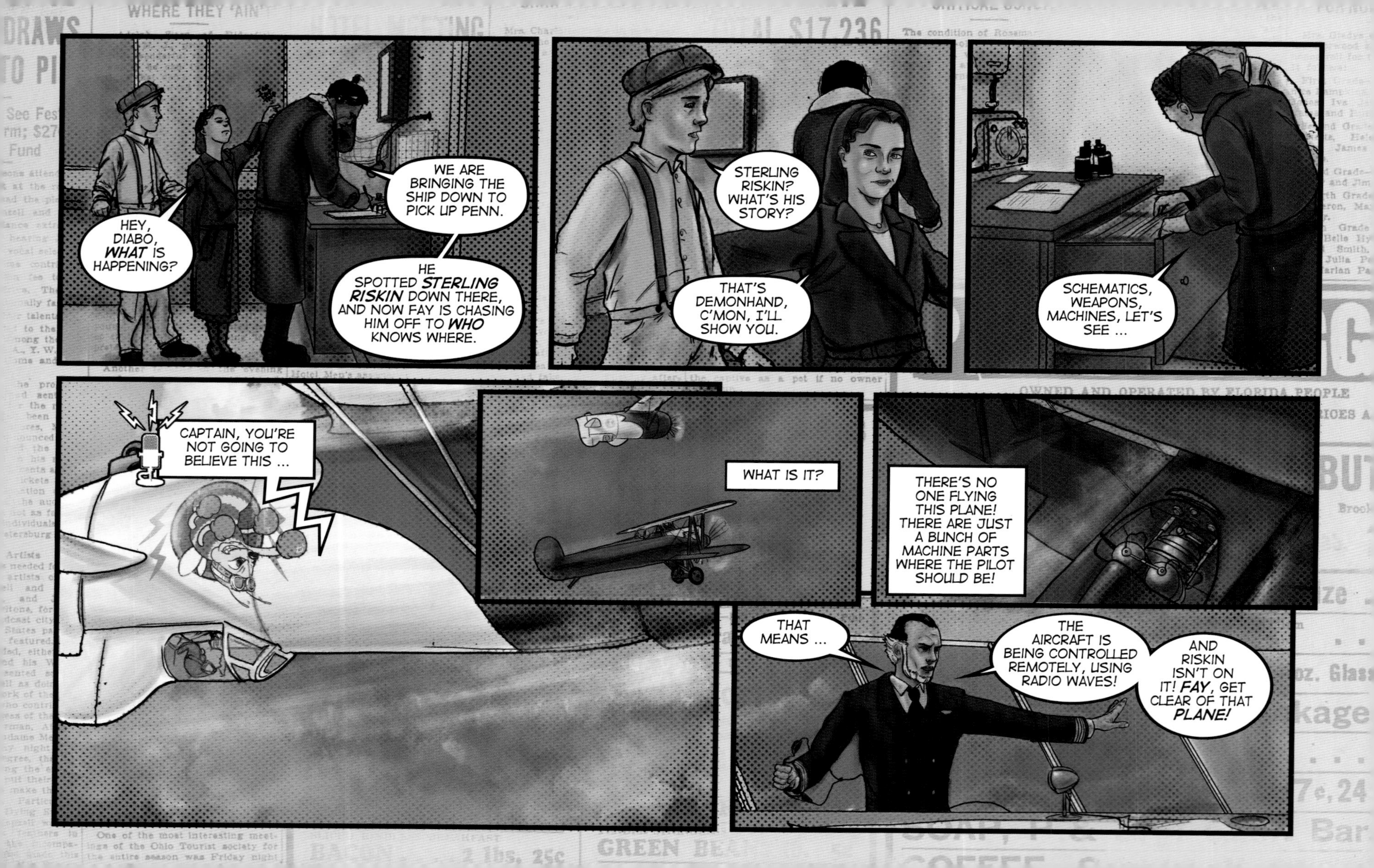
HEY, DIABO, WHAT IS HAPPENING?
WE ARE BRINGING THE SHIP DOWN TO PICK UP PENN.
HE SPOTTED STERLING RISKIN DOWN THERE, AND NOW FAY IS CHASING HIM OFF TO WHO KNOWS WHERE.
STERLING RISKIN? WHAT'S HIS STORY?
THAT'S DEMONHAND, C'MON, I'LL SHOW YOU.
SCHEMATICS, WEAPONS, MACHINES, LET'S SEE ...
CAPTAIN, YOU'RE NOT GOING TO BELIEVE THIS ...
WHAT IS IT?
THERE'S NO ONE FLYING THIS PLANE! THERE ARE JUST A BUNCH OF MACHINE PARTS WHERE THE PILOT SHOULD BE!
THAT MEANS ...
THE AIRCRAFT IS BEING CONTROLLED REMOTELY, USING RADIO WAVES!
AND RISKIN ISN'T ON IT! FAY, GET CLEAR OF THAT PLANE!

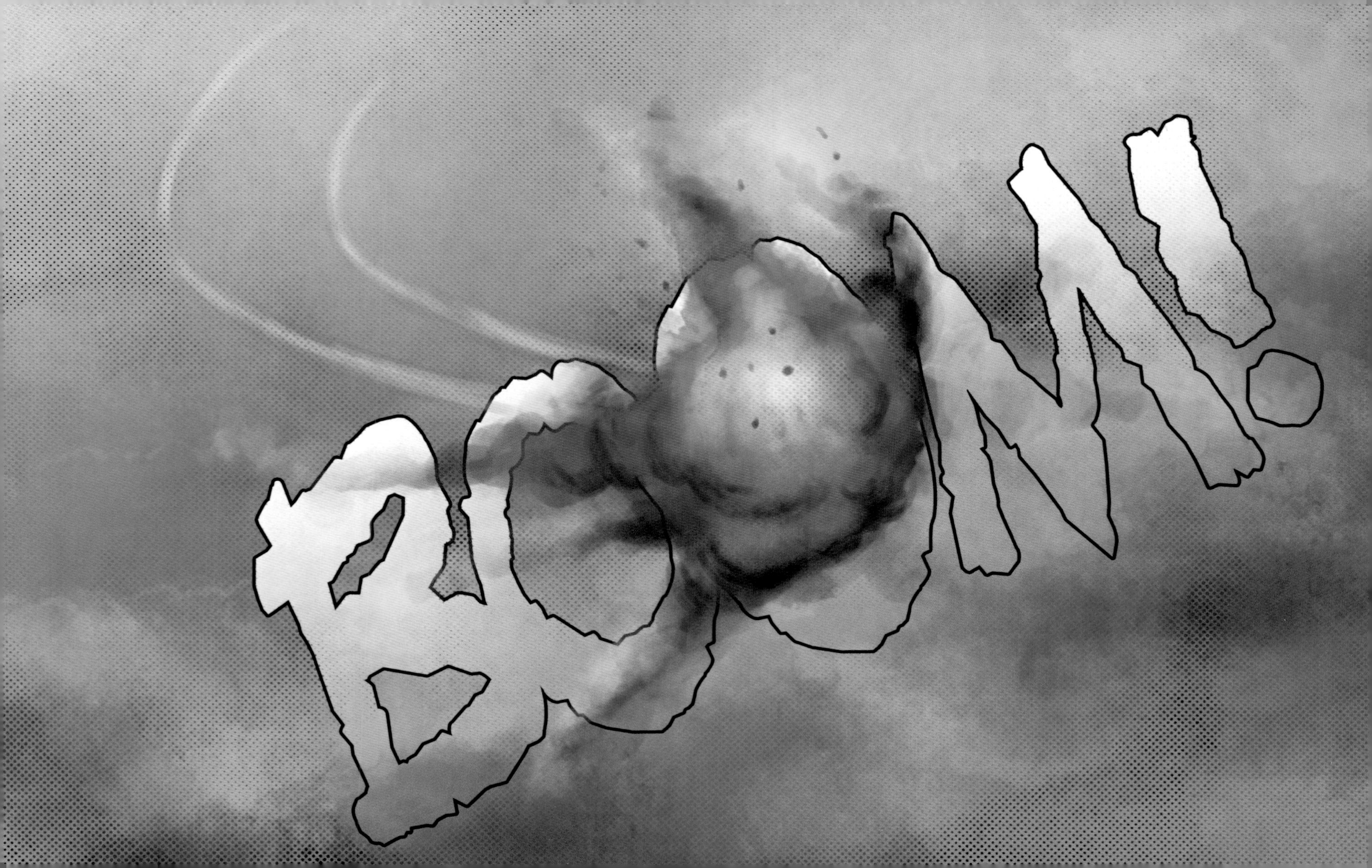
BOOM!

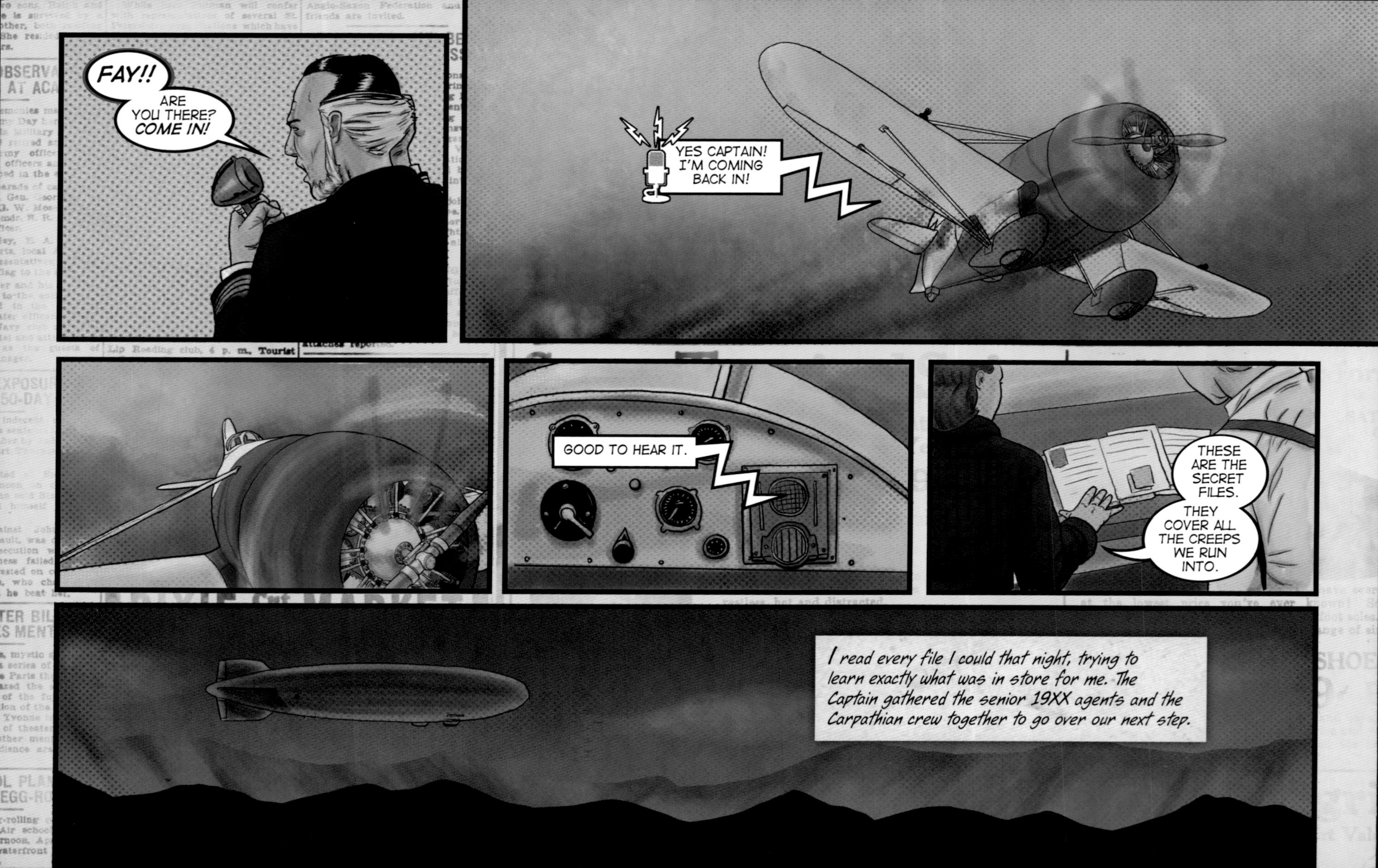

FAY!! ARE YOU THERE? COME IN!
YES CAPTAIN! I'M COMING BACK IN!
GOOD TO HEAR IT.
THESE ARE THE SECRET FILES.
THEY COVER ALL THE CREEPS WE RUN INTO.
I read every file I could that night, trying to learn exactly what was in store for me. The Captain gathered the senior 19XX agents and the Carpathian crew together to go over our next step.

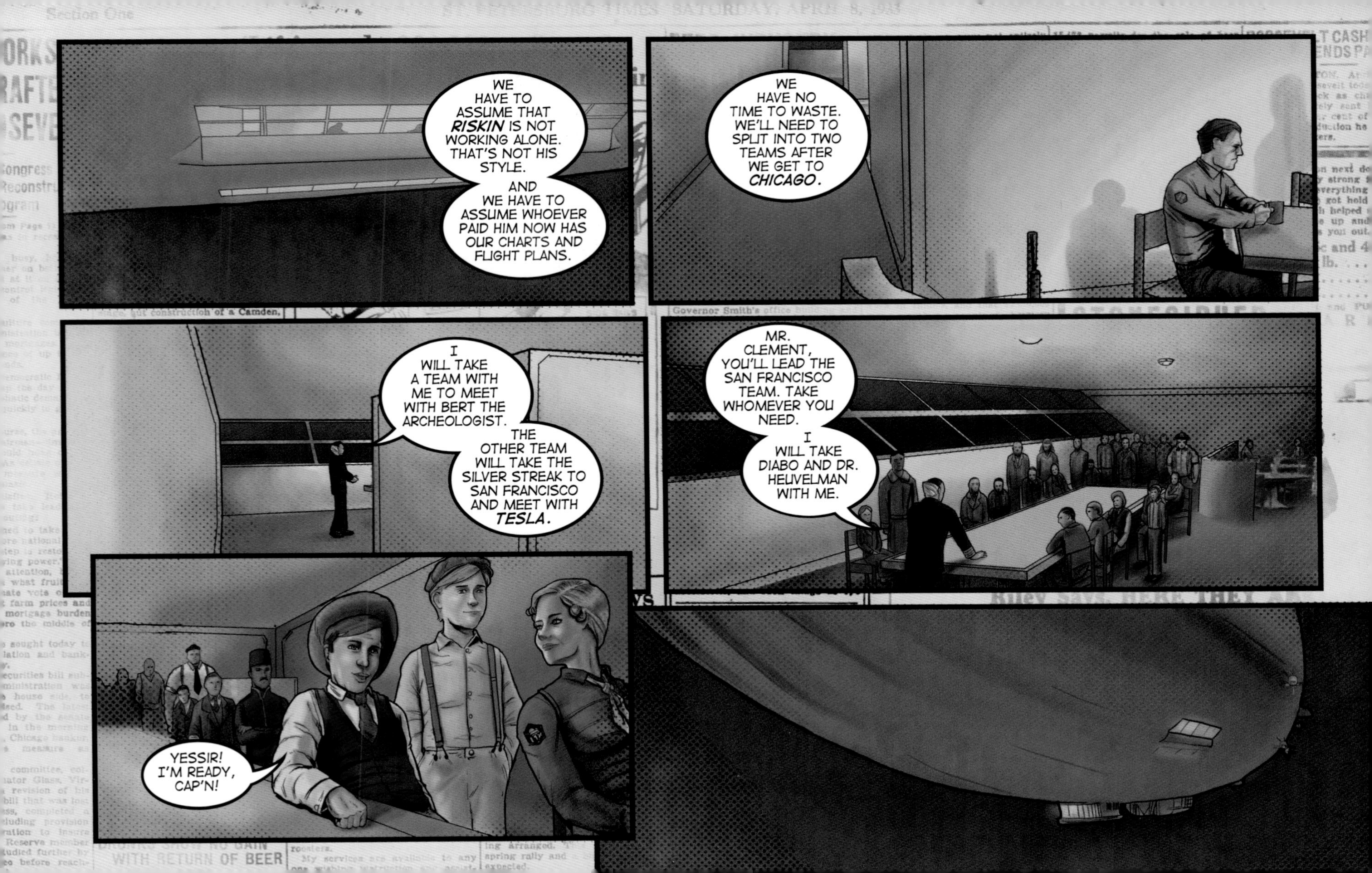
WE HAVE TO ASSUME THAT RISKIN IS NOT WORKING ALONE. THAT'S NOT HIS STYLE.
AND WE HAVE TO ASSUME WHOEVER PAID HIM NOW HAS OUR CHARTS AND FLIGHT PLANS.
WE HAVE NO TIME TO WASTE. WE'LL NEED TO SPLIT INTO TWO TEAMS AFTER WE GET TO CHICAGO.
I WILL TAKE A TEAM WITH ME TO MEET WITH BERT THE ARCHEOLOGIST.
THE OTHER TEAM WILL TAKE THE SILVER STREAK TO SAN FRANCISCO AND MEET WITH TESLA.
MR. CLEMENT, YOU'LL LEAD THE SAN FRANCISCO TEAM. TAKE WHOMEVER YOU NEED.
I WILL TAKE DIABO AND DR. HEUVELMAN WITH ME.
YESSIR! I'M READY, CAP'N!

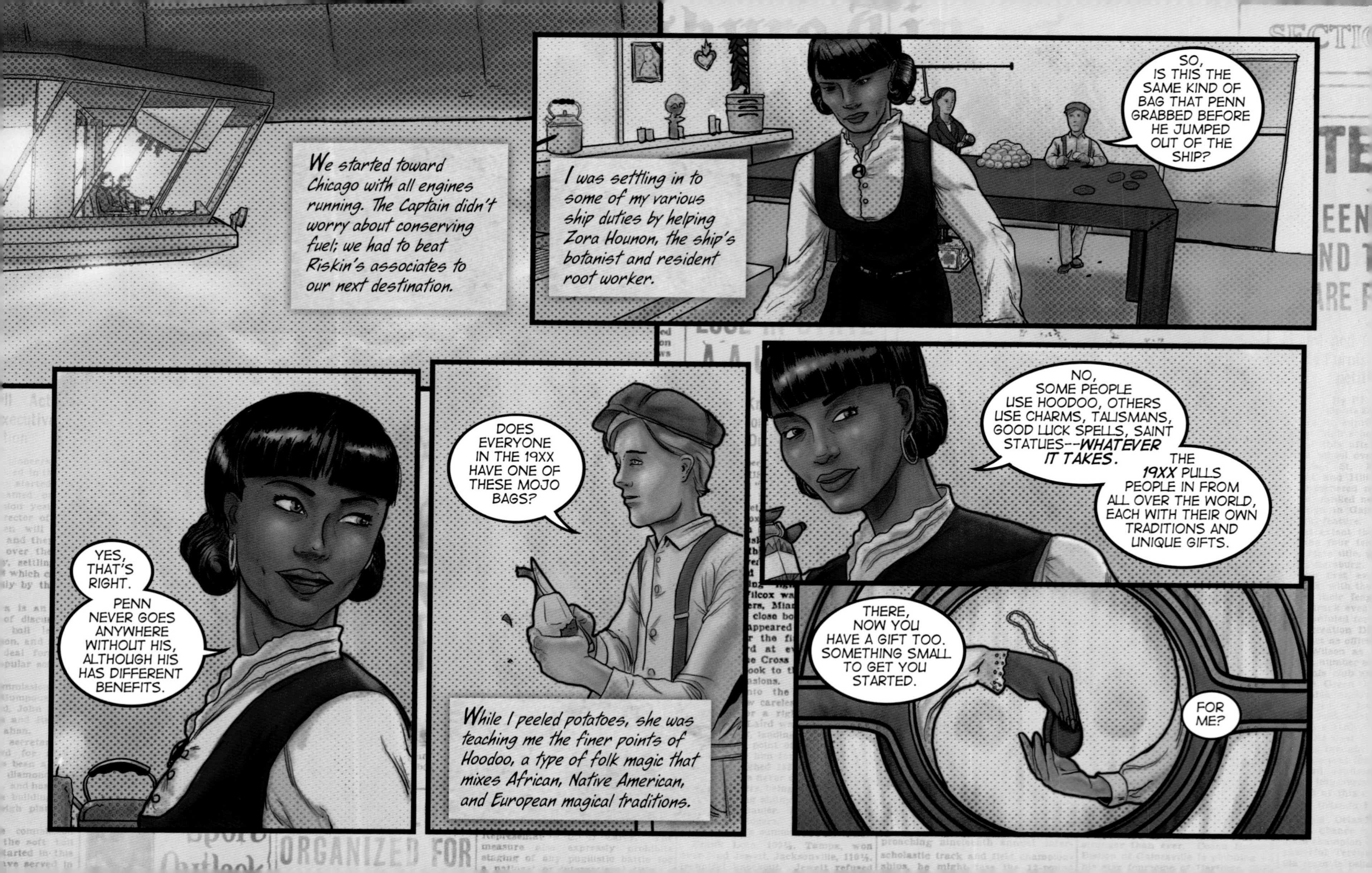

We started toward Chicago with all engines running. The Captain didn't worry about conserving fuel; we had to beat Riskin's associates to our next destination.
I was settling in to some of my various ship duties by helping Zora Hounon, the ship's botanist and resident root worker.
SO, IS THIS THE SAME KIND OF BAG THAT PENN GRABBED BEFORE HE JUMPED OUT OF THE SHIP?
YES, THAT'S RIGHT.
PENN NEVER GOES ANYWHERE WITHOUT HIS, ALTHOUGH HIS HAS DIFFERENT BENEFITS.
DOES EVERYONE IN THE 19XX HAVE ONE OF THESE MOJO BAGS?
While I peeled potatoes, she was teaching me the finer points of Hoodoo, a type of folk magic that mixes African, Native American, and European magical traditions.
NO, SOME PEOPLE USE HOODOO, OTHERS USE CHARMS, TALISMANS, GOOD LUCK SPELLS, SAINT STATUES--*WHATEVER IT TAKES.*
THE *19XX* PULLS PEOPLE IN FROM ALL OVER THE WORLD, EACH WITH THEIR OWN TRADITIONS AND UNIQUE GIFTS.
THERE, NOW YOU HAVE A GIFT TOO. SOMETHING SMALL TO GET YOU STARTED.
FOR ME?

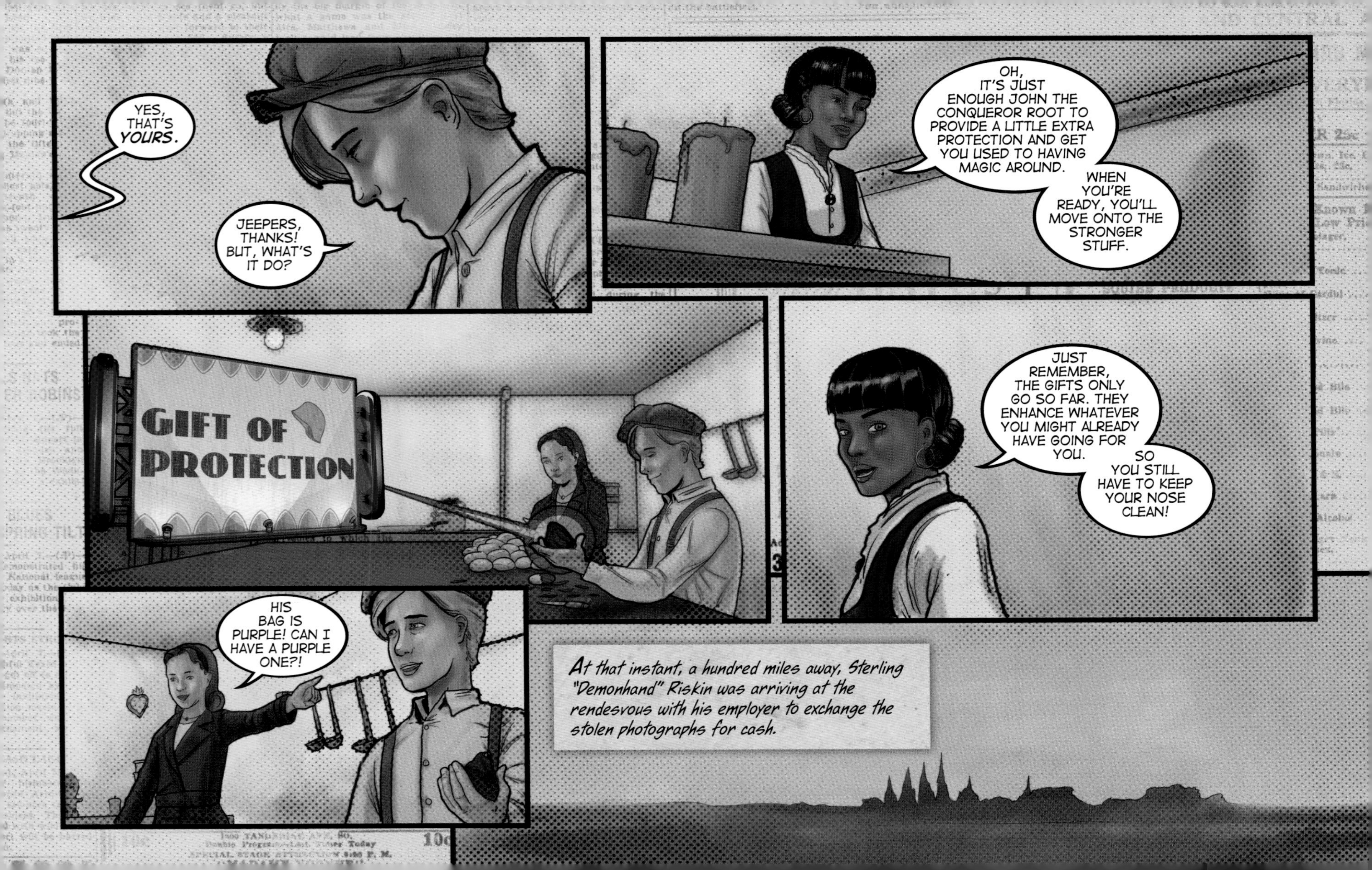
YES, THAT'S YOURS.
JEEPERS, THANKS! BUT, WHAT'S IT DO?
OH, IT'S JUST ENOUGH JOHN THE CONQUEROR ROOT TO PROVIDE A LITTLE EXTRA PROTECTION AND GET YOU USED TO HAVING MAGIC AROUND.
WHEN YOU'RE READY, YOU'LL MOVE ONTO THE STRONGER STUFF.
GIFT OF PROTECTION
JUST REMEMBER, THE GIFTS ONLY GO SO FAR. THEY ENHANCE WHATEVER YOU MIGHT ALREADY HAVE GOING FOR YOU.
SO YOU STILL HAVE TO KEEP YOUR NOSE CLEAN!
HIS BAG IS PURPLE! CAN I HAVE A PURPLE ONE?!
At that instant, a hundred miles away, Sterling "Demonhand" Riskin was arriving at the rendesvous with his employer to exchange the stolen photographs for cash.

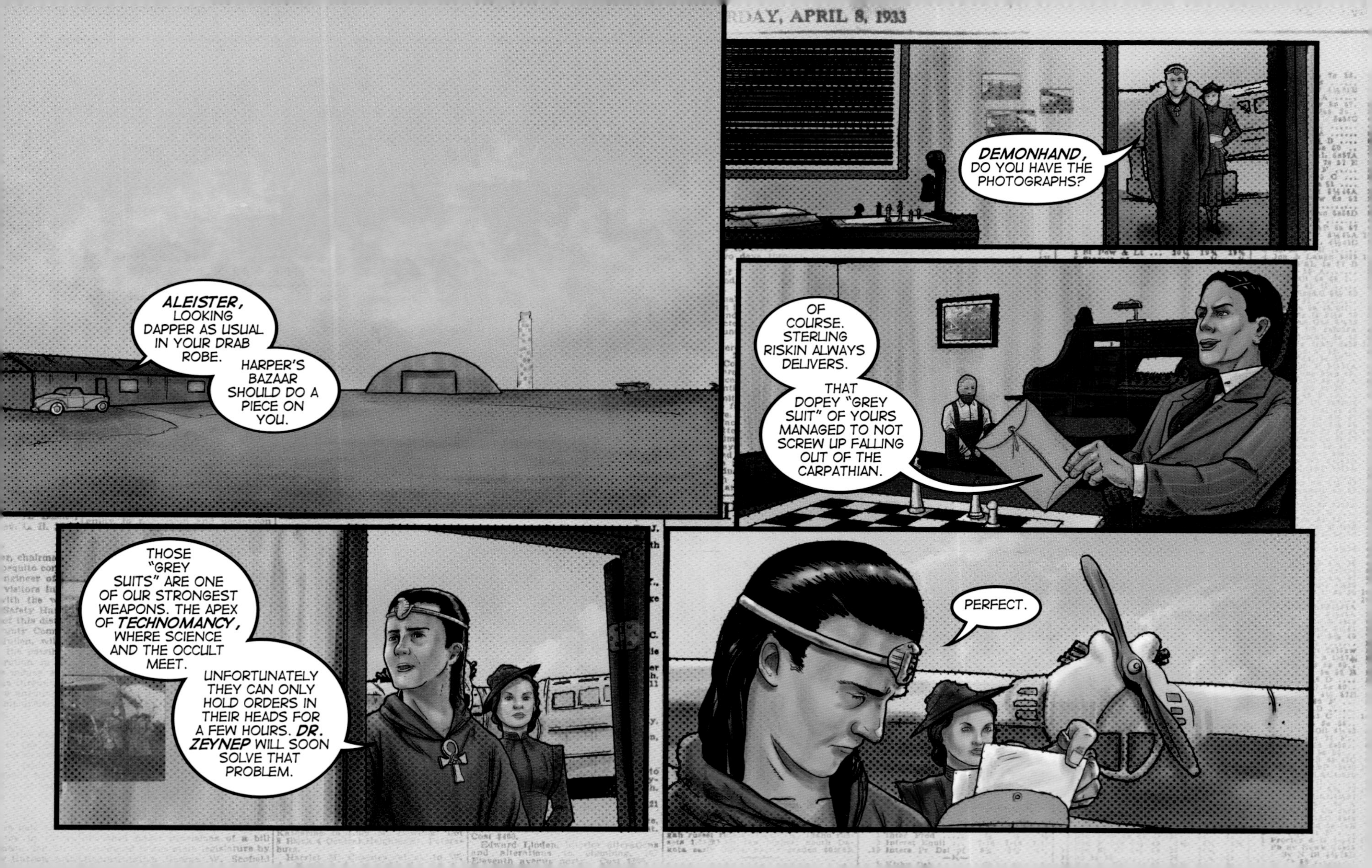

SATURDAY, APRIL 8, 1933
ALEISTER, LOOKING DAPPER AS USUAL IN YOUR DRAB ROBE.
HARPER'S BAZAAR SHOULD DO A PIECE ON YOU.
DEMONHAND, DO YOU HAVE THE PHOTOGRAPHS?
OF COURSE. STERLING RISKIN ALWAYS DELIVERS.
THAT DOPEY "GREY SUIT" OF YOURS MANAGED TO NOT SCREW UP FALLING OUT OF THE CARPATHIAN.
THOSE "GREY SUITS" ARE ONE OF OUR STRONGEST WEAPONS. THE APEX OF TECHNOMANCY, WHERE SCIENCE AND THE OCCULT MEET.
UNFORTUNATELY THEY CAN ONLY HOLD ORDERS IN THEIR HEADS FOR A FEW HOURS. DR. ZEYNEP WILL SOON SOLVE THAT PROBLEM.
PERFECT.

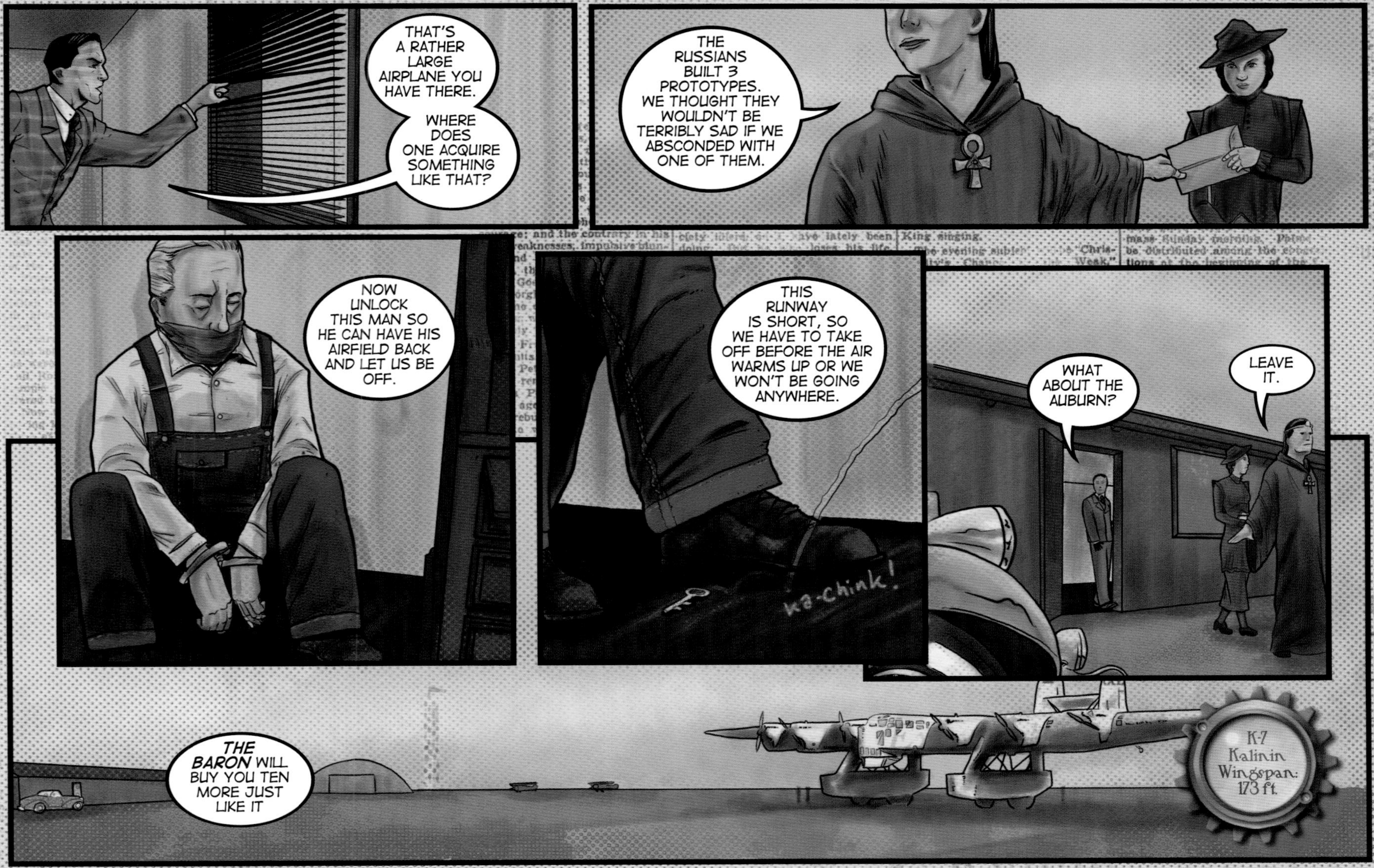
THAT'S A RATHER LARGE AIRPLANE YOU HAVE THERE.
WHERE DOES ONE ACQUIRE SOMETHING LIKE THAT?
THE RUSSIANS BUILT 3 PROTOTYPES. WE THOUGHT THEY WOULDN'T BE TERRIBLY SAD IF WE ABSCONDED WITH ONE OF THEM.
NOW UNLOCK THIS MAN SO HE CAN HAVE HIS AIRFIELD BACK AND LET US BE OFF.
THIS RUNWAY IS SHORT, SO WE HAVE TO TAKE OFF BEFORE THE AIR WARMS UP OR WE WON'T BE GOING ANYWHERE.
ka-chink!
WHAT ABOUT THE AUBURN?
LEAVE IT.
THE BARON WILL BUY YOU TEN MORE JUST LIKE IT
K-7 Kalinin Wingspan: 173 ft.

CHAPTER 2

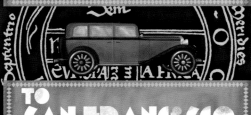

FROM CHICAGO TO SAN FRANCISCO

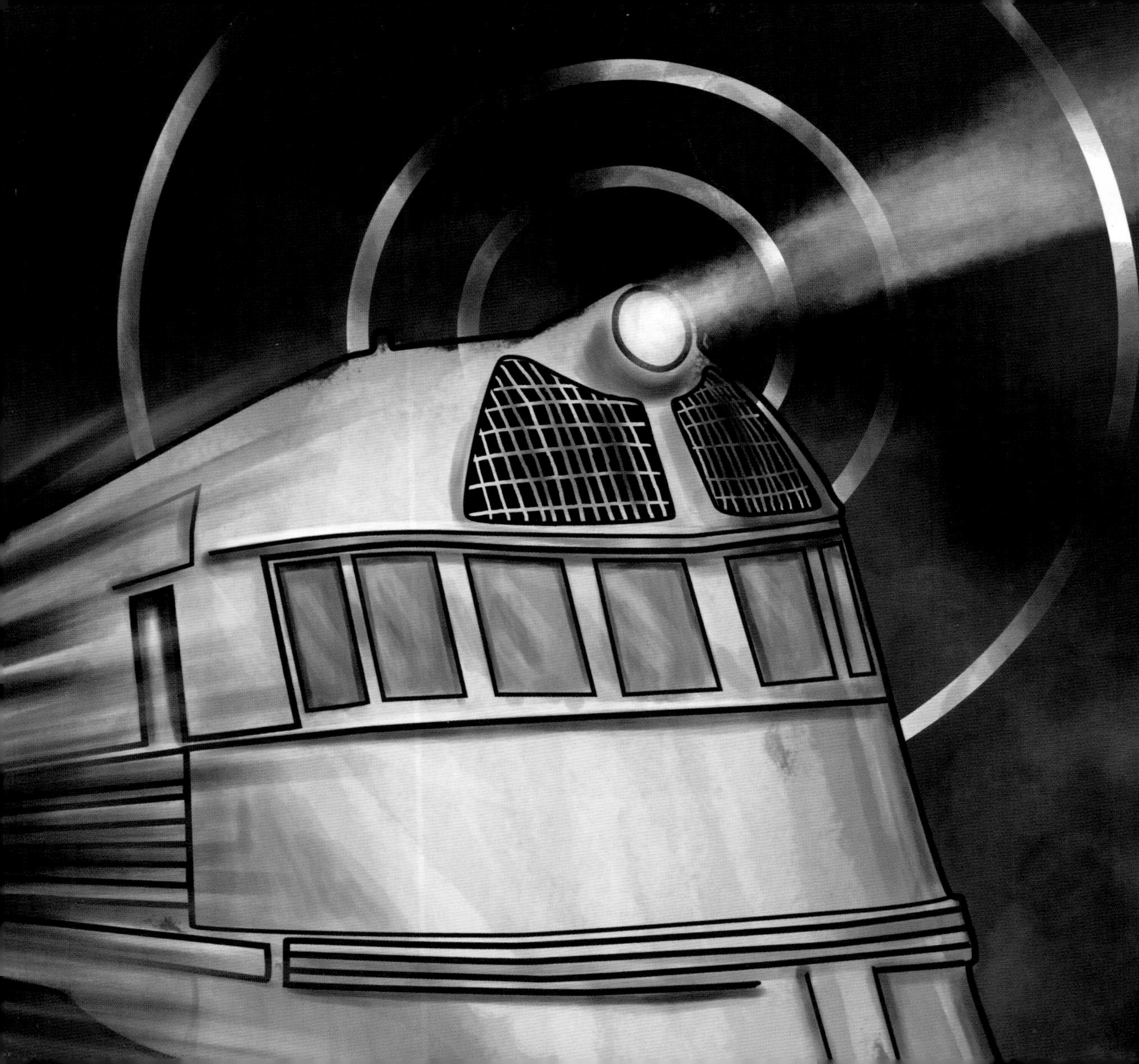

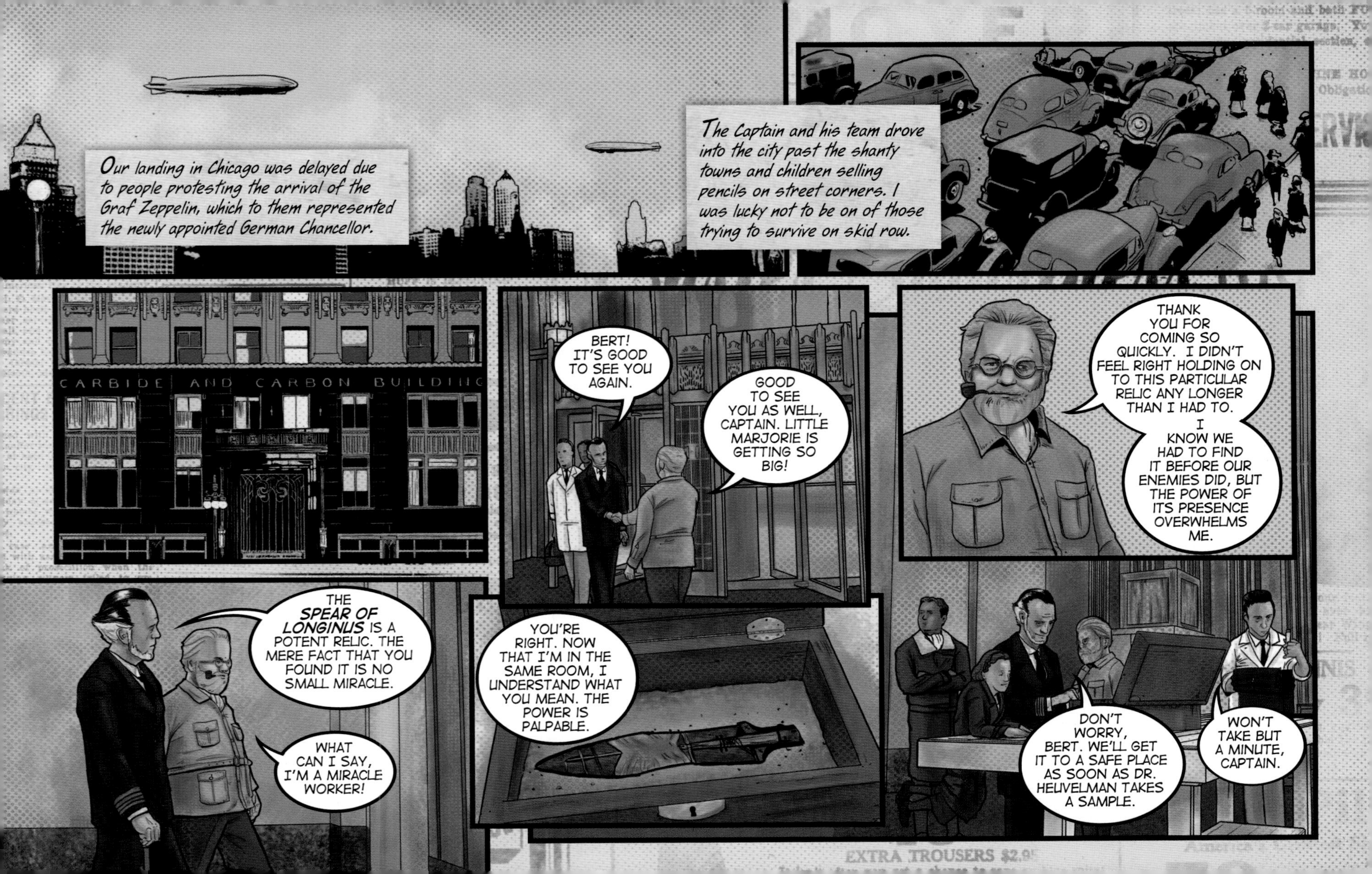
Our landing in Chicago was delayed due to people protesting the arrival of the Graf Zeppelin, which to them represented the newly appointed German Chancellor.
The Captain and his team drove into the city past the shanty towns and children selling pencils on street corners. I was lucky not to be on of those trying to survive on skid row.
CARBIDE AND CARBON BUILDING
BERT! IT'S GOOD TO SEE YOU AGAIN.
GOOD TO SEE YOU AS WELL, CAPTAIN. LITTLE MARJORIE IS GETTING SO BIG!
THANK YOU FOR COMING SO QUICKLY. I DIDN'T FEEL RIGHT HOLDING ON TO THIS PARTICULAR RELIC ANY LONGER THAN I HAD TO.
I KNOW WE HAD TO FIND IT BEFORE OUR ENEMIES DID, BUT THE POWER OF ITS PRESENCE OVERWHELMS ME.
THE **SPEAR OF LONGINUS** IS A POTENT RELIC. THE MERE FACT THAT YOU FOUND IT IS NO SMALL MIRACLE.
WHAT CAN I SAY, I'M A MIRACLE WORKER!
YOU'RE RIGHT. NOW THAT I'M IN THE SAME ROOM, I UNDERSTAND WHAT YOU MEAN. THE POWER IS PALPABLE.
DON'T WORRY, BERT. WE'LL GET IT TO A SAFE PLACE AS SOON AS DR. HEUVELMAN TAKES A SAMPLE.
WON'T TAKE BUT A MINUTE, CAPTAIN.
EXTRA TROUSERS $2.95

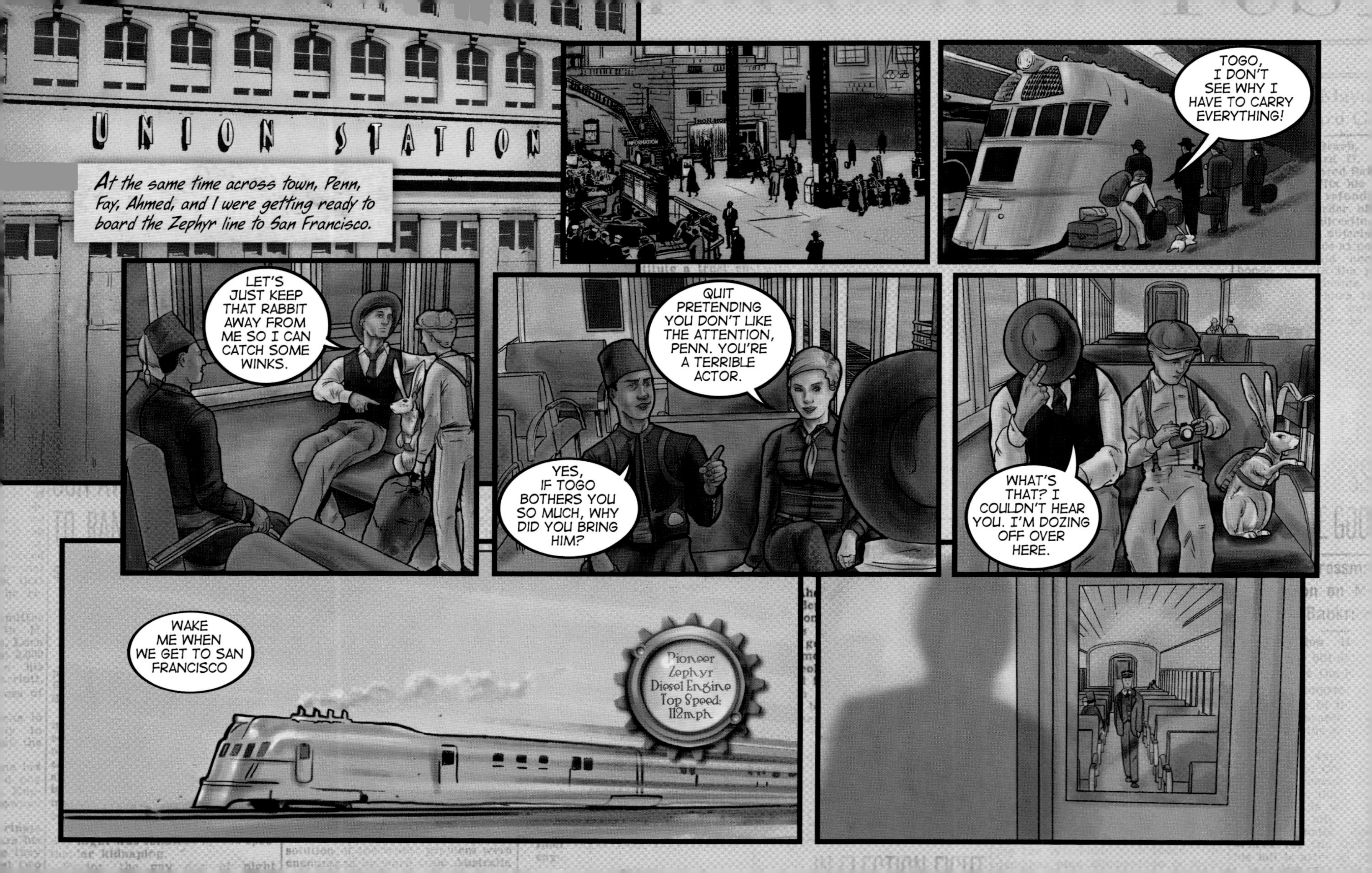
UNION STATION
At the same time across town, Penn, Fay, Ahmed, and I were getting ready to board the Zephyr line to San Francisco.
TOGO, I DON'T SEE WHY I HAVE TO CARRY EVERYTHING!
LET'S JUST KEEP THAT RABBIT AWAY FROM ME SO I CAN CATCH SOME WINKS.
QUIT PRETENDING YOU DON'T LIKE THE ATTENTION, PENN. YOU'RE A TERRIBLE ACTOR.
YES, IF TOGO BOTHERS YOU SO MUCH, WHY DID YOU BRING HIM?
WHAT'S THAT? I COULDN'T HEAR YOU. I'M DOZING OFF OVER HERE.
WAKE ME WHEN WE GET TO SAN FRANCISCO
Pioneer Zephyr Diesel Engine Top Speed: 112mph

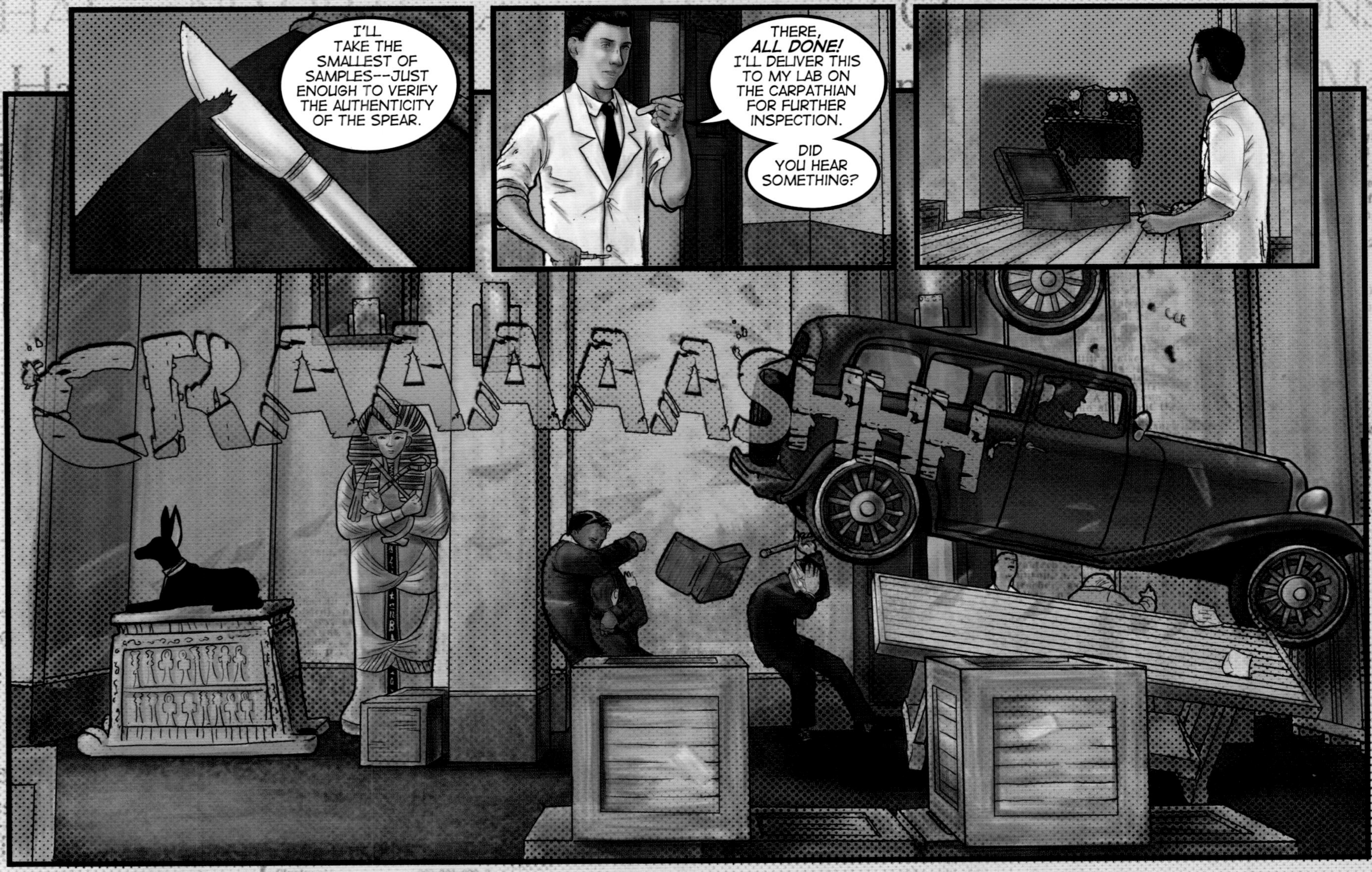
I'LL TAKE THE SMALLEST OF SAMPLES--JUST ENOUGH TO VERIFY THE AUTHENTICITY OF THE SPEAR.
THERE, ALL DONE! I'LL DELIVER THIS TO MY LAB ON THE CARPATHIAN FOR FURTHER INSPECTION.
DID YOU HEAR SOMETHING?
CRAAAAASHHH

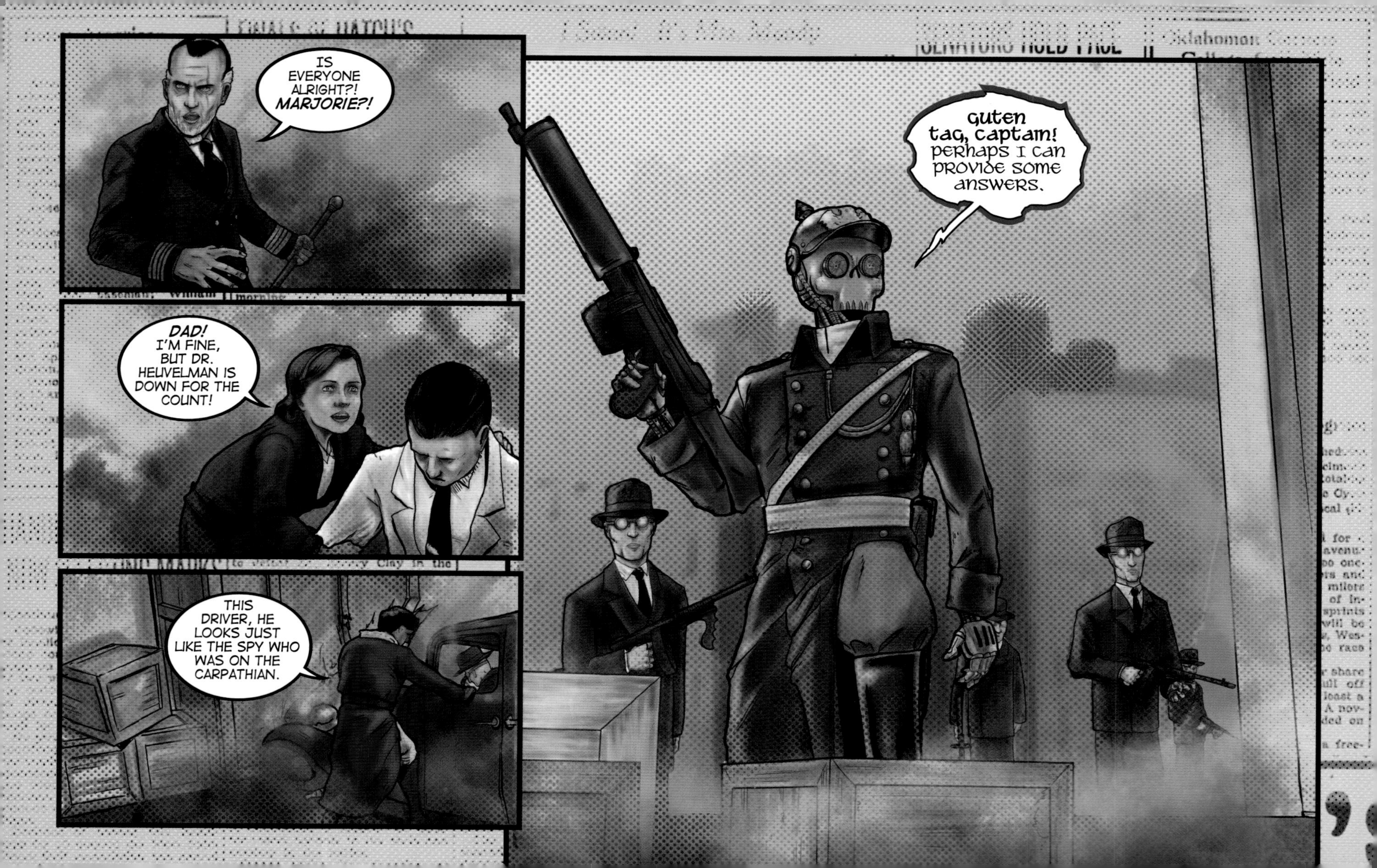
IS EVERYONE ALRIGHT?! MARJORIE?!
DAD! I'M FINE, BUT DR. HEUVELMAN IS DOWN FOR THE COUNT!
THIS DRIVER, HE LOOKS JUST LIKE THE SPY WHO WAS ON THE CARPATHIAN.
Guten tag, captain! Perhaps I can provide some answers.

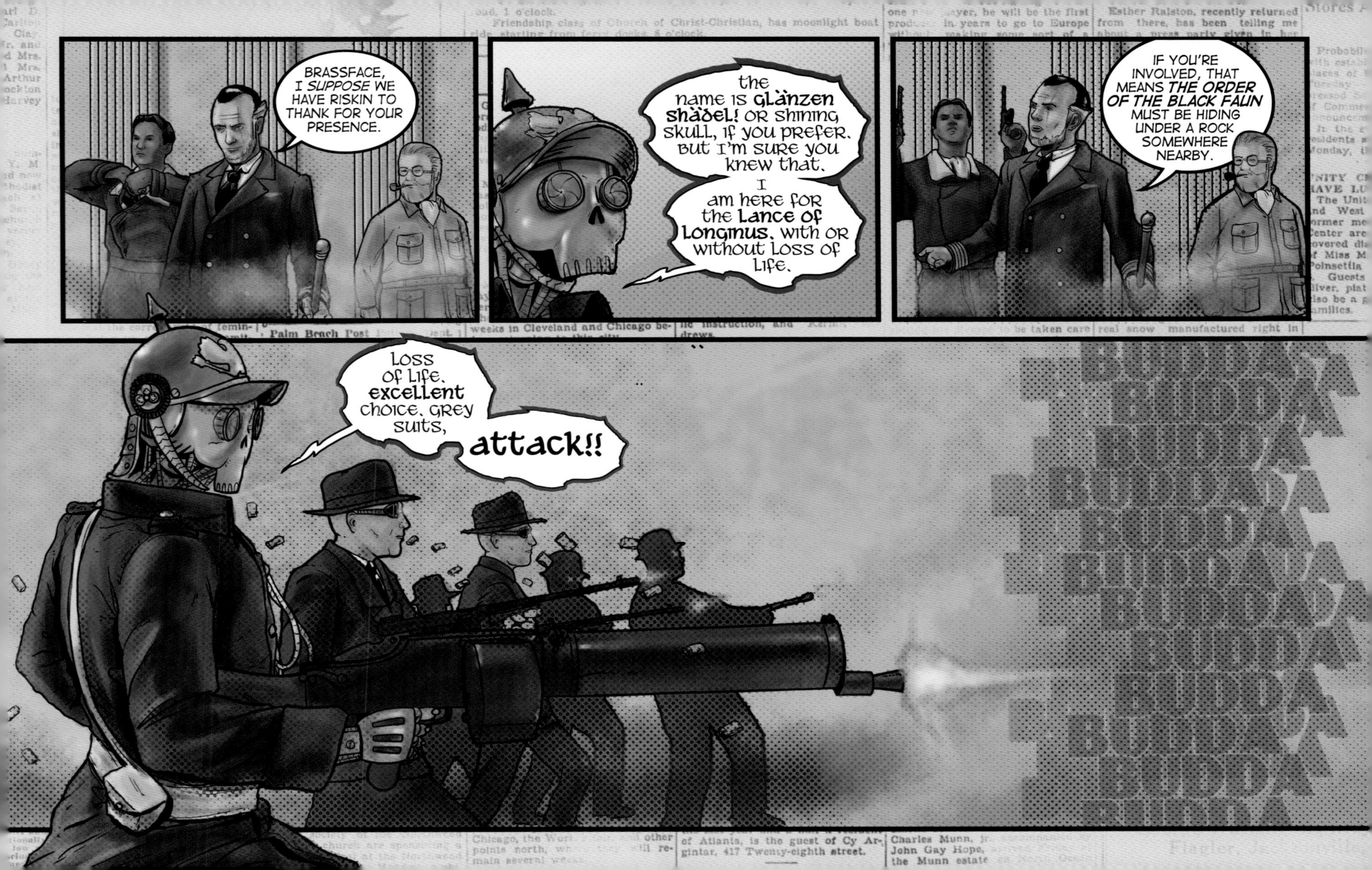
BRASSFACE, I SUPPOSE WE HAVE RISKIN TO THANK FOR YOUR PRESENCE.
the name is Glänzen Shädel! or shining skull, if you prefer. But I'm sure you knew that.
I am here for the Lance of Longmus, with or without loss of life.
IF YOU'RE INVOLVED, THAT MEANS THE ORDER OF THE BLACK FAUN MUST BE HIDING UNDER A ROCK SOMEWHERE NEARBY.
Loss of Life. excellent choice. Grey suits,
attack!!
BUDDA BUDDA BUDDA BUDDA BUDDA BUDDA BUDDA BUDDA BUDDA

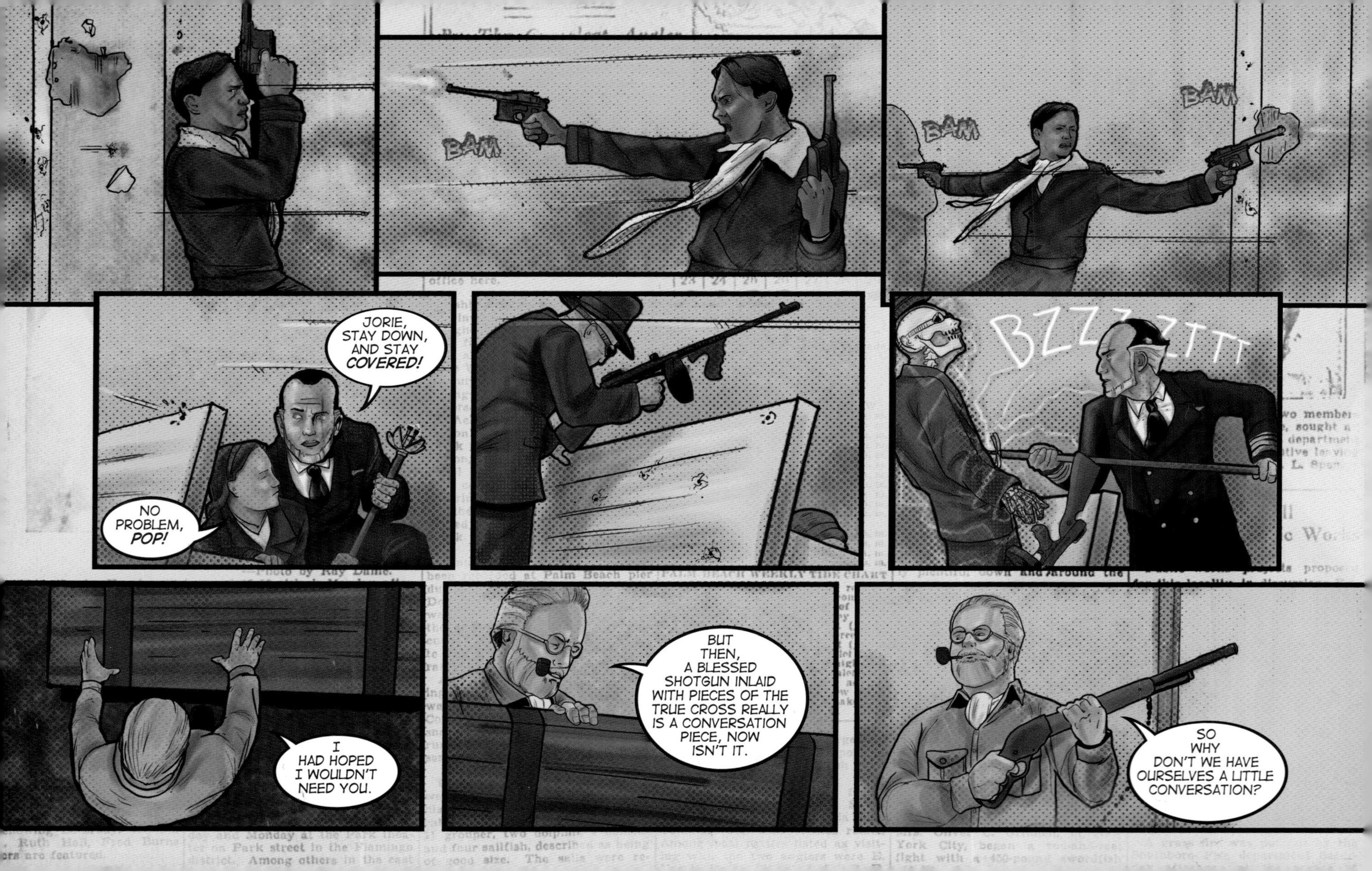
BAM
BAM
BAM
JORIE, STAY DOWN, AND STAY *COVERED!*
NO PROBLEM, *POP!*
BZZZ ZTTT
I HAD HOPED I WOULDN'T NEED YOU.
BUT THEN, A BLESSED SHOTGUN INLAID WITH PIECES OF THE TRUE CROSS REALLY IS A CONVERSATION PIECE, NOW ISN'T IT.
SO WHY DON'T WE HAVE OURSELVES A LITTLE CONVERSATION?

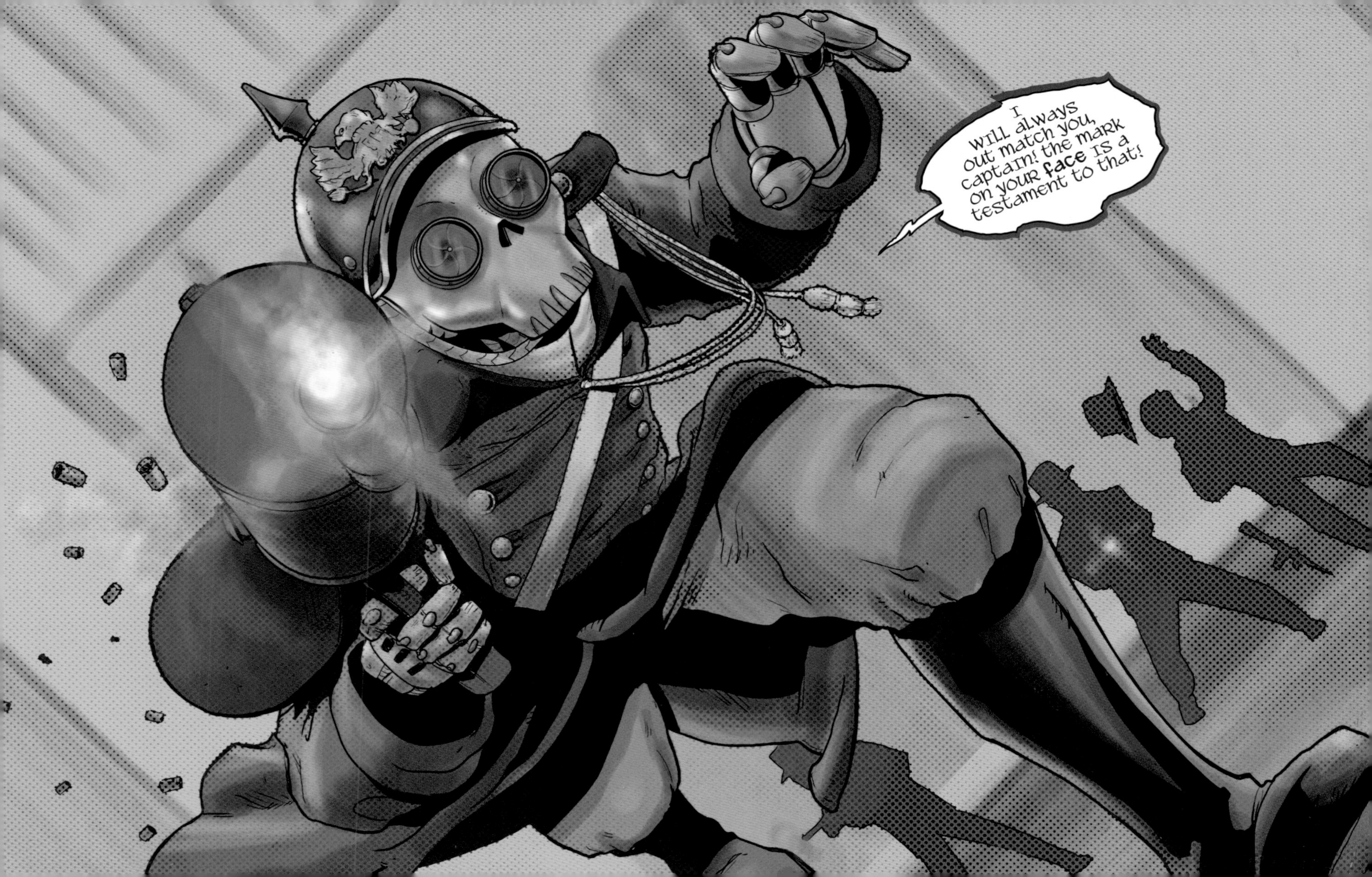
I WILL always out match you, captain! the mark on your face IS a testament to that!

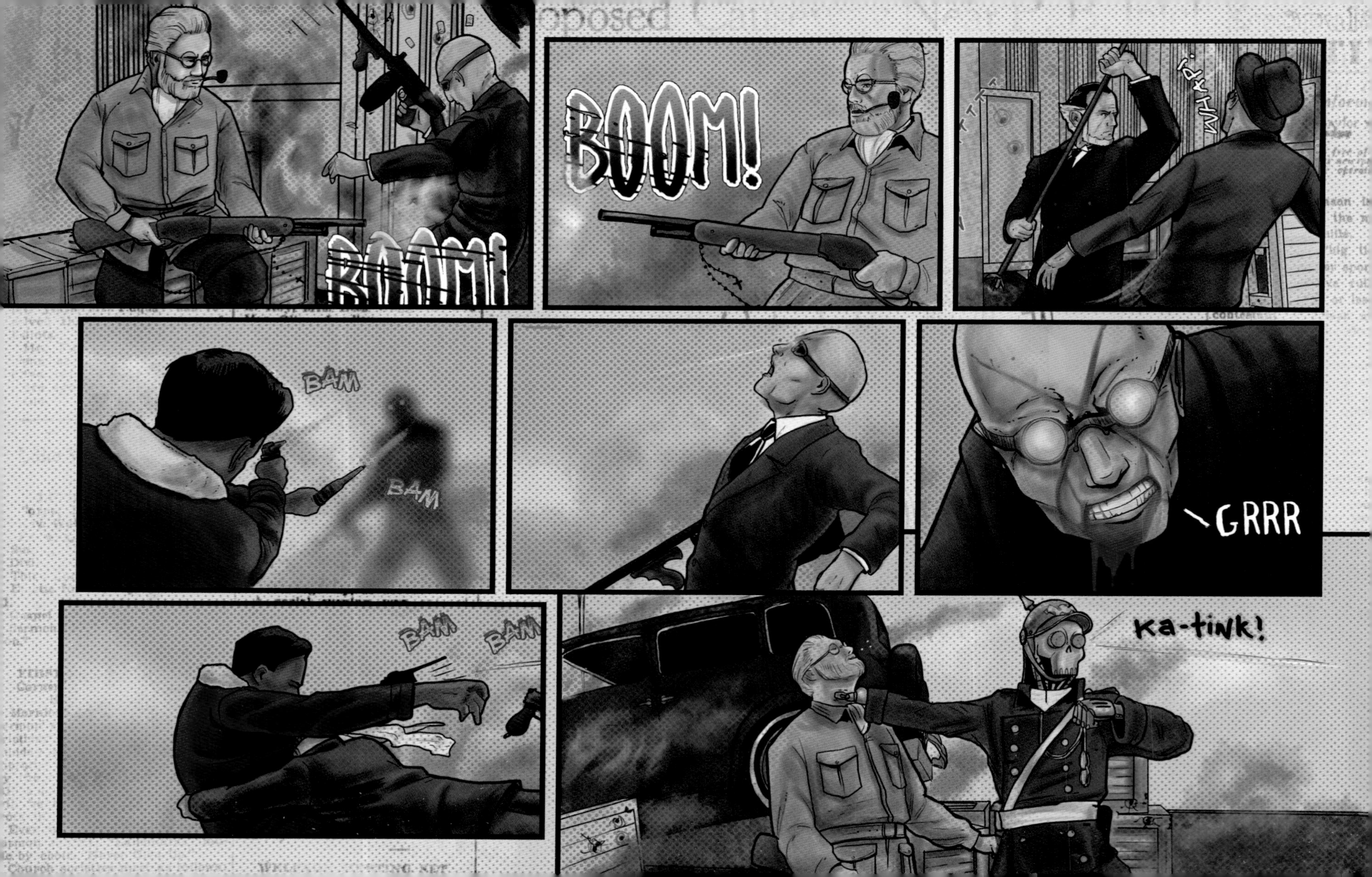
BOOM!
BOOM!
WHAP!
BAM
BAM
GRRR
BAM
BAM
Ka-tink!

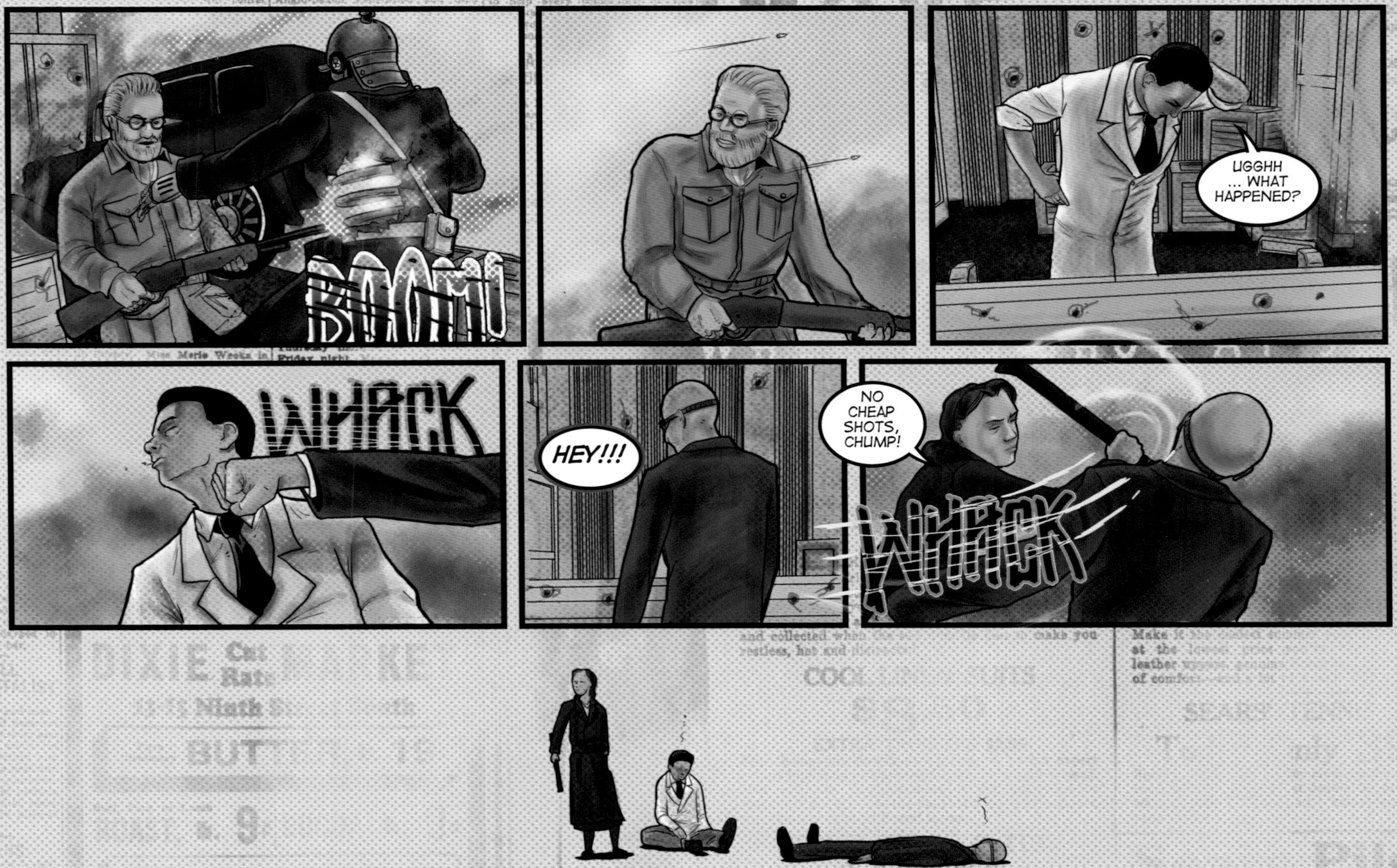
BOOM!
UGGHH ... WHAT HAPPENED?
WHACK
HEY!!!
NO CHEAP SHOTS, CHUMP!
WHACK

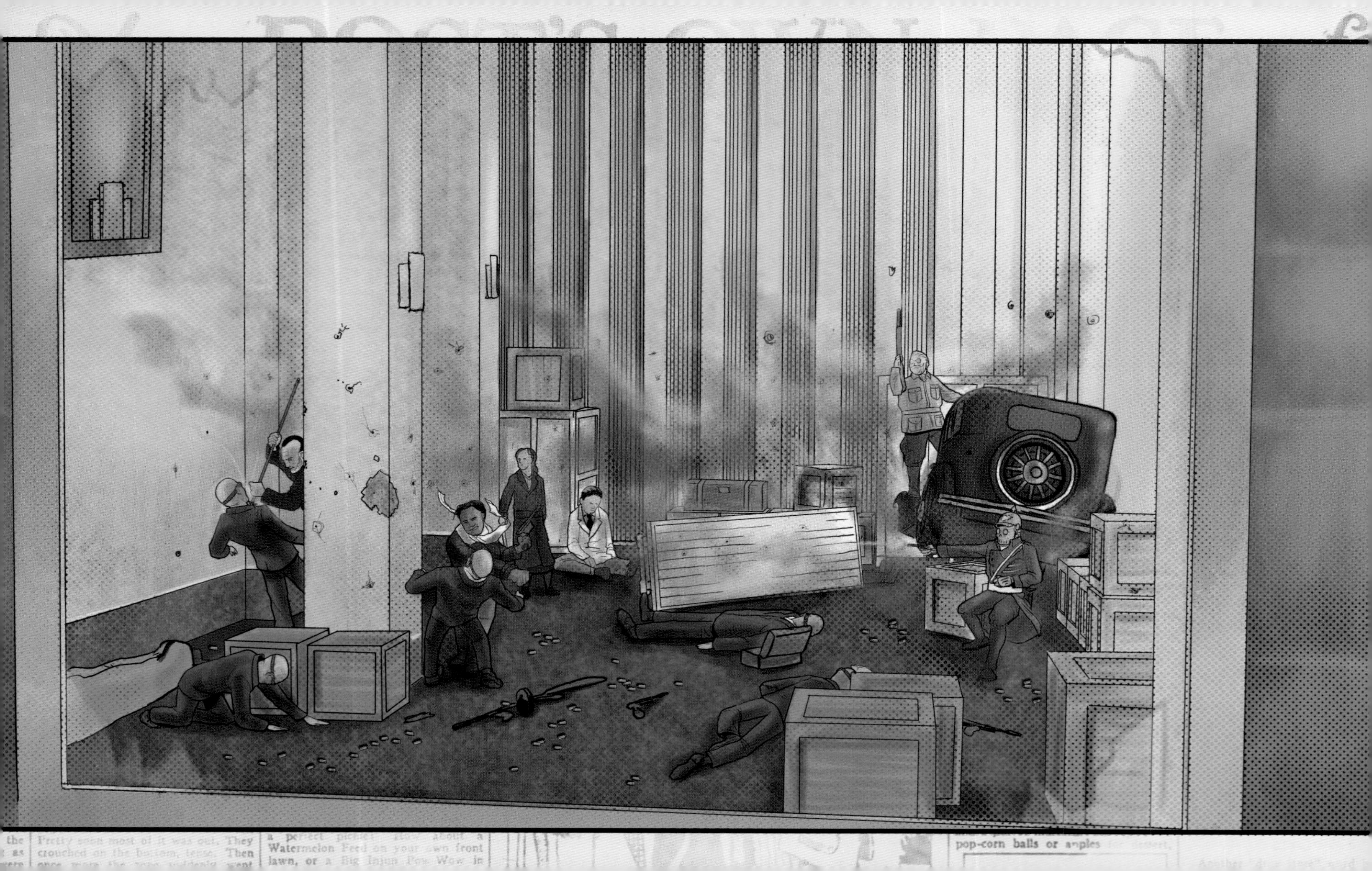
Pretty soon most of it was out. They
crouched on the bottom, tense. Then
Watermelon Feed on your own front
lawn, or a Big Injun Pow Wow in
pop-corn balls or apples

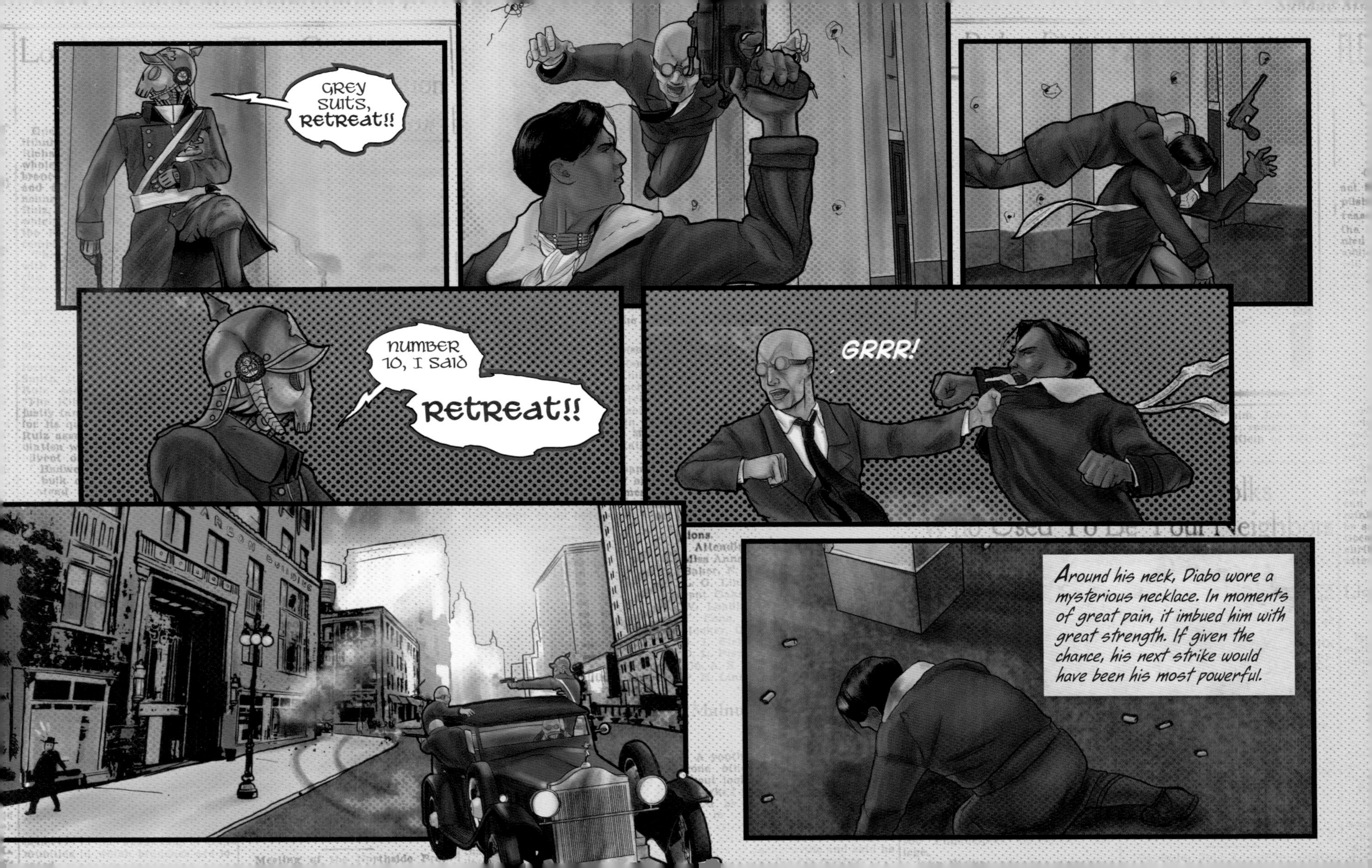
GREY SUITS, RETREAT!!
NUMBER 10, I SAID
RETREAT!!
GRRR!
Around his neck, Diabo wore a mysterious necklace. In moments of great pain, it imbued him with great strength. If given the chance, his next strike would have been his most powerful.

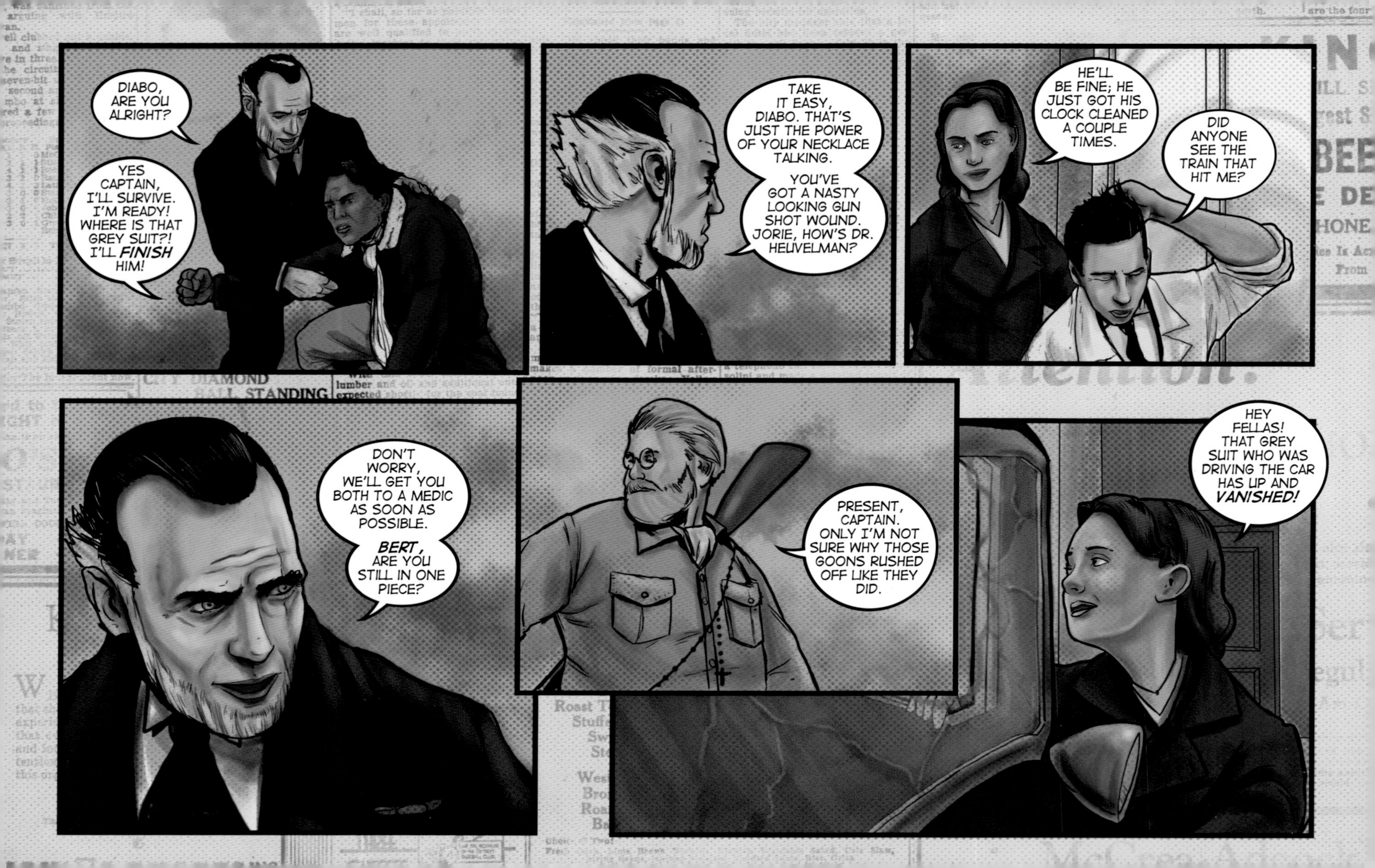

DIABO, ARE YOU ALRIGHT?
YES CAPTAIN, I'LL SURVIVE. I'M READY! WHERE IS THAT GREY SUIT?! I'LL *FINISH* HIM!
TAKE IT EASY, DIABO. THAT'S JUST THE POWER OF YOUR NECKLACE TALKING.
YOU'VE GOT A NASTY LOOKING GUN SHOT WOUND. JORIE, HOW'S DR. HEUVELMAN?
HE'LL BE FINE; HE JUST GOT HIS CLOCK CLEANED A COUPLE TIMES.
DID ANYONE SEE THE TRAIN THAT HIT ME?
DON'T WORRY, WE'LL GET YOU BOTH TO A MEDIC AS SOON AS POSSIBLE.
BERT, ARE YOU STILL IN ONE PIECE?
PRESENT, CAPTAIN. ONLY I'M NOT SURE WHY THOSE GOONS RUSHED OFF LIKE THEY DID.
HEY FELLAS! THAT GREY SUIT WHO WAS DRIVING THE CAR HAS UP AND *VANISHED!*

THE SPEAR?!

Smoke from the engine fire filled the room. Shell casings covered the floor. Bert found the box containing the spear on the ground and opened it.

THE BOX, IT'S HERE! IT'S...

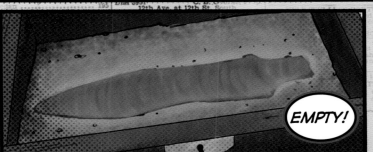

EMPTY!

HEUVELMAN! DO YOU STILL HAVE THE SAMPLE?

RIGHT HERE, *CAPTAIN*. SAFE AND SOUND!

GOOD, THAT'S A START. AT LEAST WE MIGHT BE ABLE TO DETERMINE THE TRUE POWER THE SPEAR MAY HOLD.

AND MAYBE SOME WAY TO COUNTERACT IT.

HEY, THIS ONE HERE IS STILL BREATHING! YOU WANT I SHOULD *KNOCK* HIS BLOCK OFF?!

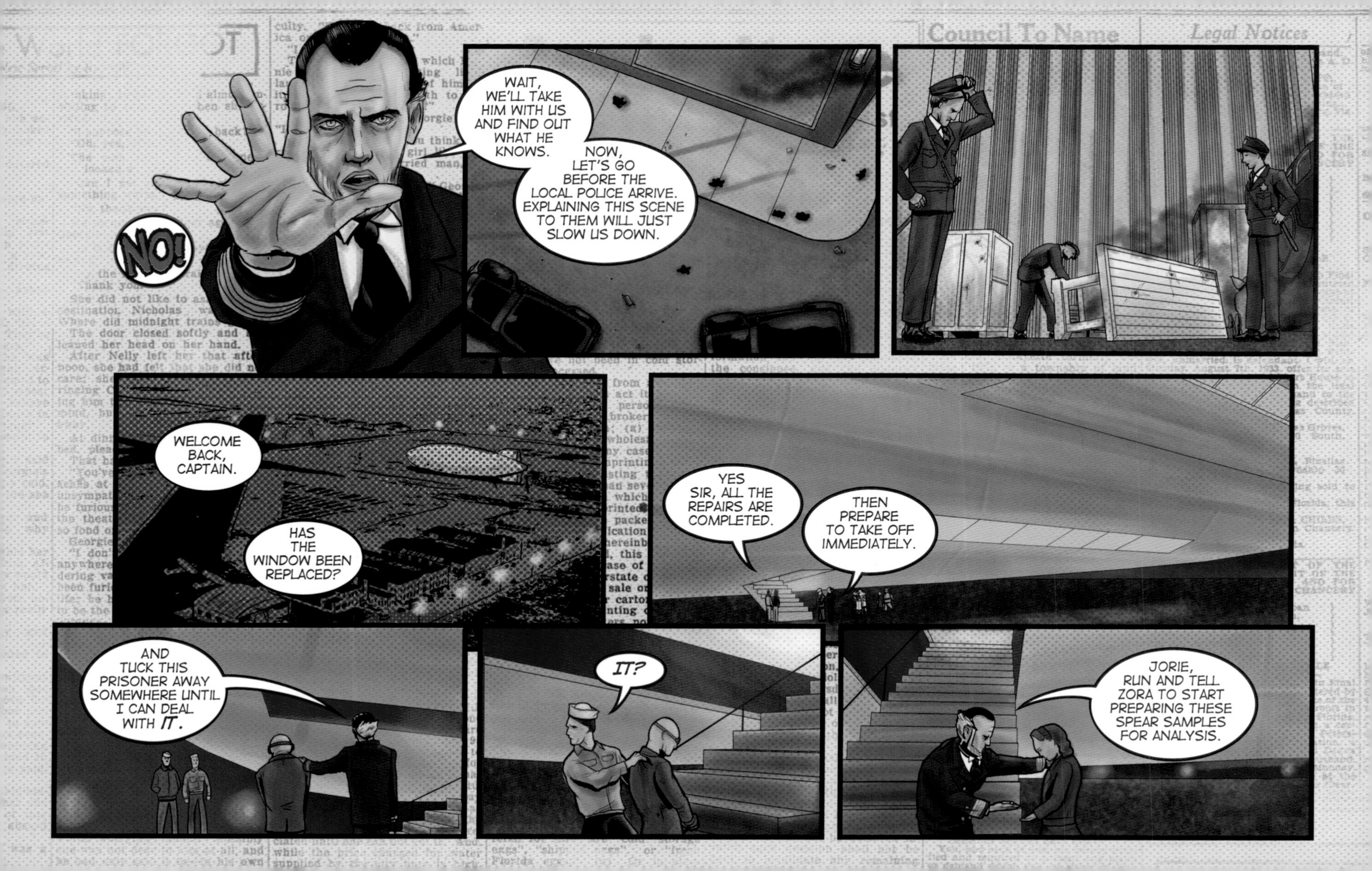
NO!
WAIT, WE'LL TAKE HIM WITH US AND FIND OUT WHAT HE KNOWS.
NOW, LET'S GO BEFORE THE LOCAL POLICE ARRIVE. EXPLAINING THIS SCENE TO THEM WILL JUST SLOW US DOWN.
WELCOME BACK, CAPTAIN.
HAS THE WINDOW BEEN REPLACED?
YES SIR, ALL THE REPAIRS ARE COMPLETED.
THEN PREPARE TO TAKE OFF IMMEDIATELY.
AND TUCK THIS PRISONER AWAY SOMEWHERE UNTIL I CAN DEAL WITH IT.
IT?
JORIE, RUN AND TELL ZORA TO START PREPARING THESE SPEAR SAMPLES FOR ANALYSIS.

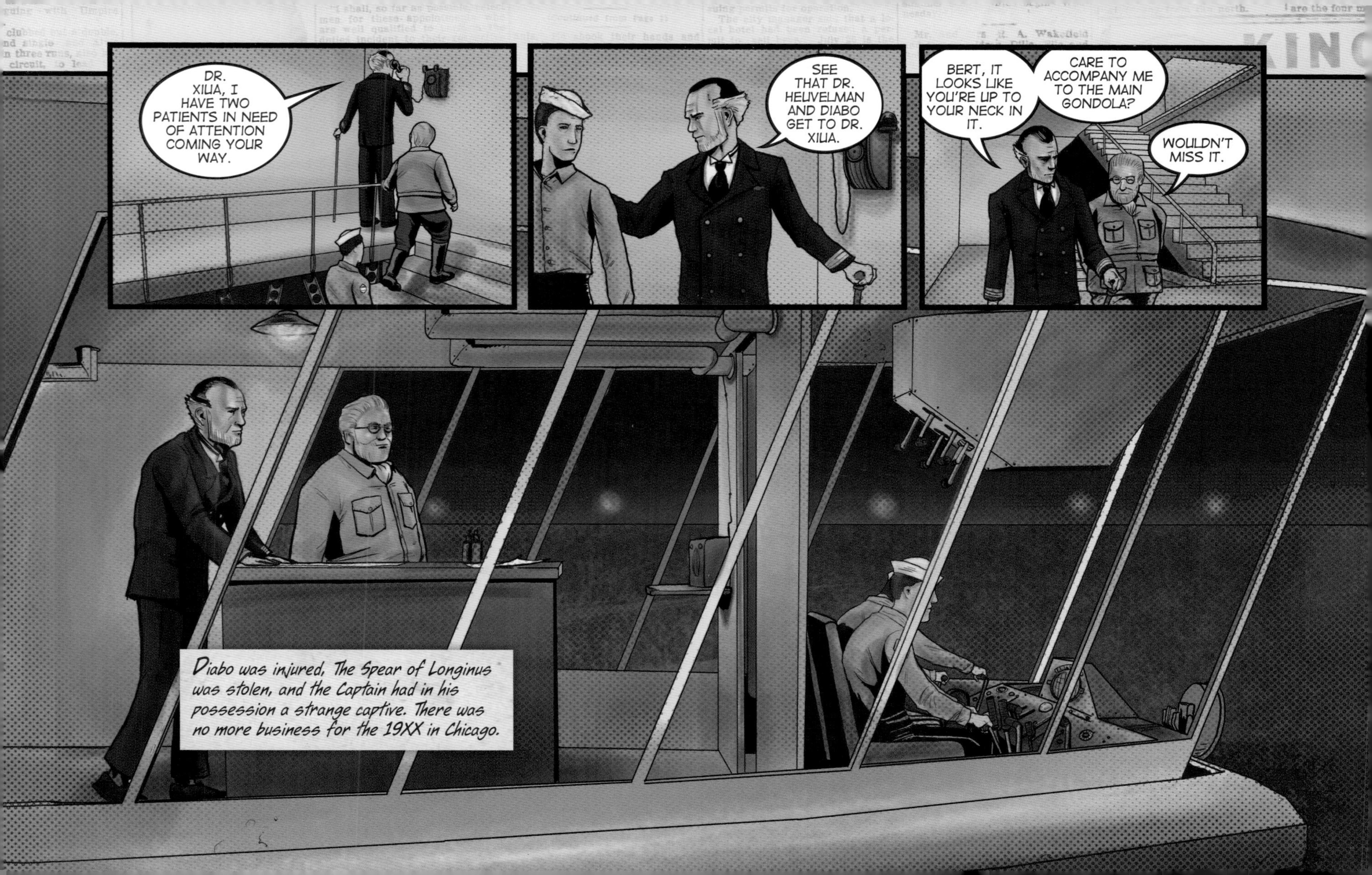
DR. XIUA, I HAVE TWO PATIENTS IN NEED OF ATTENTION COMING YOUR WAY.
SEE THAT DR. HEUVELMAN AND DIABO GET TO DR. XIUA.
BERT, IT LOOKS LIKE YOU'RE UP TO YOUR NECK IN IT.
CARE TO ACCOMPANY ME TO THE MAIN GONDOLA?
WOULDN'T MISS IT.
Diabo was injured, The Spear of Longinus was stolen, and the Captain had in his possession a strange captive. There was no more business for the 19XX in Chicago.

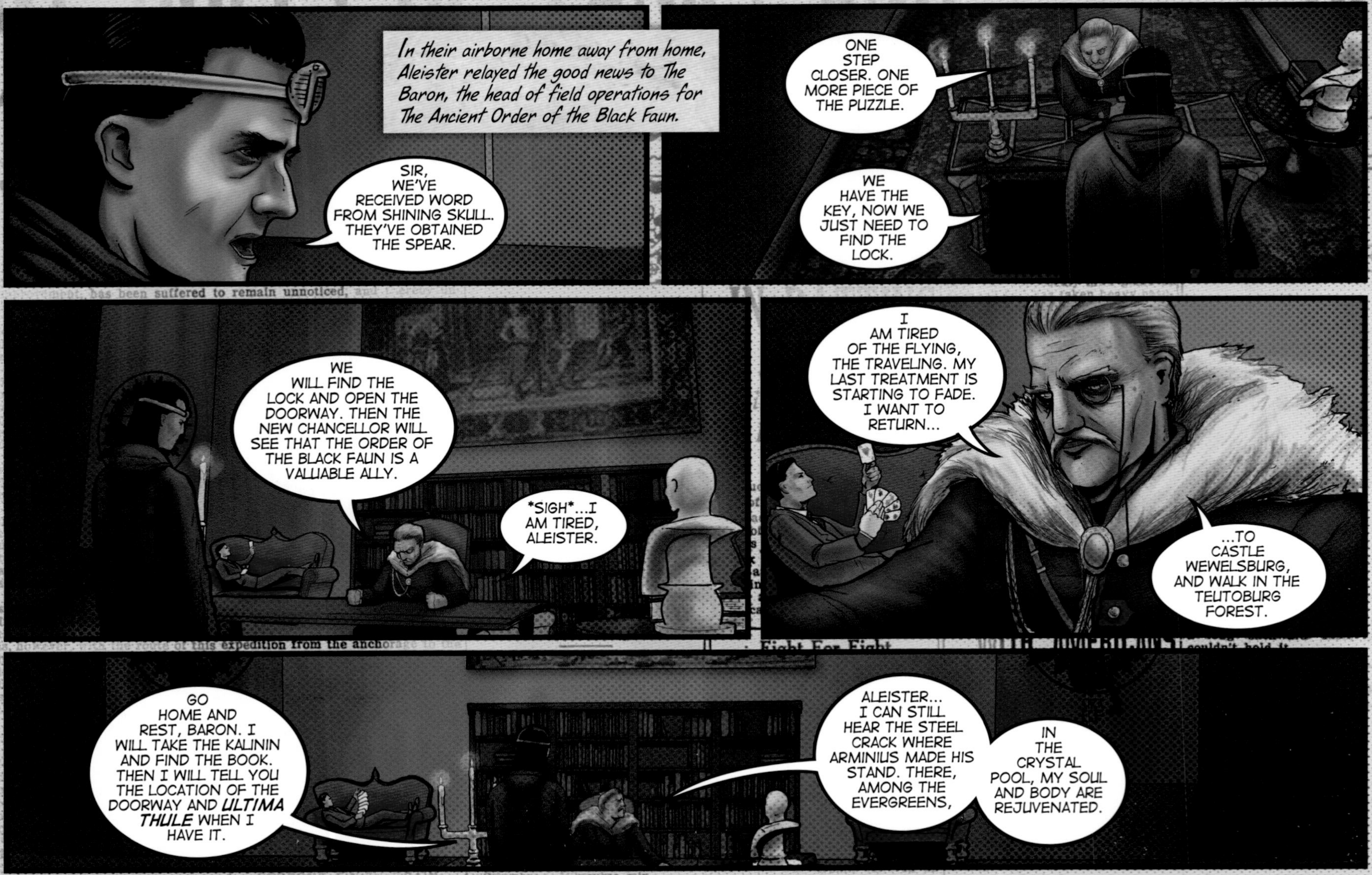
In their airborne home away from home, Aleister relayed the good news to The Baron, the head of field operations for The Ancient Order of the Black Faun.
SIR, WE'VE RECEIVED WORD FROM SHINING SKULL. THEY'VE OBTAINED THE SPEAR.
ONE STEP CLOSER. ONE MORE PIECE OF THE PUZZLE.
WE HAVE THE KEY, NOW WE JUST NEED TO FIND THE LOCK.
WE WILL FIND THE LOCK AND OPEN THE DOORWAY. THEN THE NEW CHANCELLOR WILL SEE THAT THE ORDER OF THE BLACK FAUN IS A VALUABLE ALLY.
SIGH...I AM TIRED, ALEISTER.
I AM TIRED OF THE FLYING, THE TRAVELING. MY LAST TREATMENT IS STARTING TO FADE. I WANT TO RETURN...
...TO CASTLE WEWELSBURG, AND WALK IN THE TEUTOBURG FOREST.
GO HOME AND REST, BARON. I WILL TAKE THE KALININ AND FIND THE BOOK. THEN I WILL TELL YOU THE LOCATION OF THE DOORWAY AND ULTIMA THULE WHEN I HAVE IT.
ALEISTER... I CAN STILL HEAR THE STEEL CRACK WHERE ARMINIUS MADE HIS STAND. THERE, AMONG THE EVERGREENS,
IN THE CRYSTAL POOL, MY SOUL AND BODY ARE REJUVENATED.

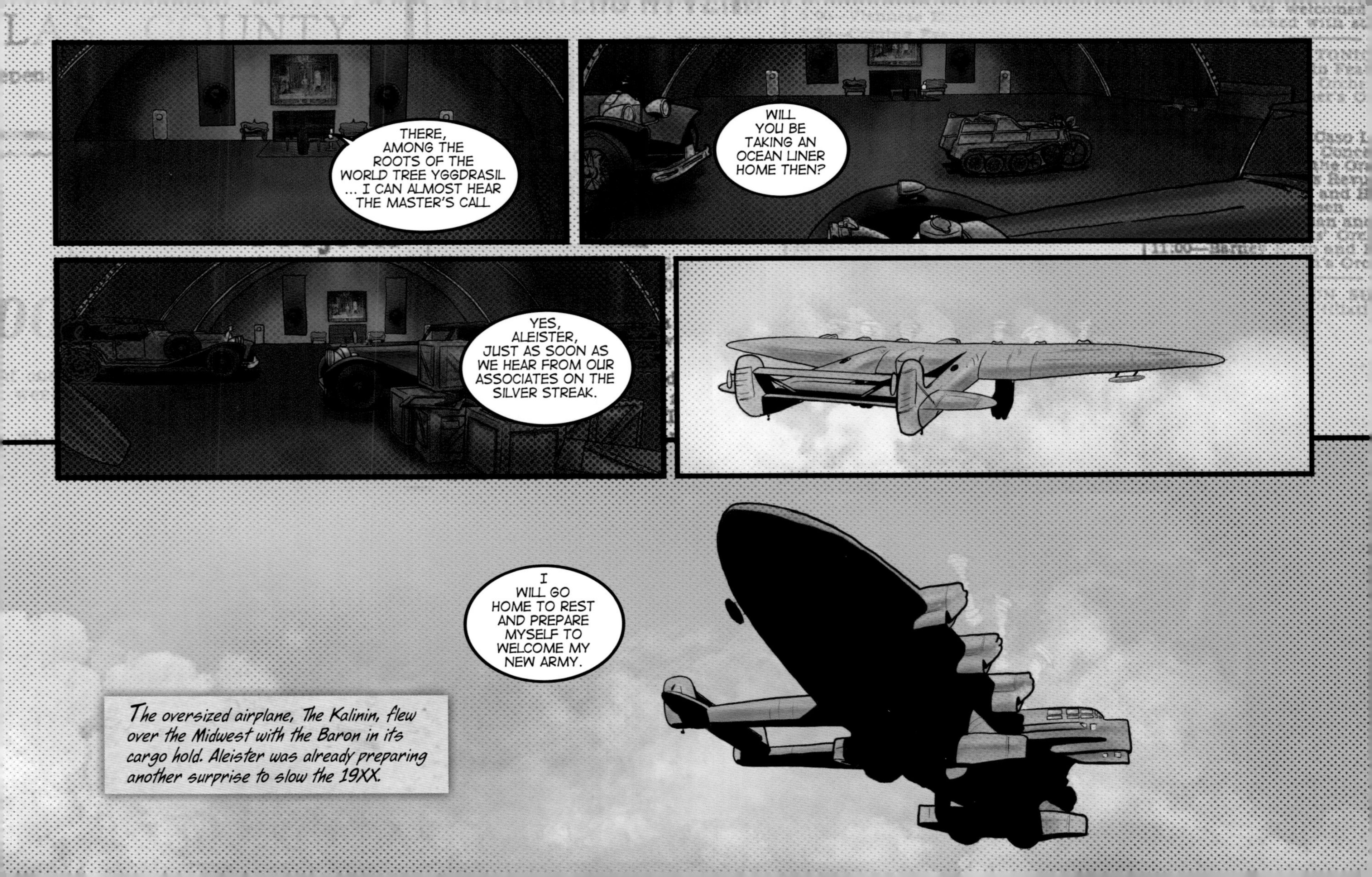

THERE, AMONG THE ROOTS OF THE WORLD TREE YGGDRASIL ... I CAN ALMOST HEAR THE MASTER'S CALL
WILL YOU BE TAKING AN OCEAN LINER HOME THEN?
YES, ALEISTER, JUST AS SOON AS WE HEAR FROM OUR ASSOCIATES ON THE SILVER STREAK.
I WILL GO HOME TO REST AND PREPARE MYSELF TO WELCOME MY NEW ARMY.
The oversized airplane, The Kalinin, flew over the Midwest with the Baron in its cargo hold. Aleister was already preparing another surprise to slow the 19XX.

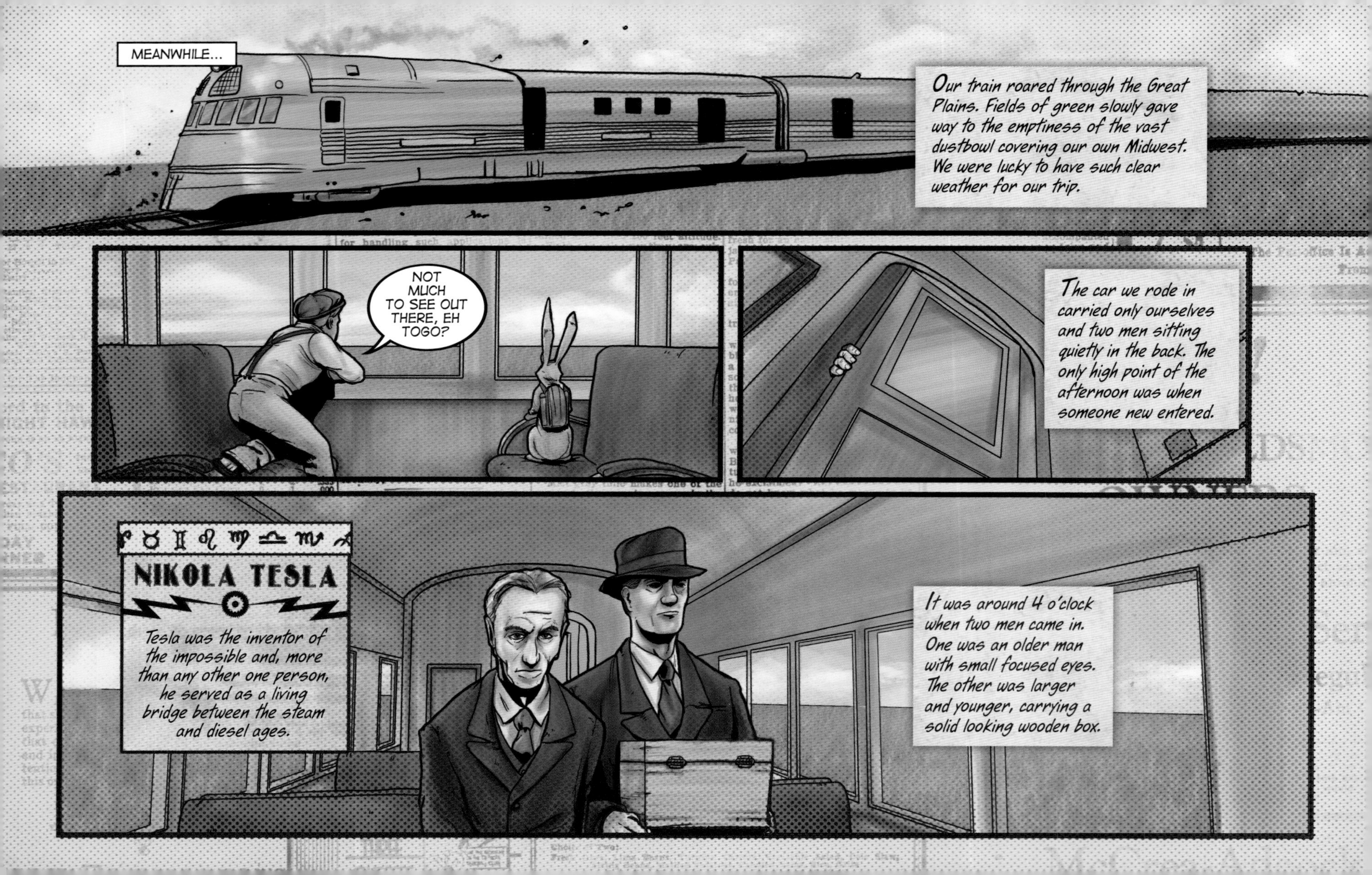

MEANWHILE...
Our train roared through the Great Plains. Fields of green slowly gave way to the emptiness of the vast dustbowl covering our own Midwest. We were lucky to have such clear weather for our trip.
NOT MUCH TO SEE OUT THERE, EH TOGO?
The car we rode in carried only ourselves and two men sitting quietly in the back. The only high point of the afternoon was when someone new entered.
NIKOLA TESLA
Tesla was the inventor of the impossible and, more than any other one person, he served as a living bridge between the steam and diesel ages.
It was around 4 o'clock when two men came in. One was an older man with small focused eyes. The other was larger and younger, carrying a solid looking wooden box.

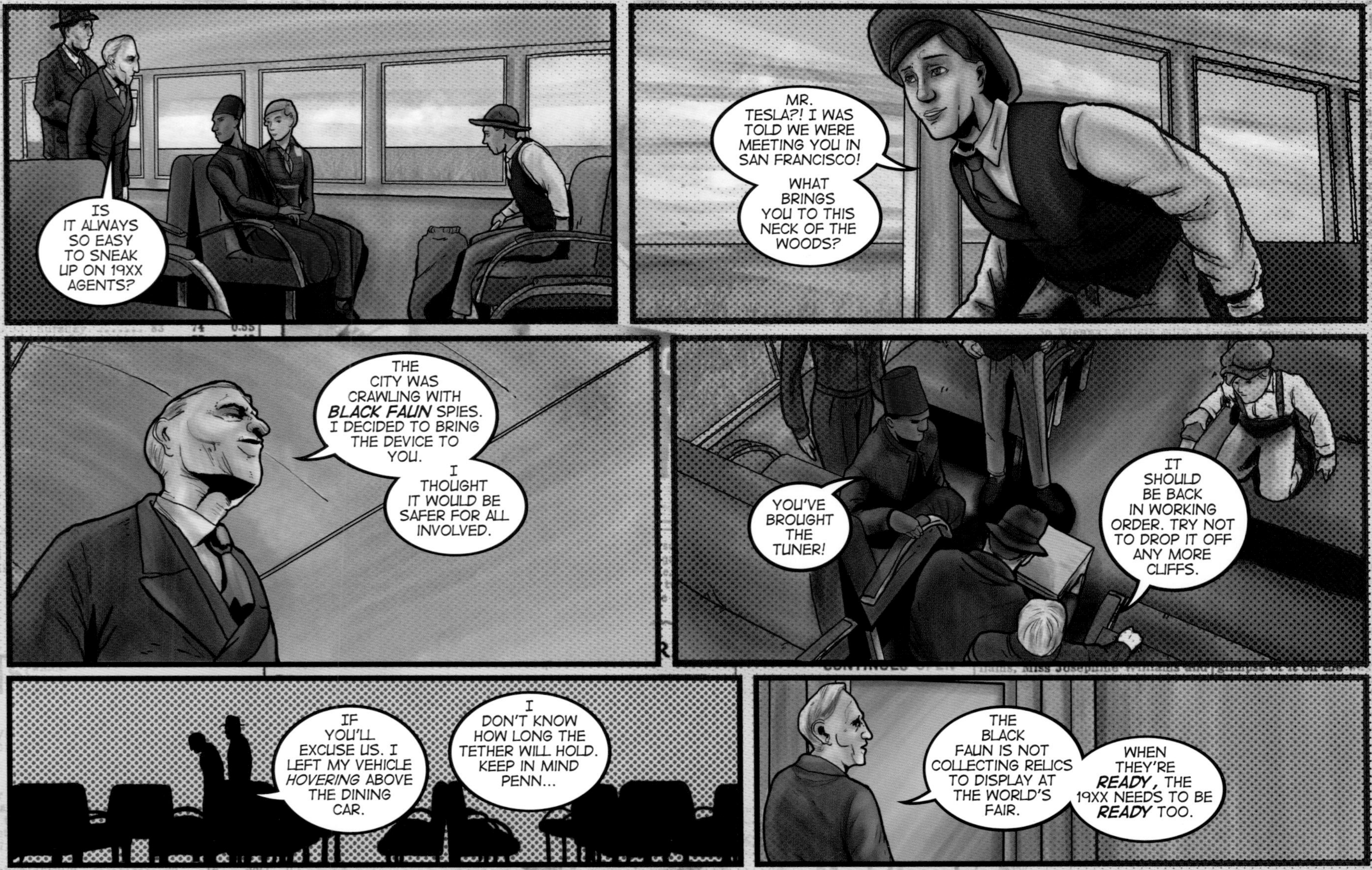
IS IT ALWAYS SO EASY TO SNEAK UP ON 19XX AGENTS?
MR. TESLA?! I WAS TOLD WE WERE MEETING YOU IN SAN FRANCISCO!
WHAT BRINGS YOU TO THIS NECK OF THE WOODS?
THE CITY WAS CRAWLING WITH BLACK FAUN SPIES. I DECIDED TO BRING THE DEVICE TO YOU.
I THOUGHT IT WOULD BE SAFER FOR ALL INVOLVED.
YOU'VE BROUGHT THE TUNER!
IT SHOULD BE BACK IN WORKING ORDER. TRY NOT TO DROP IT OFF ANY MORE CLIFFS.
IF YOU'LL EXCUSE US. I LEFT MY VEHICLE HOVERING ABOVE THE DINING CAR.
I DON'T KNOW HOW LONG THE TETHER WILL HOLD. KEEP IN MIND PENN...
THE BLACK FAUN IS NOT COLLECTING RELICS TO DISPLAY AT THE WORLD'S FAIR.
WHEN THEY'RE READY, THE 19XX NEEDS TO BE READY TOO.

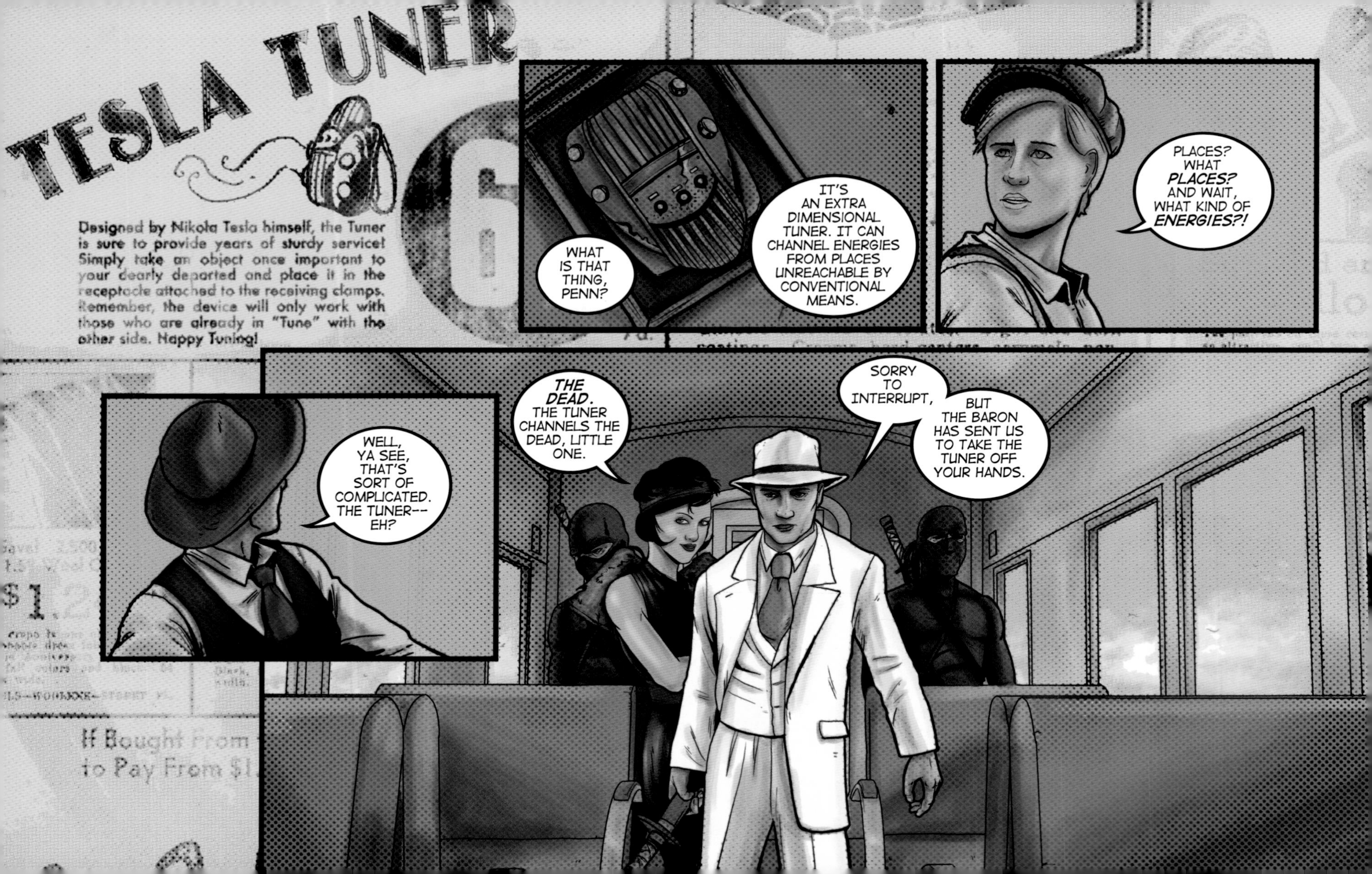
TESLA TUNER
6
Designed by Nikola Tesla himself, the Tuner is sure to provide years of sturdy service! Simply take an object once important to your dearly departed and place it in the receptacle attached to the receiving clamps. Remember, the device will only work with those who are already in "Tune" with the other side. Happy Tuning!
WHAT IS THAT THING, PENN?
IT'S AN EXTRA DIMENSIONAL TUNER. IT CAN CHANNEL ENERGIES FROM PLACES UNREACHABLE BY CONVENTIONAL MEANS.
PLACES? WHAT *PLACES?* AND WAIT, WHAT KIND OF *ENERGIES?!*
WELL, YA SEE, THAT'S SORT OF COMPLICATED. THE TUNER-- EH?
THE DEAD. THE TUNER CHANNELS THE DEAD, LITTLE ONE.
SORRY TO INTERRUPT,
BUT THE BARON HAS SENT US TO TAKE THE TUNER OFF YOUR HANDS.

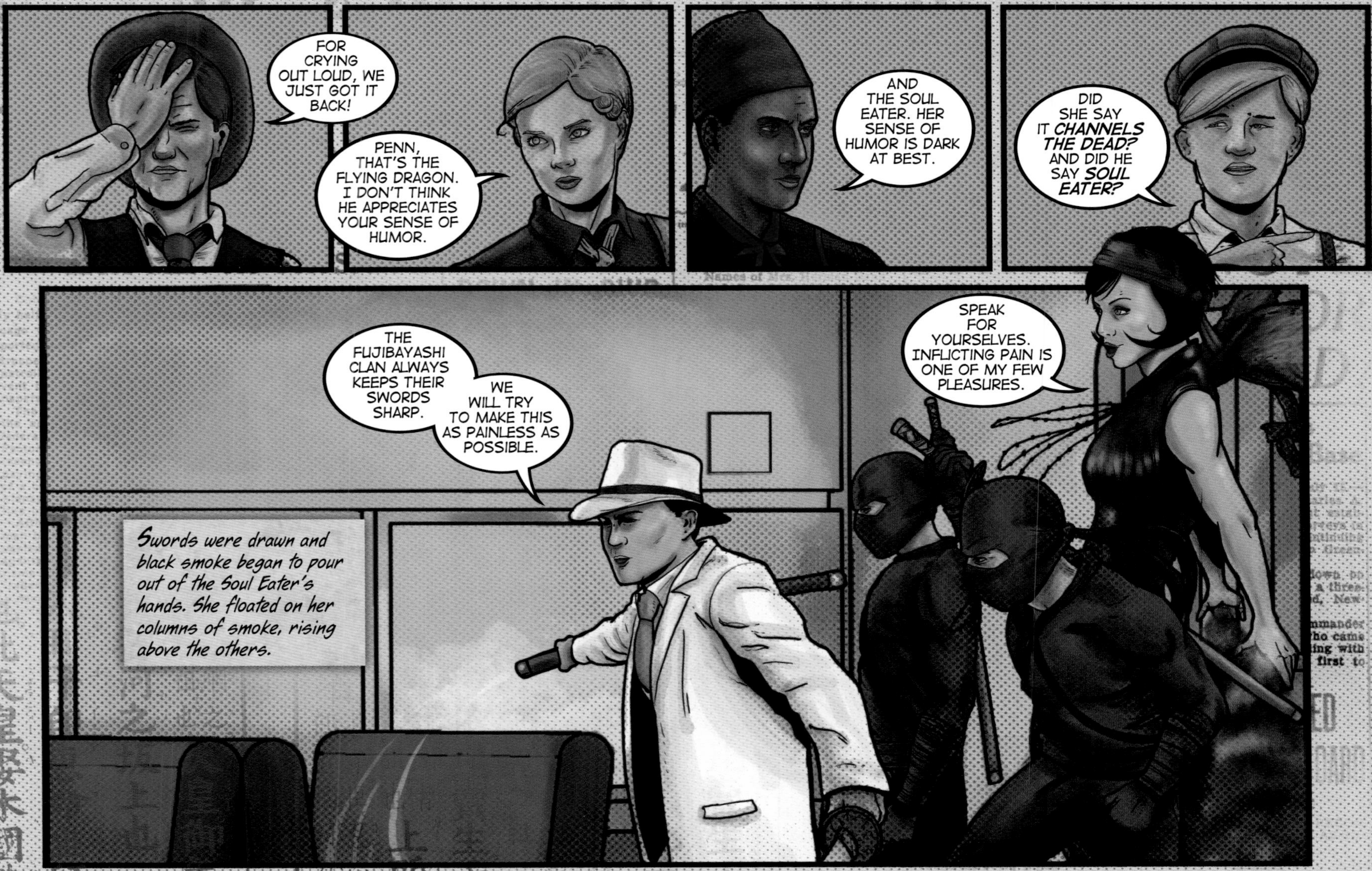
FOR CRYING OUT LOUD, WE JUST GOT IT BACK!
PENN, THAT'S THE FLYING DRAGON. I DON'T THINK HE APPRECIATES YOUR SENSE OF HUMOR.
AND THE SOUL EATER. HER SENSE OF HUMOR IS DARK AT BEST.
DID SHE SAY IT CHANNELS THE DEAD? AND DID HE SAY SOUL EATER?
THE FUJIBAYASHI CLAN ALWAYS KEEPS THEIR SWORDS SHARP.
WE WILL TRY TO MAKE THIS AS PAINLESS AS POSSIBLE.
SPEAK FOR YOURSELVES. INFLICTING PAIN IS ONE OF MY FEW PLEASURES.
Swords were drawn and black smoke began to pour out of the Soul Eater's hands. She floated on her columns of smoke, rising above the others.

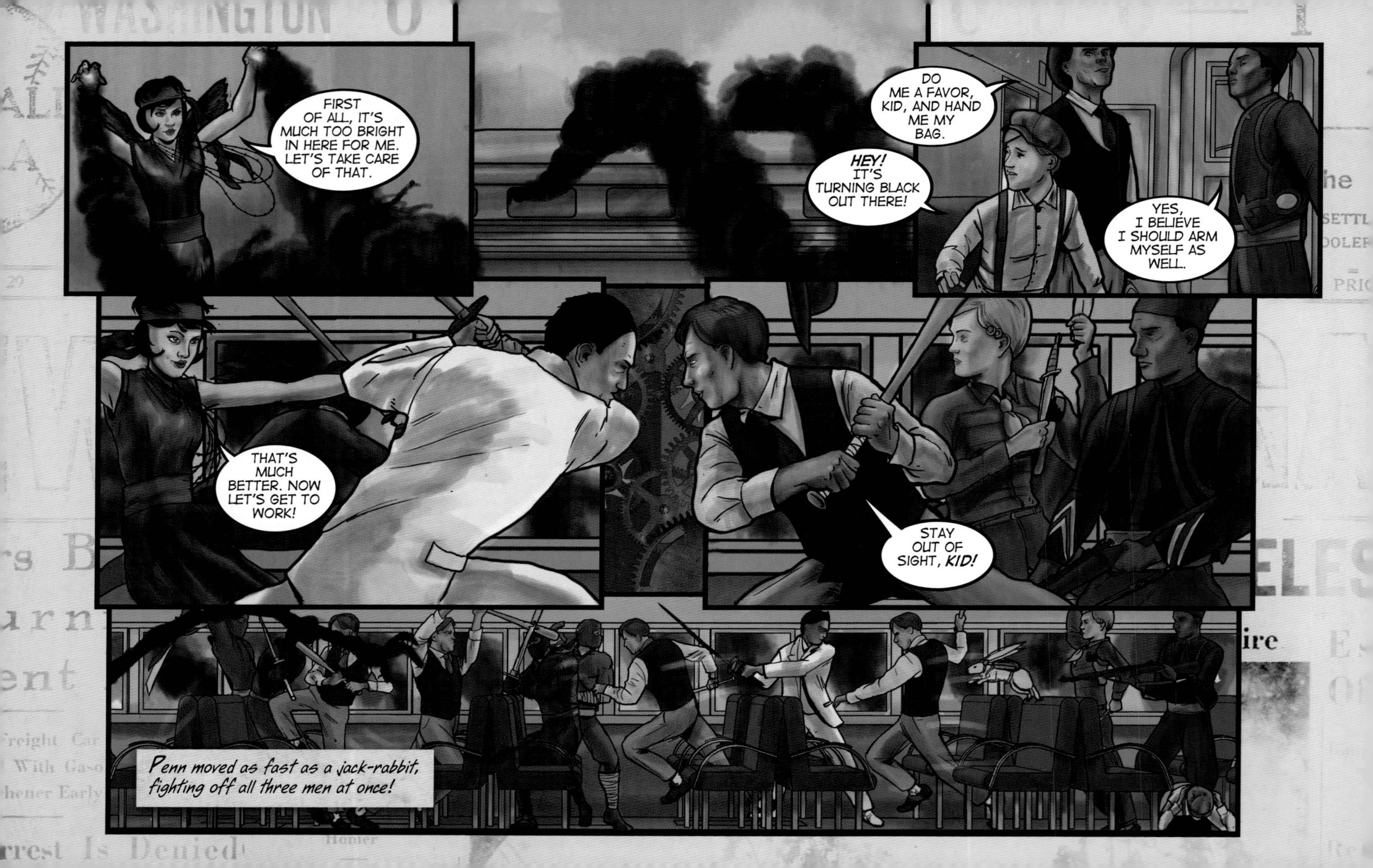
FIRST OF ALL, IT'S MUCH TOO BRIGHT IN HERE FOR ME. LET'S TAKE CARE OF THAT.
DO ME A FAVOR, KID, AND HAND ME MY BAG.
HEY! IT'S TURNING BLACK OUT THERE!
YES, I BELIEVE I SHOULD ARM MYSELF AS WELL.
THAT'S MUCH BETTER. NOW LET'S GET TO WORK!
STAY OUT OF SIGHT, *KID!*
Penn moved as fast as a jack-rabbit, fighting off all three men at once!

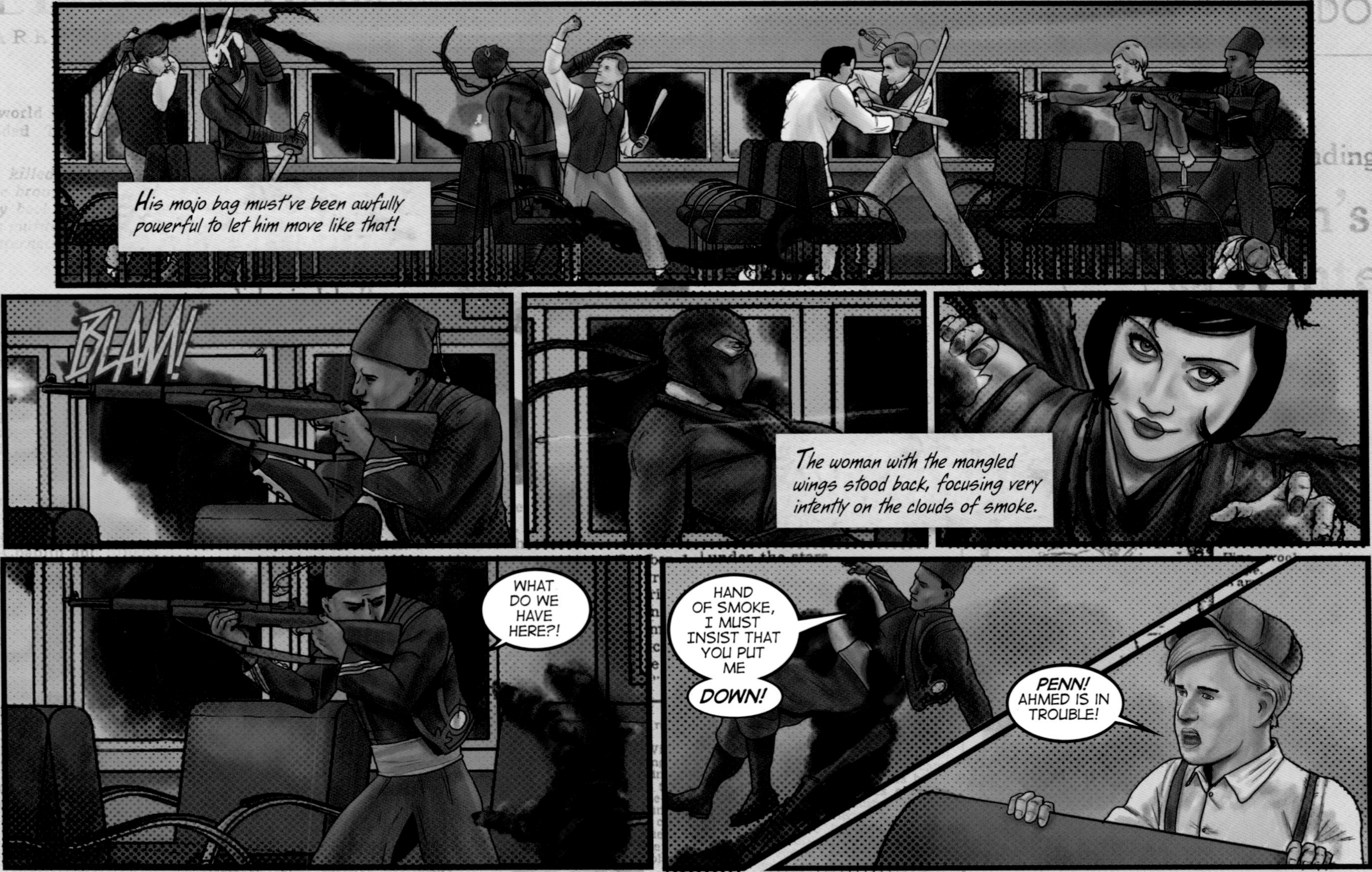
His mojo bag must've been awfully powerful to let him move like that!
BLAM!
The woman with the mangled wings stood back, focusing very intently on the clouds of smoke.
WHAT DO WE HAVE HERE?!
HAND OF SMOKE, I MUST INSIST THAT YOU PUT ME DOWN!
PENN! AHMED IS IN TROUBLE!

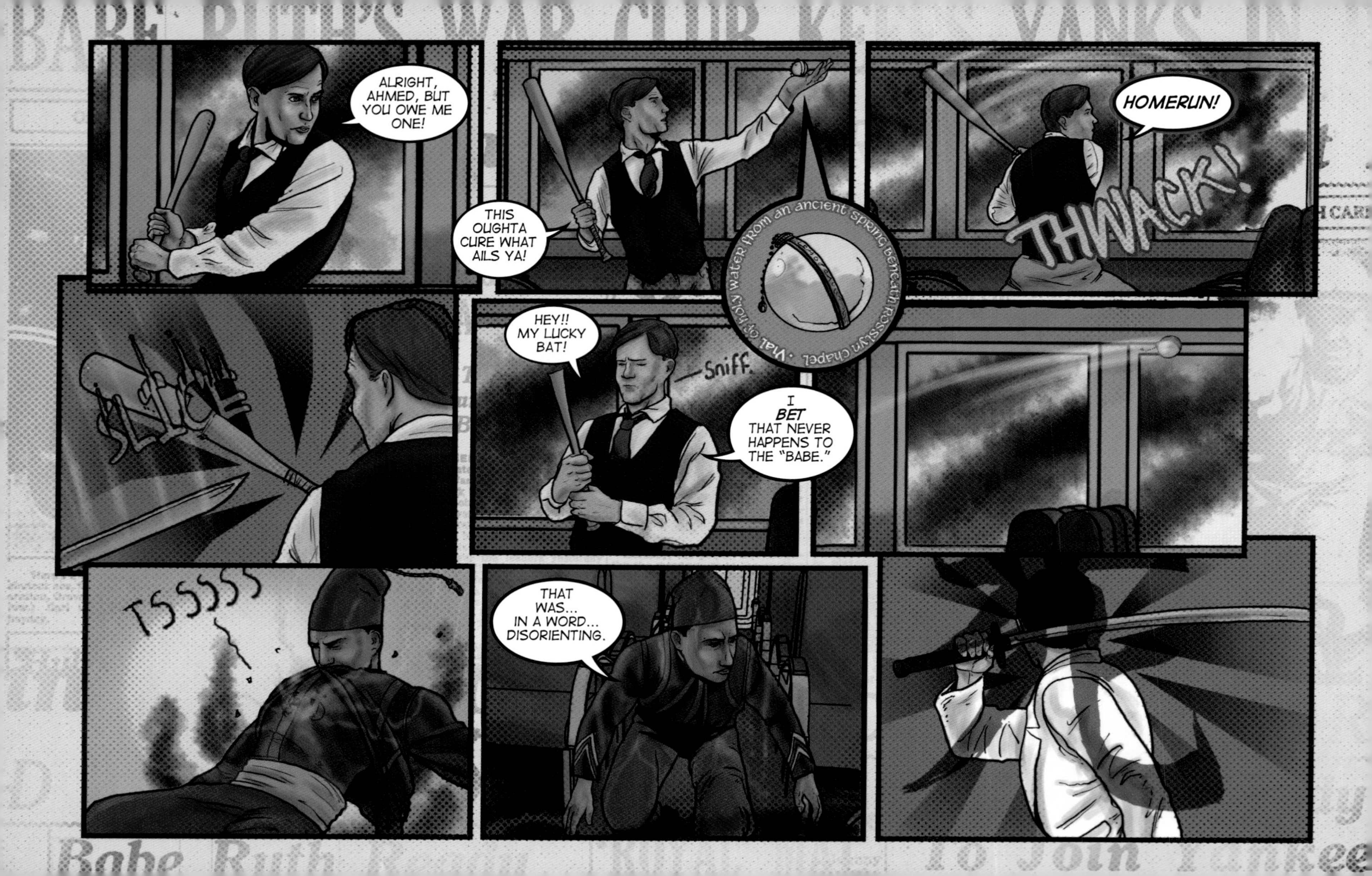
ALRIGHT, AHMED, BUT YOU OWE ME ONE!
THIS OUGHTA CURE WHAT AILS YA!
Vial of holy water from an ancient spring beneath Rosslyn chapel.
HOMERUN!
THWACK!
HEY!! MY LUCKY BAT!
Sniff.
I BET THAT NEVER HAPPENS TO THE "BABE."
TSSSSS
THAT WAS... IN A WORD... DISORIENTING.

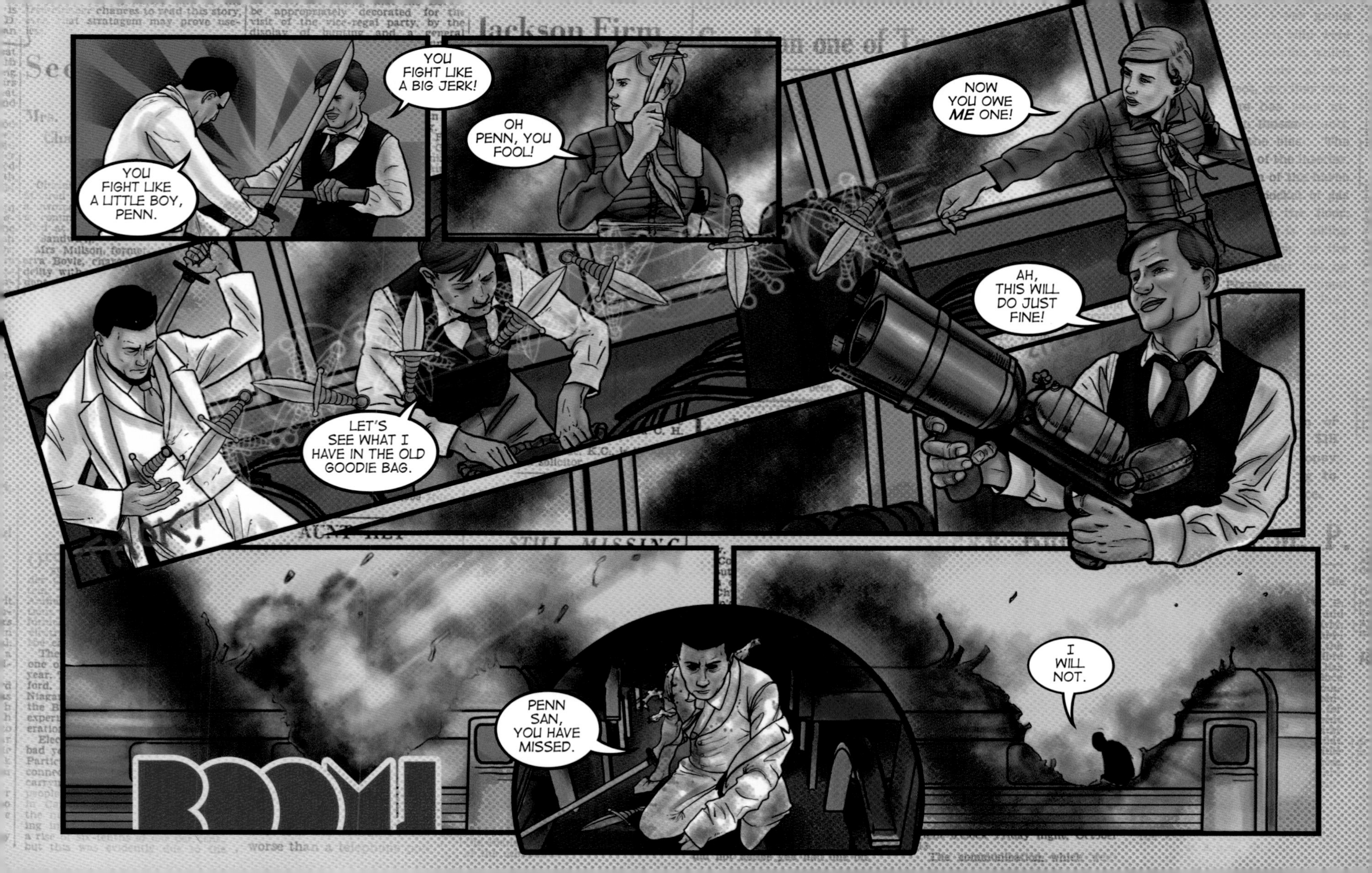
YOU FIGHT LIKE A LITTLE BOY, PENN.
YOU FIGHT LIKE A BIG JERK!
OH PENN, YOU FOOL!
NOW YOU OWE ME ONE!
LET'S SEE WHAT I HAVE IN THE OLD GOODIE BAG.
AH, THIS WILL DO JUST FINE!
BOOM!
PENN SAN, YOU HAVE MISSED.
I WILL NOT.

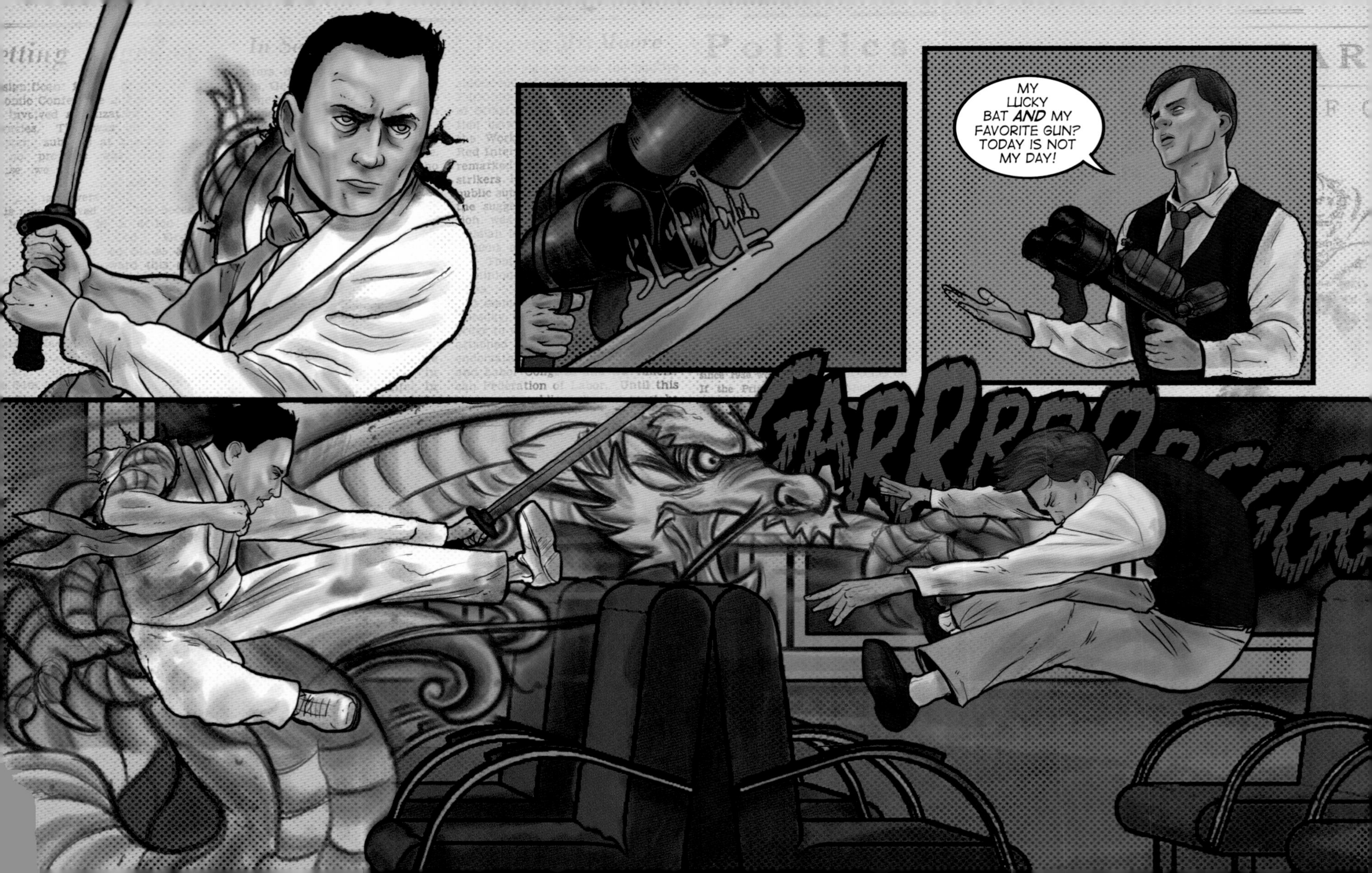
SLICE
MY LUCKY BAT AND MY FAVORITE GUN? TODAY IS NOT MY DAY!
GARRR

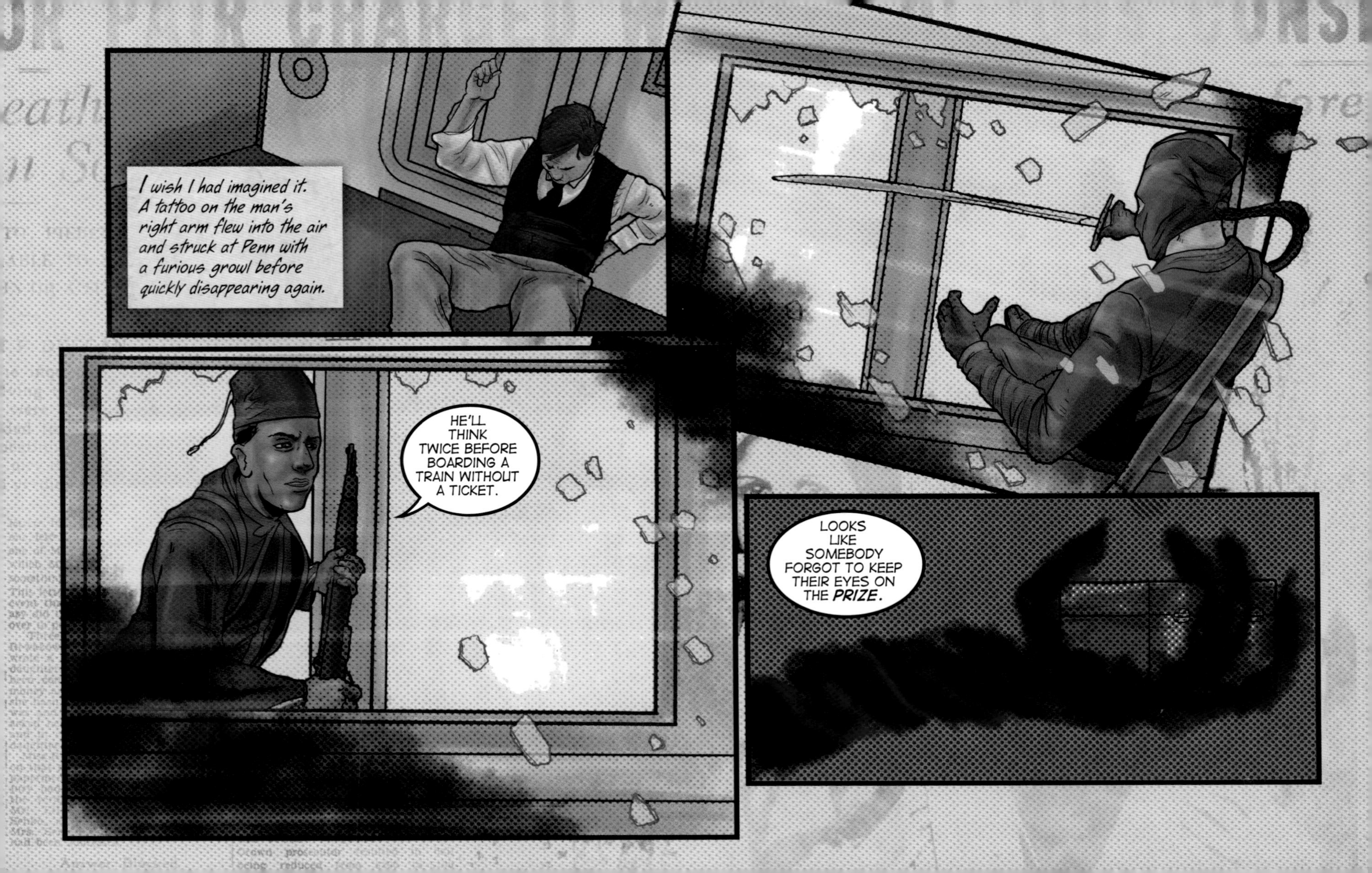
I wish I had imagined it. A tattoo on the man's right arm flew into the air and struck at Penn with a furious growl before quickly disappearing again.
HE'LL THINK TWICE BEFORE BOARDING A TRAIN WITHOUT A TICKET.
LOOKS LIKE SOMEBODY FORGOT TO KEEP THEIR EYES ON THE PRIZE.

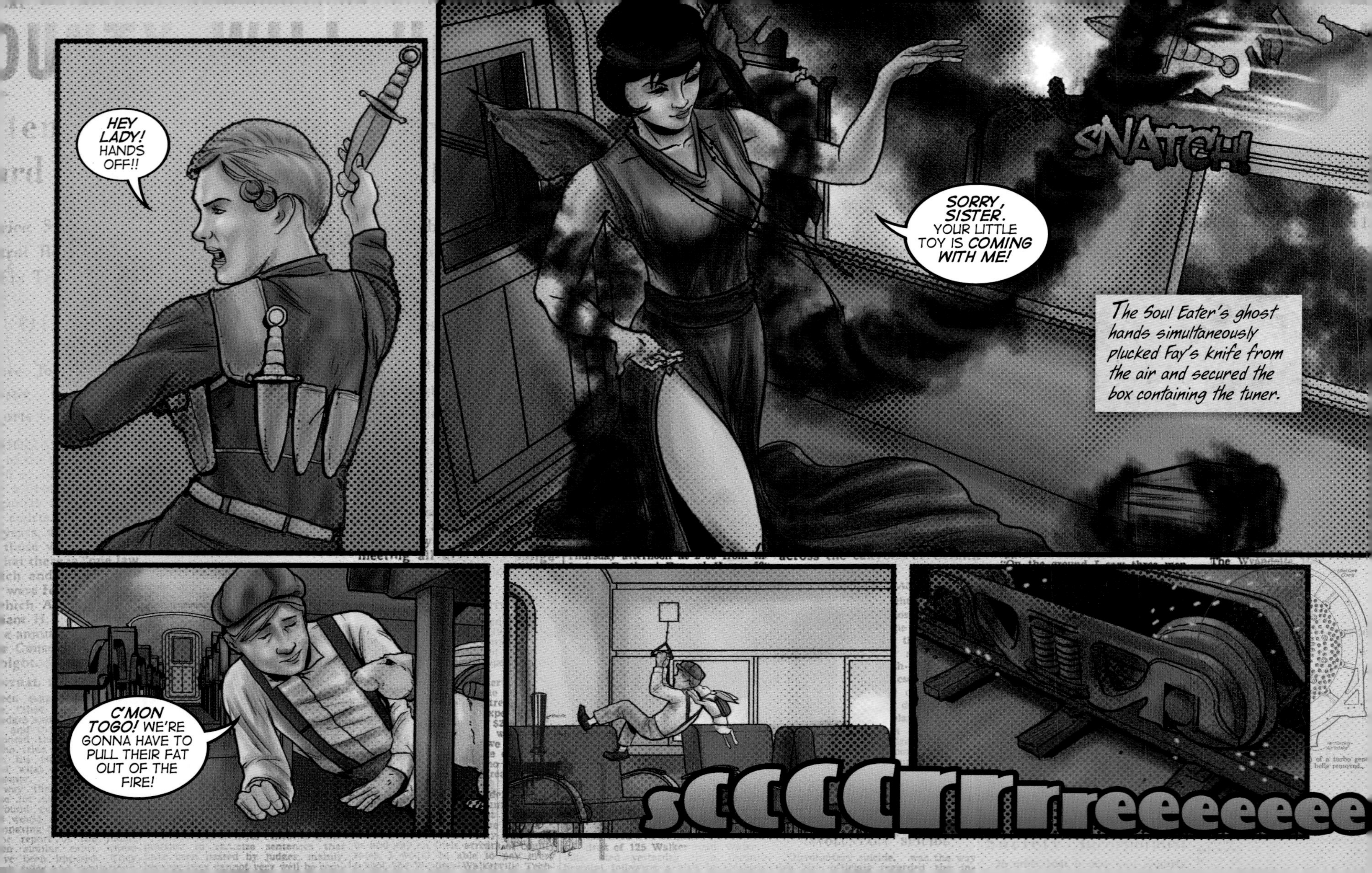
HEY LADY! HANDS OFF!!
SNATCH!
SORRY, SISTER. YOUR LITTLE TOY IS COMING WITH ME!
The Soul Eater's ghost hands simultaneously plucked Fay's knife from the air and secured the box containing the tuner.
C'MON TOGO! WE'RE GONNA HAVE TO PULL THEIR FAT OUT OF THE FIRE!
sCCCCrrrreeeeeee

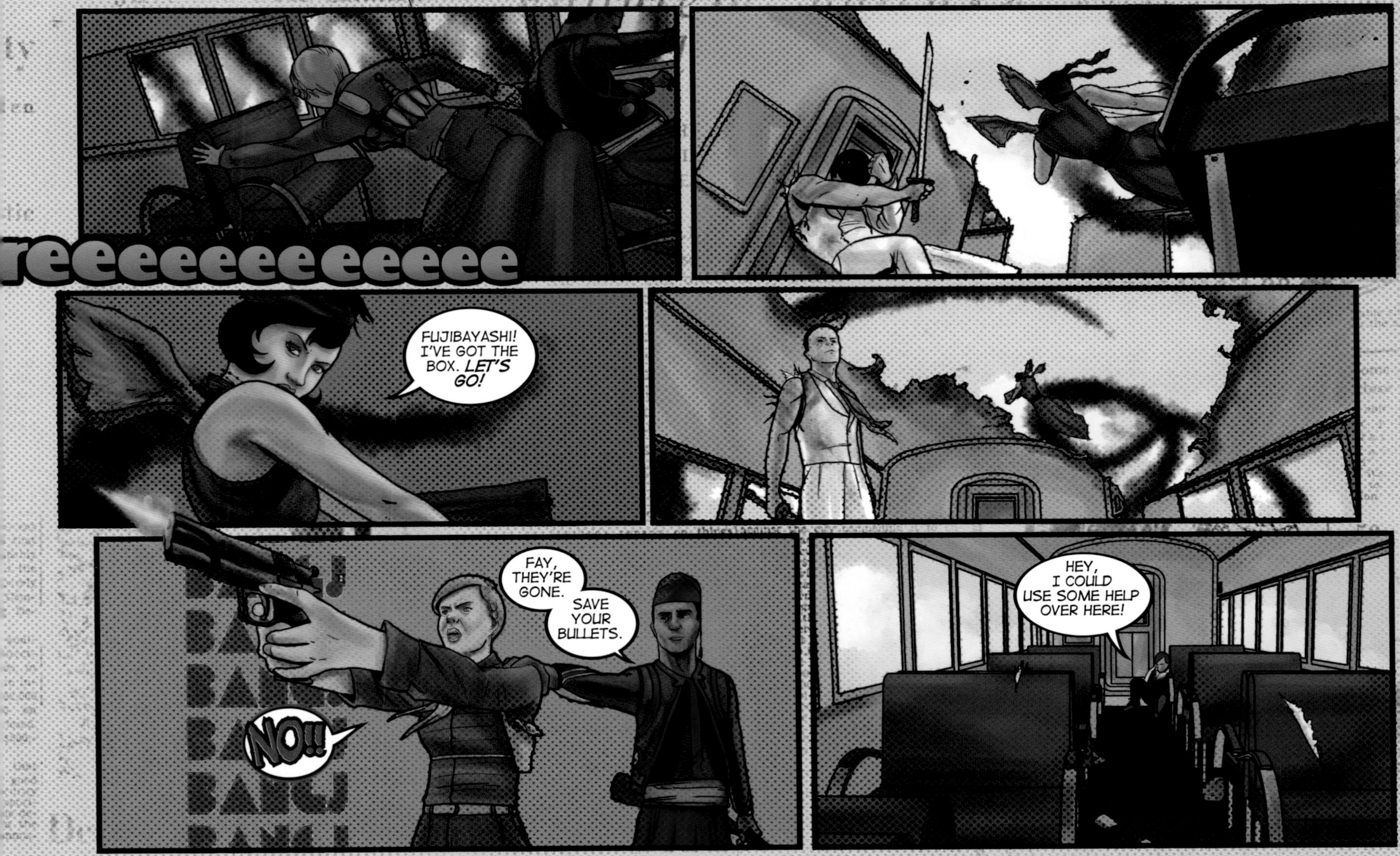

reeeeeeeeeeeee
FUJIBAYASHI! I'VE GOT THE BOX. LET'S GO!
FAY, THEY'RE GONE.
SAVE YOUR BULLETS.
NO!!
HEY, I COULD USE SOME HELP OVER HERE!

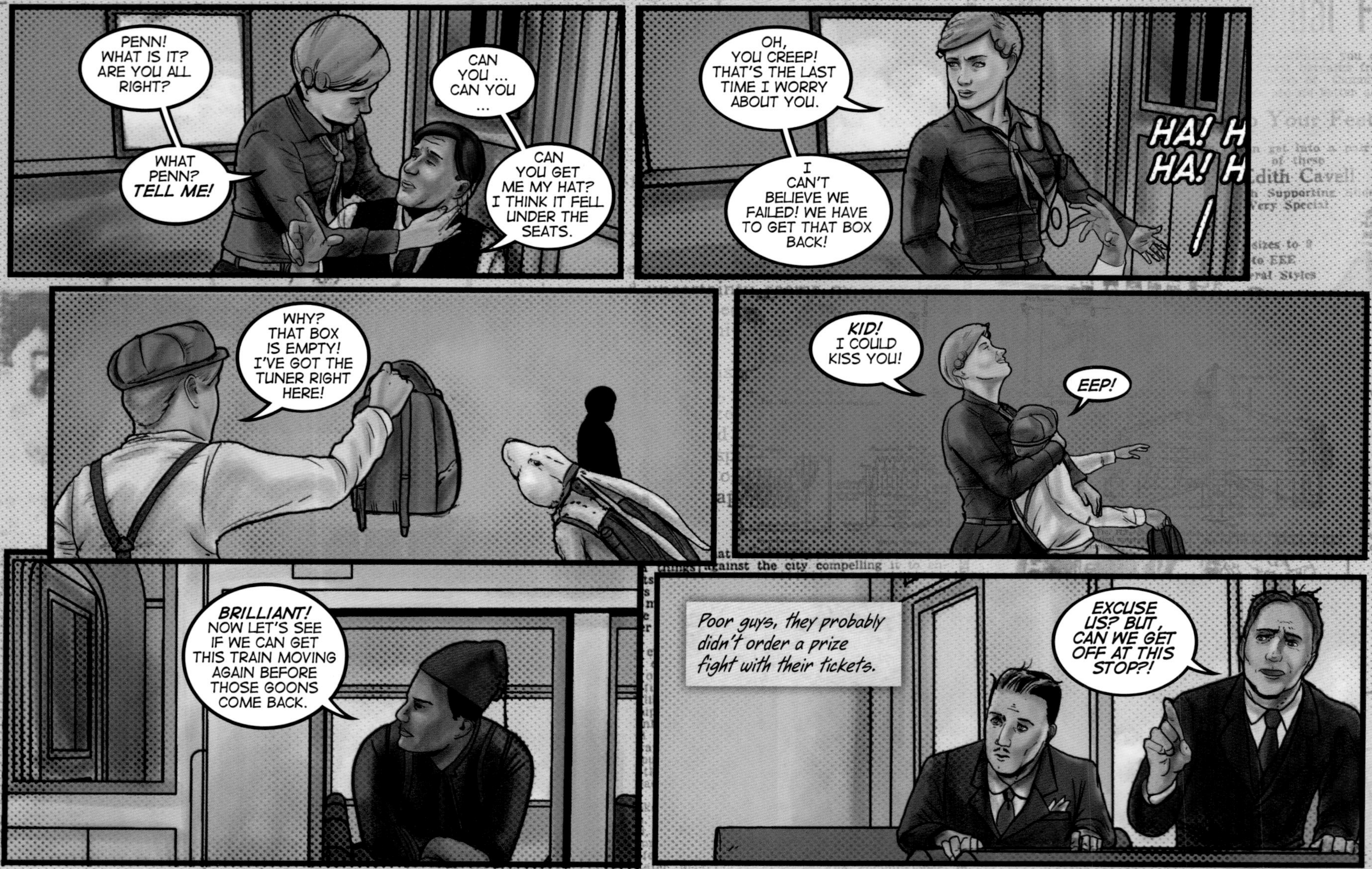
PENN! WHAT IS IT? ARE YOU ALL RIGHT?
CAN YOU ... CAN YOU ...
WHAT PENN? TELL ME!
CAN YOU GET ME MY HAT? I THINK IT FELL UNDER THE SEATS.
OH, YOU CREEP! THAT'S THE LAST TIME I WORRY ABOUT YOU.
I CAN'T BELIEVE WE FAILED! WE HAVE TO GET THAT BOX BACK!
HA! H HA! H
WHY? THAT BOX IS EMPTY! I'VE GOT THE TUNER RIGHT HERE!
KID! I COULD KISS YOU!
EEP!
BRILLIANT! NOW LET'S SEE IF WE CAN GET THIS TRAIN MOVING AGAIN BEFORE THOSE GOONS COME BACK.
Poor guys, they probably didn't order a prize fight with their tickets.
EXCUSE US? BUT, CAN WE GET OFF AT THIS STOP?!

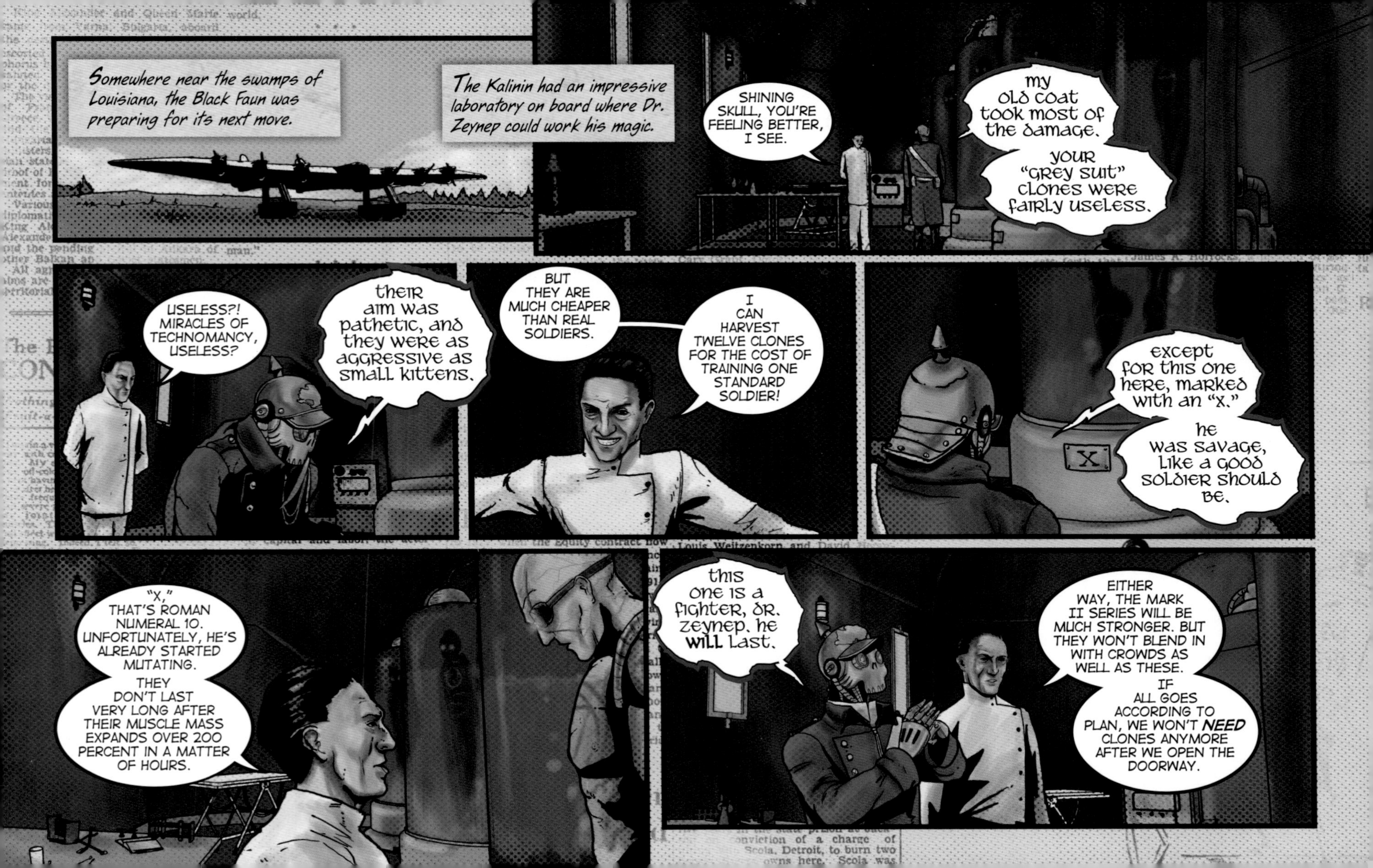

Somewhere near the swamps of Louisiana, the Black Faun was preparing for its next move.
The Kalinin had an impressive laboratory on board where Dr. Zeynep could work his magic.
SHINING SKULL, YOU'RE FEELING BETTER, I SEE.
my old coat took most of the damage.
your "grey suit" clones were fairly useless.
USELESS?! MIRACLES OF TECHNOMANCY, USELESS?
their aim was pathetic, and they were as aggressive as small kittens.
BUT THEY ARE MUCH CHEAPER THAN REAL SOLDIERS.
I CAN HARVEST TWELVE CLONES FOR THE COST OF TRAINING ONE STANDARD SOLDIER!
except for this one here, marked with an "x."
he was savage, like a good soldier should be.
X
"X," THAT'S ROMAN NUMERAL 10. UNFORTUNATELY, HE'S ALREADY STARTED MUTATING.
THEY DON'T LAST VERY LONG AFTER THEIR MUSCLE MASS EXPANDS OVER 200 PERCENT IN A MATTER OF HOURS.
this one is a fighter, dr. zeynep. he **will** last.
EITHER WAY, THE MARK II SERIES WILL BE MUCH STRONGER. BUT THEY WON'T BLEND IN WITH CROWDS AS WELL AS THESE.
IF ALL GOES ACCORDING TO PLAN, WE WON'T ***NEED*** CLONES ANYMORE AFTER WE OPEN THE DOORWAY.

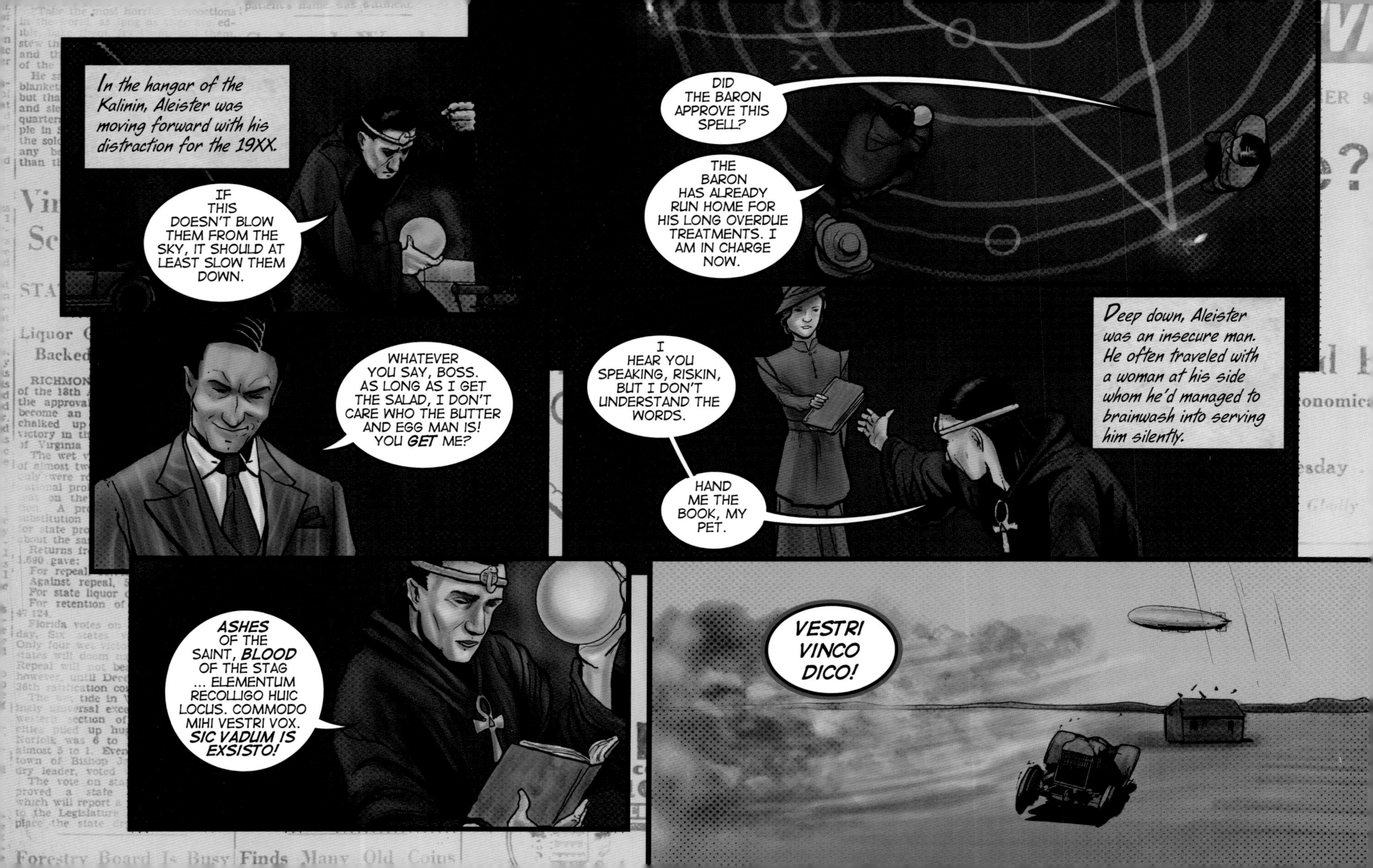
In the hangar of the Kalinin, Aleister was moving forward with his distraction for the 19XX.
IF THIS DOESN'T BLOW THEM FROM THE SKY, IT SHOULD AT LEAST SLOW THEM DOWN.
DID THE BARON APPROVE THIS SPELL?
THE BARON HAS ALREADY RUN HOME FOR HIS LONG OVERDUE TREATMENTS. I AM IN CHARGE NOW.
WHATEVER YOU SAY, BOSS. AS LONG AS I GET THE SALAD, I DON'T CARE WHO THE BUTTER AND EGG MAN IS! YOU GET ME?
I HEAR YOU SPEAKING, RISKIN, BUT I DON'T UNDERSTAND THE WORDS.
HAND ME THE BOOK, MY PET.
Deep down, Aleister was an insecure man. He often traveled with a woman at his side whom he'd managed to brainwash into serving him silently.
ASHES OF THE SAINT, BLOOD OF THE STAG ... ELEMENTUM RECOLLIGO HUIC LOCUS. COMMODO MIHI VESTRI VOX. SIC VADUM IS EXSISTO!
VESTRI VINCO DICO!

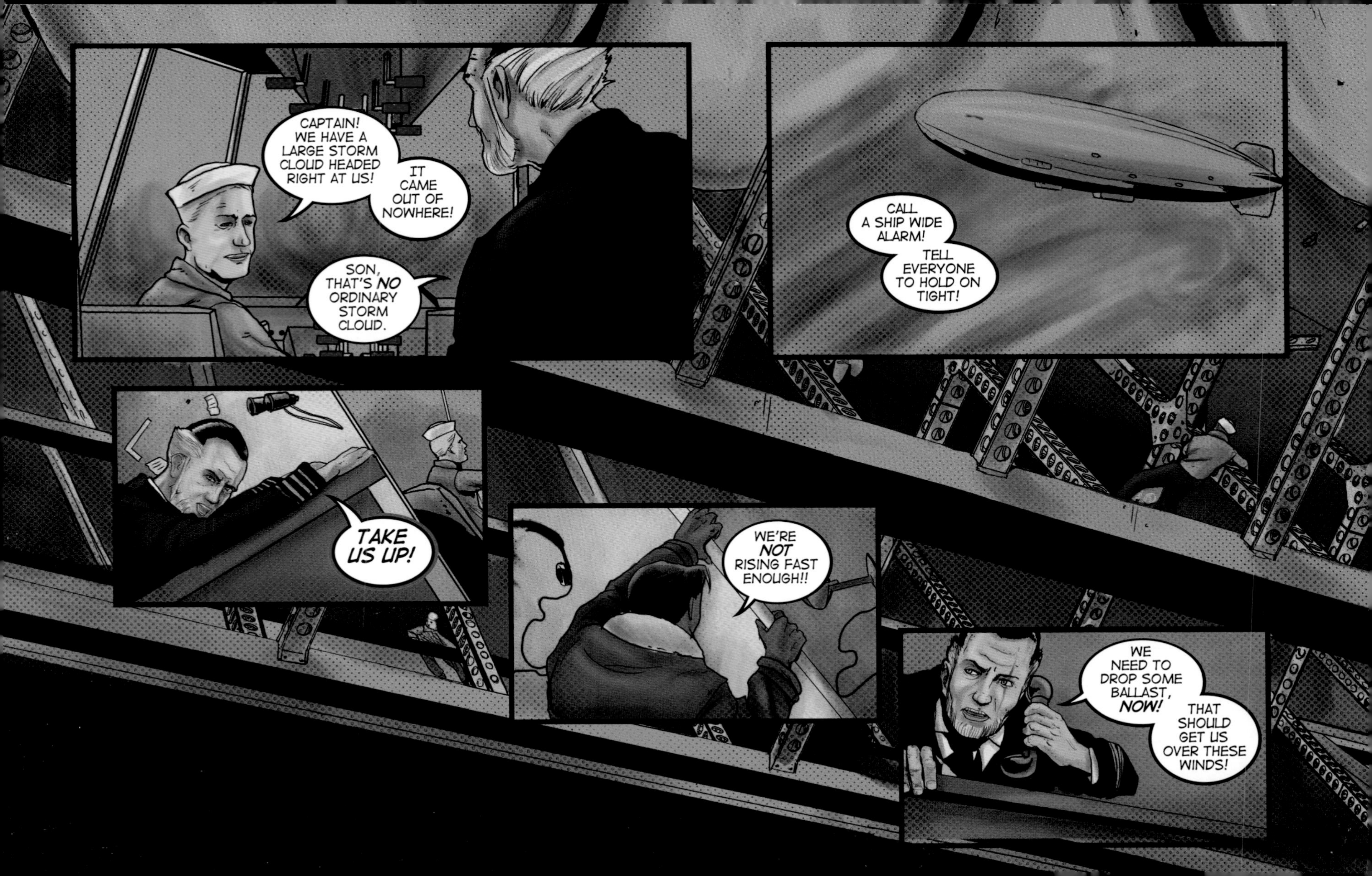
CAPTAIN! WE HAVE A LARGE STORM CLOUD HEADED RIGHT AT US!
IT CAME OUT OF NOWHERE!
SON, THAT'S NO ORDINARY STORM CLOUD.
CALL A SHIP WIDE ALARM!
TELL EVERYONE TO HOLD ON TIGHT!
TAKE US UP!
WE'RE NOT RISING FAST ENOUGH!!
WE NEED TO DROP SOME BALLAST, NOW!
THAT SHOULD GET US OVER THESE WINDS!

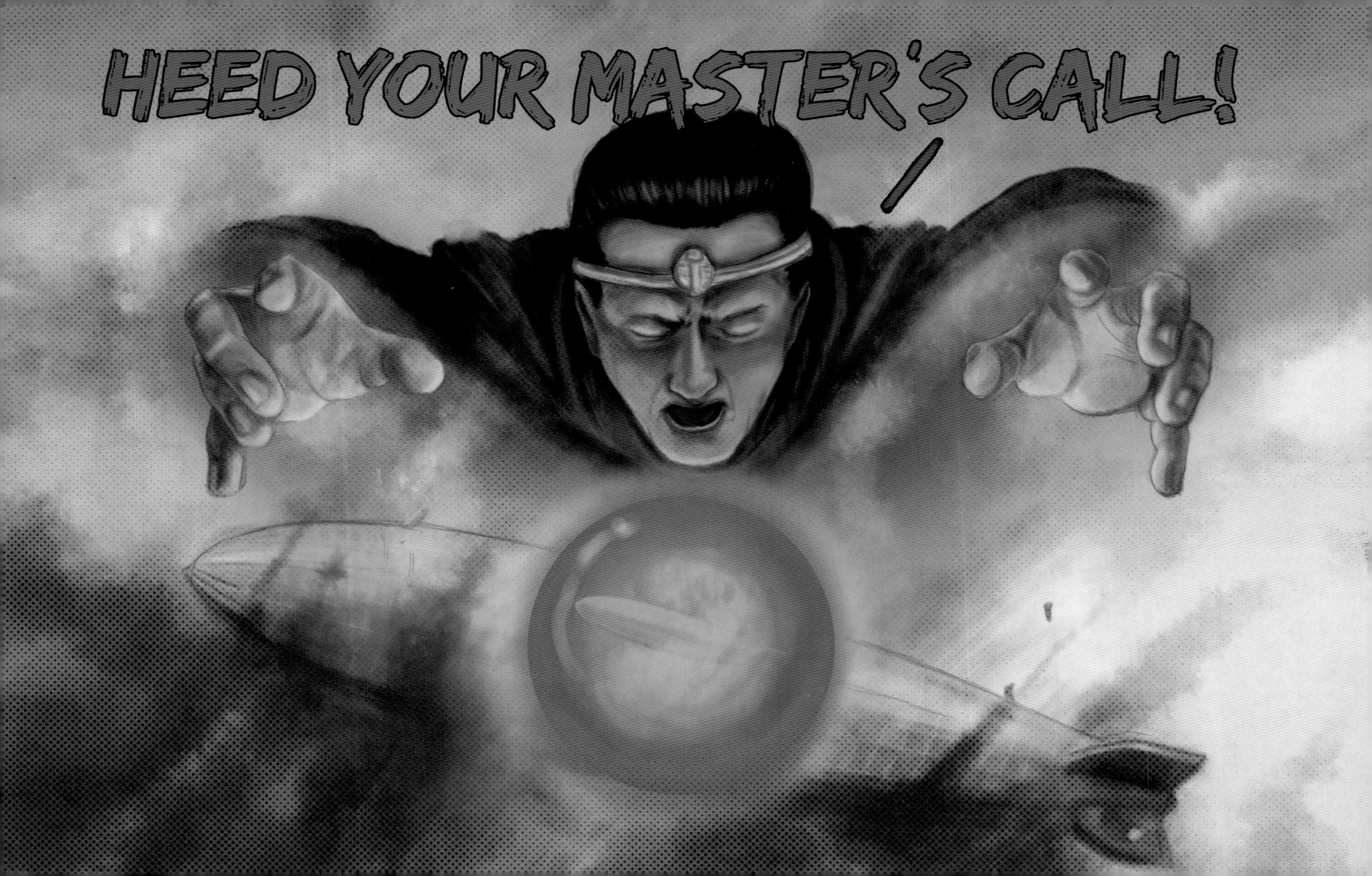
HEED YOUR MASTER'S CALL!

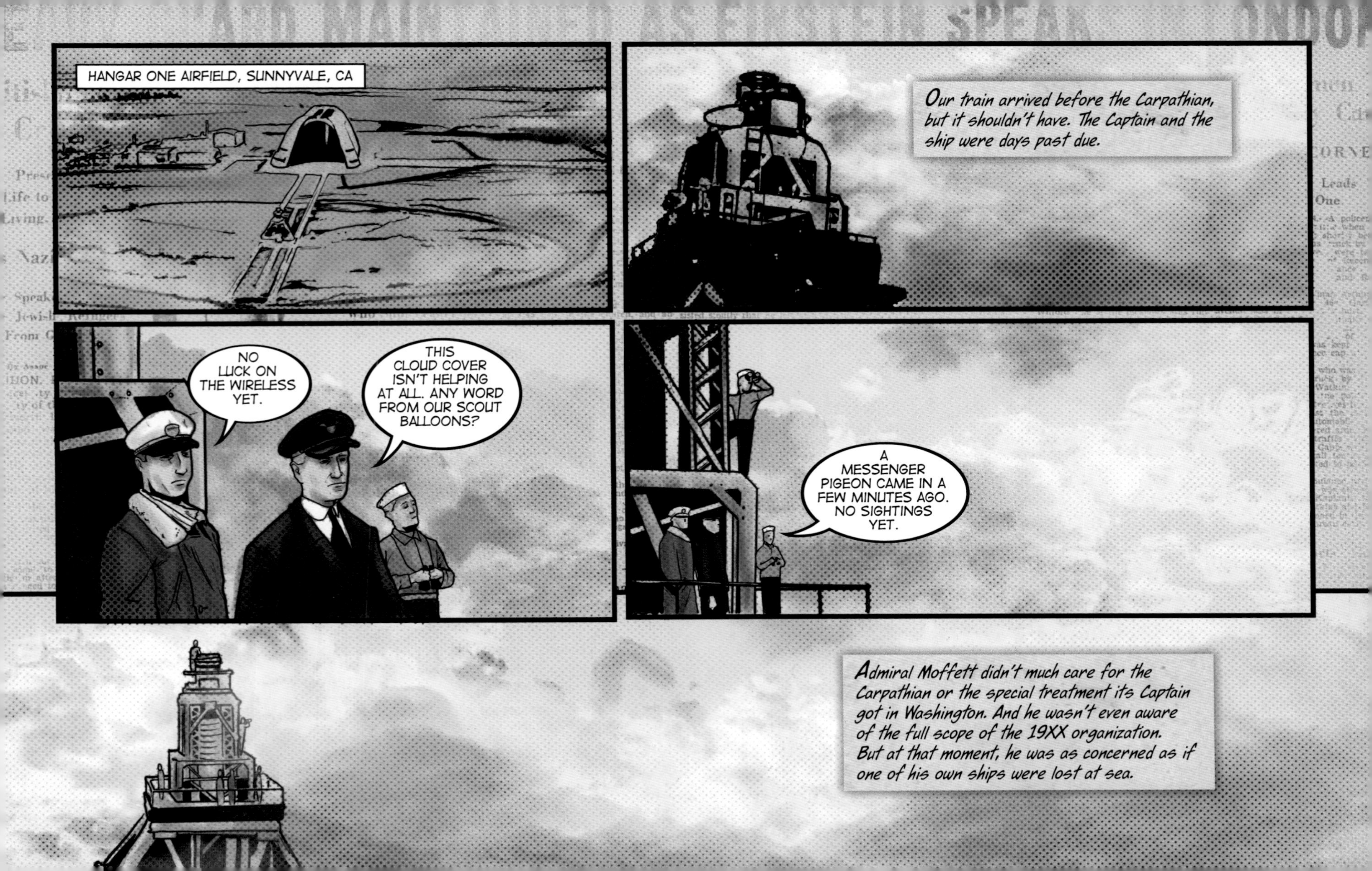
HANGAR ONE AIRFIELD, SUNNYVALE, CA
Our train arrived before the Carpathian, but it shouldn't have. The Captain and the ship were days past due.
NO LUCK ON THE WIRELESS YET.
THIS CLOUD COVER ISN'T HELPING AT ALL. ANY WORD FROM OUR SCOUT BALLOONS?
A MESSENGER PIGEON CAME IN A FEW MINUTES AGO. NO SIGHTINGS YET.
Admiral Moffett didn't much care for the Carpathian or the special treatment its Captain got in Washington. And he wasn't even aware of the full scope of the 19XX organization. But at that moment, he was as concerned as if one of his own ships were lost at sea.

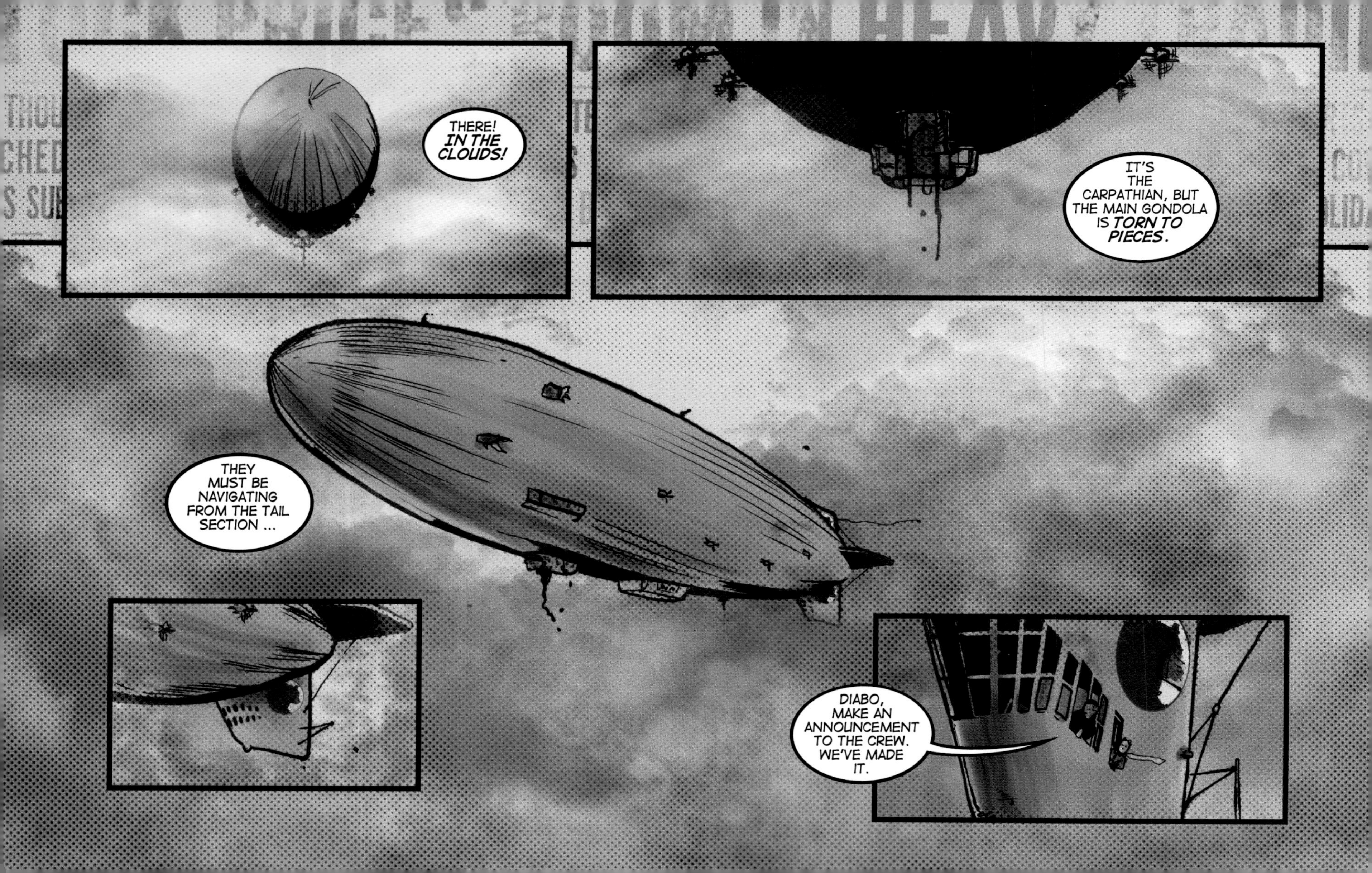
THERE! IN THE CLOUDS!
IT'S THE CARPATHIAN, BUT THE MAIN GONDOLA IS TORN TO PIECES.
THEY MUST BE NAVIGATING FROM THE TAIL SECTION ...
DIABO, MAKE AN ANNOUNCEMENT TO THE CREW. WE'VE MADE IT.

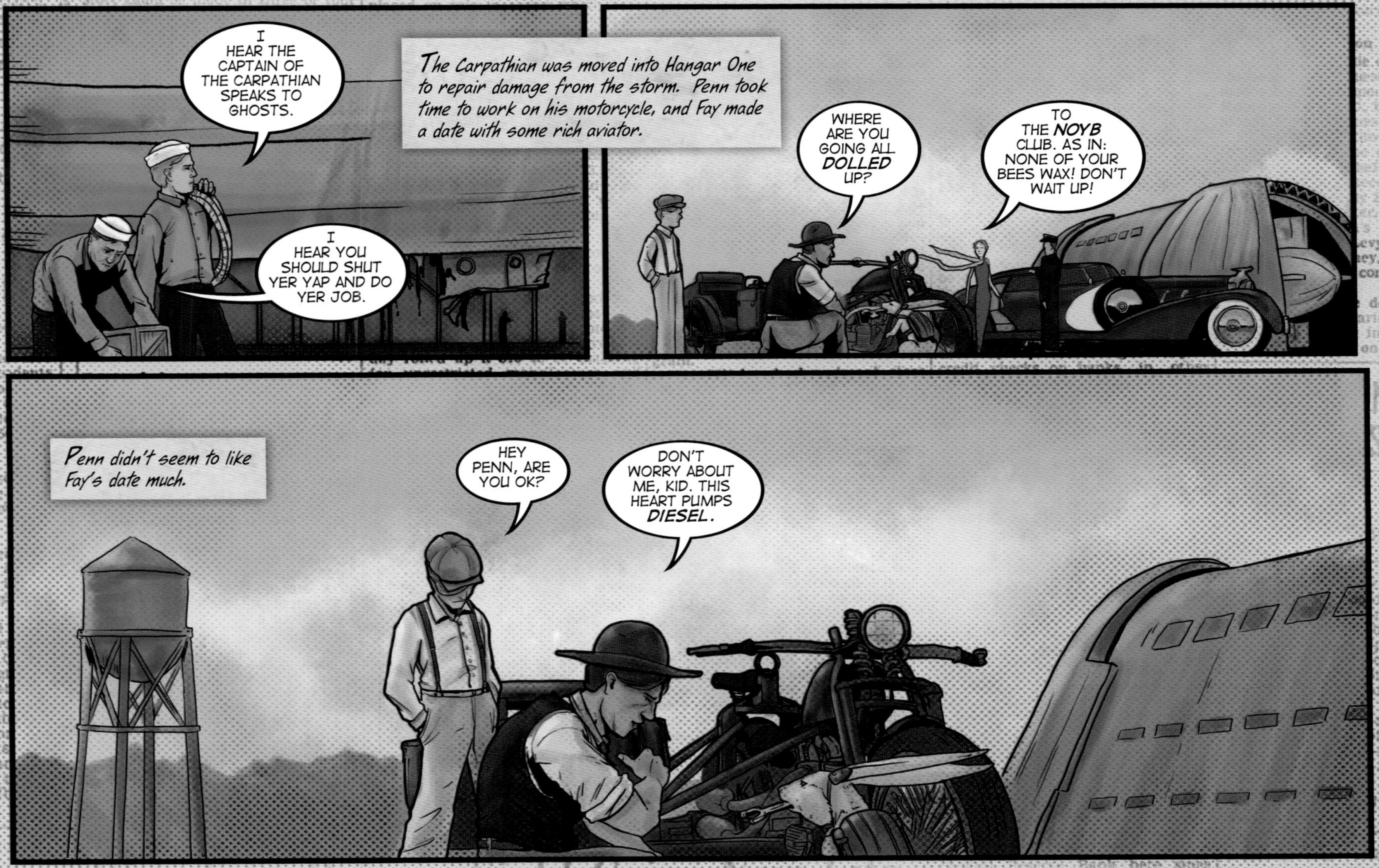

I HEAR THE CAPTAIN OF THE CARPATHIAN SPEAKS TO GHOSTS.
The Carpathian was moved into Hangar One to repair damage from the storm. Penn took time to work on his motorcycle, and Fay made a date with some rich aviator.
I HEAR YOU SHOULD SHUT YER YAP AND DO YER JOB.
WHERE ARE YOU GOING ALL DOLLED UP?
TO THE NOYB CLUB. AS IN: NONE OF YOUR BEES WAX! DON'T WAIT UP!
Penn didn't seem to like Fay's date much.
HEY PENN, ARE YOU OK?
DON'T WORRY ABOUT ME, KID. THIS HEART PUMPS DIESEL.

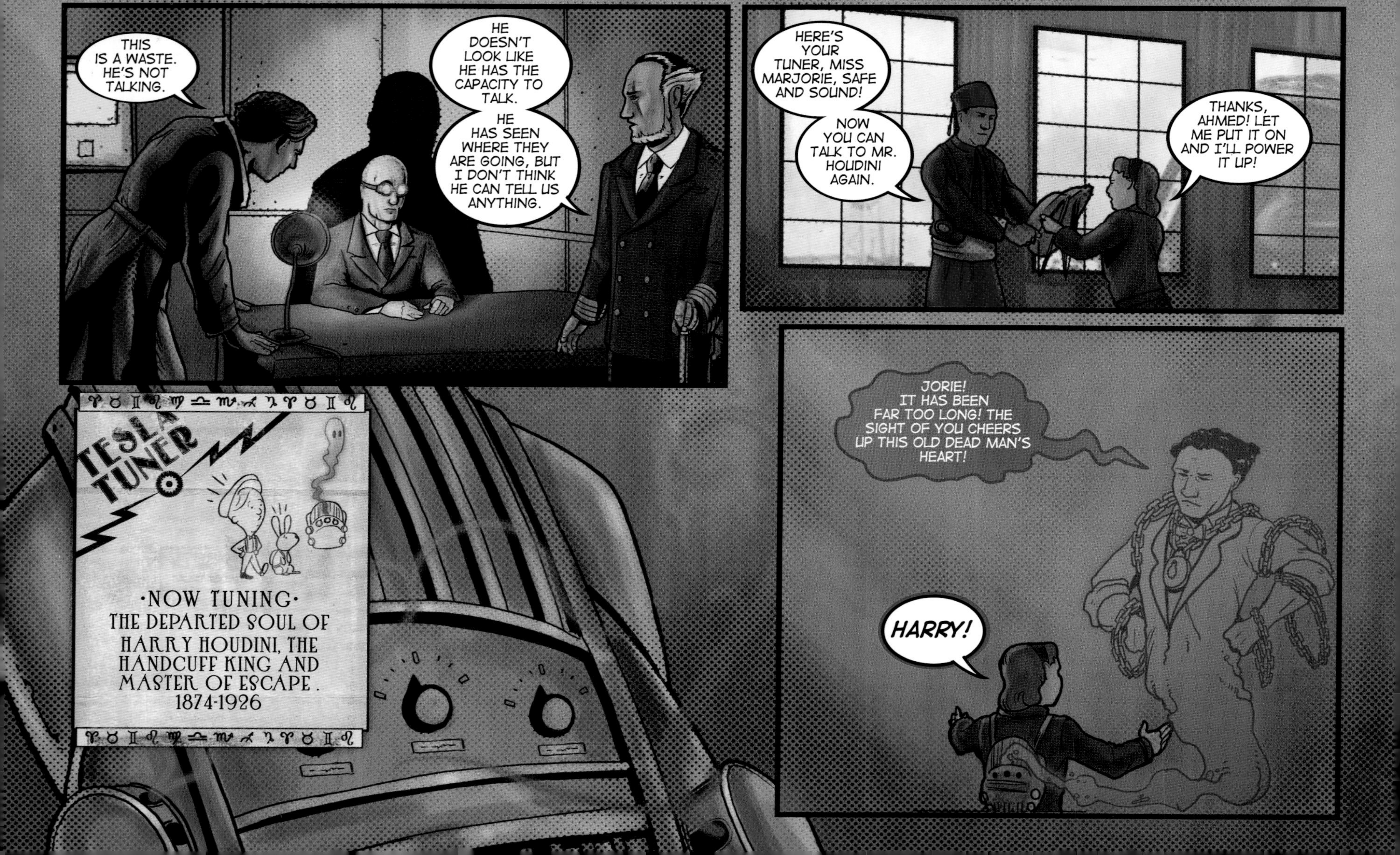

THIS IS A WASTE. HE'S NOT TALKING.
HE DOESN'T LOOK LIKE HE HAS THE CAPACITY TO TALK.
HE HAS SEEN WHERE THEY ARE GOING, BUT I DON'T THINK HE CAN TELL US ANYTHING.
HERE'S YOUR TUNER, MISS MARJORIE, SAFE AND SOUND!
NOW YOU CAN TALK TO MR. HOUDINI AGAIN.
THANKS, AHMED! LET ME PUT IT ON AND I'LL POWER IT UP!
TESLA TUNER
·NOW TUNING·
THE DEPARTED SOUL OF HARRY HOUDINI, THE HANDCUFF KING AND MASTER OF ESCAPE.
1874-1926
JORIE! IT HAS BEEN FAR TOO LONG! THE SIGHT OF YOU CHEERS UP THIS OLD DEAD MAN'S HEART!
HARRY!

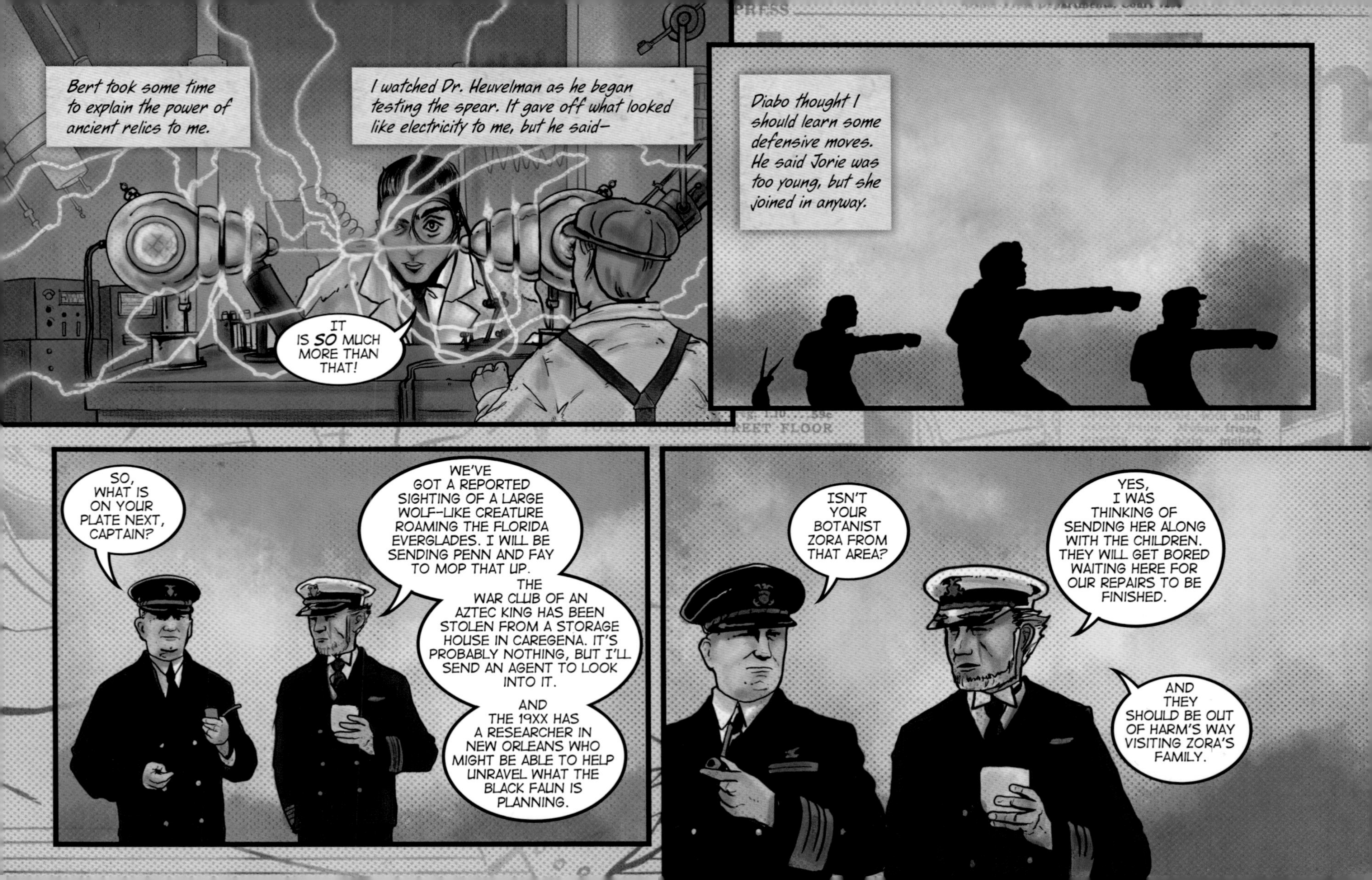
Bert took some time to explain the power of ancient relics to me.
I watched Dr. Heuvelman as he began testing the spear. It gave off what looked like electricity to me, but he said—
IT IS SO MUCH MORE THAN THAT!
Diabo thought I should learn some defensive moves. He said Jorie was too young, but she joined in anyway.
SO, WHAT IS ON YOUR PLATE NEXT, CAPTAIN?
WE'VE GOT A REPORTED SIGHTING OF A LARGE WOLF-LIKE CREATURE ROAMING THE FLORIDA EVERGLADES. I WILL BE SENDING PENN AND FAY TO MOP THAT UP.
THE WAR CLUB OF AN AZTEC KING HAS BEEN STOLEN FROM A STORAGE HOUSE IN CAREGENA. IT'S PROBABLY NOTHING, BUT I'LL SEND AN AGENT TO LOOK INTO IT.
AND THE 19XX HAS A RESEARCHER IN NEW ORLEANS WHO MIGHT BE ABLE TO HELP UNRAVEL WHAT THE BLACK FAUN IS PLANNING.
ISN'T YOUR BOTANIST ZORA FROM THAT AREA?
YES, I WAS THINKING OF SENDING HER ALONG WITH THE CHILDREN. THEY WILL GET BORED WAITING HERE FOR OUR REPAIRS TO BE FINISHED.
AND THEY SHOULD BE OUT OF HARM'S WAY VISITING ZORA'S FAMILY.

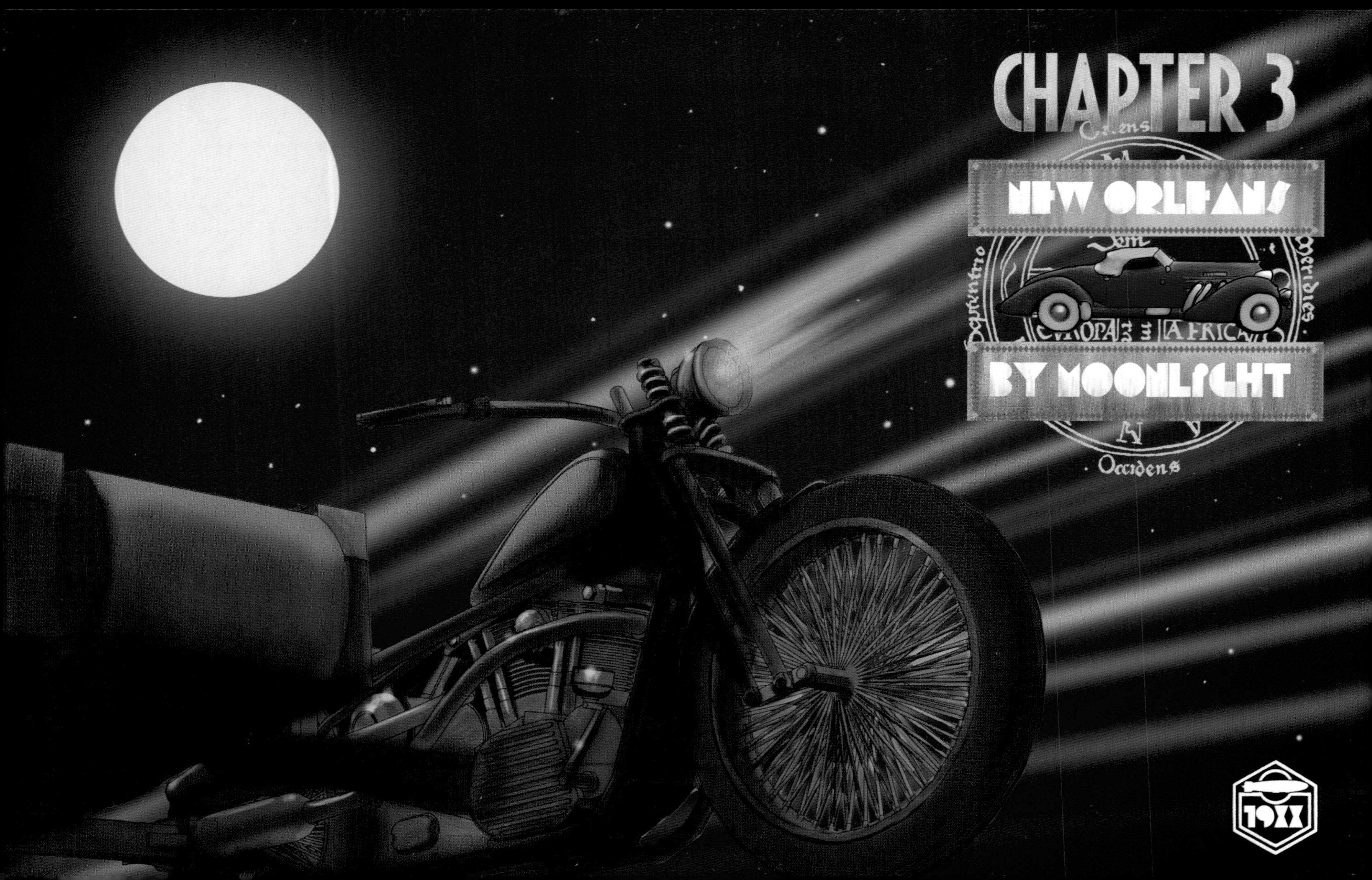
CHAPTER 3
NEW ORLEANS
BY MOONLIGHT
Occidens
Meridies

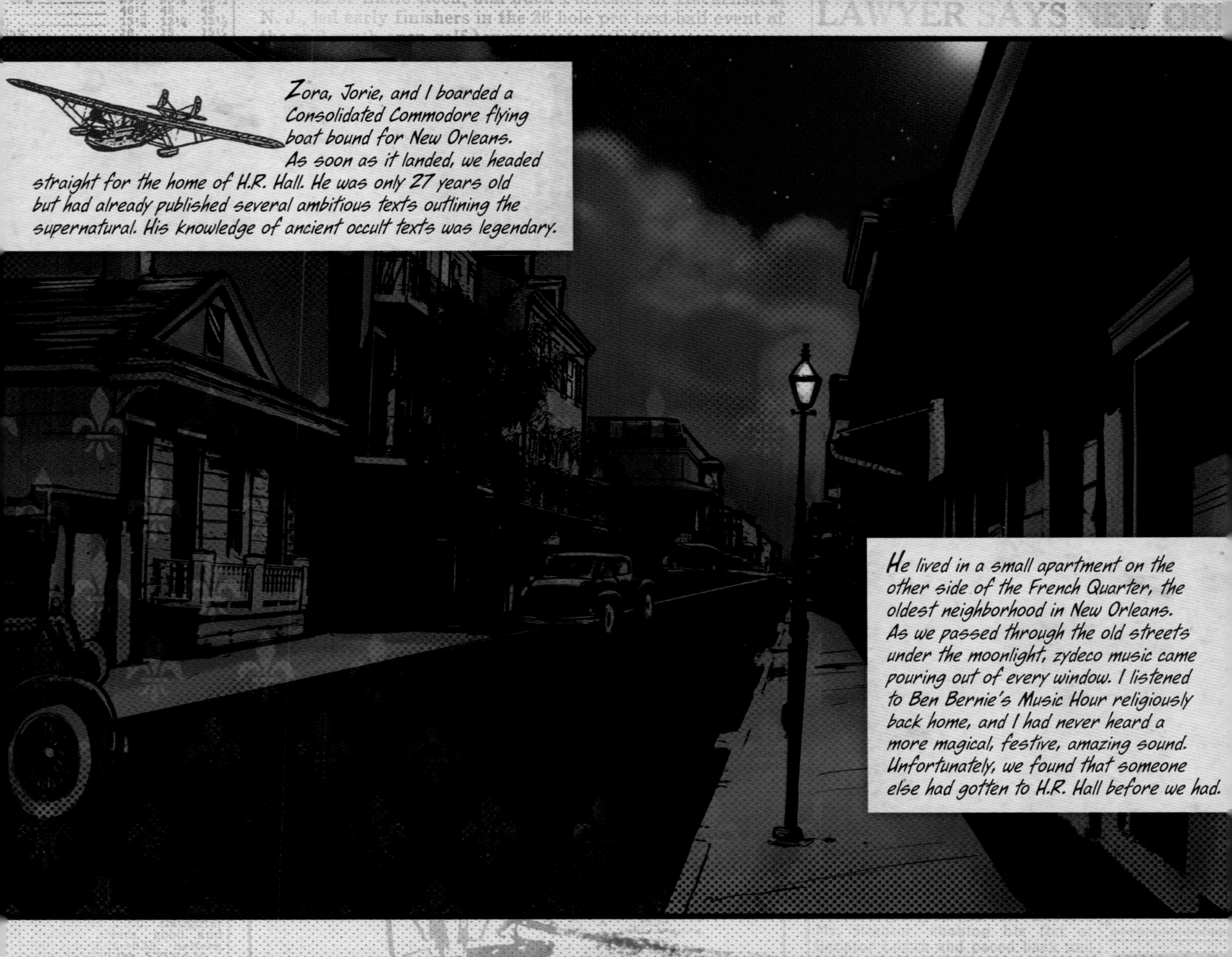
Zora, Jorie, and I boarded a Consolidated Commodore flying boat bound for New Orleans. As soon as it landed, we headed straight for the home of H.R. Hall. He was only 27 years old but had already published several ambitious texts outlining the supernatural. His knowledge of ancient occult texts was legendary.
He lived in a small apartment on the other side of the French Quarter, the oldest neighborhood in New Orleans. As we passed through the old streets under the moonlight, zydeco music came pouring out of every window. I listened to Ben Bernie's Music Hour religiously back home, and I had never heard a more magical, festive, amazing sound. Unfortunately, we found that someone else had gotten to H.R. Hall before we had.

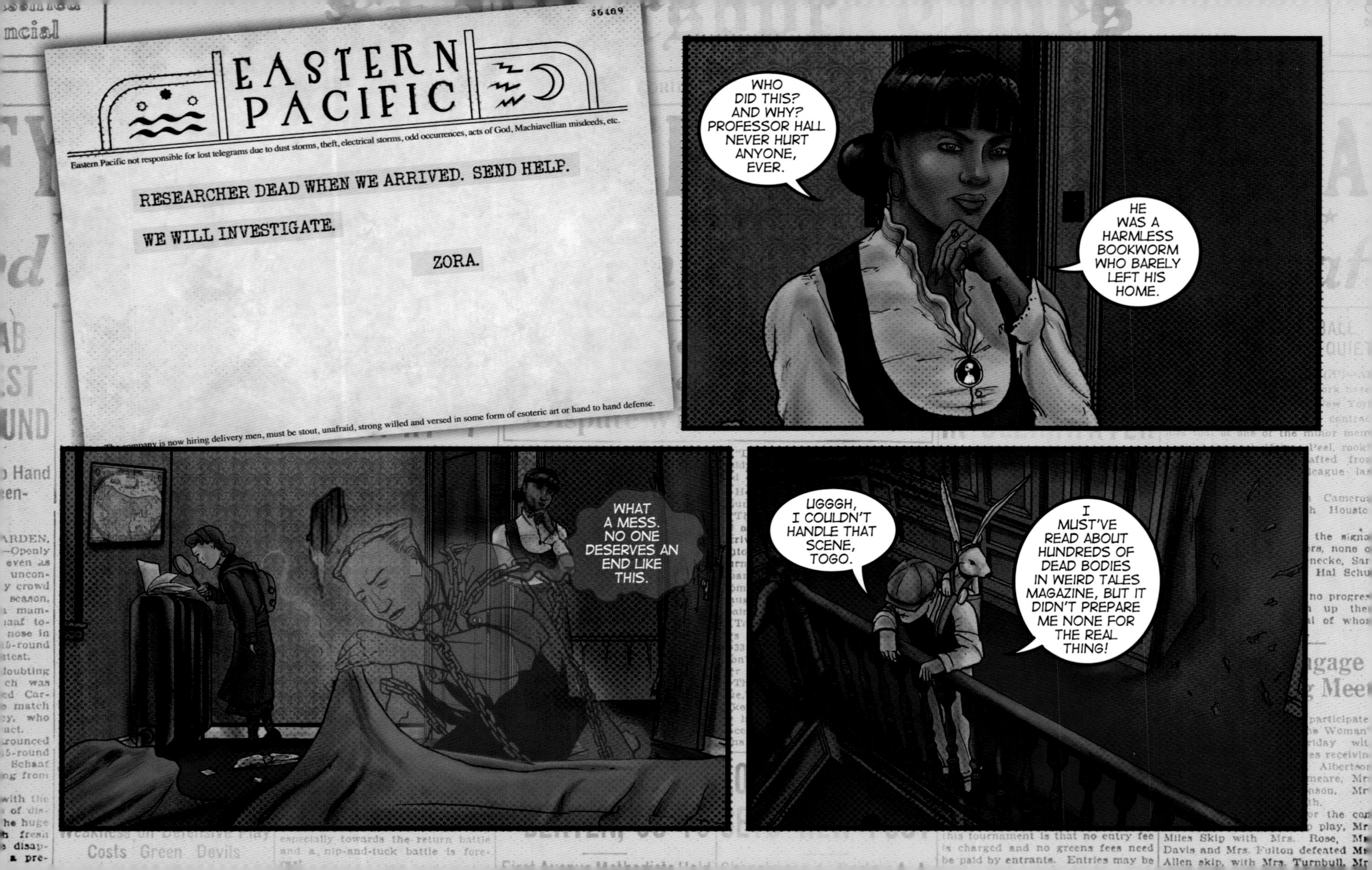
EASTERN PACIFIC
Eastern Pacific not responsible for lost telegrams due to dust storms, theft, electrical storms, odd occurrences, acts of God, Machiavellian misdeeds, etc.
RESEARCHER DEAD WHEN WE ARRIVED. SEND HELP.
WE WILL INVESTIGATE.
ZORA.
The company is now hiring delivery men, must be stout, unafraid, strong willed and versed in some form of esoteric art or hand to hand defense.
WHO DID THIS? AND WHY? PROFESSOR HALL NEVER HURT ANYONE, EVER.
HE WAS A HARMLESS BOOKWORM WHO BARELY LEFT HIS HOME.
WHAT A MESS. NO ONE DESERVES AN END LIKE THIS.
UGGGH, I COULDN'T HANDLE THAT SCENE, TOGO.
I MUST'VE READ ABOUT HUNDREDS OF DEAD BODIES IN WEIRD TALES MAGAZINE, BUT IT DIDN'T PREPARE ME NONE FOR THE REAL THING!

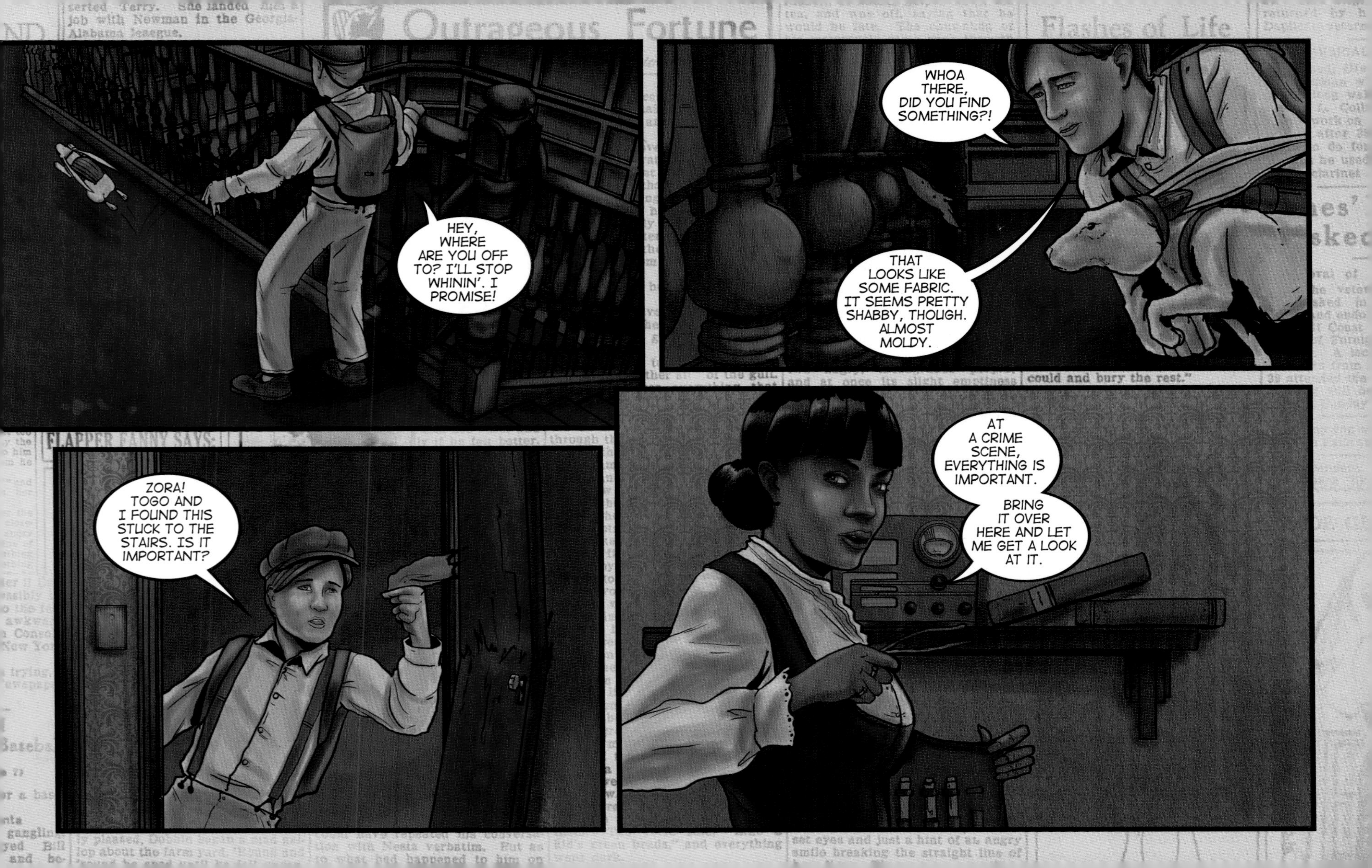
HEY, WHERE ARE YOU OFF TO? I'LL STOP WHININ'. I PROMISE!
WHOA THERE, DID YOU FIND SOMETHING?!
THAT LOOKS LIKE SOME FABRIC. IT SEEMS PRETTY SHABBY, THOUGH. ALMOST MOLDY.
ZORA! TOGO AND I FOUND THIS STUCK TO THE STAIRS. IS IT IMPORTANT?
AT A CRIME SCENE, EVERYTHING IS IMPORTANT.
BRING IT OVER HERE AND LET ME GET A LOOK AT IT.

LET'S REVIEW THE CLUES.

A STRANGE SYMBOL WAS DRAWN IN BLOOD ON THIS TABLE...

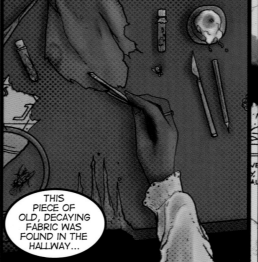

THIS PIECE OF OLD, DECAYING FABRIC WAS FOUND IN THE HALLWAY...

THERE ARE SARCOPHAGIDAE AT VARIOUS STAGES OF DEVELOPMENT AROUND THE ROOM.

FLESH FLIES FEED ON DECAYING FLESH. HALL HAS BEEN DEAD LESS THEN A DAY, BUT ALONG WITH THE LARVAE, I SEE FULLY GROWN SPECIMENS HERE.

THOSE TAKE SEVERAL DAYS TO DEVELOP ON A BODY.

THE FRONT DOOR WAS DESTROYED BY AN UNNATURAL PHYSICAL FORCE.

ALL OF HIS BOOKS AND PAPERS WERE THROWN ABOUT IN A MAD SEARCH FOR SOMETHING.

I KNOW THE BLACK FAUN WAS BEHIND THIS, BUT WHAT EXACTLY WERE THEY SEARCHING FOR?

AND MORE IMPORTANTLY, DID THEY FIND IT?

THERE ARE SO MANY BOOKS HERE. IT COULD HAVE BEEN ANY ONE OF THEM!

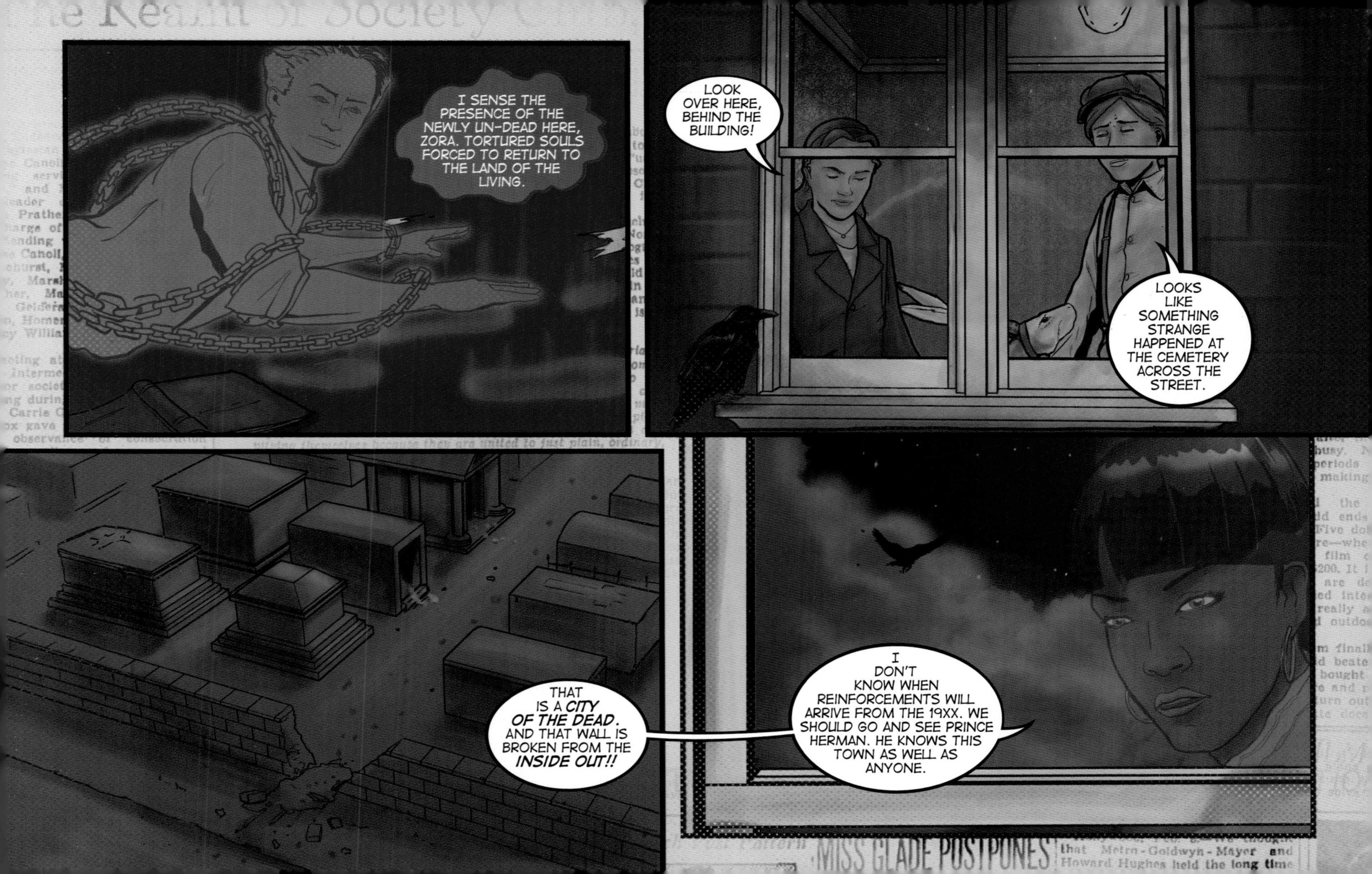
I SENSE THE PRESENCE OF THE NEWLY UN-DEAD HERE, ZORA. TORTURED SOULS FORCED TO RETURN TO THE LAND OF THE LIVING.
LOOK OVER HERE, BEHIND THE BUILDING!
LOOKS LIKE SOMETHING STRANGE HAPPENED AT THE CEMETERY ACROSS THE STREET.
THAT IS A *CITY OF THE DEAD*. AND THAT WALL IS BROKEN FROM THE *INSIDE OUT!!*
I DON'T KNOW WHEN REINFORCEMENTS WILL ARRIVE FROM THE 19XX. WE SHOULD GO AND SEE PRINCE HERMAN. HE KNOWS THIS TOWN AS WELL AS ANYONE.
MISS GLADE POSTPONES!
that Metro-Goldwyn-Mayer and Howard Hughes held the long time

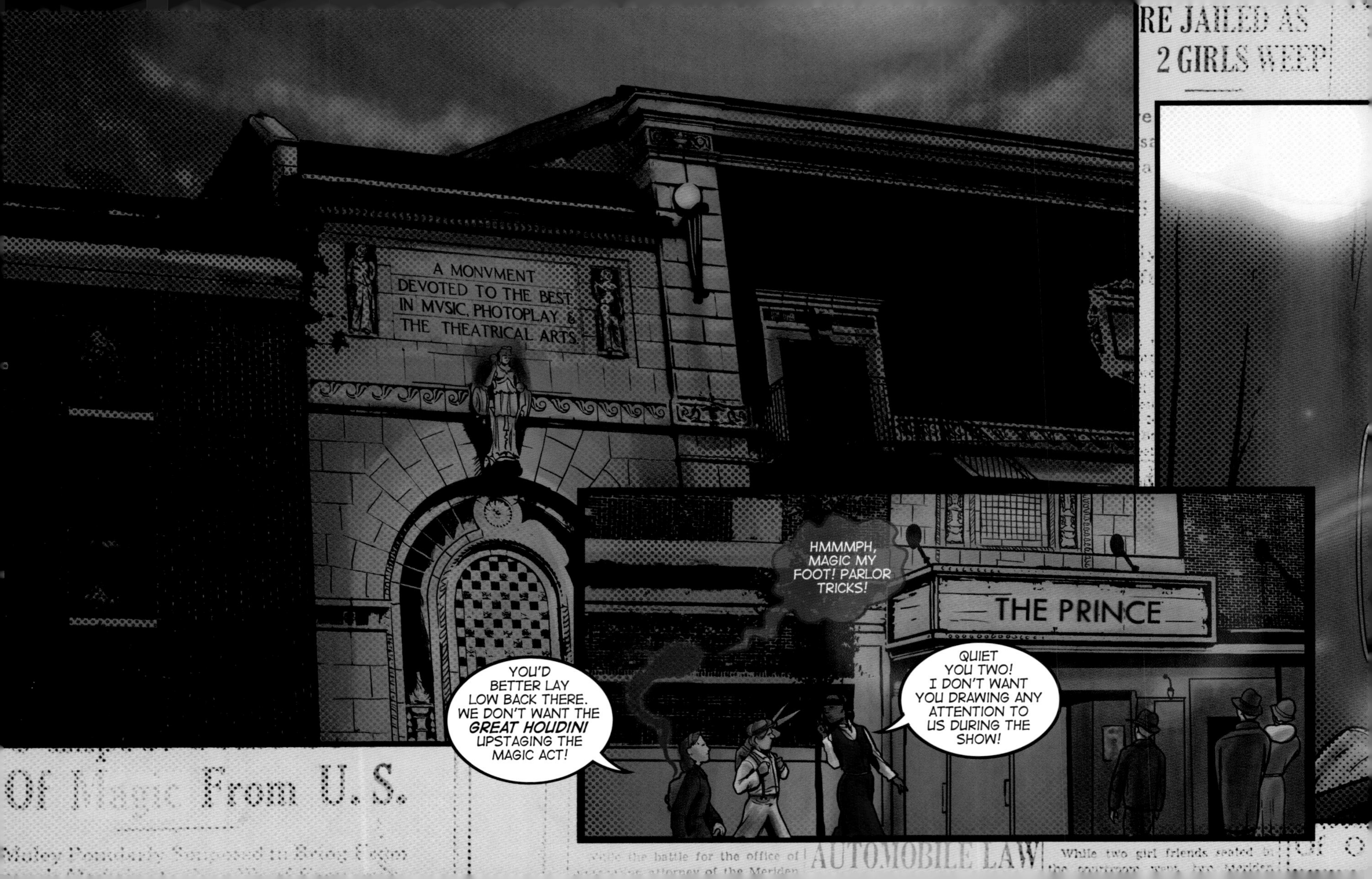
RE JAILED AS
2 GIRLS WEEP
A MONVMENT DEVOTED TO THE BEST IN MVSIC, PHOTOPLAY & THE THEATRICAL ARTS.
THE PRINCE
YOU'D BETTER LAY LOW BACK THERE. WE DON'T WANT THE *GREAT HOUDINI* UPSTAGING THE MAGIC ACT!
HMMMPH, MAGIC MY FOOT! PARLOR TRICKS!
QUIET YOU TWO! I DON'T WANT YOU DRAWING ANY ATTENTION TO US DURING THE SHOW!
Of Magic From U.S.
While the battle for the office of
AUTOMOBILE LAW
While two girl friends seated in

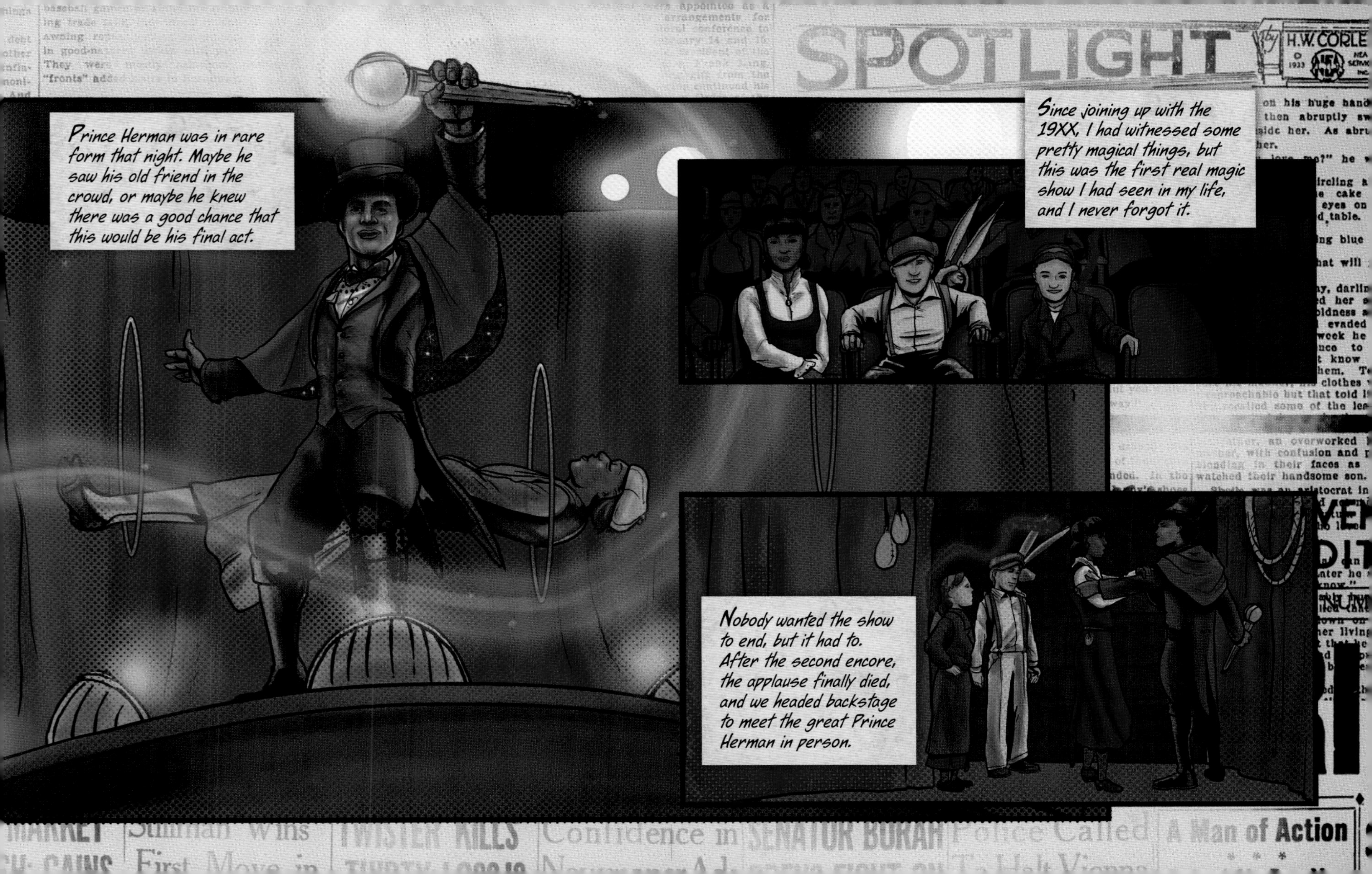
Prince Herman was in rare form that night. Maybe he saw his old friend in the crowd, or maybe he knew there was a good chance that this would be his final act.
Since joining up with the 19XX, I had witnessed some pretty magical things, but this was the first real magic show I had seen in my life, and I never forgot it.
Nobody wanted the show to end, but it had to. After the second encore, the applause finally died, and we headed backstage to meet the great Prince Herman in person.

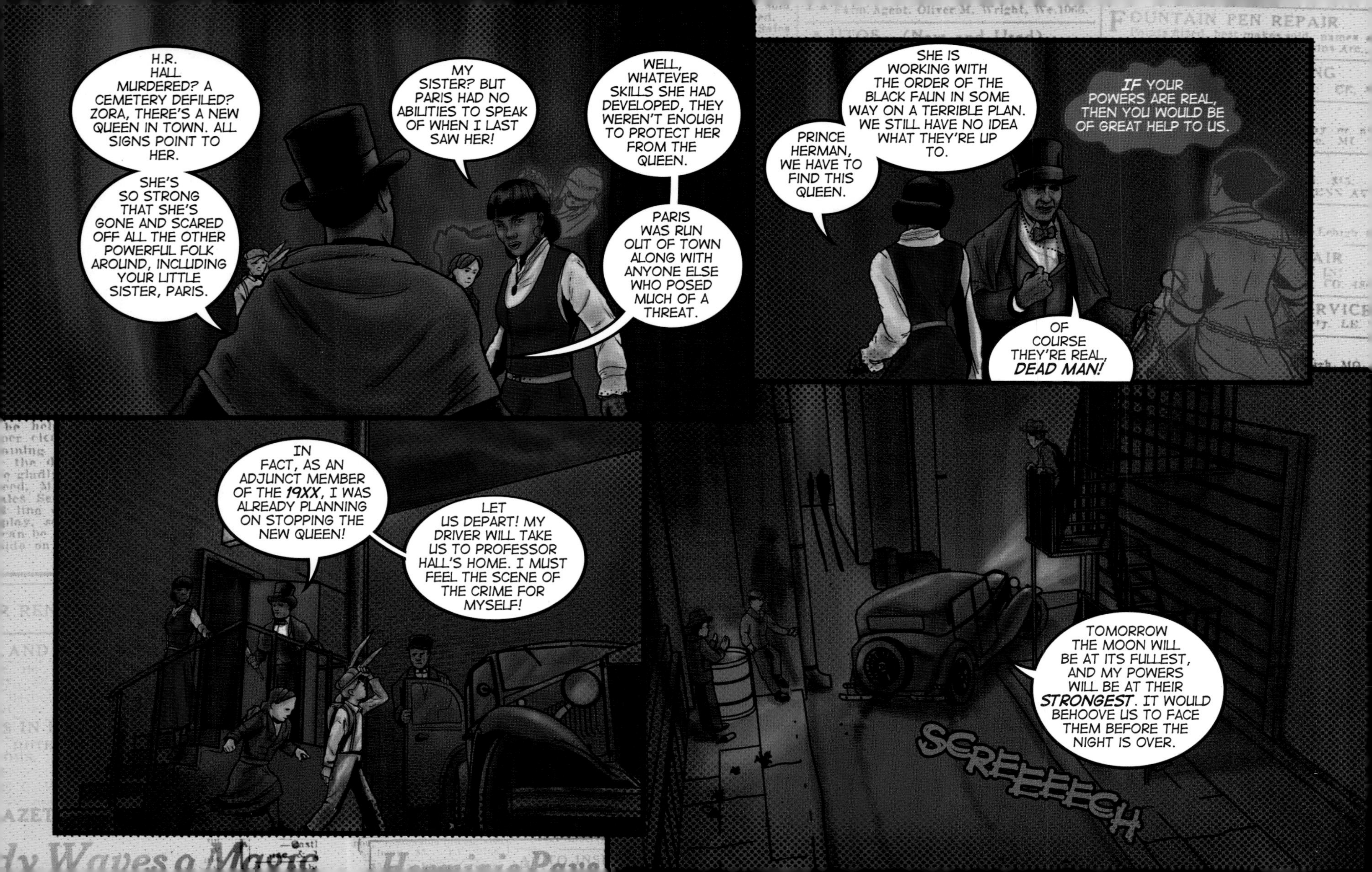
H.R. HALL MURDERED? A CEMETERY DEFILED? ZORA, THERE'S A NEW QUEEN IN TOWN. ALL SIGNS POINT TO HER.
SHE'S SO STRONG THAT SHE'S GONE AND SCARED OFF ALL THE OTHER POWERFUL FOLK AROUND, INCLUDING YOUR LITTLE SISTER, PARIS.
MY SISTER? BUT PARIS HAD NO ABILITIES TO SPEAK OF WHEN I LAST SAW HER!
WELL, WHATEVER SKILLS SHE HAD DEVELOPED, THEY WEREN'T ENOUGH TO PROTECT HER FROM THE QUEEN.
PARIS WAS RUN OUT OF TOWN ALONG WITH ANYONE ELSE WHO POSED MUCH OF A THREAT.
PRINCE HERMAN, WE HAVE TO FIND THIS QUEEN.
SHE IS WORKING WITH THE ORDER OF THE BLACK FAUN IN SOME WAY ON A TERRIBLE PLAN. WE STILL HAVE NO IDEA WHAT THEY'RE UP TO.
IF YOUR POWERS ARE REAL, THEN YOU WOULD BE OF GREAT HELP TO US.
OF COURSE THEY'RE REAL, DEAD MAN!
IN FACT, AS AN ADJUNCT MEMBER OF THE 19XX, I WAS ALREADY PLANNING ON STOPPING THE NEW QUEEN!
LET US DEPART! MY DRIVER WILL TAKE US TO PROFESSOR HALL'S HOME. I MUST FEEL THE SCENE OF THE CRIME FOR MYSELF!
TOMORROW THE MOON WILL BE AT ITS FULLEST, AND MY POWERS WILL BE AT THEIR STRONGEST. IT WOULD BEHOOVE US TO FACE THEM BEFORE THE NIGHT IS OVER.
SCREEEECH

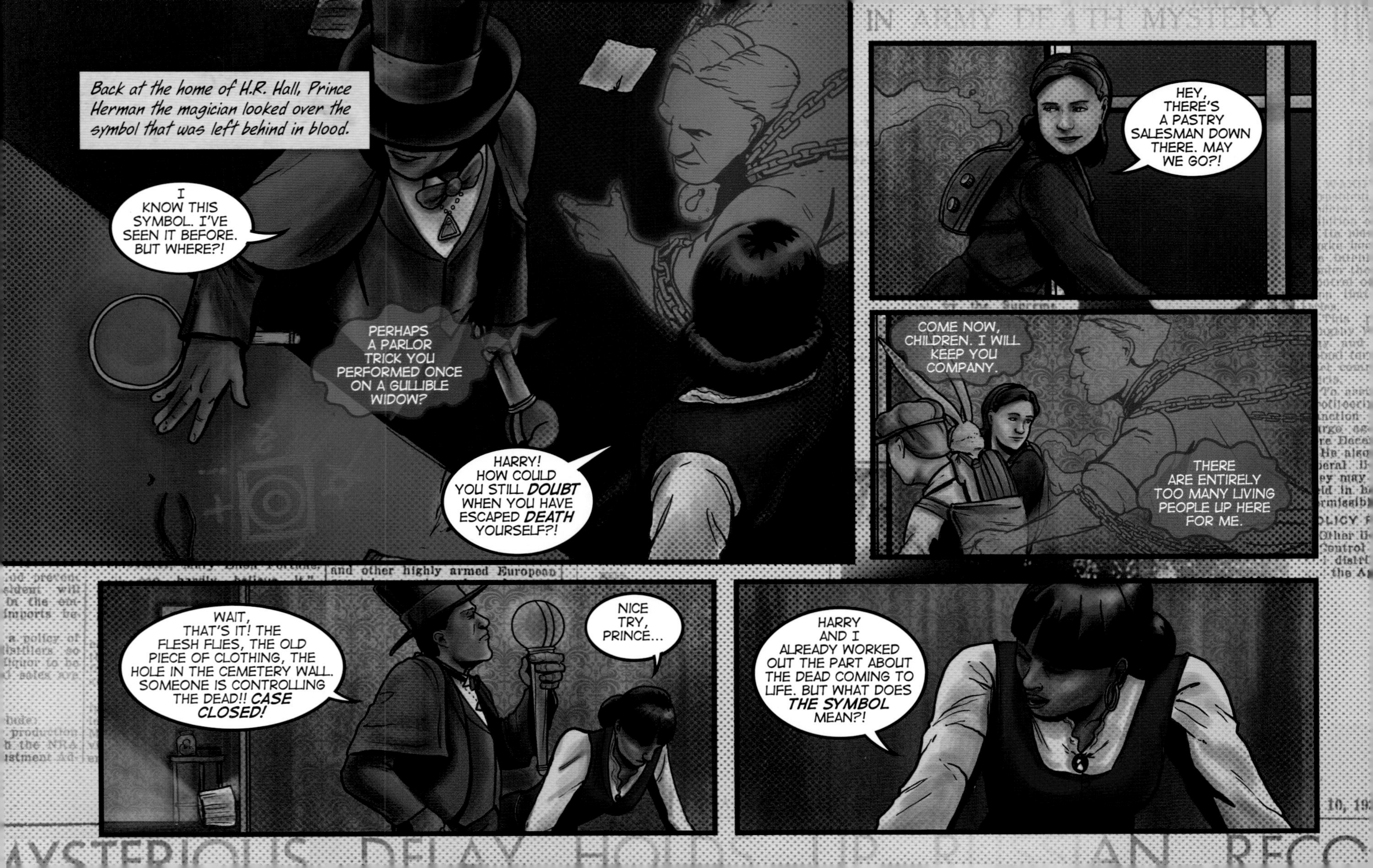
Back at the home of H.R. Hall, Prince Herman the magician looked over the symbol that was left behind in blood.
I KNOW THIS SYMBOL. I'VE SEEN IT BEFORE. BUT WHERE?!
PERHAPS A PARLOR TRICK YOU PERFORMED ONCE ON A GULLIBLE WIDOW?
HARRY! HOW COULD YOU STILL *DOUBT* WHEN YOU HAVE ESCAPED *DEATH* YOURSELF?!
HEY, THERE'S A PASTRY SALESMAN DOWN THERE. MAY WE GO?!
COME NOW, CHILDREN. I WILL KEEP YOU COMPANY.
THERE ARE ENTIRELY TOO MANY LIVING PEOPLE UP HERE FOR ME.
WAIT, THAT'S IT! THE FLESH FLIES, THE OLD PIECE OF CLOTHING, THE HOLE IN THE CEMETERY WALL. SOMEONE IS CONTROLLING THE DEAD!! *CASE CLOSED!*
NICE TRY, PRINCE...
HARRY AND I ALREADY WORKED OUT THE PART ABOUT THE DEAD COMING TO LIFE. BUT WHAT DOES *THE SYMBOL* MEAN?!

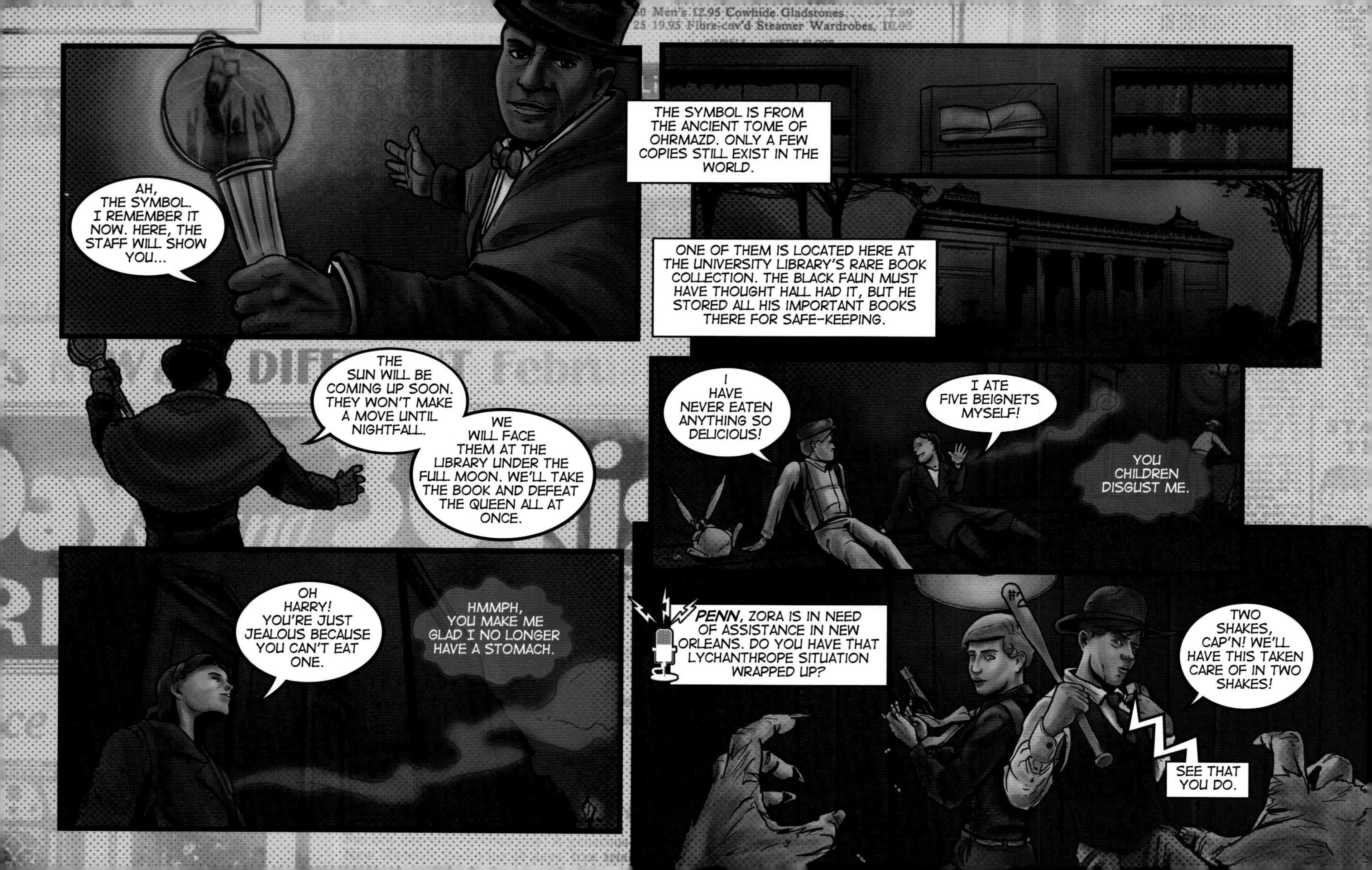
AH, THE SYMBOL. I REMEMBER IT NOW. HERE, THE STAFF WILL SHOW YOU...
THE SYMBOL IS FROM THE ANCIENT TOME OF OHRMAZD. ONLY A FEW COPIES STILL EXIST IN THE WORLD.
ONE OF THEM IS LOCATED HERE AT THE UNIVERSITY LIBRARY'S RARE BOOK COLLECTION. THE BLACK FAUN MUST HAVE THOUGHT HALL HAD IT, BUT HE STORED ALL HIS IMPORTANT BOOKS THERE FOR SAFE-KEEPING.
THE SUN WILL BE COMING UP SOON. THEY WON'T MAKE A MOVE UNTIL NIGHTFALL.
WE WILL FACE THEM AT THE LIBRARY UNDER THE FULL MOON. WE'LL TAKE THE BOOK AND DEFEAT THE QUEEN ALL AT ONCE.
I HAVE NEVER EATEN ANYTHING SO DELICIOUS!
I ATE FIVE BEIGNETS MYSELF!
YOU CHILDREN DISGUST ME.
OH HARRY! YOU'RE JUST JEALOUS BECAUSE YOU CAN'T EAT ONE.
HMMPH, YOU MAKE ME GLAD I NO LONGER HAVE A STOMACH.
PENN, ZORA IS IN NEED OF ASSISTANCE IN NEW ORLEANS. DO YOU HAVE THAT LYCHANTHROPE SITUATION WRAPPED UP?
TWO SHAKES, CAP'N! WE'LL HAVE THIS TAKEN CARE OF IN TWO SHAKES!
SEE THAT YOU DO.

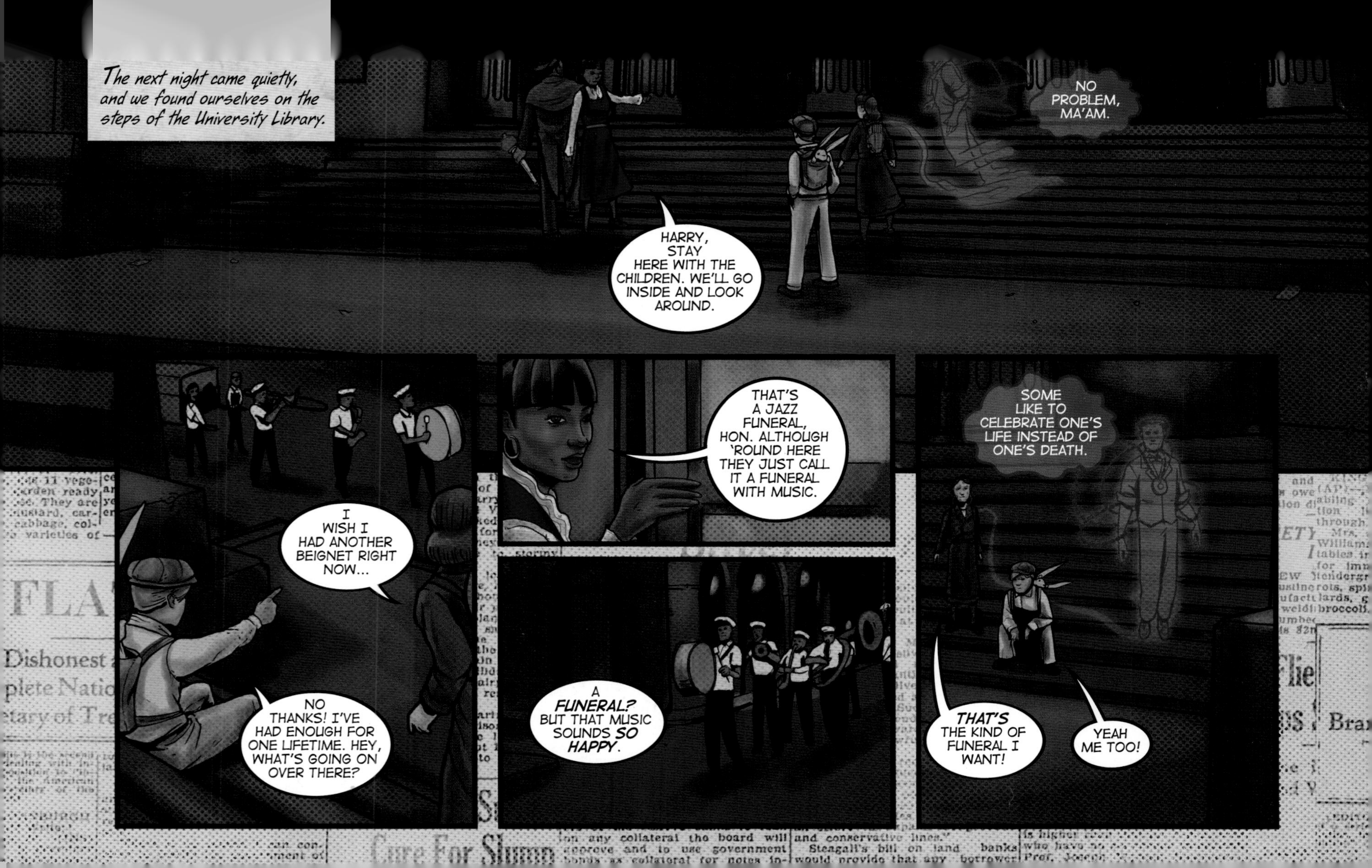
The next night came quietly, and we found ourselves on the steps of the University Library.
HARRY, STAY HERE WITH THE CHILDREN. WE'LL GO INSIDE AND LOOK AROUND.
NO PROBLEM, MA'AM.
I WISH I HAD ANOTHER BEIGNET RIGHT NOW...
NO THANKS! I'VE HAD ENOUGH FOR ONE LIFETIME. HEY, WHAT'S GOING ON OVER THERE?
THAT'S A JAZZ FUNERAL, HON. ALTHOUGH 'ROUND HERE THEY JUST CALL IT A FUNERAL WITH MUSIC.
A *FUNERAL?* BUT THAT MUSIC SOUNDS *SO HAPPY*.
SOME LIKE TO CELEBRATE ONE'S LIFE INSTEAD OF ONE'S DEATH.
THAT'S THE KIND OF FUNERAL I WANT!
YEAH ME TOO!

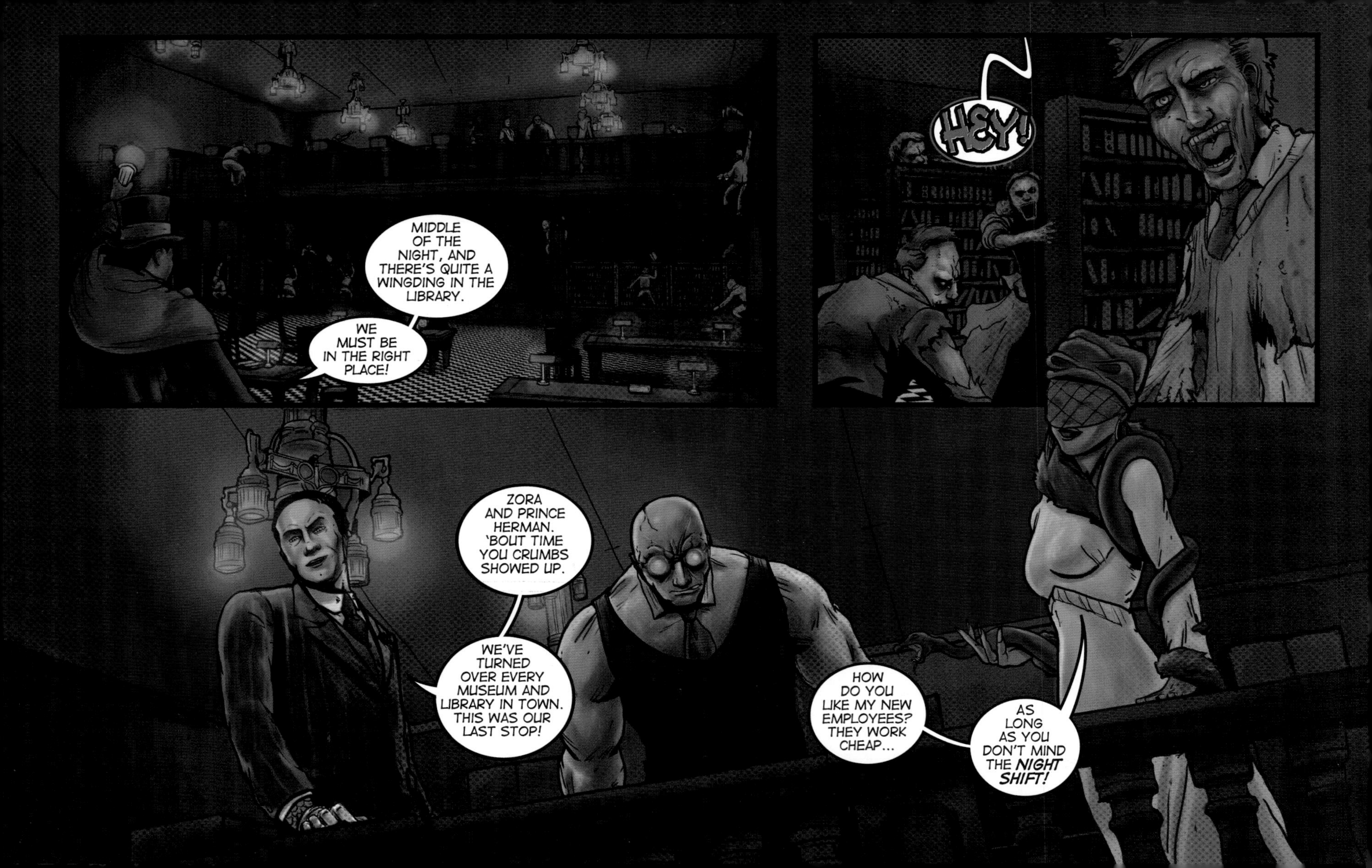
MIDDLE OF THE NIGHT, AND THERE'S QUITE A WINGDING IN THE LIBRARY.
WE MUST BE IN THE RIGHT PLACE!
HEY!
ZORA AND PRINCE HERMAN. 'BOUT TIME YOU CRUMBS SHOWED UP.
WE'VE TURNED OVER EVERY MUSEUM AND LIBRARY IN TOWN. THIS WAS OUR LAST STOP!
HOW DO YOU LIKE MY NEW EMPLOYEES? THEY WORK CHEAP...
AS LONG AS YOU DON'T MIND THE NIGHT SHIFT!

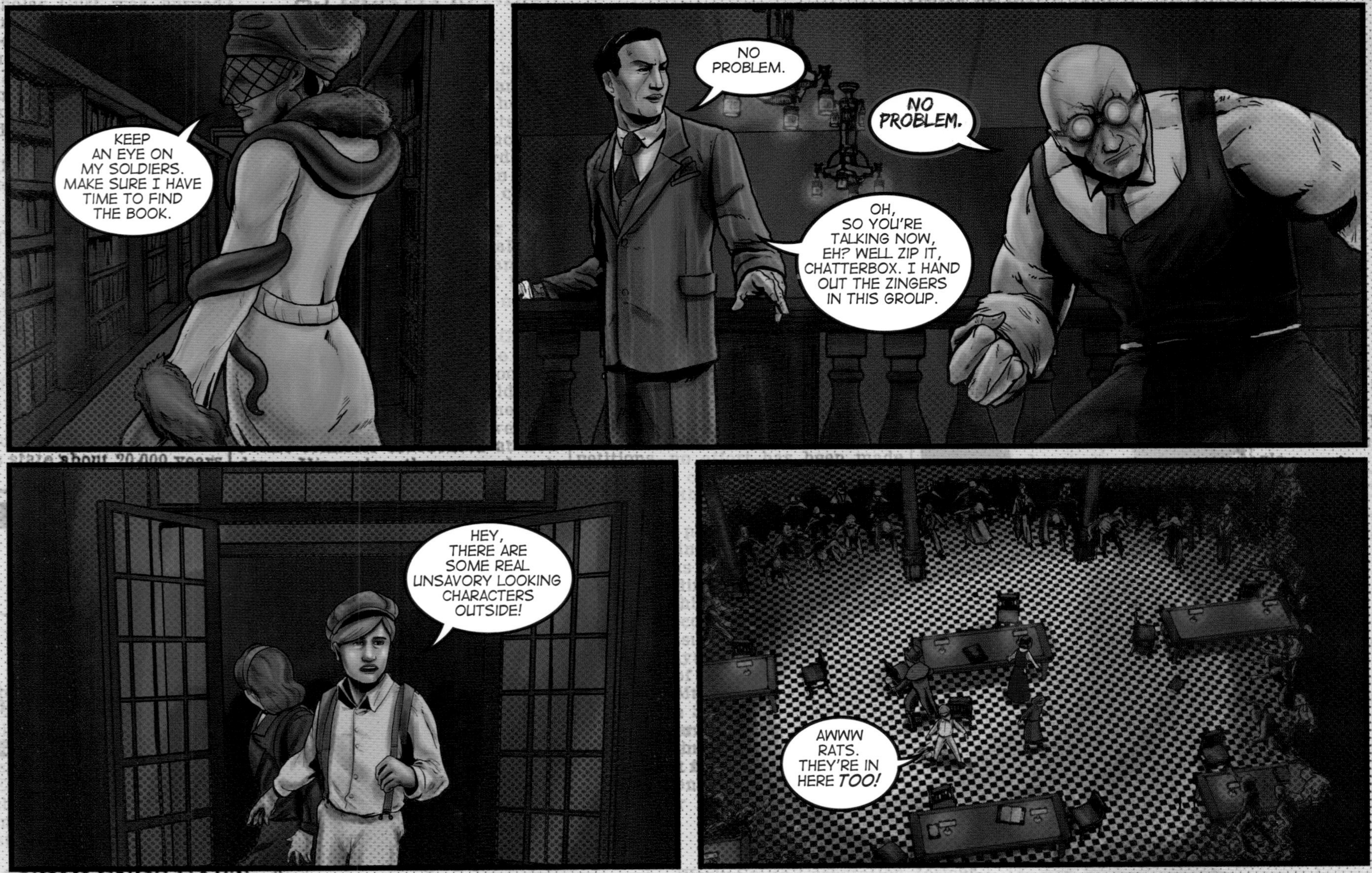

KEEP AN EYE ON MY SOLDIERS. MAKE SURE I HAVE TIME TO FIND THE BOOK.
NO PROBLEM.
NO PROBLEM.
OH, SO YOU'RE TALKING NOW, EH? WELL ZIP IT, CHATTERBOX. I HAND OUT THE ZINGERS IN THIS GROUP.
HEY, THERE ARE SOME REAL UNSAVORY LOOKING CHARACTERS OUTSIDE!
AWWW RATS. THEY'RE IN HERE *TOO!*

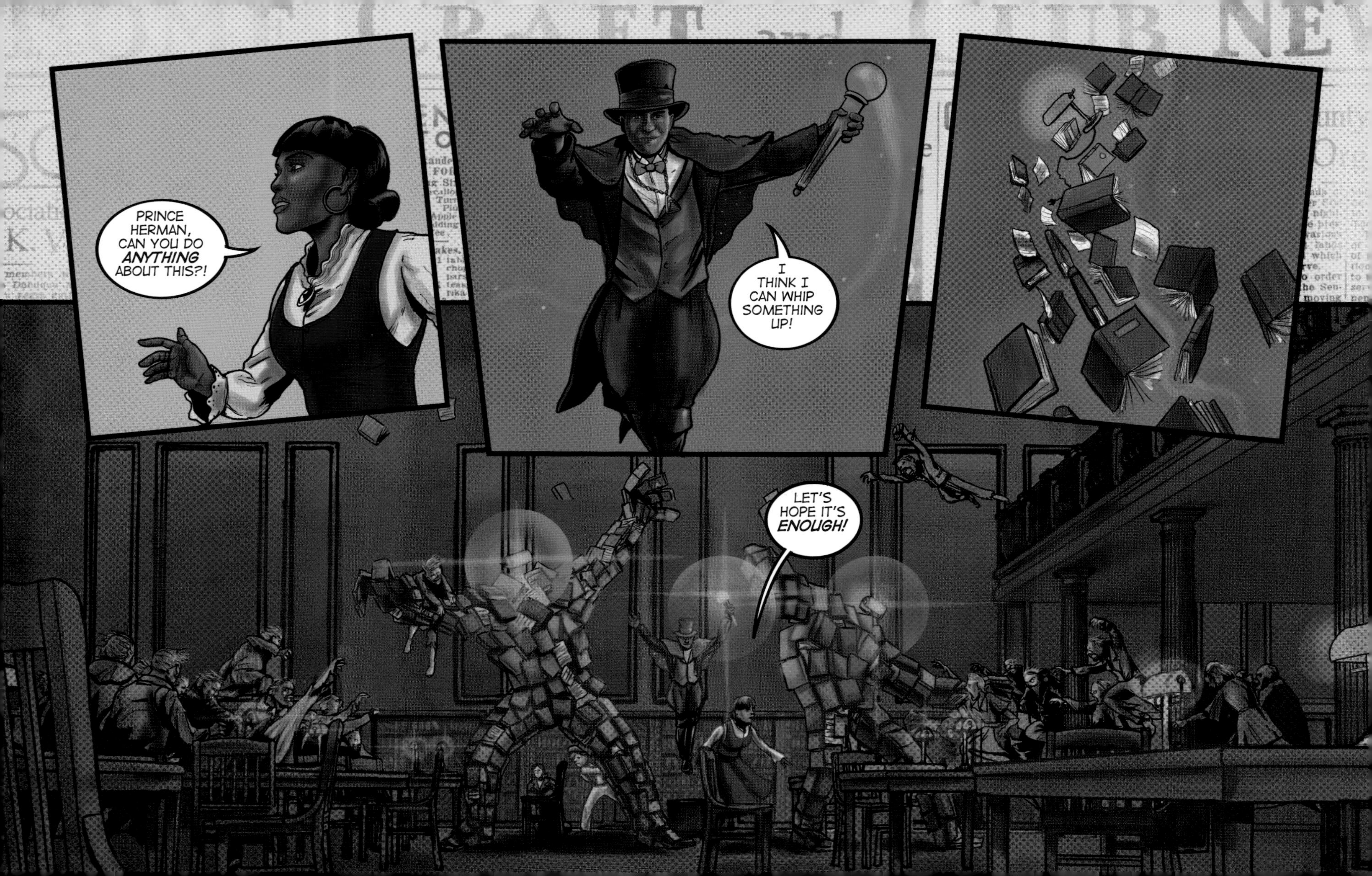
PRINCE HERMAN, CAN YOU DO ANYTHING ABOUT THIS?!
I THINK I CAN WHIP SOMETHING UP!
LET'S HOPE IT'S ENOUGH!

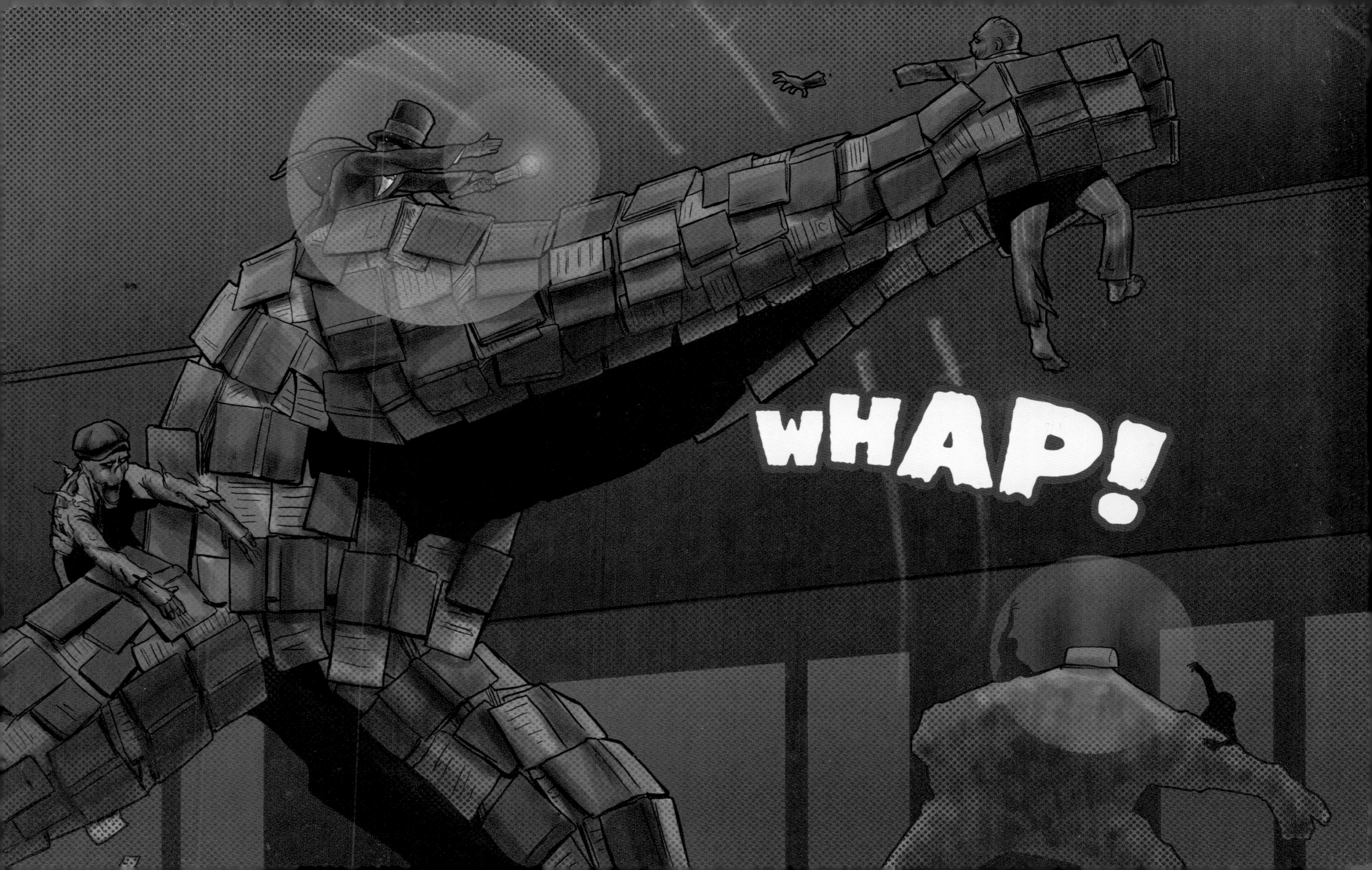
wHAP!

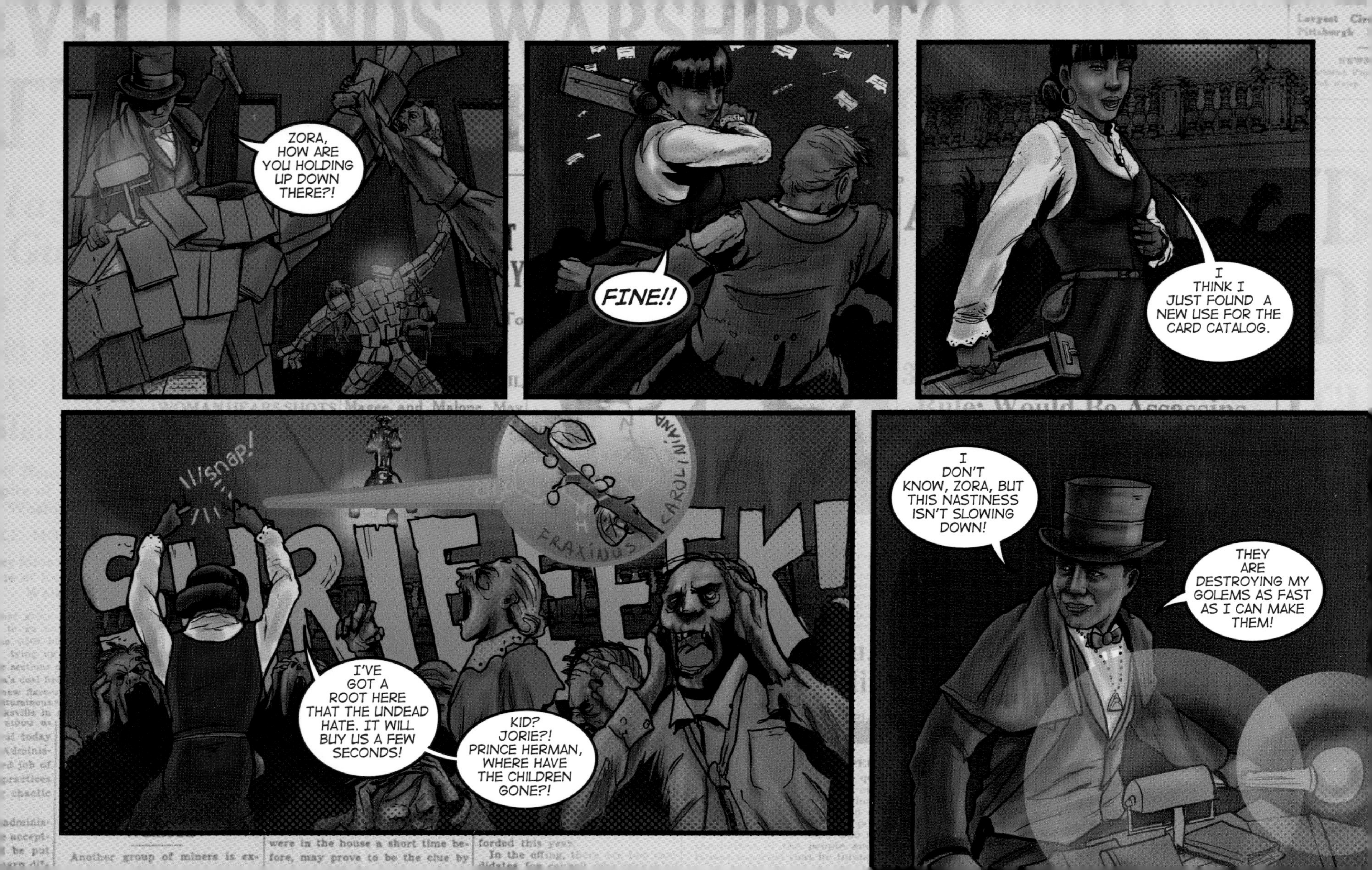

ZORA, HOW ARE YOU HOLDING UP DOWN THERE?!
FINE!!
I THINK I JUST FOUND A NEW USE FOR THE CARD CATALOG.
SNAP!
SHRIEEEK!
FRAXINUS CAROLINIANA
I'VE GOT A ROOT HERE THAT THE UNDEAD HATE. IT WILL BUY US A FEW SECONDS!
KID? JORIE?! PRINCE HERMAN, WHERE HAVE THE CHILDREN GONE?!
I DON'T KNOW, ZORA, BUT THIS NASTINESS ISN'T SLOWING DOWN!
THEY ARE DESTROYING MY GOLEMS AS FAST AS I CAN MAKE THEM!

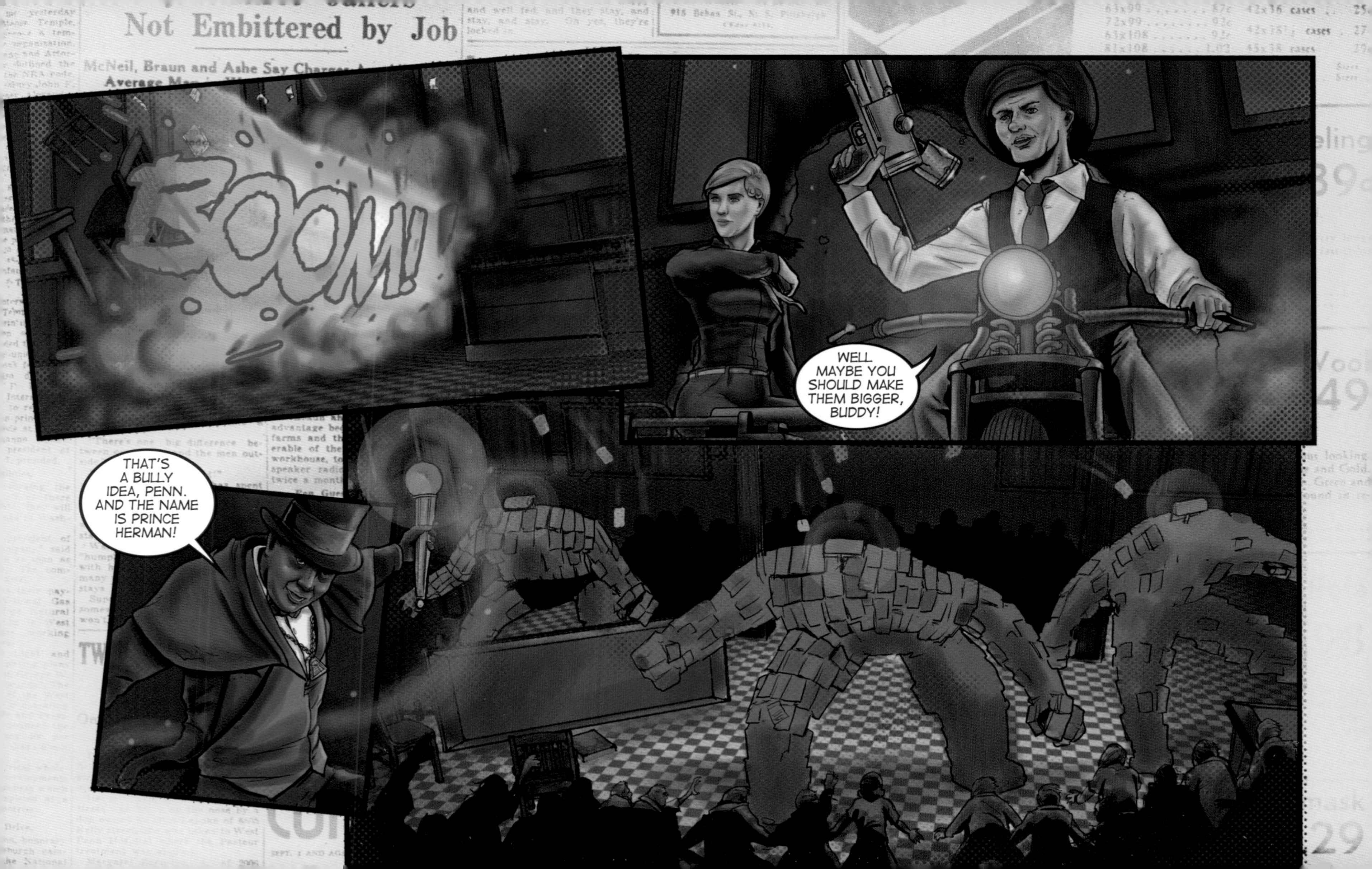
Not Embittered by Job
BOOM!
WELL MAYBE YOU SHOULD MAKE THEM BIGGER, BUDDY!
THAT'S A BULLY IDEA, PENN. AND THE NAME IS PRINCE HERMAN!

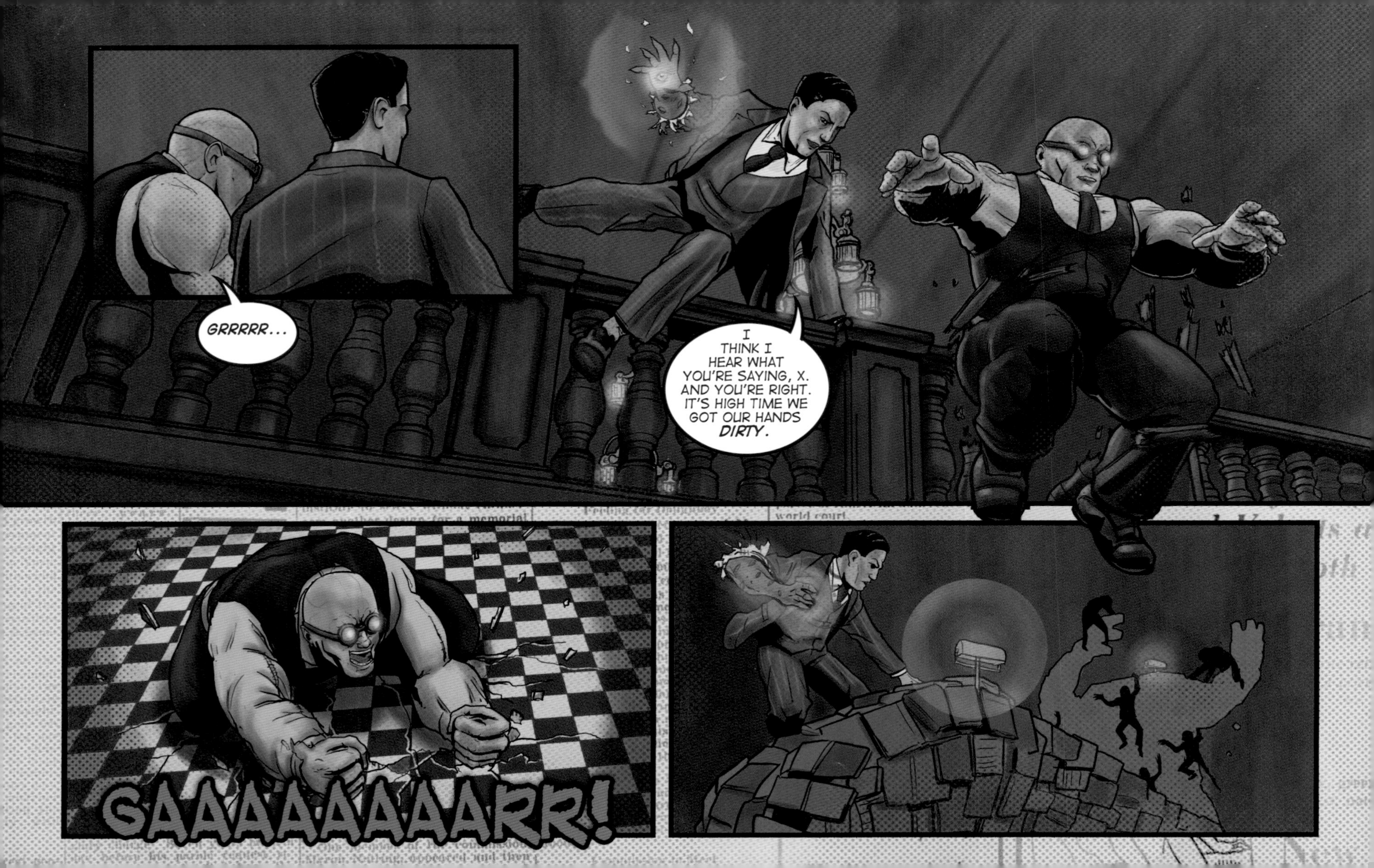
GRRRRR...
I THINK I HEAR WHAT YOU'RE SAYING, X. AND YOU'RE RIGHT. IT'S HIGH TIME WE GOT OUR HANDS DIRTY.
GAAAAAAAARR!

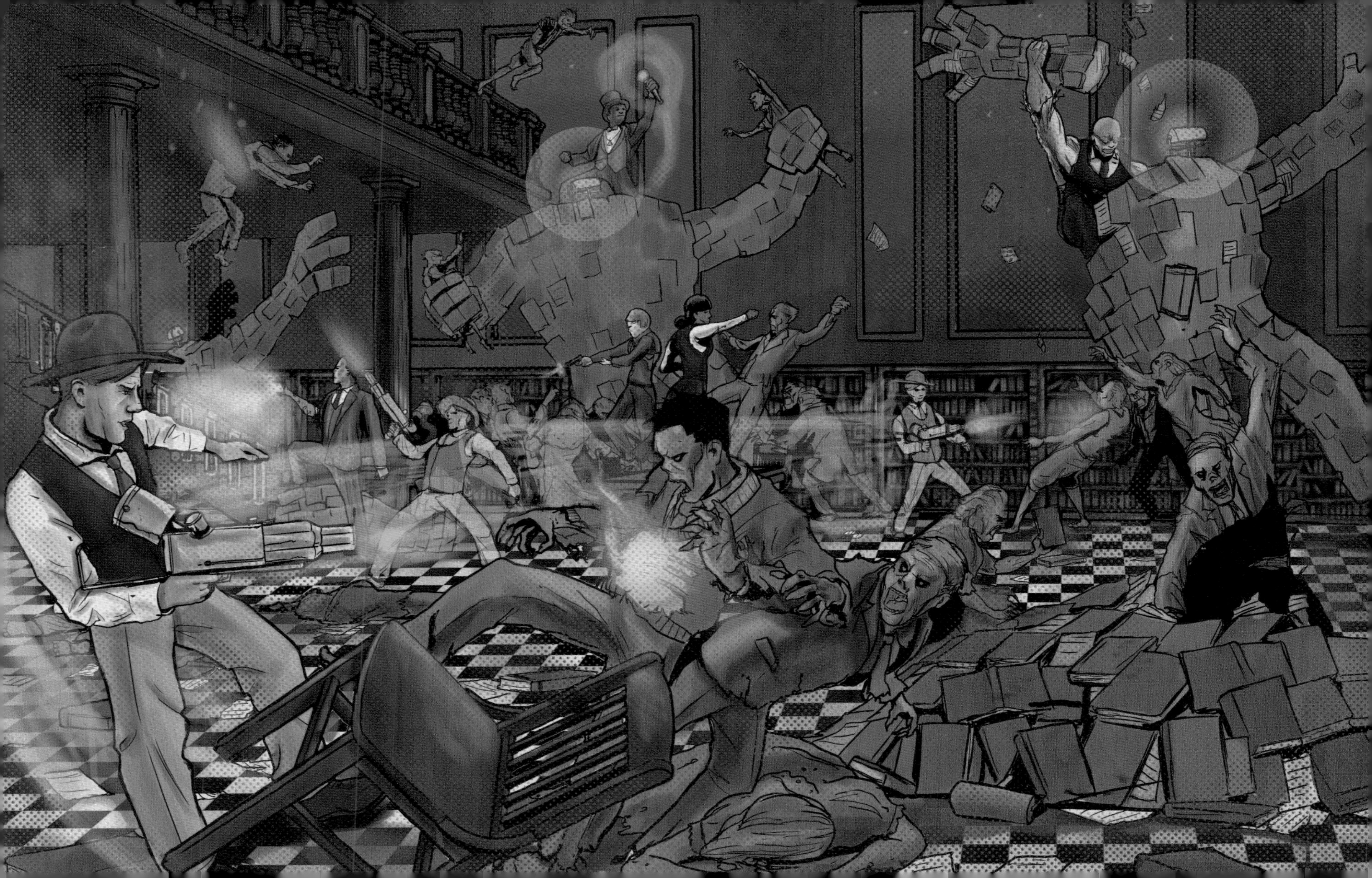

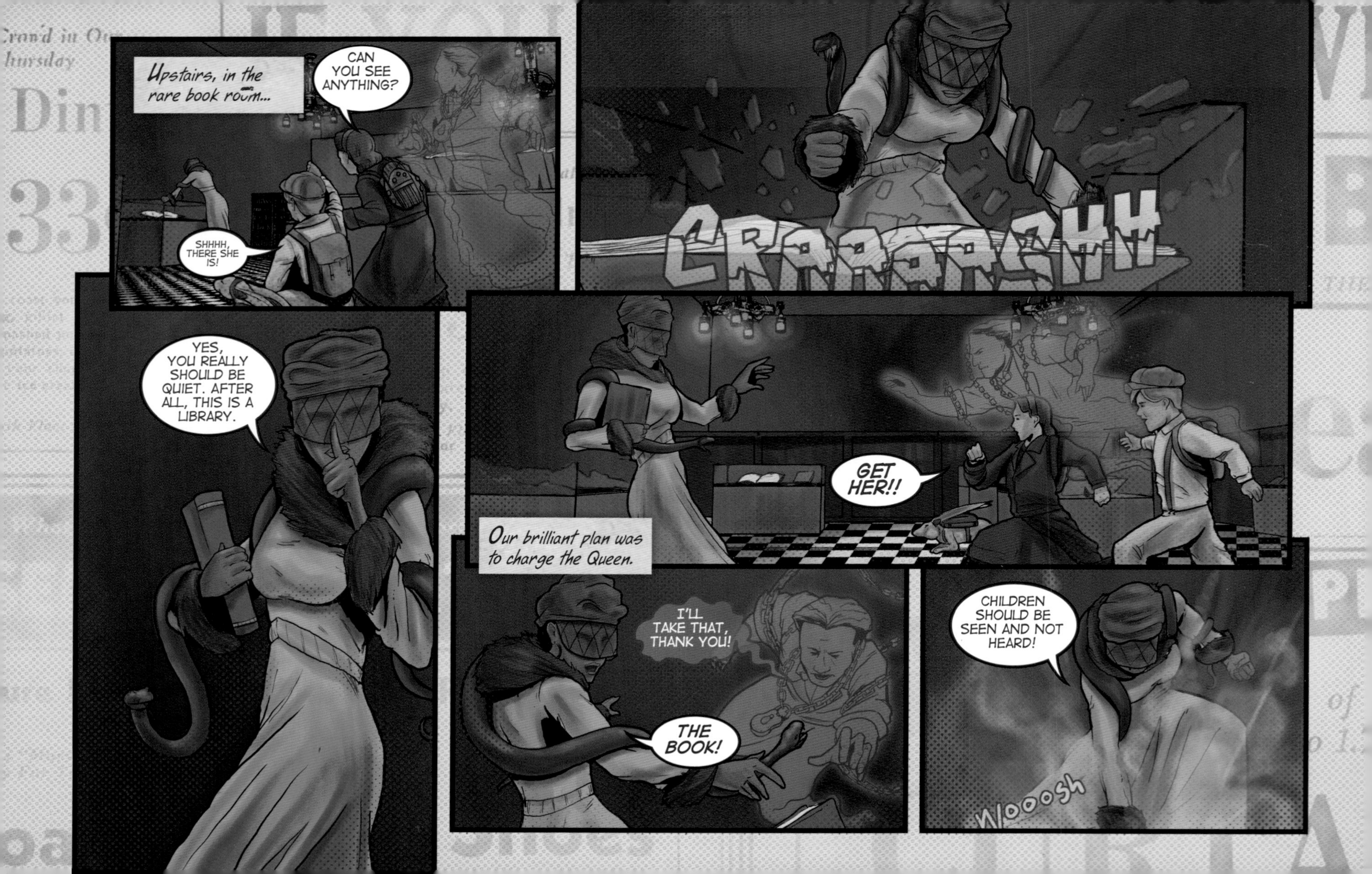

Upstairs, in the rare book room...
CAN YOU SEE ANYTHING?
SHHHH, THERE SHE IS!
CRRRRRASHH
YES, YOU REALLY SHOULD BE QUIET. AFTER ALL, THIS IS A LIBRARY.
GET HER!!
Our brilliant plan was to charge the Queen.
I'LL TAKE THAT, THANK YOU!
THE BOOK!
CHILDREN SHOULD BE SEEN AND NOT HEARD!
WOOOSH

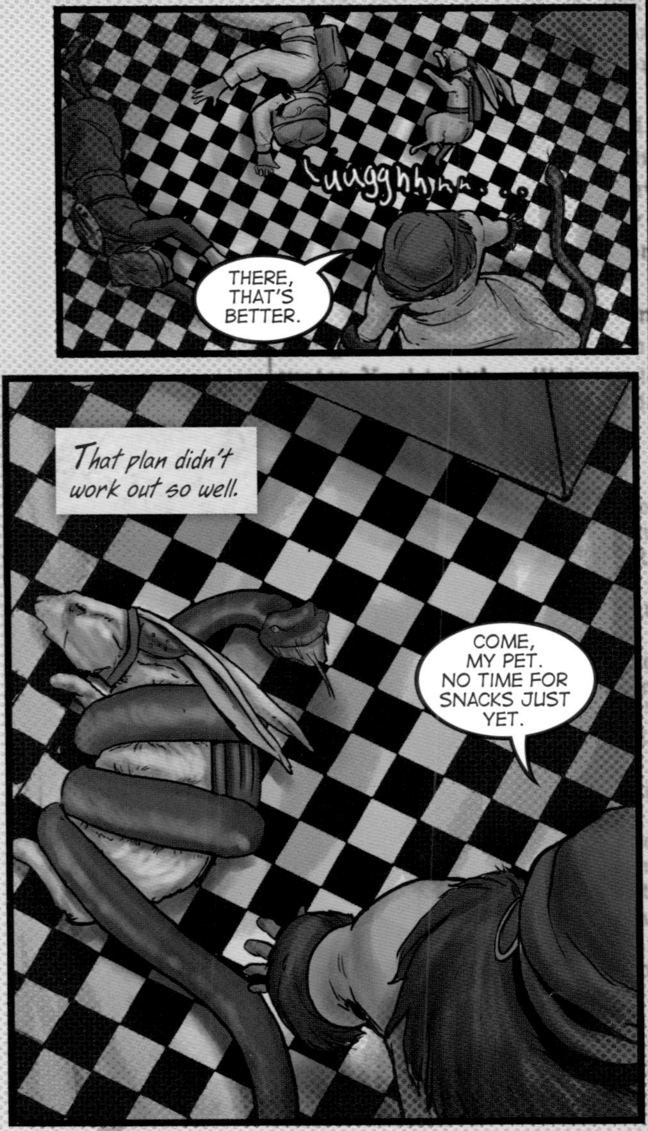
Uuggghhhh...
THERE, THAT'S BETTER.
That plan didn't work out so well.
COME, MY PET. NO TIME FOR SNACKS JUST YET.

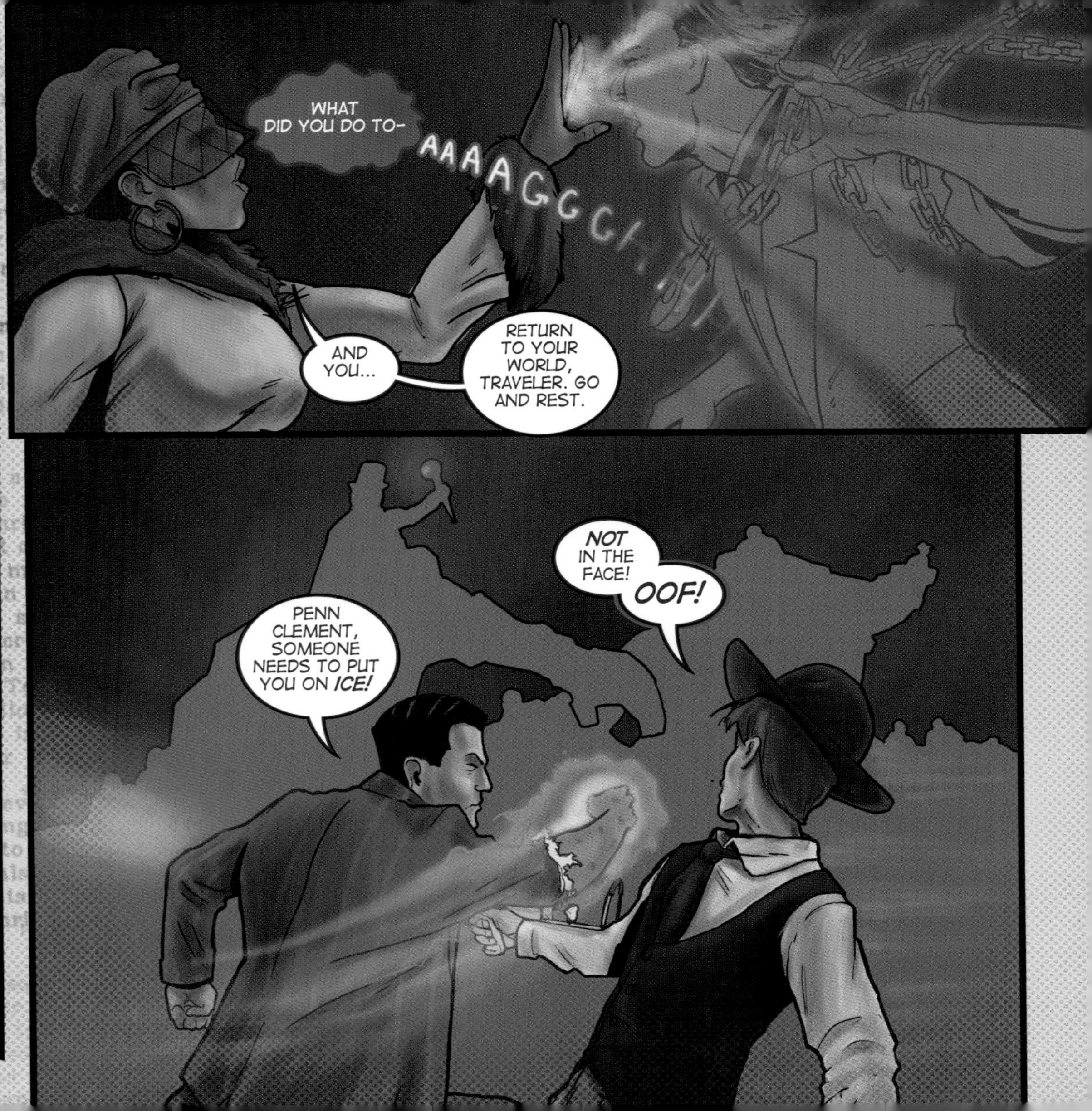
WHAT DID YOU DO TO-
AAAAGGG
AND YOU...
RETURN TO YOUR WORLD, TRAVELER. GO AND REST.
PENN CLEMENT, SOMEONE NEEDS TO PUT YOU ON *ICE!*
NOT IN THE FACE!
OOF!

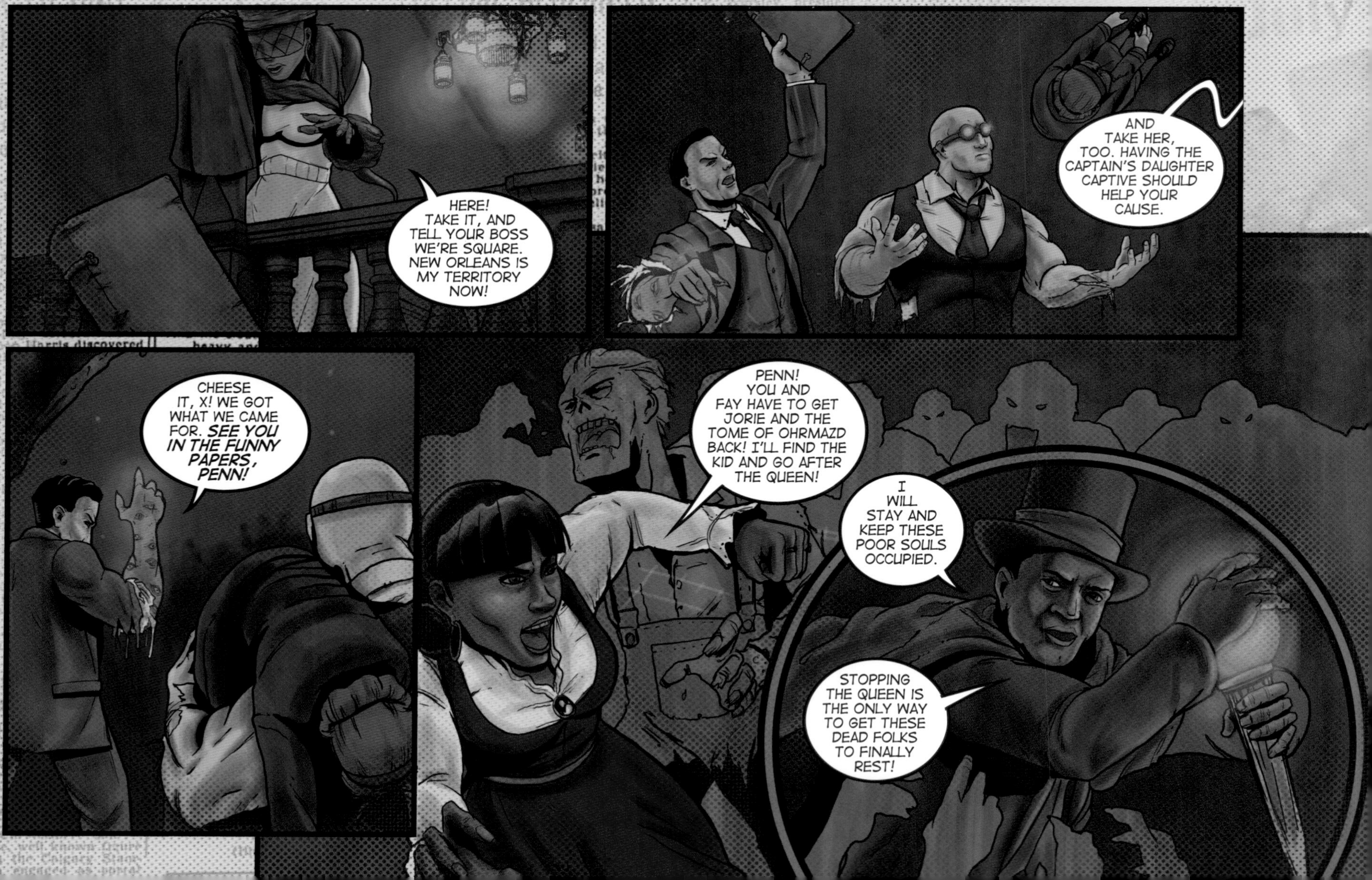
HERE! TAKE IT, AND TELL YOUR BOSS WE'RE SQUARE. NEW ORLEANS IS MY TERRITORY NOW!
AND TAKE HER, TOO. HAVING THE CAPTAIN'S DAUGHTER CAPTIVE SHOULD HELP YOUR CAUSE.
CHEESE IT, X! WE GOT WHAT WE CAME FOR. SEE YOU IN THE FUNNY PAPERS, PENN!
PENN! YOU AND FAY HAVE TO GET JORIE AND THE TOME OF OHRMAZD BACK! I'LL FIND THE KID AND GO AFTER THE QUEEN!
I WILL STAY AND KEEP THESE POOR SOULS OCCUPIED.
STOPPING THE QUEEN IS THE ONLY WAY TO GET THESE DEAD FOLKS TO FINALLY REST!

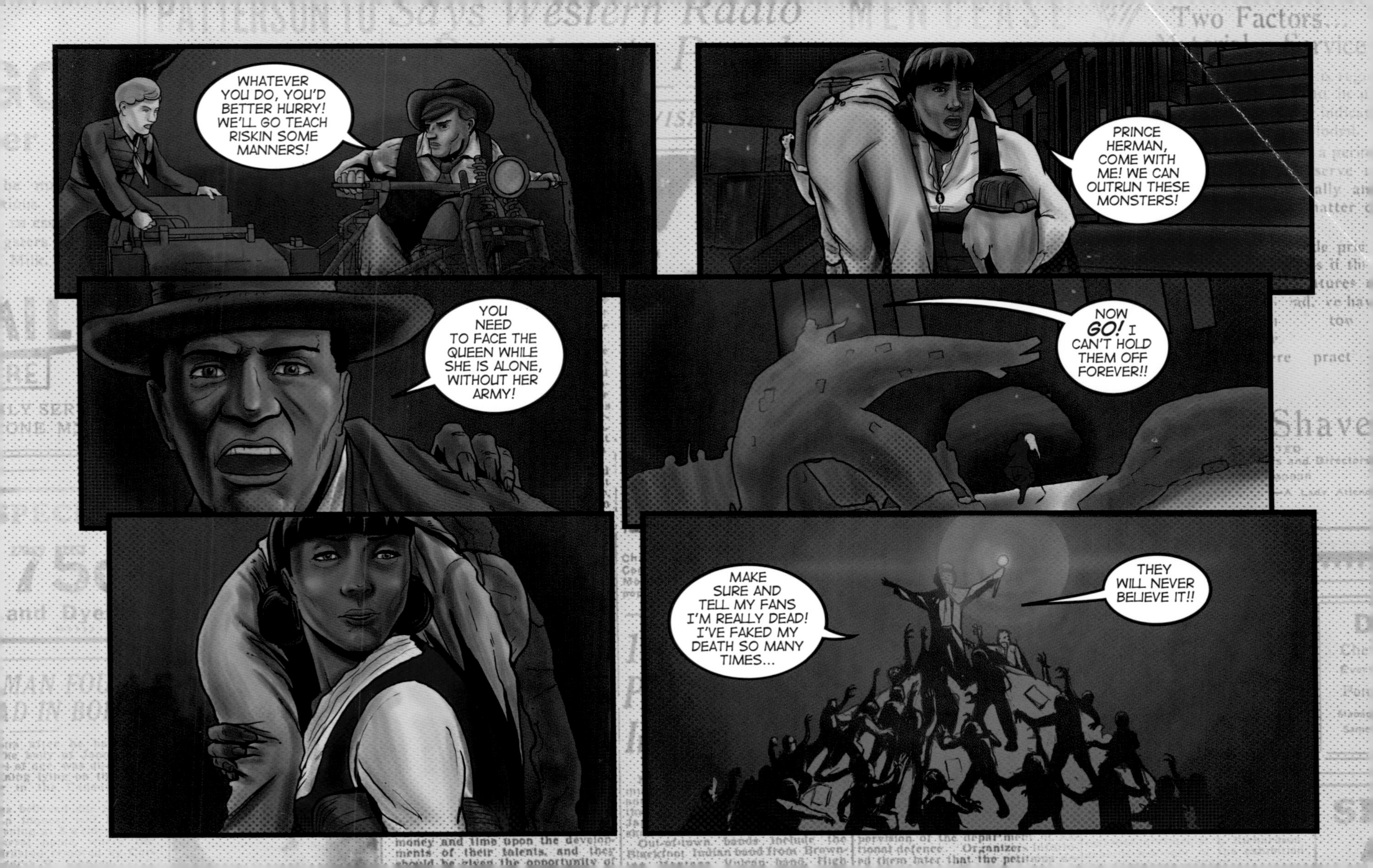
WHATEVER YOU DO, YOU'D BETTER HURRY! WE'LL GO TEACH RISKIN SOME MANNERS!
PRINCE HERMAN, COME WITH ME! WE CAN OUTRUN THESE MONSTERS!
YOU NEED TO FACE THE QUEEN WHILE SHE IS ALONE, WITHOUT HER ARMY!
NOW GO! I CAN'T HOLD THEM OFF FOREVER!!
MAKE SURE AND TELL MY FANS I'M REALLY DEAD! I'VE FAKED MY DEATH SO MANY TIMES...
THEY WILL NEVER BELIEVE IT!!

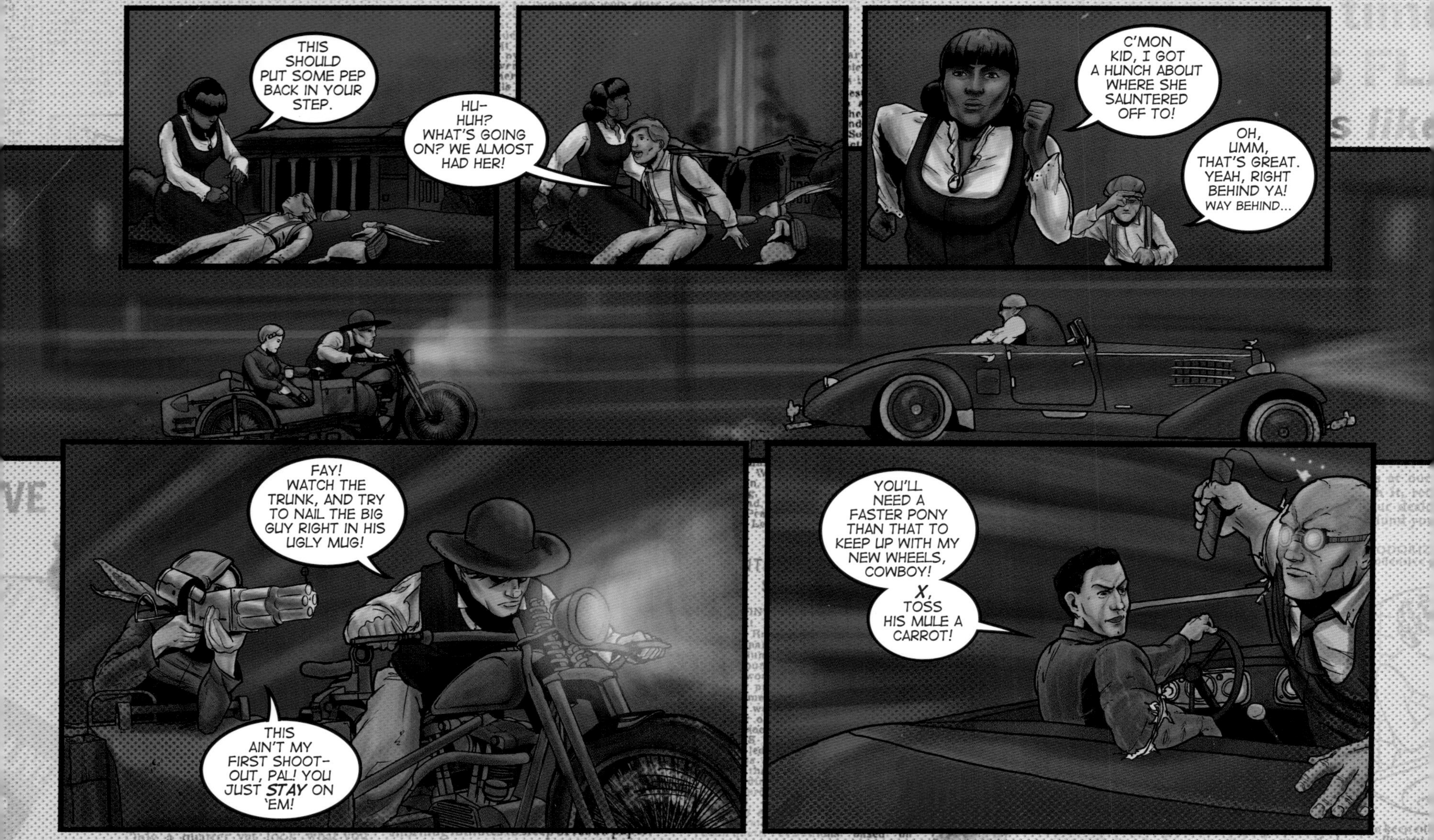

THIS SHOULD PUT SOME PEP BACK IN YOUR STEP.
HU-HUH? WHAT'S GOING ON? WE ALMOST HAD HER!
C'MON KID, I GOT A HUNCH ABOUT WHERE SHE SAUNTERED OFF TO!
OH, UMM, THAT'S GREAT. YEAH, RIGHT BEHIND YA! WAY BEHIND...
FAY! WATCH THE TRUNK, AND TRY TO NAIL THE BIG GUY RIGHT IN HIS UGLY MUG!
THIS AIN'T MY FIRST SHOOT-OUT, PAL! YOU JUST *STAY* ON 'EM!
YOU'LL NEED A FASTER PONY THAN THAT TO KEEP UP WITH MY NEW WHEELS, COWBOY!
X, TOSS HIS MULE A CARROT!

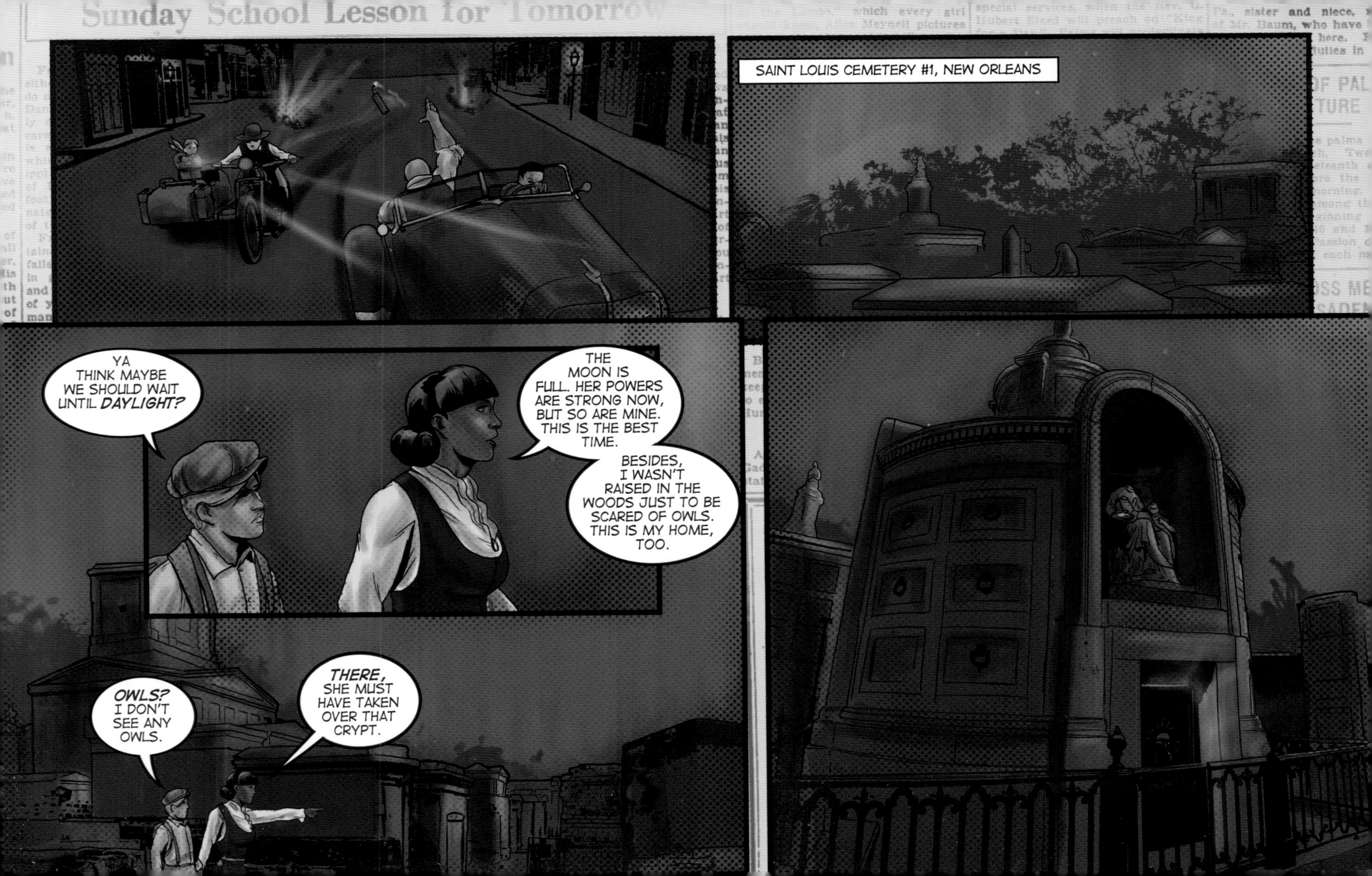
Sunday School Lesson for Tomorrow
SAINT LOUIS CEMETERY #1, NEW ORLEANS
YA THINK MAYBE WE SHOULD WAIT UNTIL *DAYLIGHT?*
THE MOON IS FULL. HER POWERS ARE STRONG NOW, BUT SO ARE MINE. THIS IS THE BEST TIME.
BESIDES, I WASN'T RAISED IN THE WOODS JUST TO BE SCARED OF OWLS. THIS IS MY HOME, TOO.
OWLS? I DON'T SEE ANY OWLS.
THERE, SHE MUST HAVE TAKEN OVER THAT CRYPT.

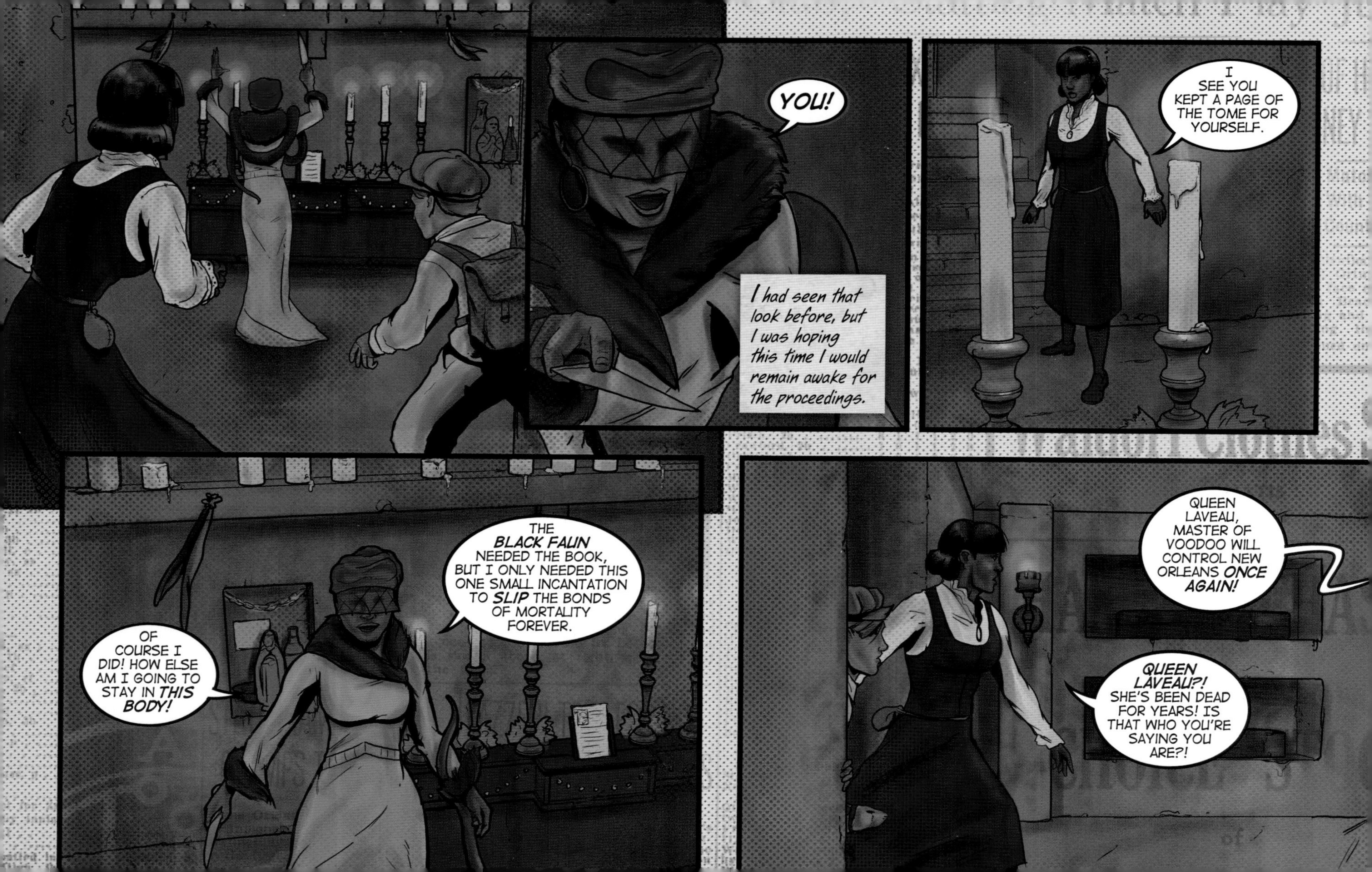
YOU!
I had seen that look before, but I was hoping this time I would remain awake for the proceedings.
I SEE YOU KEPT A PAGE OF THE TOME FOR YOURSELF.
OF COURSE I DID! HOW ELSE AM I GOING TO STAY IN THIS BODY!
THE BLACK FAUN NEEDED THE BOOK, BUT I ONLY NEEDED THIS ONE SMALL INCANTATION TO SLIP THE BONDS OF MORTALITY FOREVER.
QUEEN LAVEAU, MASTER OF VOODOO WILL CONTROL NEW ORLEANS ONCE AGAIN!
QUEEN LAVEAU?! SHE'S BEEN DEAD FOR YEARS! IS THAT WHO YOU'RE SAYING YOU ARE?!

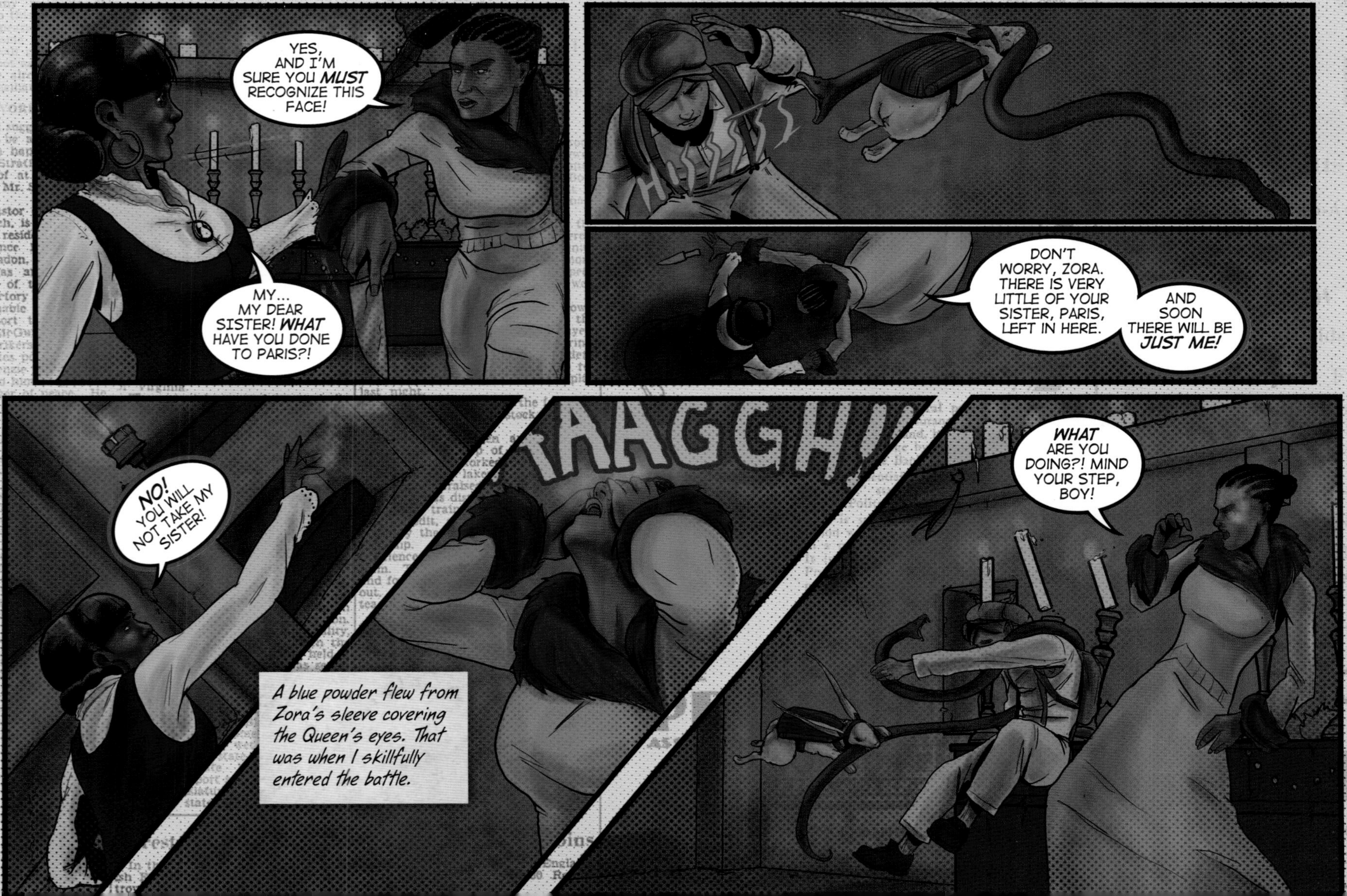

YES, AND I'M SURE YOU MUST RECOGNIZE THIS FACE!
MY... MY DEAR SISTER! WHAT HAVE YOU DONE TO PARIS?!
HISSSSS
DON'T WORRY, ZORA. THERE IS VERY LITTLE OF YOUR SISTER, PARIS, LEFT IN HERE.
AND SOON THERE WILL BE JUST ME!
NO! YOU WILL NOT TAKE MY SISTER!
RAAGGH!!
A blue powder flew from Zora's sleeve covering the Queen's eyes. That was when I skillfully entered the battle.
WHAT ARE YOU DOING?! MIND YOUR STEP, BOY!

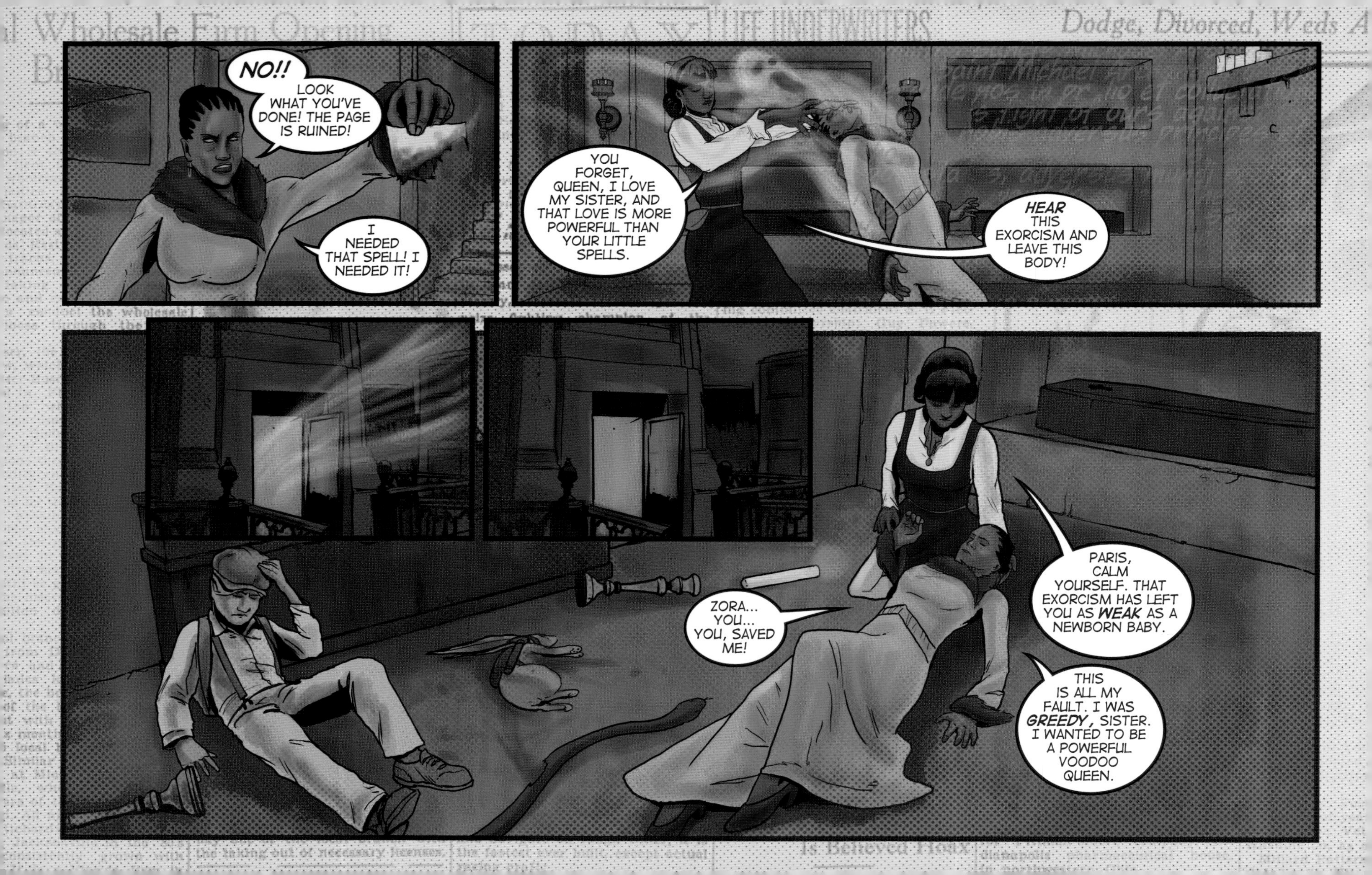
NO!! LOOK WHAT YOU'VE DONE! THE PAGE IS RUINED!
I NEEDED THAT SPELL! I NEEDED IT!
YOU FORGET, QUEEN, I LOVE MY SISTER, AND THAT LOVE IS MORE POWERFUL THAN YOUR LITTLE SPELLS.
HEAR THIS EXORCISM AND LEAVE THIS BODY!
ZORA... YOU... YOU, SAVED ME!
PARIS, CALM YOURSELF. THAT EXORCISM HAS LEFT YOU AS WEAK AS A NEWBORN BABY.
THIS IS ALL MY FAULT. I WAS GREEDY, SISTER. I WANTED TO BE A POWERFUL VOODOO QUEEN.

I JUST WANTED TO BE BETTER THAN YOU. I WAS JEALOUS. I NEEDED TO HAVE MORE POWER AND STRENGTH THAN ALL YOUR HOODOO SPELLS AND CHARMS.

I CAME TO MARIE LAVEAU'S GRAVE AND BEGAN MAKING OFFERINGS. I FELT MY POWER GROW GREATER EACH DAY.

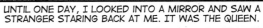
UNTIL ONE DAY, I LOOKED INTO A MIRROR AND SAW A STRANGER STARING BACK AT ME. IT WAS THE QUEEN.

PARIS,

I AM SO SORRY, ZORA. I AM SORRY FOR WHAT I **HAVE DONE** AND FOR WHAT I **ALMOST DID** TO YOU.

I FORGIVE YOU, BECAUSE YOU ARE MY SISTER, AND BLOOD IS THE STRONGEST BOND.

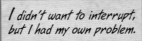
I didn't want to interrupt, but I had my own problem.

ZORA, IT'S TOGO! YOU HAVE TO HELP HIM!

Togo had helped me lick that snake, but he took quite a spill in the process.

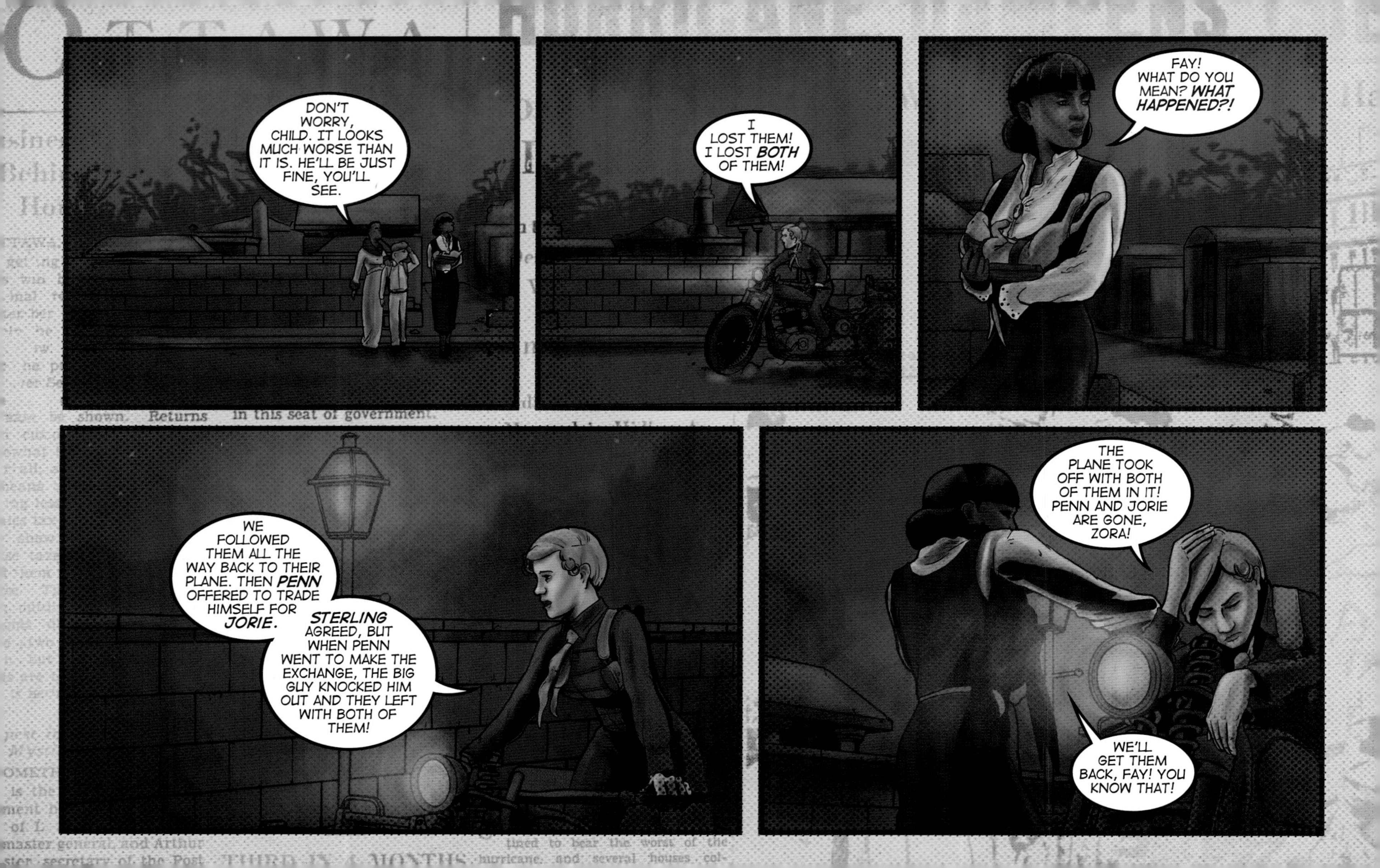
DON'T WORRY, CHILD. IT LOOKS MUCH WORSE THAN IT IS. HE'LL BE JUST FINE, YOU'LL SEE.
I LOST THEM! I LOST *BOTH* OF THEM!
FAY! WHAT DO YOU MEAN? *WHAT HAPPENED?!*
WE FOLLOWED THEM ALL THE WAY BACK TO THEIR PLANE. THEN *PENN* OFFERED TO TRADE HIMSELF FOR *JORIE*.
STERLING AGREED, BUT WHEN PENN WENT TO MAKE THE EXCHANGE, THE BIG GUY KNOCKED HIM OUT AND THEY LEFT WITH BOTH OF THEM!
THE PLANE TOOK OFF WITH BOTH OF THEM IN IT! PENN AND JORIE ARE GONE, ZORA!
WE'LL GET THEM BACK, FAY! YOU KNOW THAT!

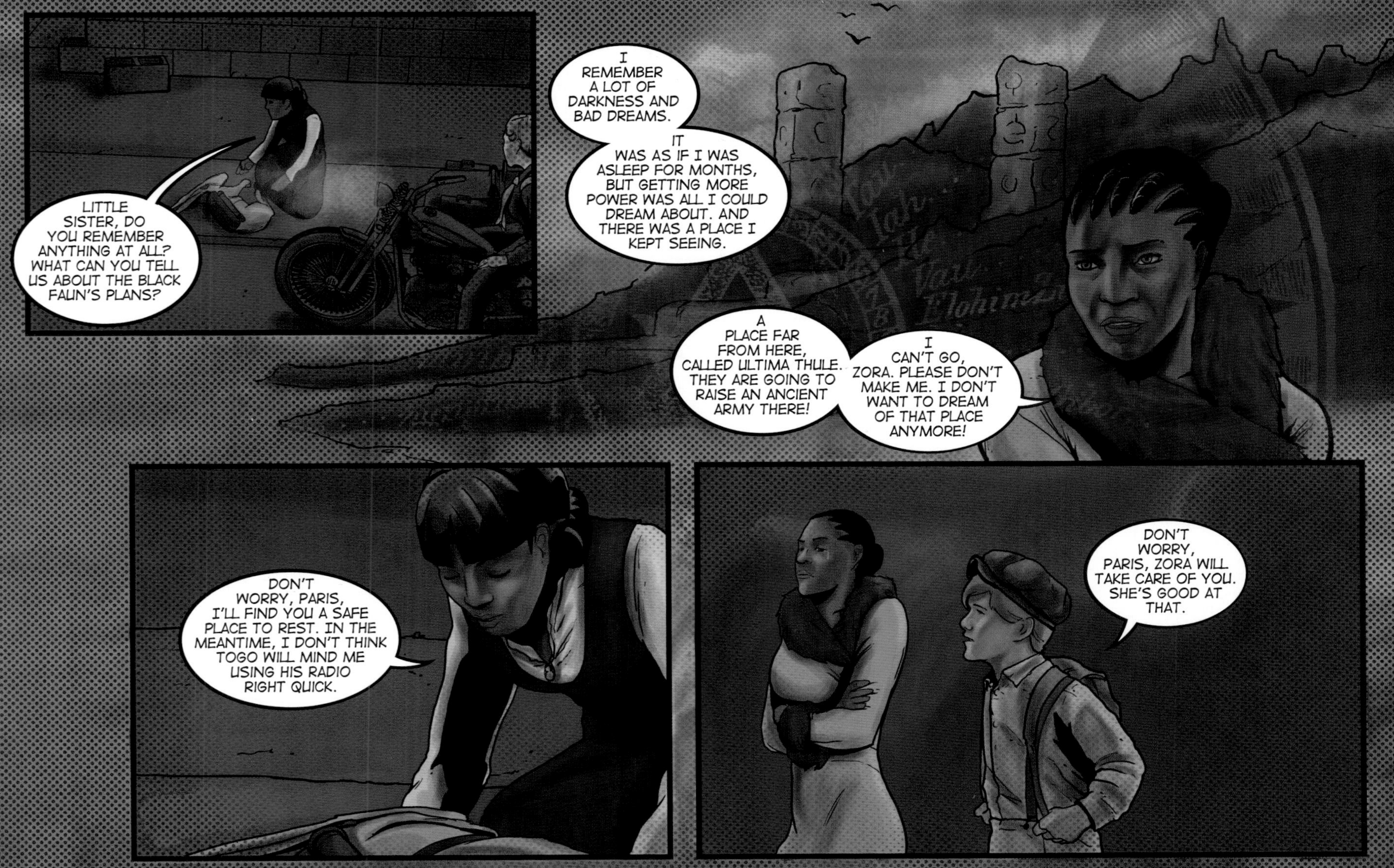
LITTLE SISTER, DO YOU REMEMBER ANYTHING AT ALL? WHAT CAN YOU TELL US ABOUT THE BLACK FAUN'S PLANS?
I REMEMBER A LOT OF DARKNESS AND BAD DREAMS.
IT WAS AS IF I WAS ASLEEP FOR MONTHS, BUT GETTING MORE POWER WAS ALL I COULD DREAM ABOUT. AND THERE WAS A PLACE I KEPT SEEING.
A PLACE FAR FROM HERE, CALLED ULTIMA THULE. THEY ARE GOING TO RAISE AN ANCIENT ARMY THERE!
I CAN'T GO, ZORA. PLEASE DON'T MAKE ME. I DON'T WANT TO DREAM OF THAT PLACE ANYMORE!
DON'T WORRY, PARIS, I'LL FIND YOU A SAFE PLACE TO REST. IN THE MEANTIME, I DON'T THINK TOGO WILL MIND ME USING HIS RADIO RIGHT QUICK.
DON'T WORRY, PARIS, ZORA WILL TAKE CARE OF YOU. SHE'S GOOD AT THAT.

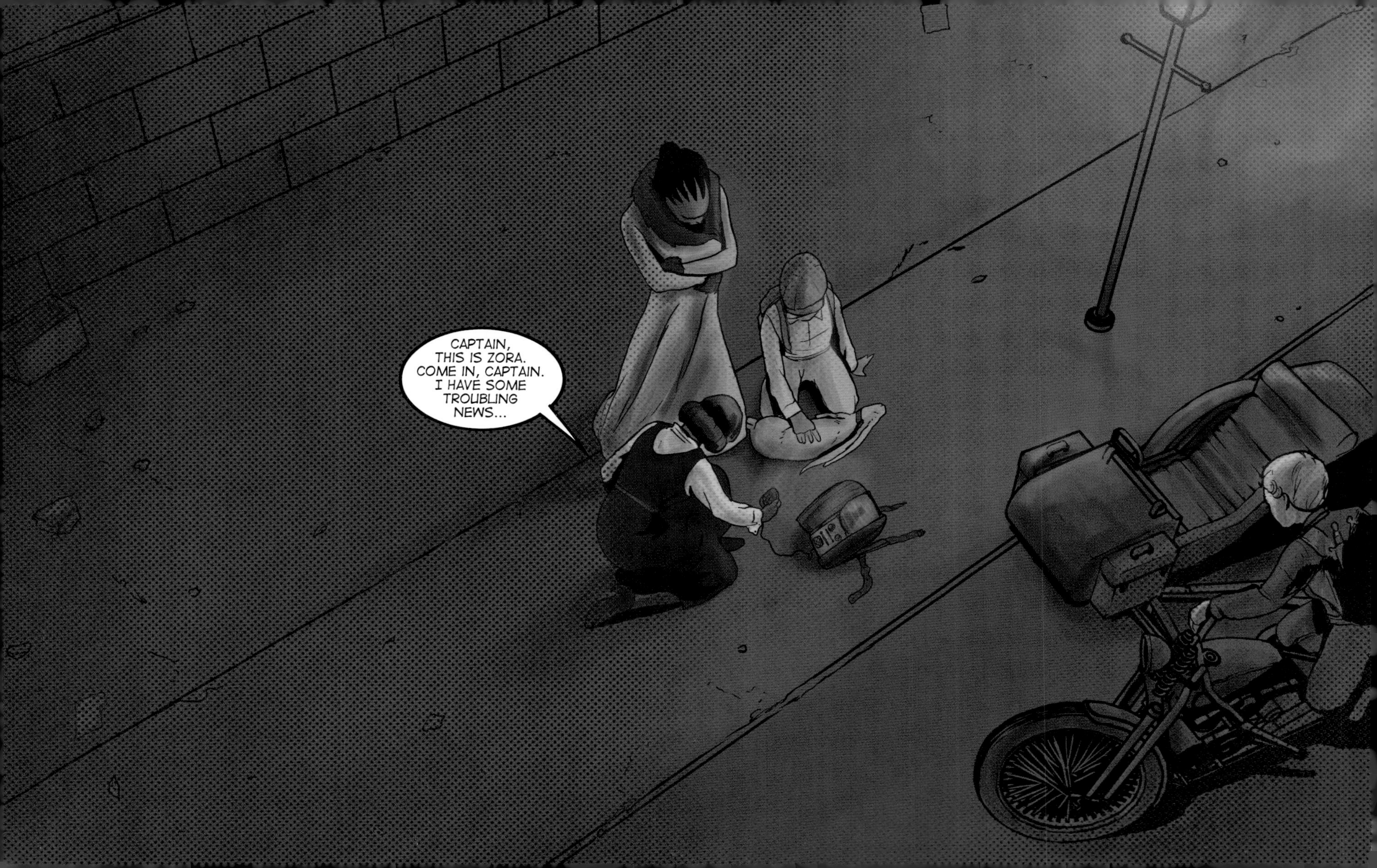
CAPTAIN, THIS IS ZORA. COME IN, CAPTAIN. I HAVE SOME TROUBLING NEWS...

CHAPTER 4

ASSAULT ON ULTIMA THULE

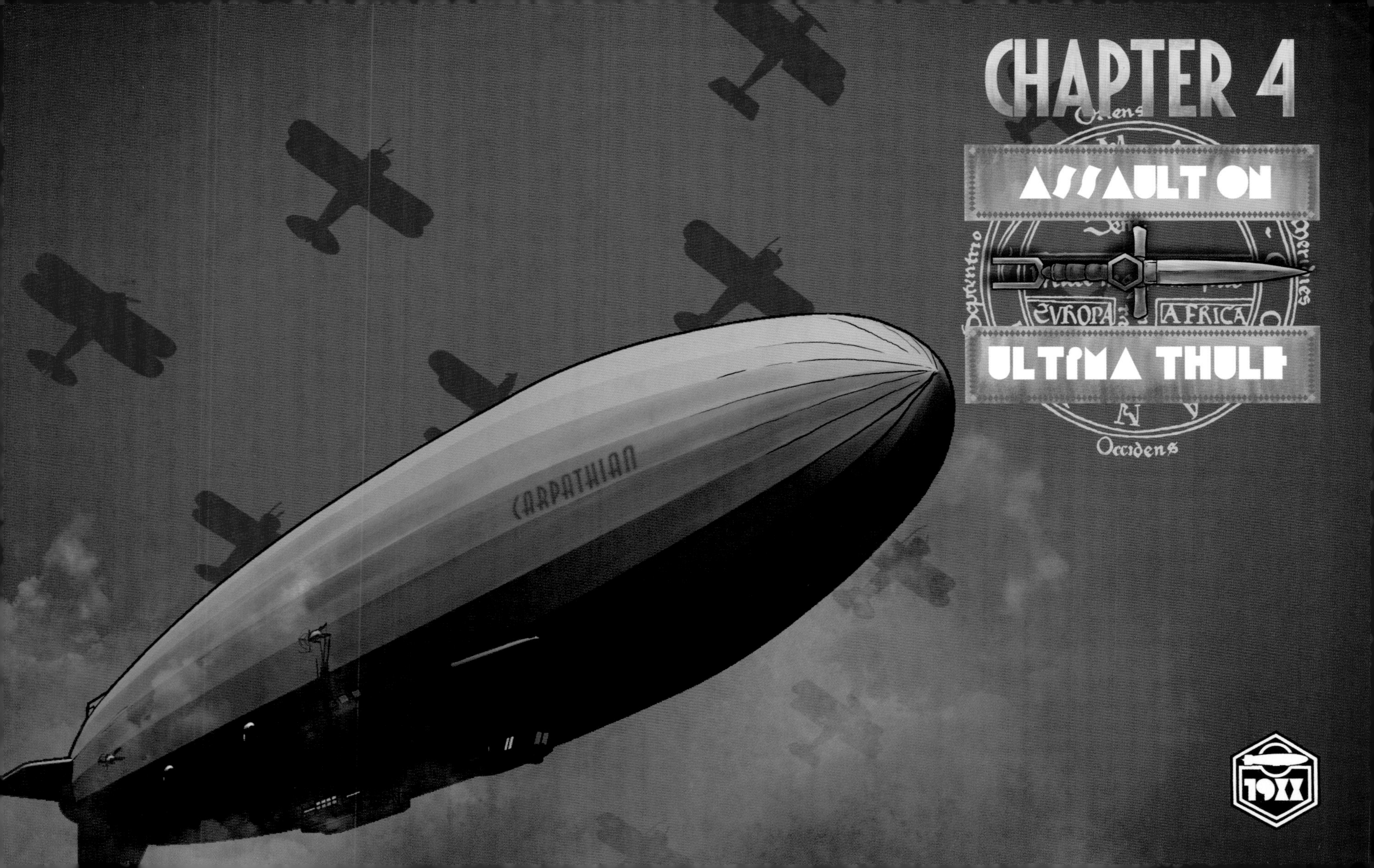

CARPATHIAN
Oriens
EVROPA
AFRICA
Occidens

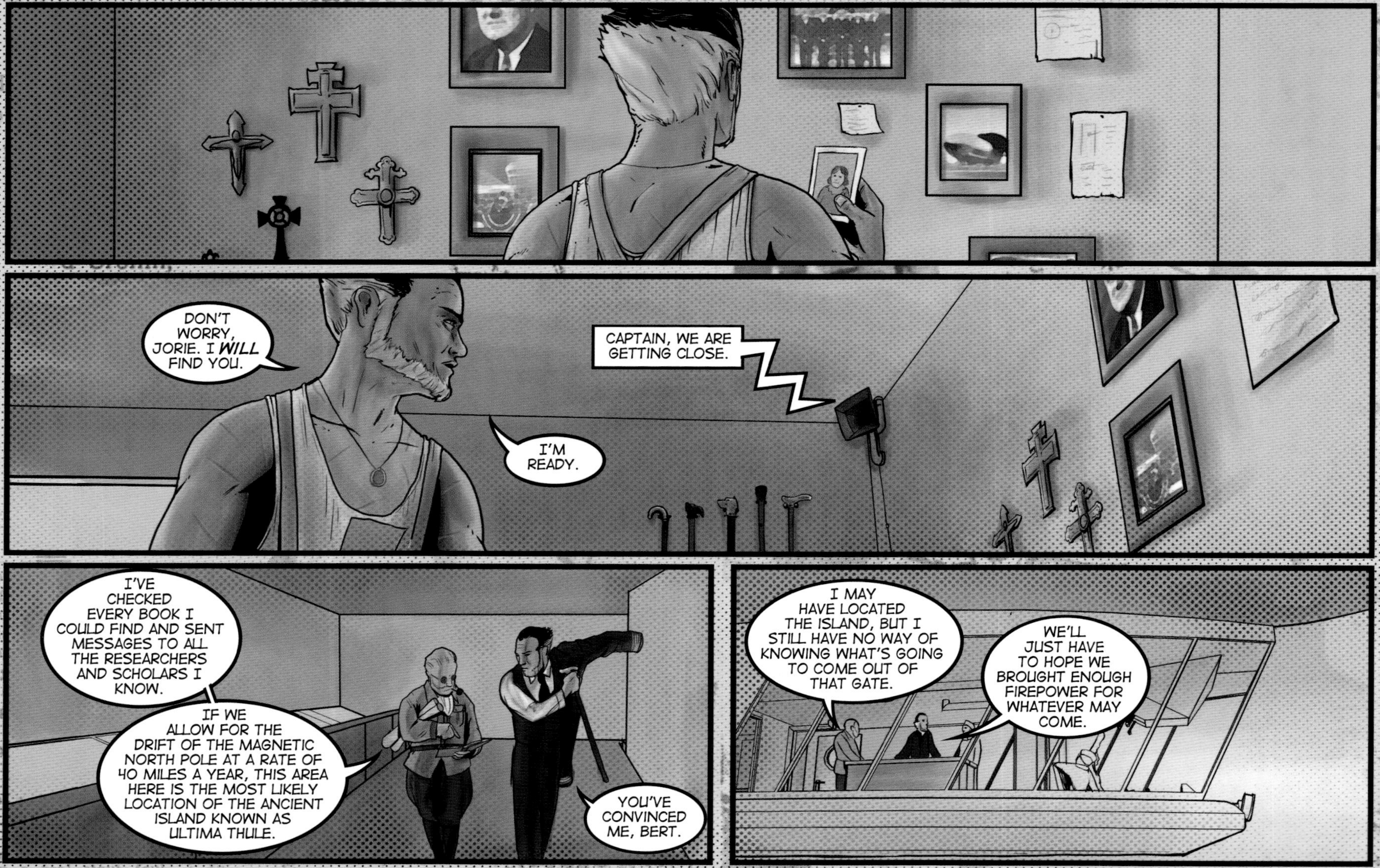
DON'T WORRY, JORIE. I *WILL* FIND YOU.
CAPTAIN, WE ARE GETTING CLOSE.
I'M READY.
I'VE CHECKED EVERY BOOK I COULD FIND AND SENT MESSAGES TO ALL THE RESEARCHERS AND SCHOLARS I KNOW.
IF WE ALLOW FOR THE DRIFT OF THE MAGNETIC NORTH POLE AT A RATE OF 40 MILES A YEAR, THIS AREA HERE IS THE MOST LIKELY LOCATION OF THE ANCIENT ISLAND KNOWN AS ULTIMA THULE.
YOU'VE CONVINCED ME, BERT.
I MAY HAVE LOCATED THE ISLAND, BUT I STILL HAVE NO WAY OF KNOWING WHAT'S GOING TO COME OUT OF THAT GATE.
WE'LL JUST HAVE TO HOPE WE BROUGHT ENOUGH FIREPOWER FOR WHATEVER MAY COME.

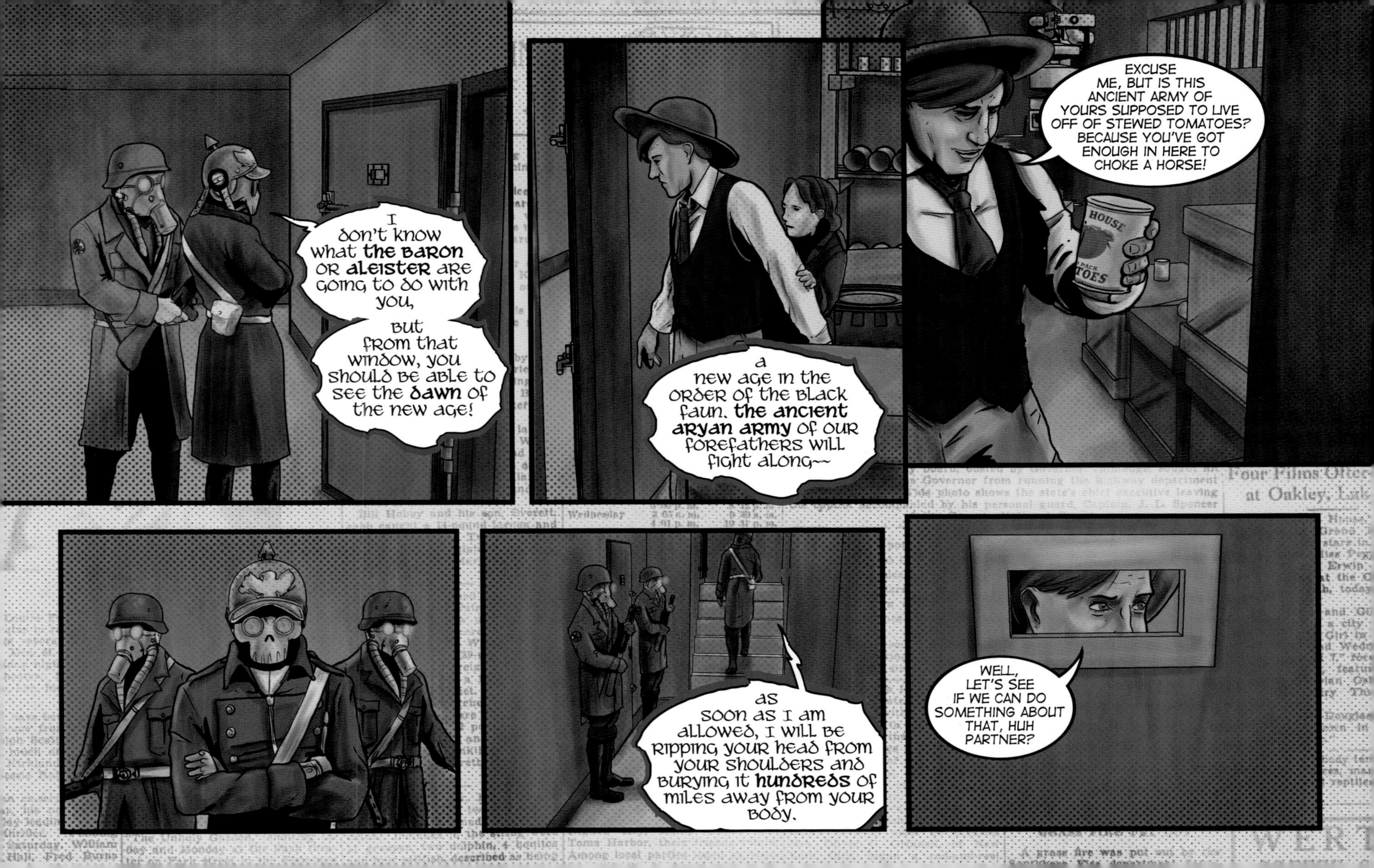
I don't know what the Baron or Aleister are going to do with you,
but from that window, you should be able to see the dawn of the new age!
a new age in the Order of the Black Faun. the ancient aryan army of our forefathers will fight along~~
EXCUSE ME, BUT IS THIS ANCIENT ARMY OF YOURS SUPPOSED TO LIVE OFF OF STEWED TOMATOES? BECAUSE YOU'VE GOT ENOUGH IN HERE TO CHOKE A HORSE!
HOUSE
TOES
as soon as I am allowed, I will be ripping your head from your shoulders and burying it hundreds of miles away from your body.
WELL, LET'S SEE IF WE CAN DO SOMETHING ABOUT THAT, HUH PARTNER?

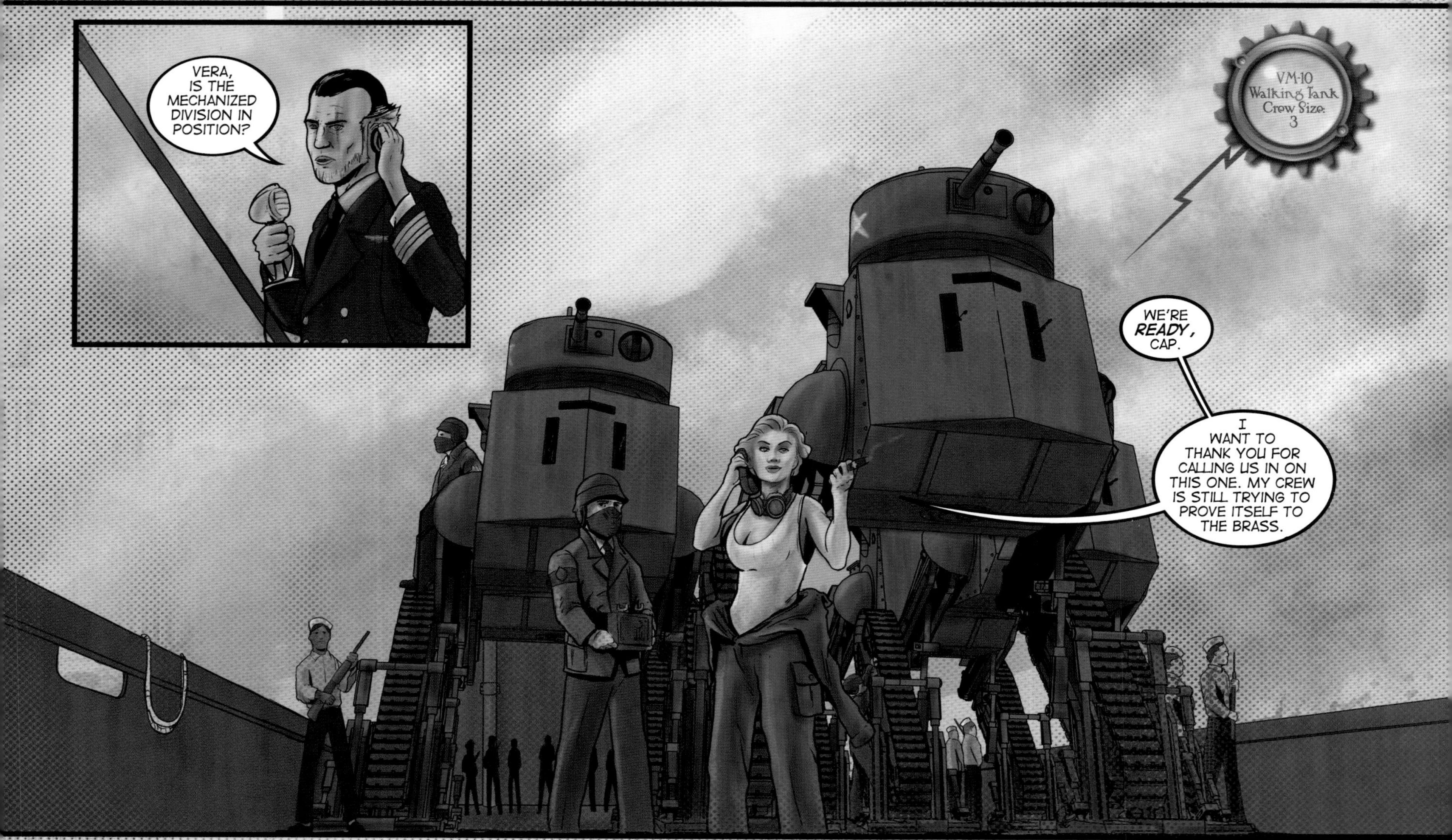
VERA, IS THE MECHANIZED DIVISION IN POSITION?
VM-10 Walking Tank Crew Size: 3
WE'RE **READY**, CAP.
I WANT TO THANK YOU FOR CALLING US IN ON THIS ONE. MY CREW IS STILL TRYING TO PROVE ITSELF TO THE BRASS.

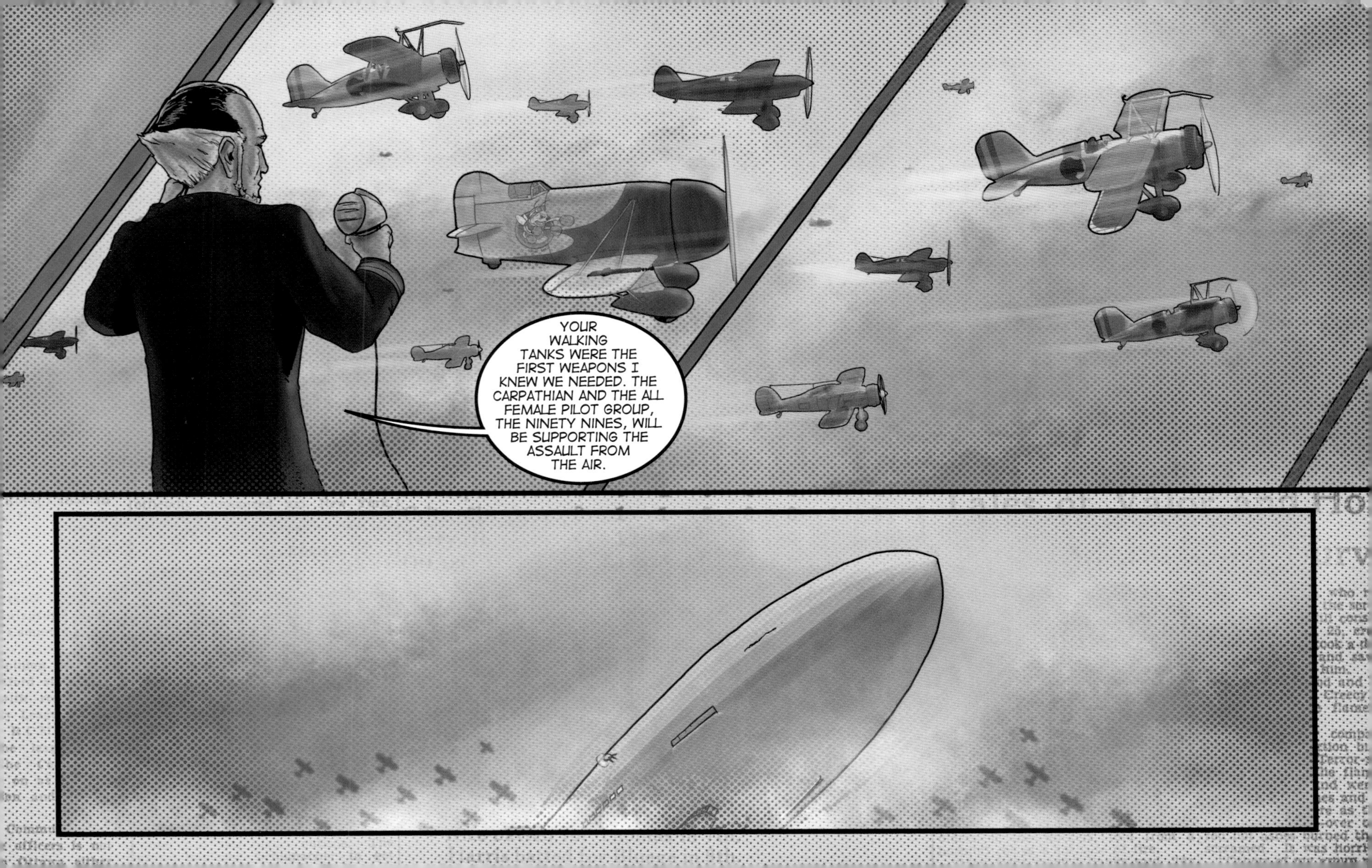
YOUR WALKING TANKS WERE THE FIRST WEAPONS I KNEW WE NEEDED. THE CARPATHIAN AND THE ALL FEMALE PILOT GROUP, THE NINETY NINES, WILL BE SUPPORTING THE ASSAULT FROM THE AIR.

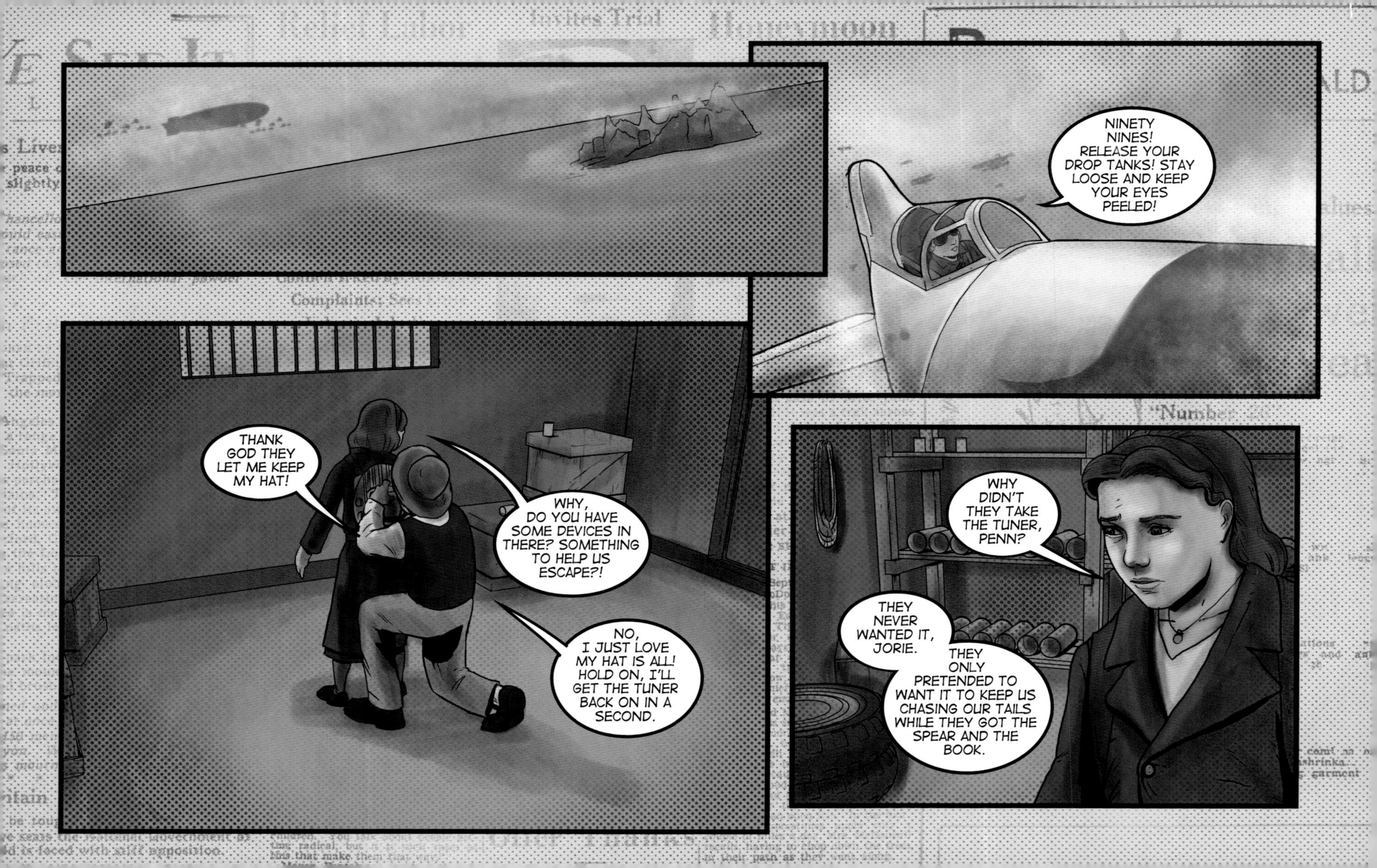
NINETY NINES! RELEASE YOUR DROP TANKS! STAY LOOSE AND KEEP YOUR EYES PEELED!
THANK GOD THEY LET ME KEEP MY HAT!
WHY, DO YOU HAVE SOME DEVICES IN THERE? SOMETHING TO HELP US ESCAPE?!
NO, I JUST LOVE MY HAT IS ALL! HOLD ON, I'LL GET THE TUNER BACK ON IN A SECOND.
WHY DIDN'T THEY TAKE THE TUNER, PENN?
THEY NEVER WANTED IT, JORIE.
THEY ONLY PRETENDED TO WANT IT TO KEEP US CHASING OUR TAILS WHILE THEY GOT THE SPEAR AND THE BOOK.

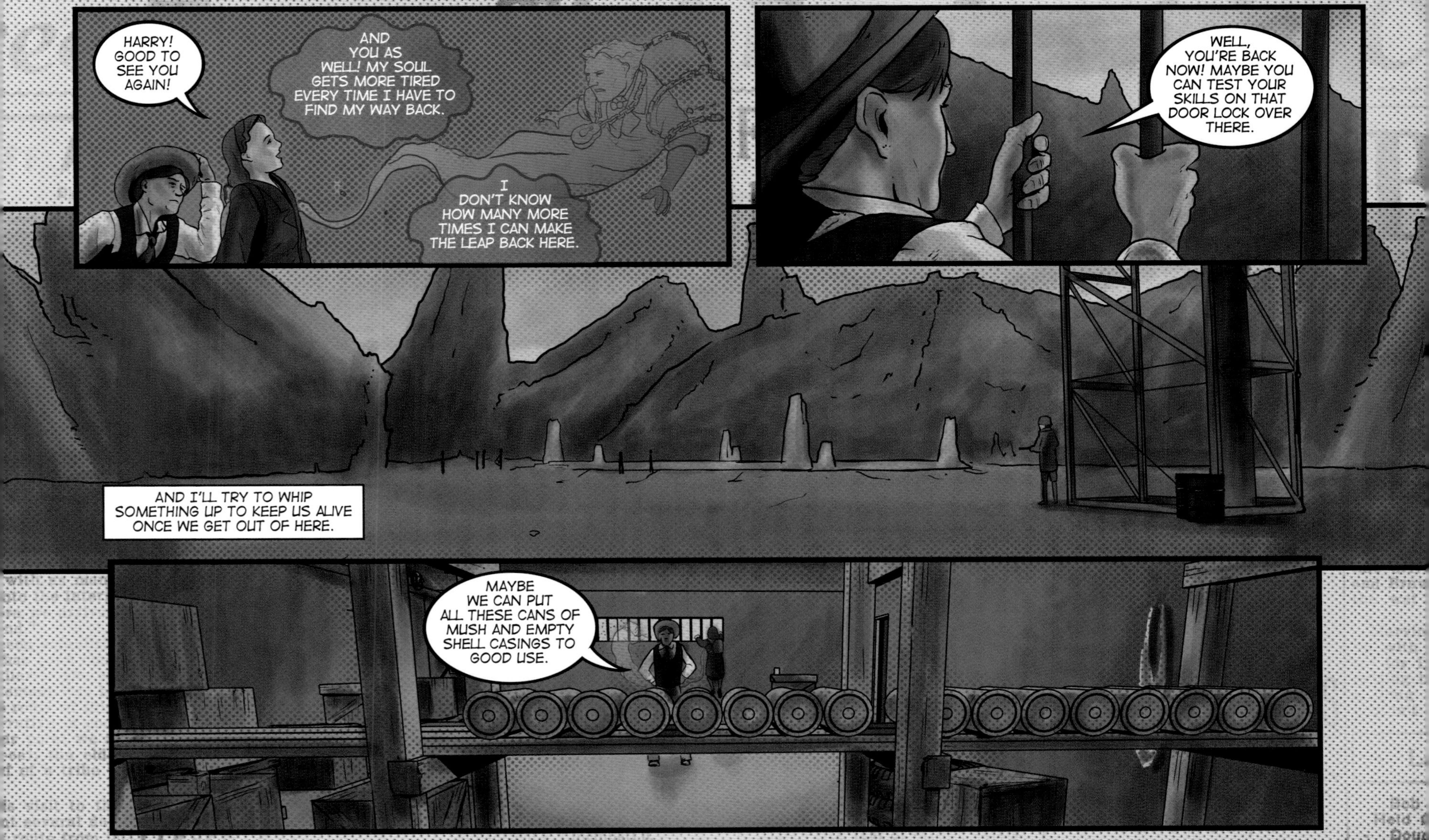
HARRY! GOOD TO SEE YOU AGAIN!
AND YOU AS WELL! MY SOUL GETS MORE TIRED EVERY TIME I HAVE TO FIND MY WAY BACK.
I DON'T KNOW HOW MANY MORE TIMES I CAN MAKE THE LEAP BACK HERE.
WELL, YOU'RE BACK NOW! MAYBE YOU CAN TEST YOUR SKILLS ON THAT DOOR LOCK OVER THERE.
AND I'LL TRY TO WHIP SOMETHING UP TO KEEP US ALIVE ONCE WE GET OUT OF HERE.
MAYBE WE CAN PUT ALL THESE CANS OF MUSH AND EMPTY SHELL CASINGS TO GOOD USE.

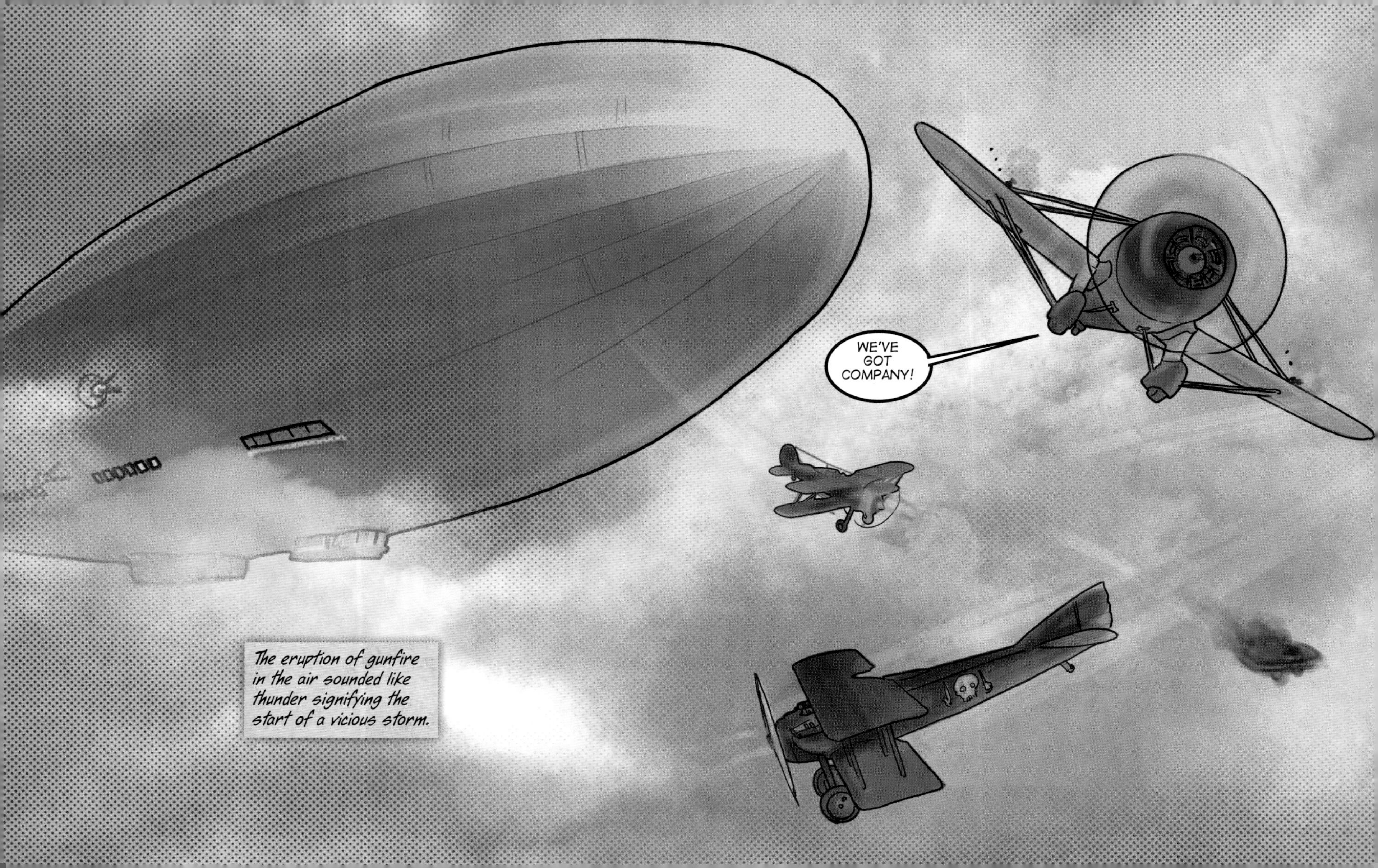
WE'VE GOT COMPANY!
The eruption of gunfire in the air sounded like thunder signifying the start of a vicious storm.

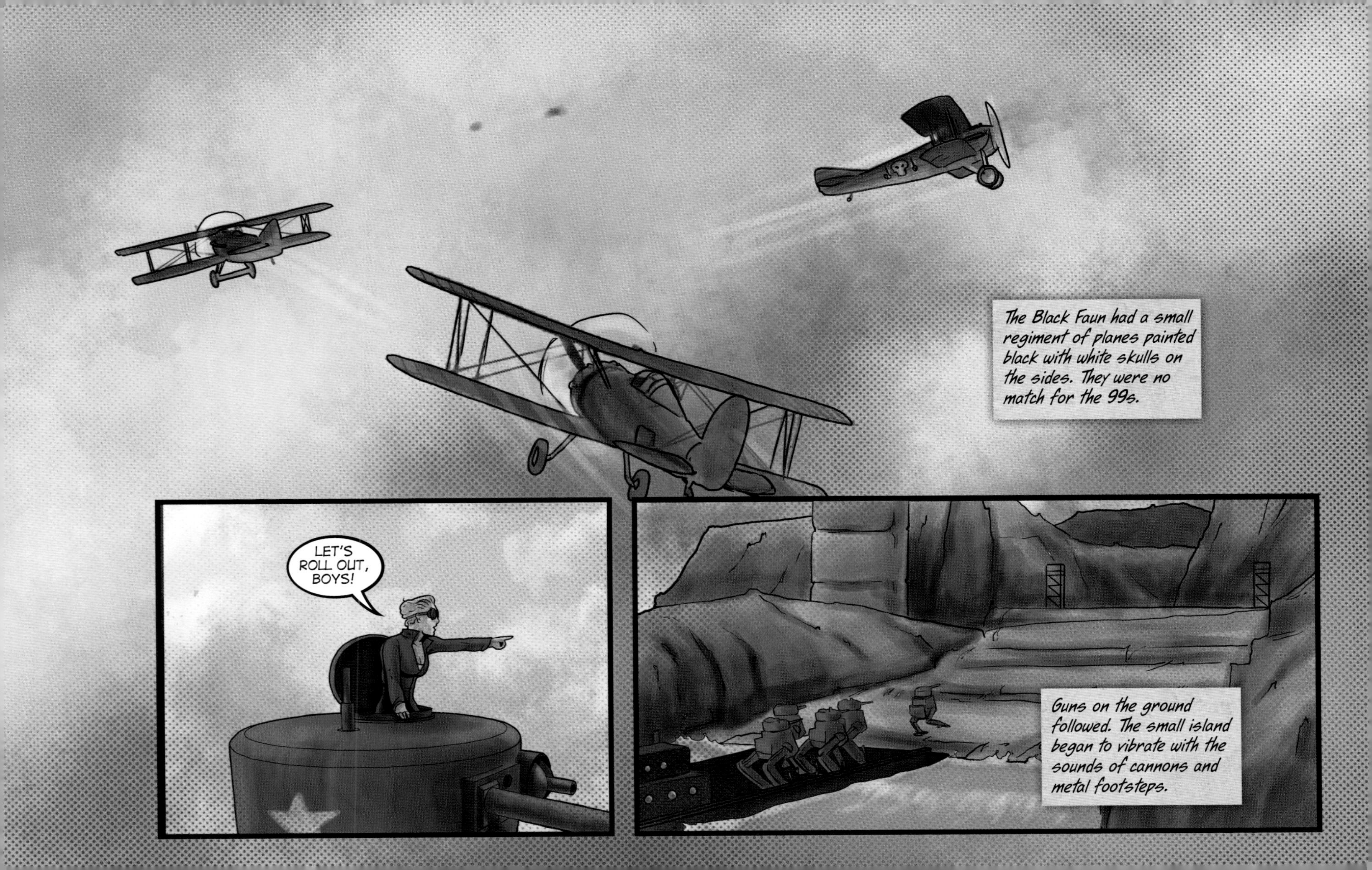
The Black Faun had a small regiment of planes painted black with white skulls on the sides. They were no match for the 99s.
LET'S ROLL OUT, BOYS!
Guns on the ground followed. The small island began to vibrate with the sounds of cannons and metal footsteps.

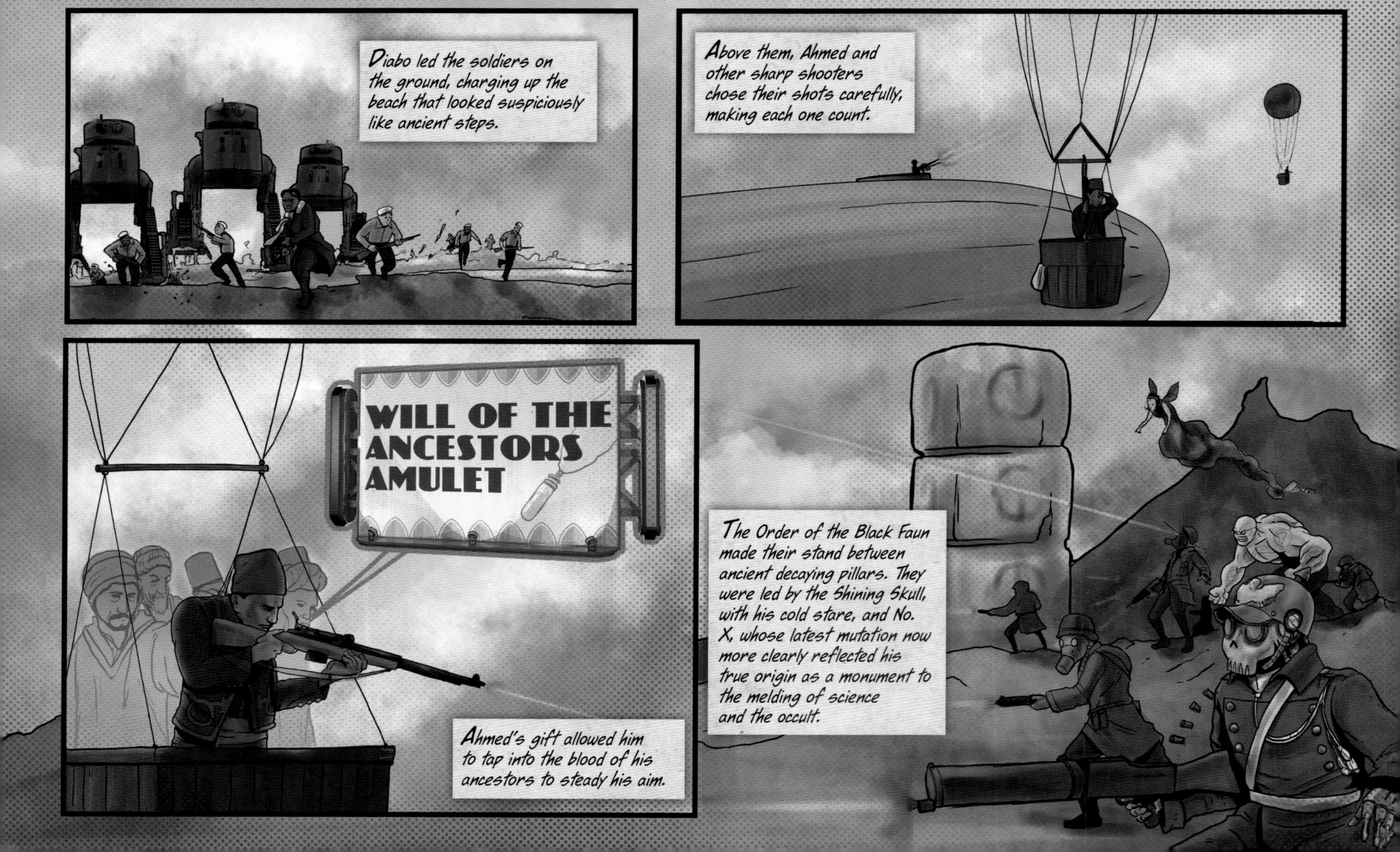
Diabo led the soldiers on the ground, charging up the beach that looked suspiciously like ancient steps.
Above them, Ahmed and other sharp shooters chose their shots carefully, making each one count.
WILL OF THE ANCESTORS AMULET
Ahmed's gift allowed him to tap into the blood of his ancestors to steady his aim.
The Order of the Black Faun made their stand between ancient decaying pillars. They were led by the Shining Skull, with his cold stare, and No. X, whose latest mutation now more clearly reflected his true origin as a monument to the melding of science and the occult.

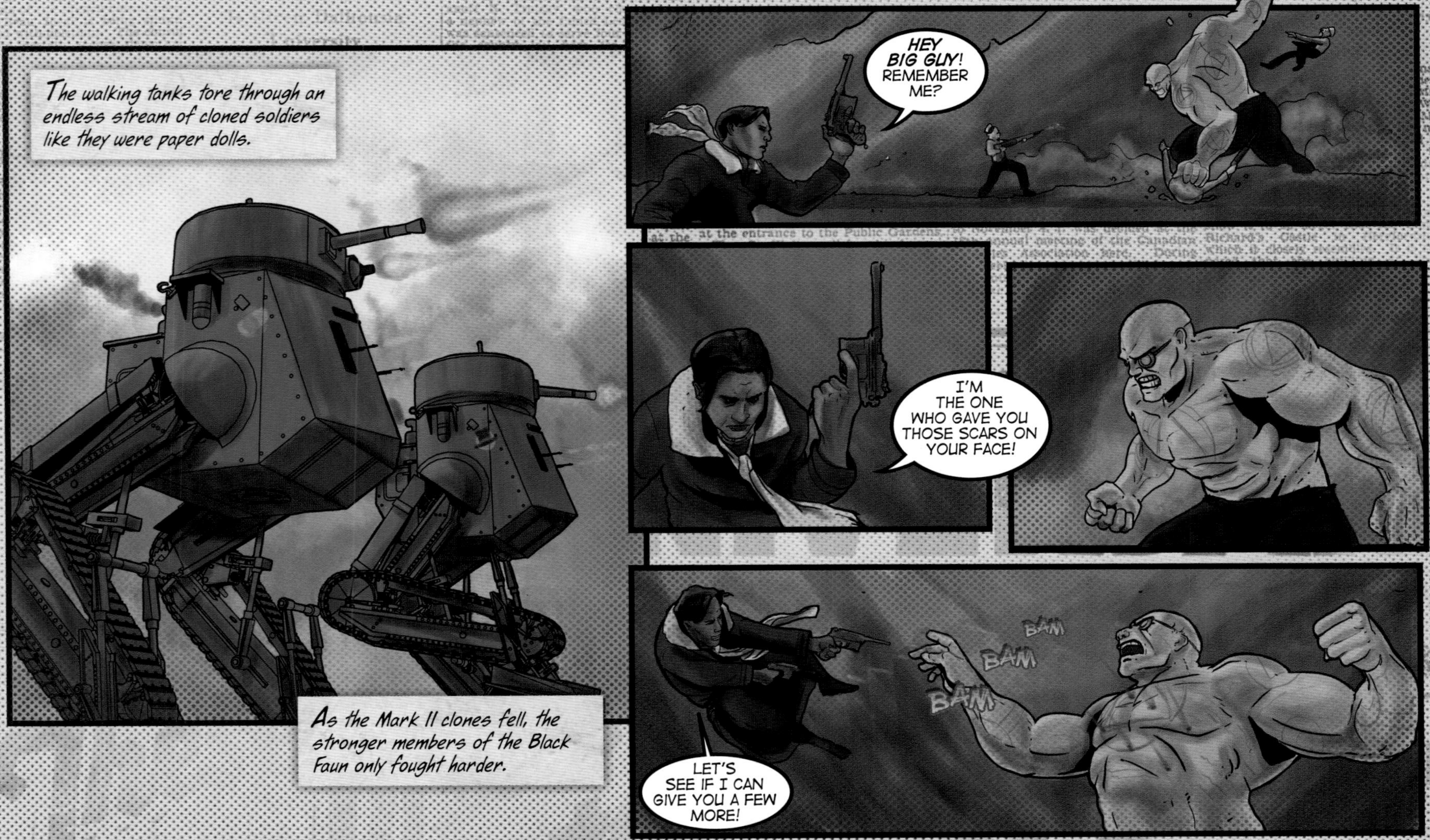
The walking tanks tore through an endless stream of cloned soldiers like they were paper dolls.
As the Mark II clones fell, the stronger members of the Black Faun only fought harder.
HEY BIG GUY! REMEMBER ME?
I'M THE ONE WHO GAVE YOU THOSE SCARS ON YOUR FACE!
BAM
BAM
BAM
LET'S SEE IF I CAN GIVE YOU A FEW MORE!

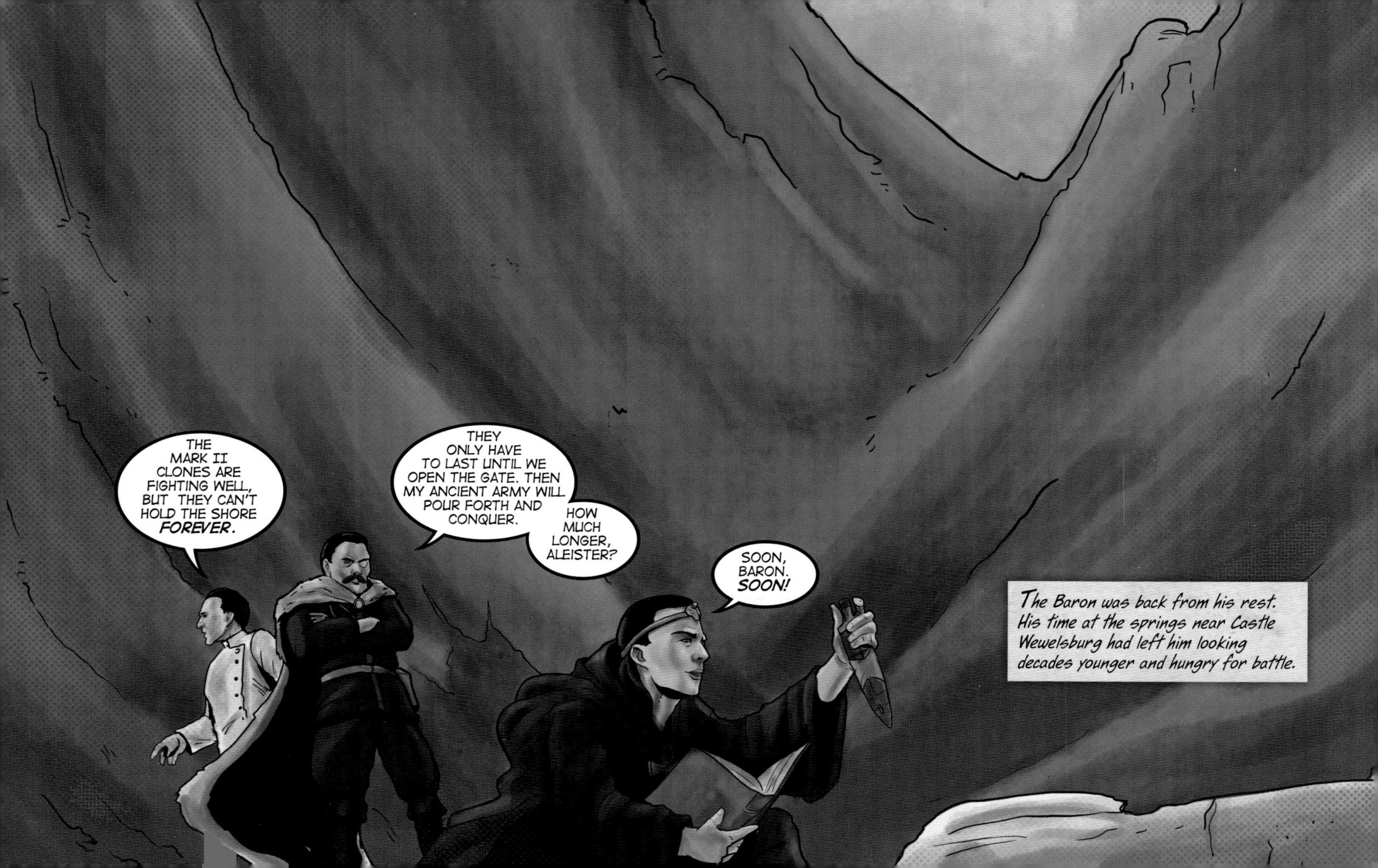
THE MARK II CLONES ARE FIGHTING WELL, BUT THEY CAN'T HOLD THE SHORE FOREVER.
THEY ONLY HAVE TO LAST UNTIL WE OPEN THE GATE. THEN MY ANCIENT ARMY WILL POUR FORTH AND CONQUER.
HOW MUCH LONGER, ALEISTER?
SOON, BARON. SOON!
The Baron was back from his rest. His time at the springs near Castle Wewelsburg had left him looking decades younger and hungry for battle.

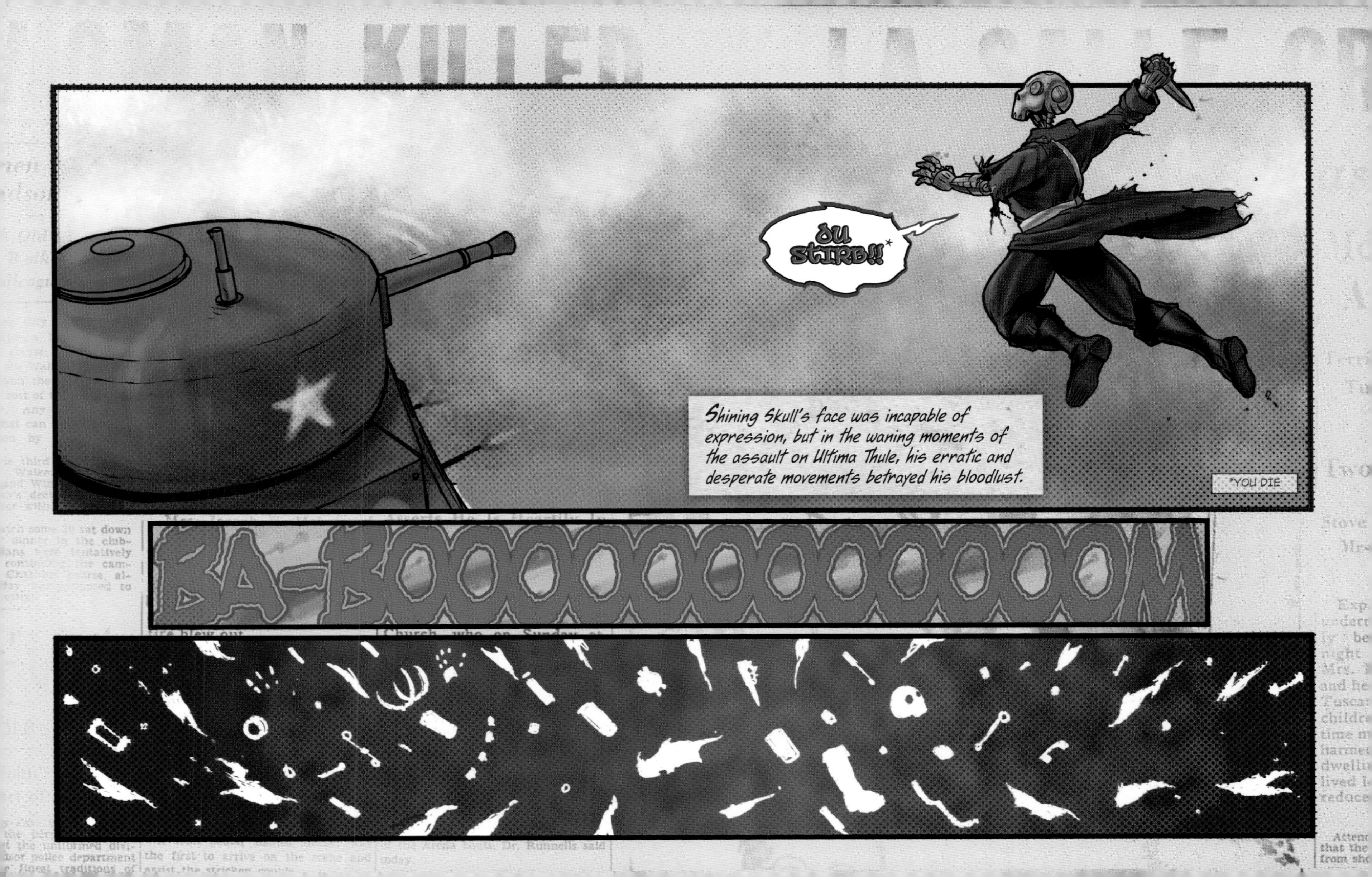
DU STIRB!!*
Shining Skull's face was incapable of expression, but in the waning moments of the assault on Ultima Thule, his erratic and desperate movements betrayed his bloodlust.
*YOU DIE
BA-BOOOOOOOOOOOOM

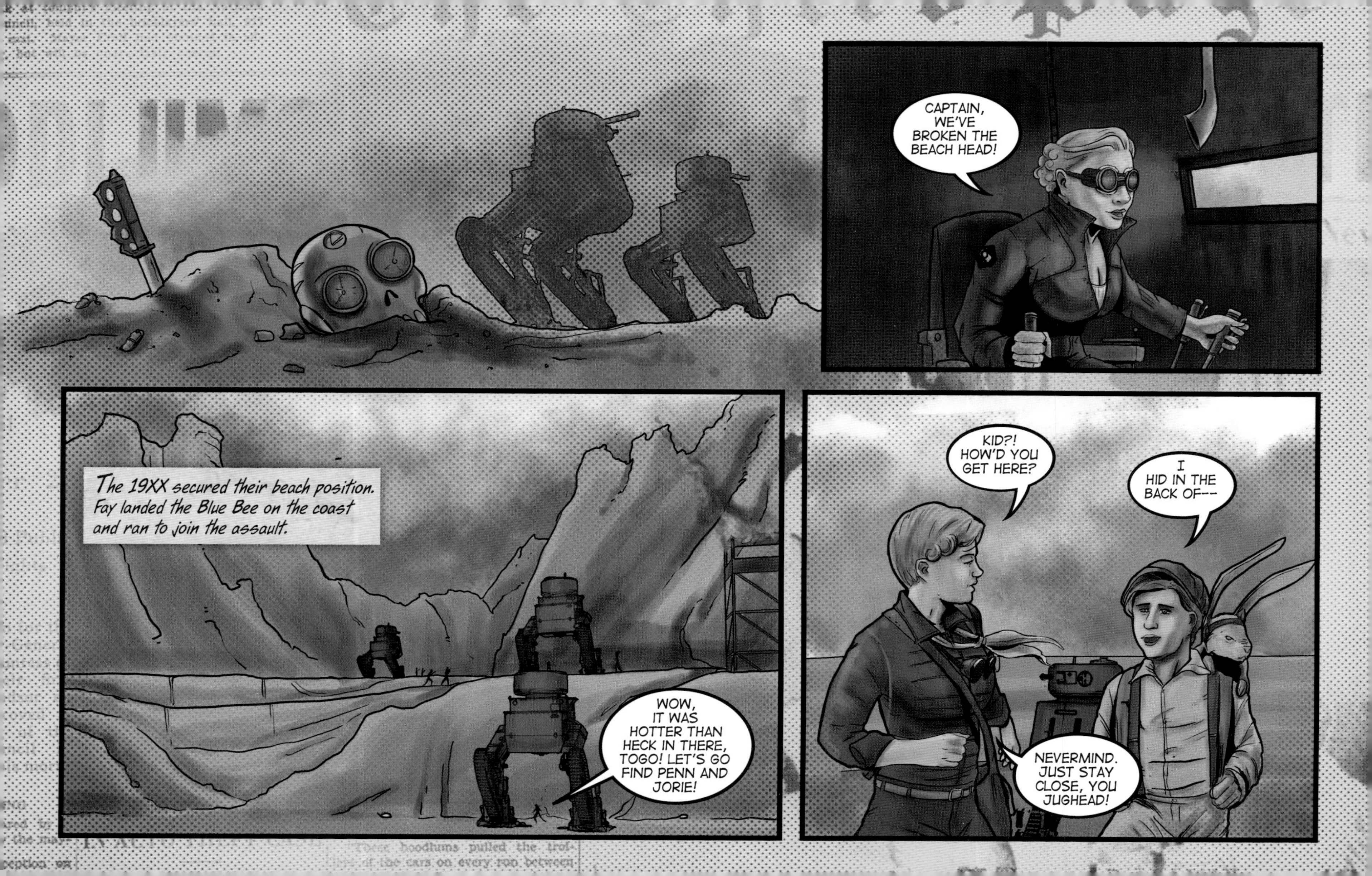
CAPTAIN, WE'VE BROKEN THE BEACH HEAD!
The 19XX secured their beach position. Fay landed the Blue Bee on the coast and ran to join the assault.
WOW, IT WAS HOTTER THAN HECK IN THERE, TOGO! LET'S GO FIND PENN AND JORIE!
KID?! HOW'D YOU GET HERE?
I HID IN THE BACK OF--
NEVERMIND. JUST STAY CLOSE, YOU JUGHEAD!

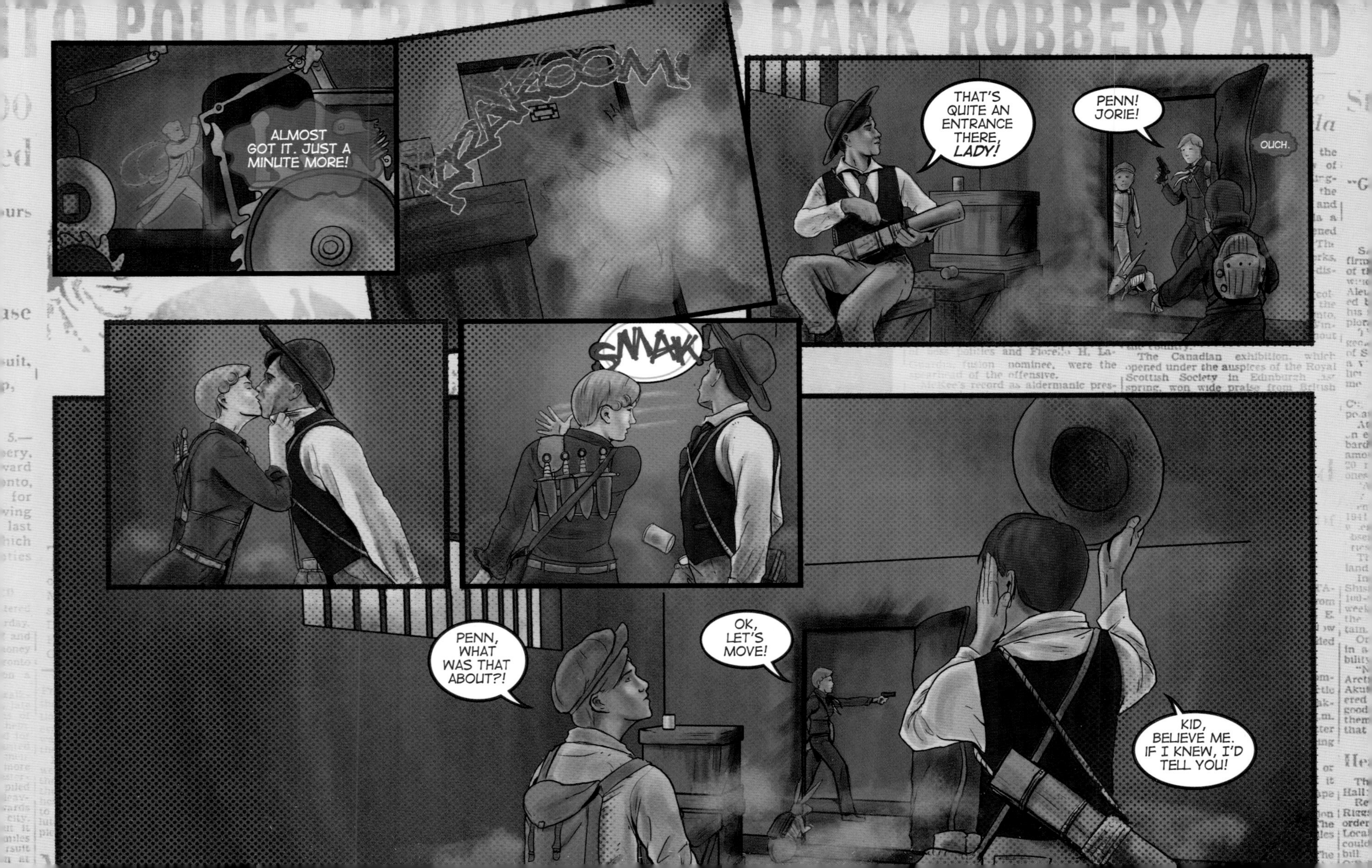
ALMOST GOT IT. JUST A MINUTE MORE!
KABLAKOOM!
THAT'S QUITE AN ENTRANCE THERE, *LADY!*
PENN! JORIE!
OUCH.
SMAK
PENN, WHAT WAS THAT ABOUT?!
OK, LET'S MOVE!
KID, BELIEVE ME. IF I KNEW, I'D TELL YOU!

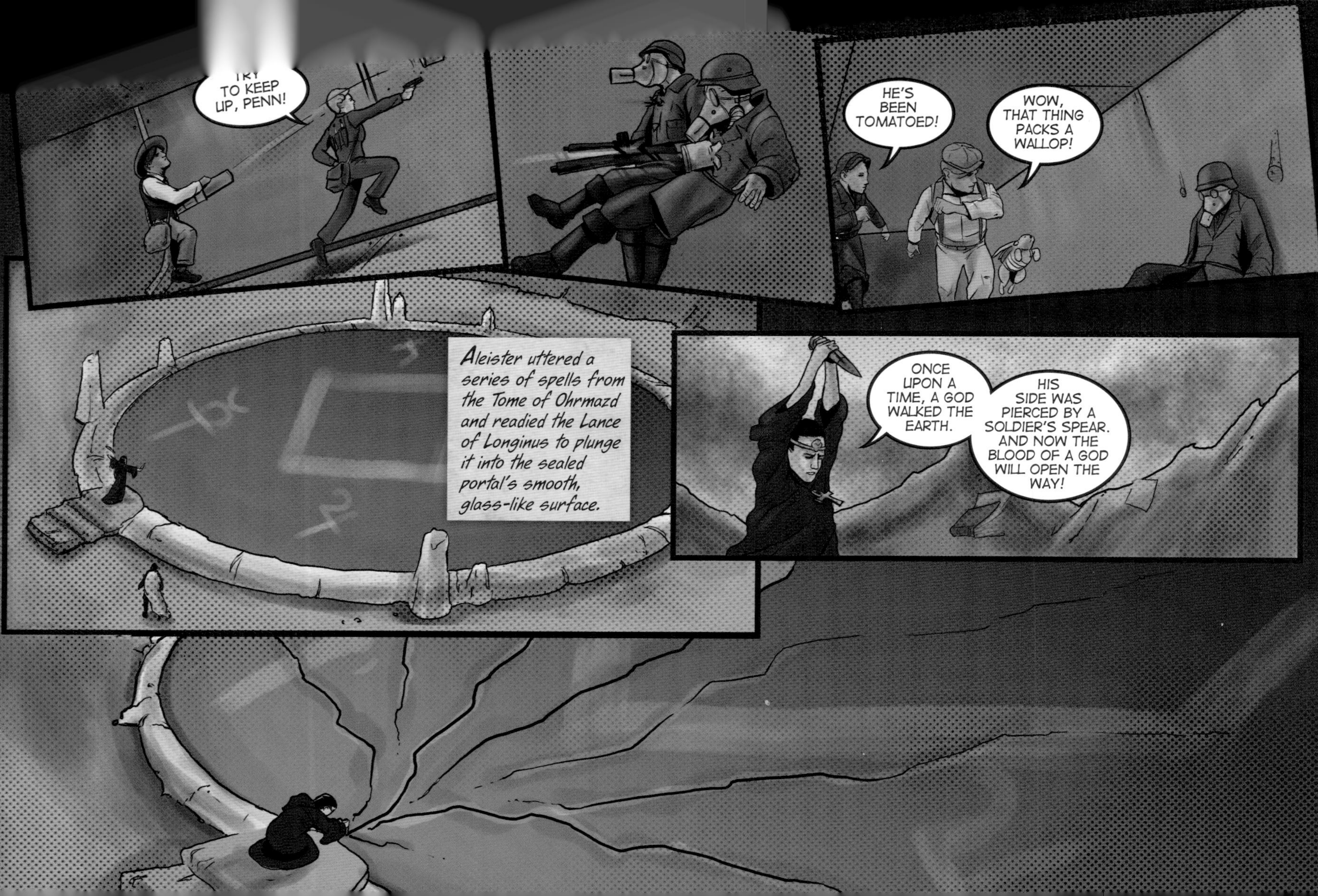

TRY TO KEEP UP, PENN!
HE'S BEEN TOMATOED!
WOW, THAT THING PACKS A WALLOP!
Aleister uttered a series of spells from the Tome of Ohrmazd and readied the Lance of Longinus to plunge it into the sealed portal's smooth, glass-like surface.
ONCE UPON A TIME, A GOD WALKED THE EARTH.
HIS SIDE WAS PIERCED BY A SOLDIER'S SPEAR. AND NOW THE BLOOD OF A GOD WILL OPEN THE WAY!

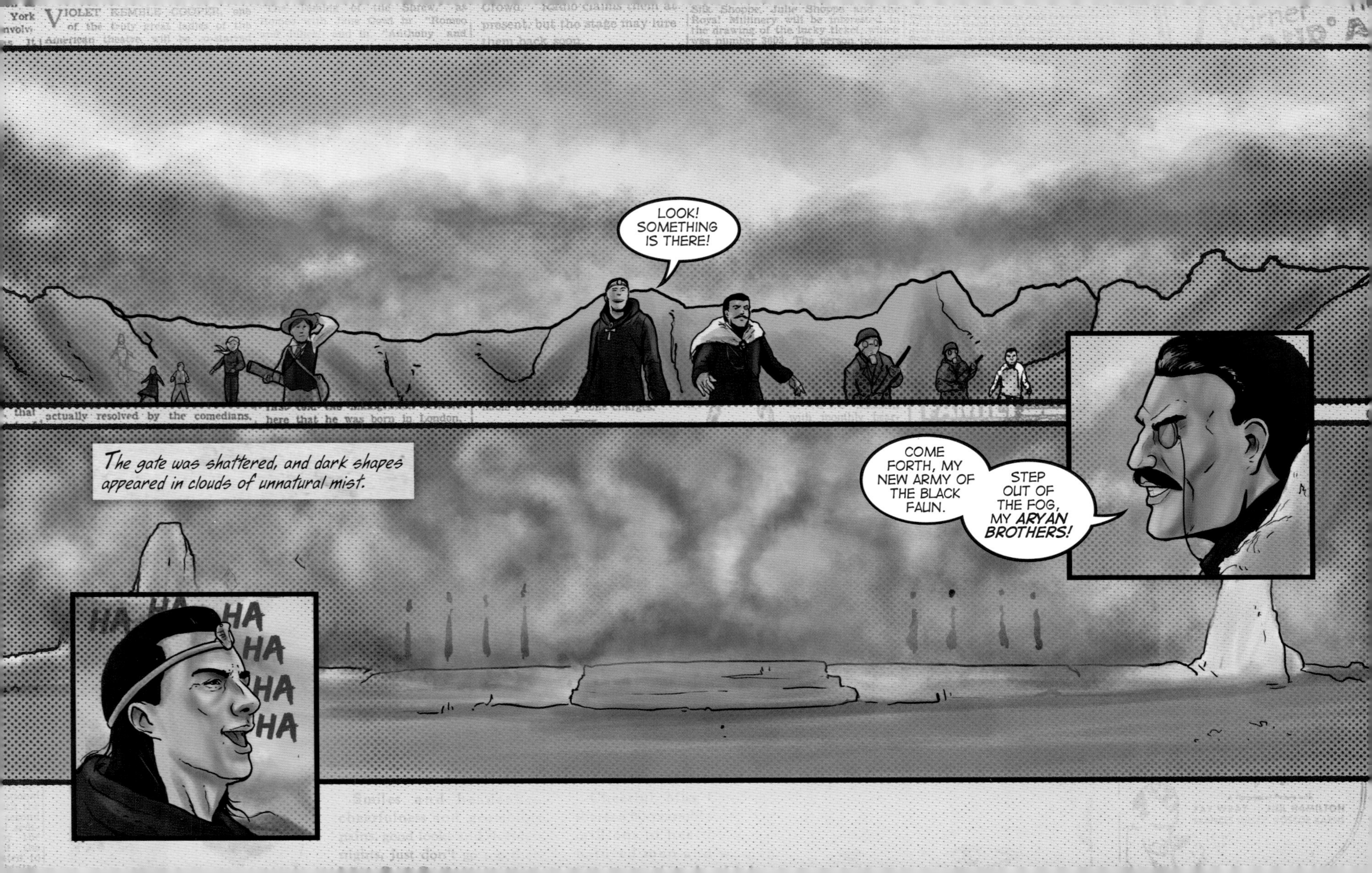
LOOK! SOMETHING IS THERE!
The gate was shattered, and dark shapes appeared in clouds of unnatural mist.
COME FORTH, MY NEW ARMY OF THE BLACK FAUN.
STEP OUT OF THE FOG, MY ARYAN BROTHERS!
HA HA HA HA HA HA

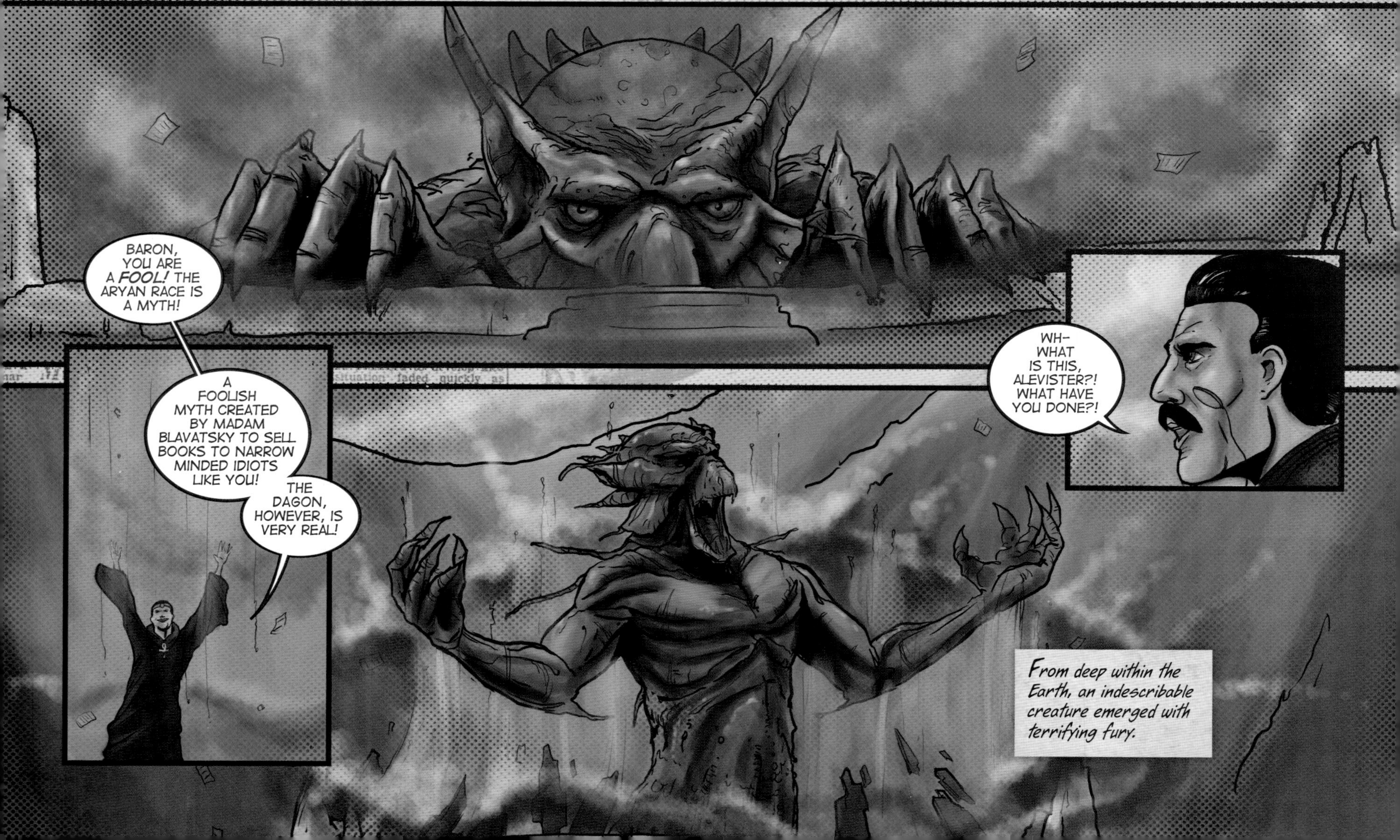
BARON, YOU ARE A ***FOOL!*** THE ARYAN RACE IS A MYTH!
A FOOLISH MYTH CREATED BY MADAM BLAVATSKY TO SELL BOOKS TO NARROW MINDED IDIOTS LIKE YOU!
THE DAGON, HOWEVER, IS VERY REAL!
WH- WHAT IS THIS, ALEVISTER?! WHAT HAVE YOU DONE?!
From deep within the Earth, an indescribable creature emerged with terrifying fury.

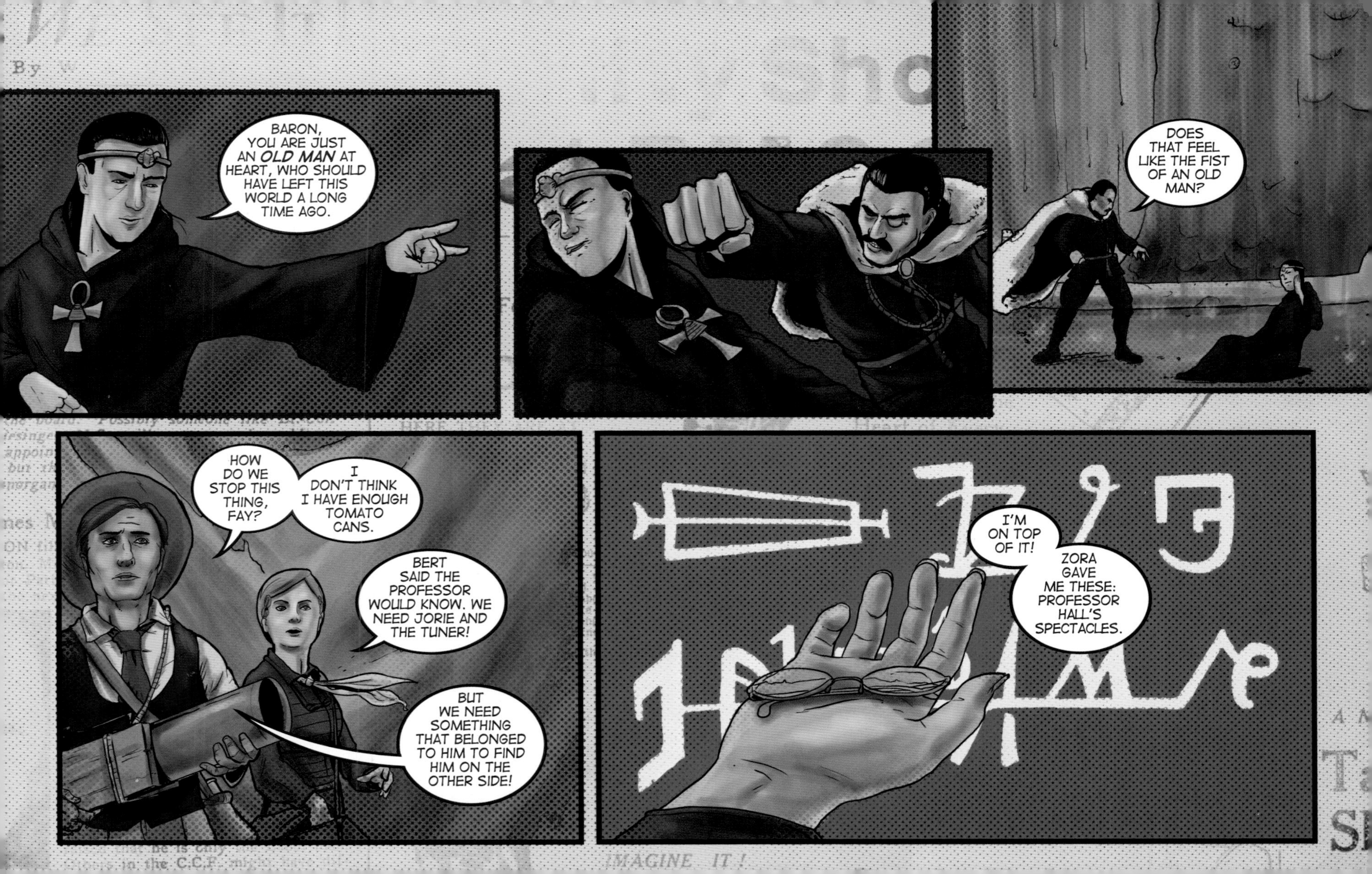
BARON, YOU ARE JUST AN OLD MAN AT HEART, WHO SHOULD HAVE LEFT THIS WORLD A LONG TIME AGO.
DOES THAT FEEL LIKE THE FIST OF AN OLD MAN?
HOW DO WE STOP THIS THING, FAY?
I DON'T THINK I HAVE ENOUGH TOMATO CANS.
BERT SAID THE PROFESSOR WOULD KNOW. WE NEED JORIE AND THE TUNER!
BUT WE NEED SOMETHING THAT BELONGED TO HIM TO FIND HIM ON THE OTHER SIDE!
I'M ON TOP OF IT!
ZORA GAVE ME THESE: PROFESSOR HALL'S SPECTACLES.

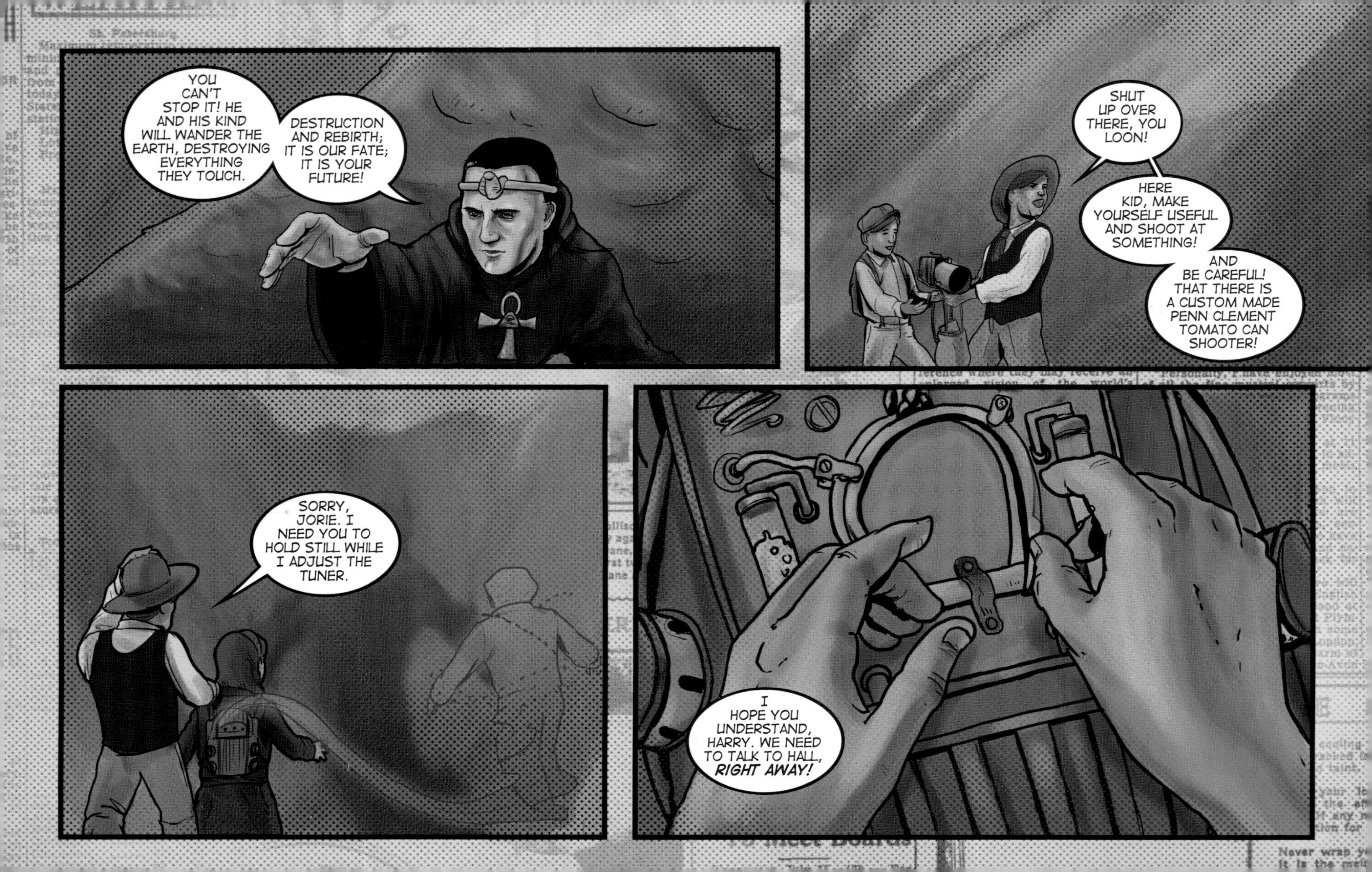
YOU CAN'T STOP IT! HE AND HIS KIND WILL WANDER THE EARTH, DESTROYING EVERYTHING THEY TOUCH.
DESTRUCTION AND REBIRTH; IT IS OUR FATE; IT IS YOUR FUTURE!
SHUT UP OVER THERE, YOU LOON!
HERE KID, MAKE YOURSELF USEFUL AND SHOOT AT SOMETHING!
AND BE CAREFUL! THAT THERE IS A CUSTOM MADE PENN CLEMENT TOMATO CAN SHOOTER!
SORRY, JORIE. I NEED YOU TO HOLD STILL WHILE I ADJUST THE TUNER.
I HOPE YOU UNDERSTAND, HARRY. WE NEED TO TALK TO HALL, **RIGHT AWAY!**

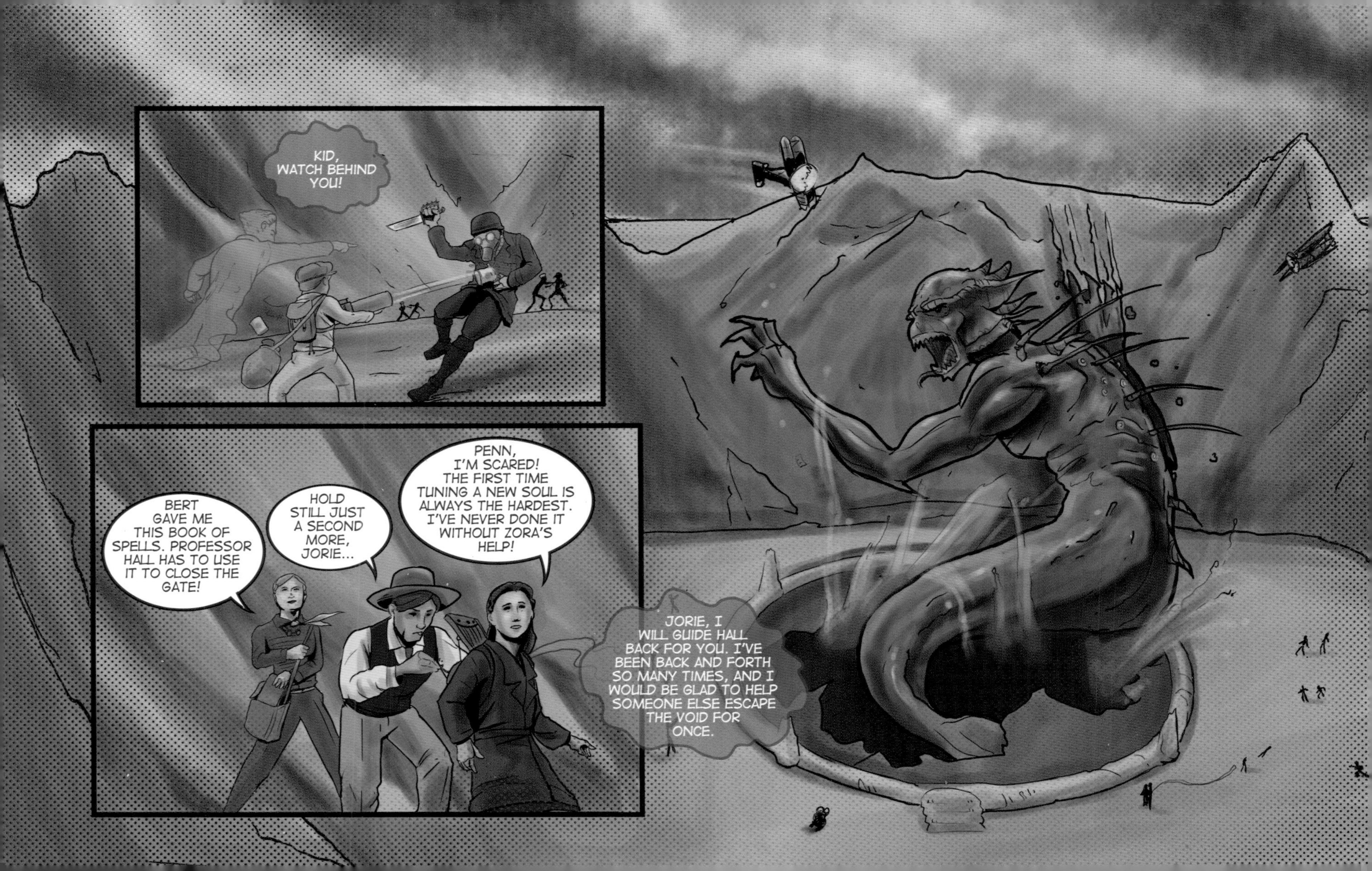
KID, WATCH BEHIND YOU!
BERT GAVE ME THIS BOOK OF SPELLS. PROFESSOR HALL HAS TO USE IT TO CLOSE THE GATE!
HOLD STILL JUST A SECOND MORE, JORIE...
PENN, I'M SCARED! THE FIRST TIME TUNING A NEW SOUL IS ALWAYS THE HARDEST. I'VE NEVER DONE IT WITHOUT ZORA'S HELP!
JORIE, I WILL GUIDE HALL BACK FOR YOU. I'VE BEEN BACK AND FORTH SO MANY TIMES, AND I WOULD BE GLAD TO HELP SOMEONE ELSE ESCAPE THE VOID FOR ONCE.

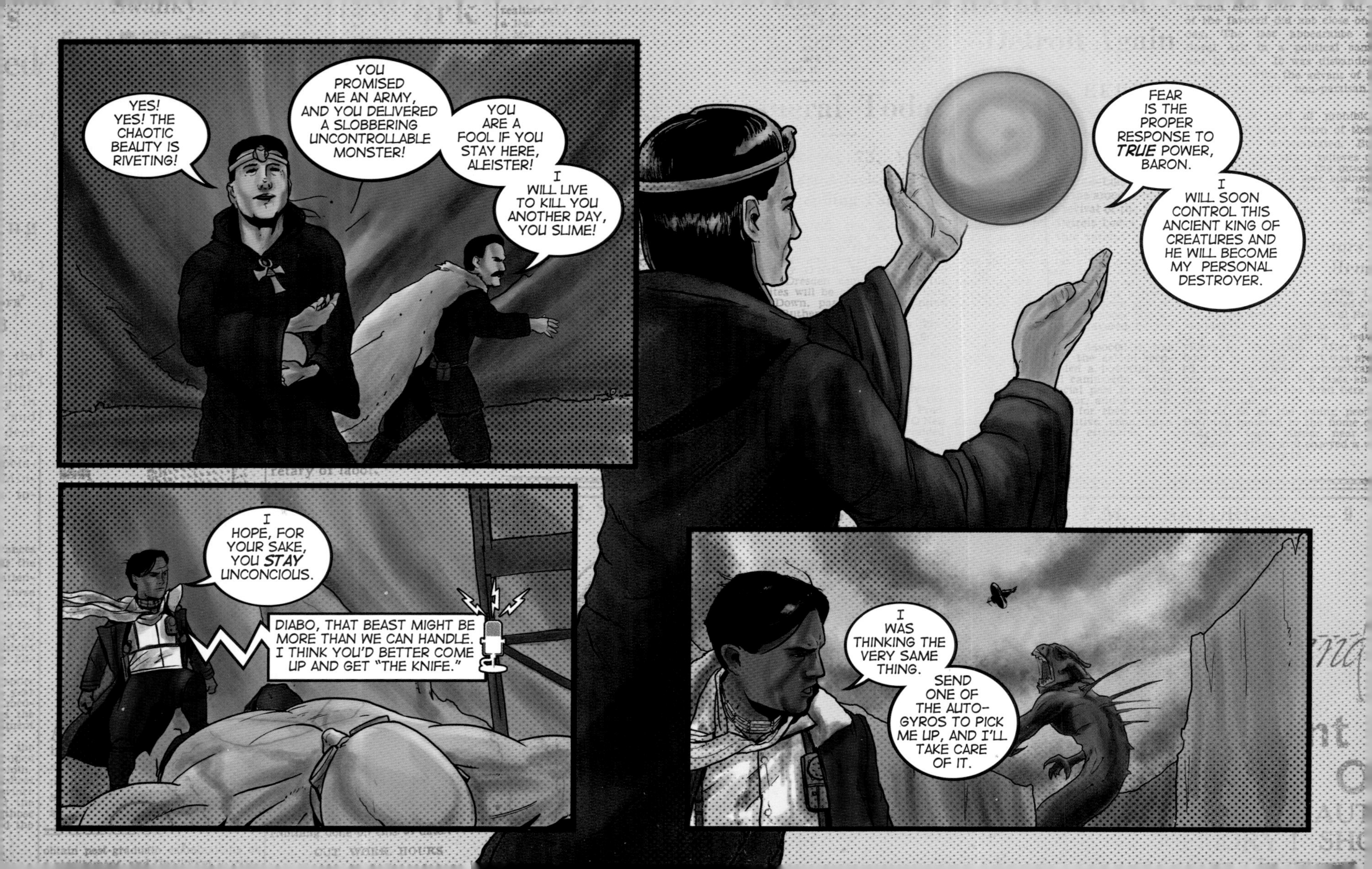
YES! YES! THE CHAOTIC BEAUTY IS RIVETING!
YOU PROMISED ME AN ARMY, AND YOU DELIVERED A SLOBBERING UNCONTROLLABLE MONSTER!
YOU ARE A FOOL IF YOU STAY HERE, ALEISTER!
I WILL LIVE TO KILL YOU ANOTHER DAY, YOU SLIME!
FEAR IS THE PROPER RESPONSE TO TRUE POWER, BARON.
I WILL SOON CONTROL THIS ANCIENT KING OF CREATURES AND HE WILL BECOME MY PERSONAL DESTROYER.
I HOPE, FOR YOUR SAKE, YOU STAY UNCONCIOUS.
DIABO, THAT BEAST MIGHT BE MORE THAN WE CAN HANDLE. I THINK YOU'D BETTER COME UP AND GET "THE KNIFE."
I WAS THINKING THE VERY SAME THING.
SEND ONE OF THE AUTO-GYROS TO PICK ME UP, AND I'LL TAKE CARE OF IT.

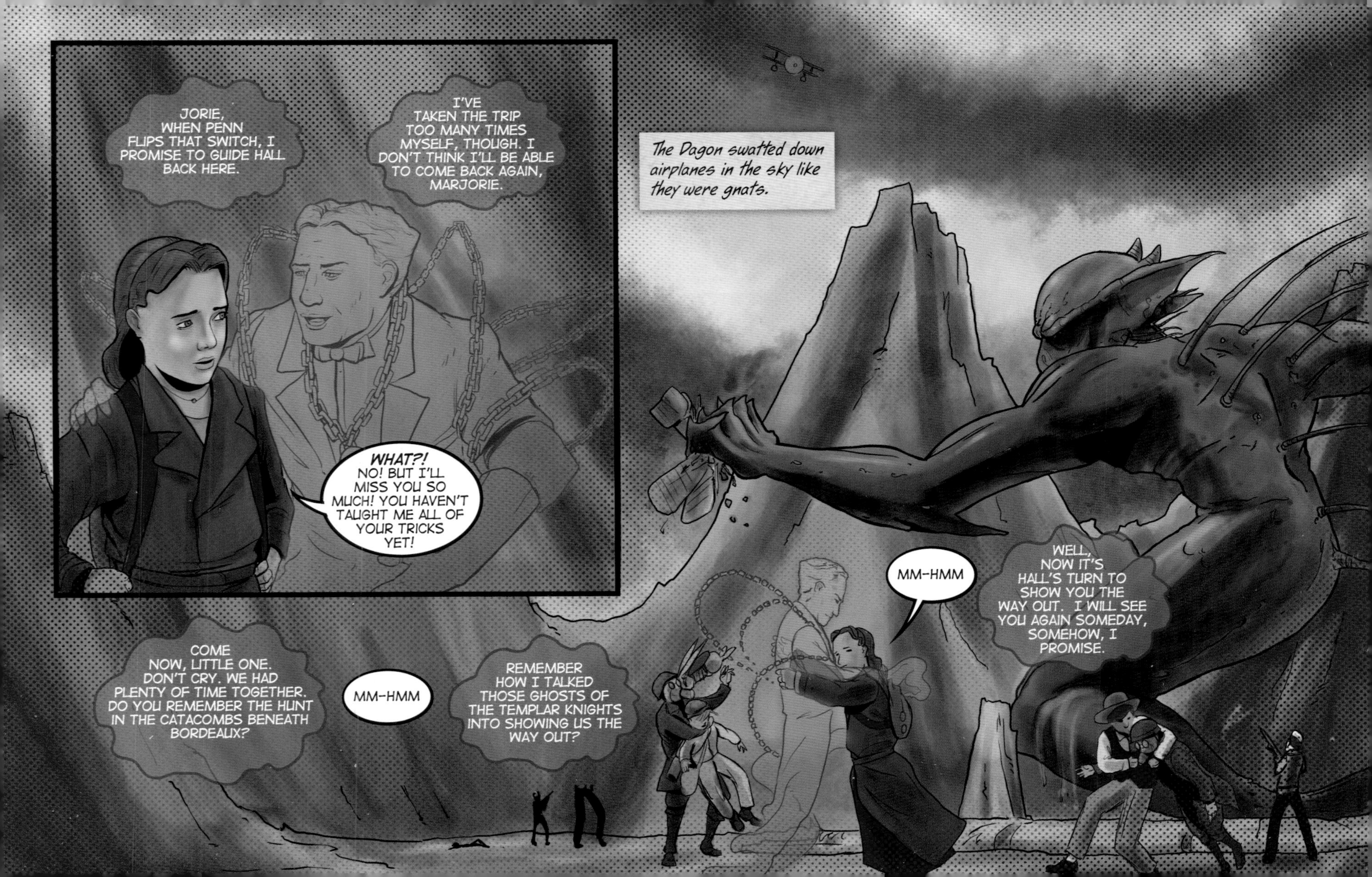

JORIE, WHEN PENN FLIPS THAT SWITCH, I PROMISE TO GUIDE HALL BACK HERE.
I'VE TAKEN THE TRIP TOO MANY TIMES MYSELF, THOUGH. I DON'T THINK I'LL BE ABLE TO COME BACK AGAIN, MARJORIE.
WHAT?! NO! BUT I'LL MISS YOU SO MUCH! YOU HAVEN'T TAUGHT ME ALL OF YOUR TRICKS YET!
The Dagon swatted down airplanes in the sky like they were gnats.
COME NOW, LITTLE ONE. DON'T CRY. WE HAD PLENTY OF TIME TOGETHER. DO YOU REMEMBER THE HUNT IN THE CATACOMBS BENEATH BORDEAUX?
MM-HMM
REMEMBER HOW I TALKED THOSE GHOSTS OF THE TEMPLAR KNIGHTS INTO SHOWING US THE WAY OUT?
MM-HMM
WELL, NOW IT'S HALL'S TURN TO SHOW YOU THE WAY OUT. I WILL SEE YOU AGAIN SOMEDAY, SOMEHOW, I PROMISE.

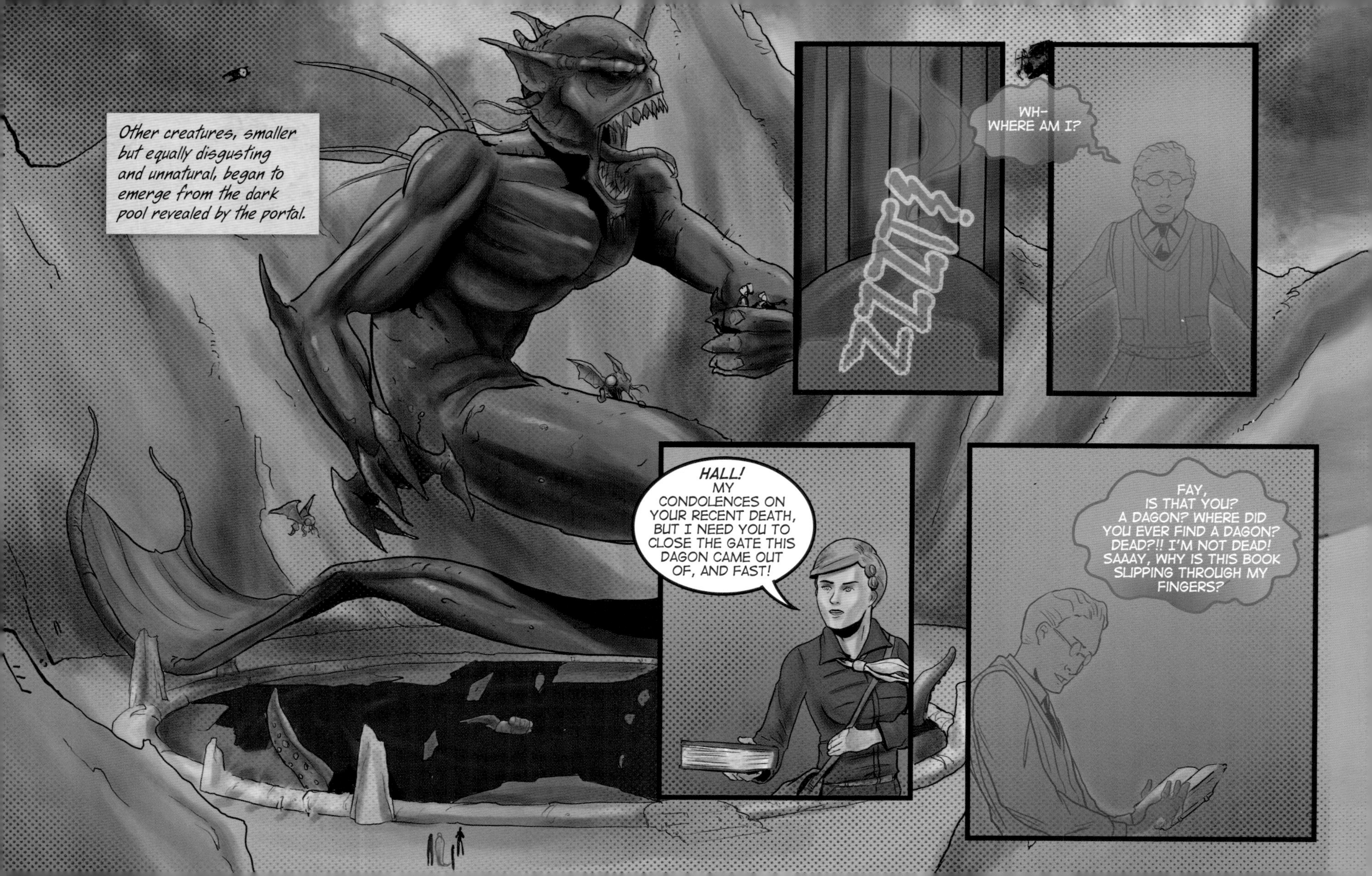
Other creatures, smaller but equally disgusting and unnatural, began to emerge from the dark pool revealed by the portal.
ZZZT!
WH- WHERE AM I?
HALL! MY CONDOLENCES ON YOUR RECENT DEATH, BUT I NEED YOU TO CLOSE THE GATE THIS DAGON CAME OUT OF, AND FAST!
FAY, IS THAT YOU? A DAGON? WHERE DID YOU EVER FIND A DAGON? DEAD?!! I'M NOT DEAD! SAAAY, WHY IS THIS BOOK SLIPPING THROUGH MY FINGERS?

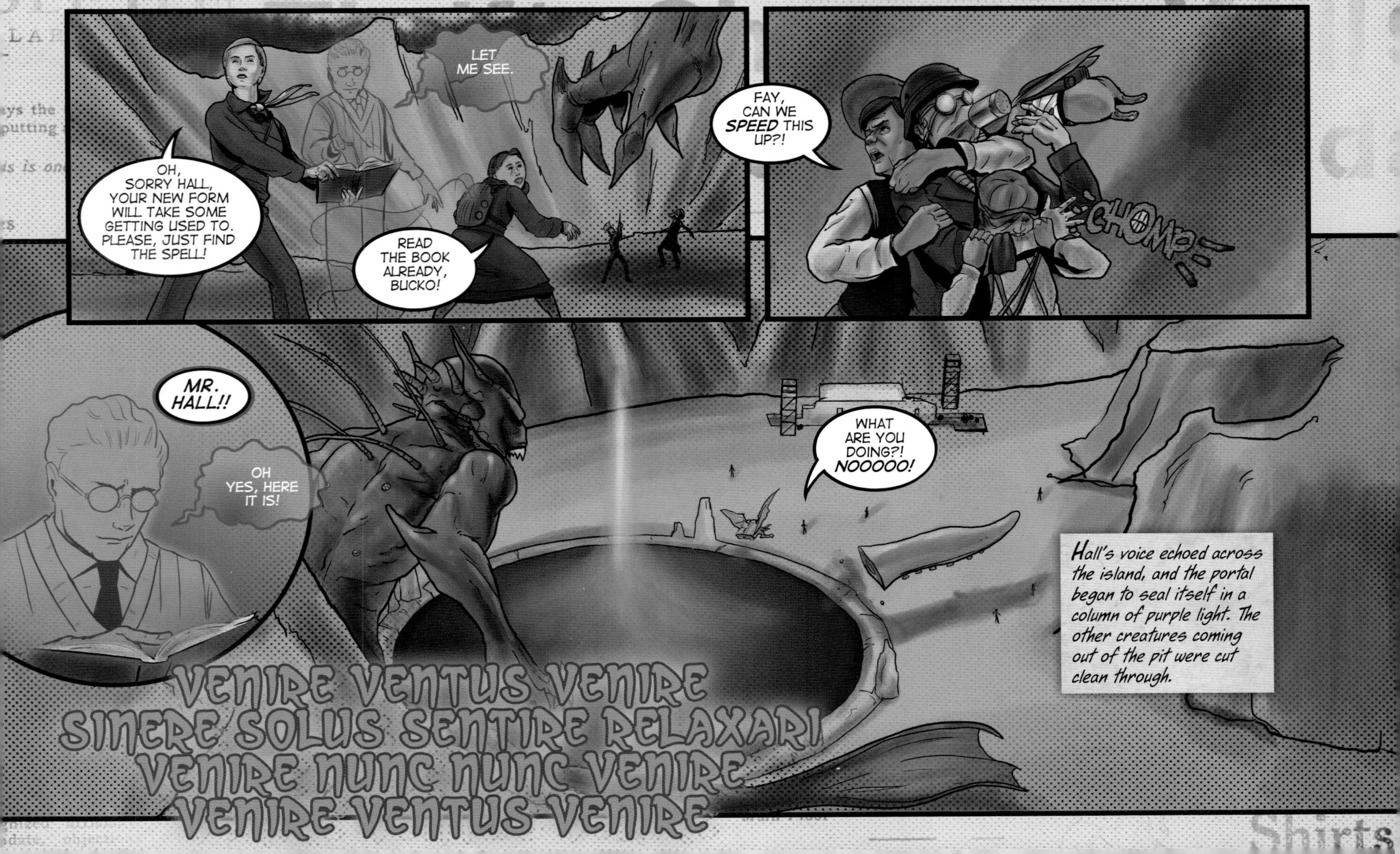
LET ME SEE.
OH, SORRY HALL, YOUR NEW FORM WILL TAKE SOME GETTING USED TO. PLEASE, JUST FIND THE SPELL!
READ THE BOOK ALREADY, BUCKO!
FAY, CAN WE SPEED THIS UP?!
CHOMP!
MR. HALL!!
OH YES, HERE IT IS!
WHAT ARE YOU DOING?! NOOOOO!
Hall's voice echoed across the island, and the portal began to seal itself in a column of purple light. The other creatures coming out of the pit were cut clean through.
VENIRE VENTUS VENIRE
SINERE SOLUS SENTIRE RELAXARI
VENIRE NUNC NUNC VENIRE
VENIRE VENTUS VENIRE

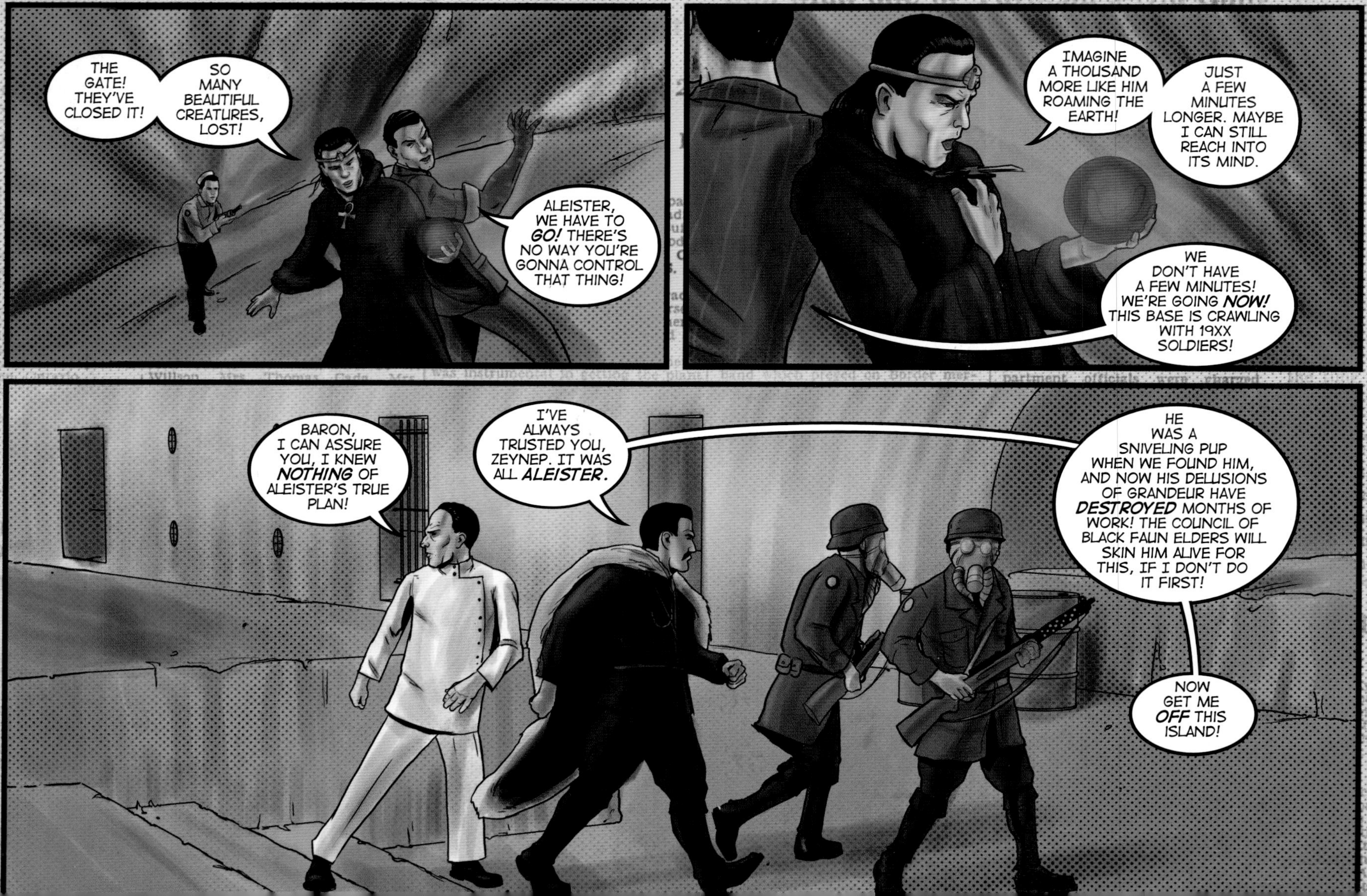

THE GATE! THEY'VE CLOSED IT!
SO MANY BEAUTIFUL CREATURES, LOST!
ALEISTER, WE HAVE TO *GO!* THERE'S NO WAY YOU'RE GONNA CONTROL THAT THING!
IMAGINE A THOUSAND MORE LIKE HIM ROAMING THE EARTH!
JUST A FEW MINUTES LONGER. MAYBE I CAN STILL REACH INTO ITS MIND.
WE DON'T HAVE A FEW MINUTES! WE'RE GOING *NOW!* THIS BASE IS CRAWLING WITH 19XX SOLDIERS!
BARON, I CAN ASSURE YOU, I KNEW *NOTHING* OF ALEISTER'S TRUE PLAN!
I'VE ALWAYS TRUSTED YOU, ZEYNEP. IT WAS ALL *ALEISTER*.
HE WAS A SNIVELING PUP WHEN WE FOUND HIM, AND NOW HIS DELUSIONS OF GRANDEUR HAVE *DESTROYED* MONTHS OF WORK! THE COUNCIL OF BLACK FAUN ELDERS WILL SKIN HIM ALIVE FOR THIS, IF I DON'T DO IT FIRST!
NOW GET ME *OFF* THIS ISLAND!

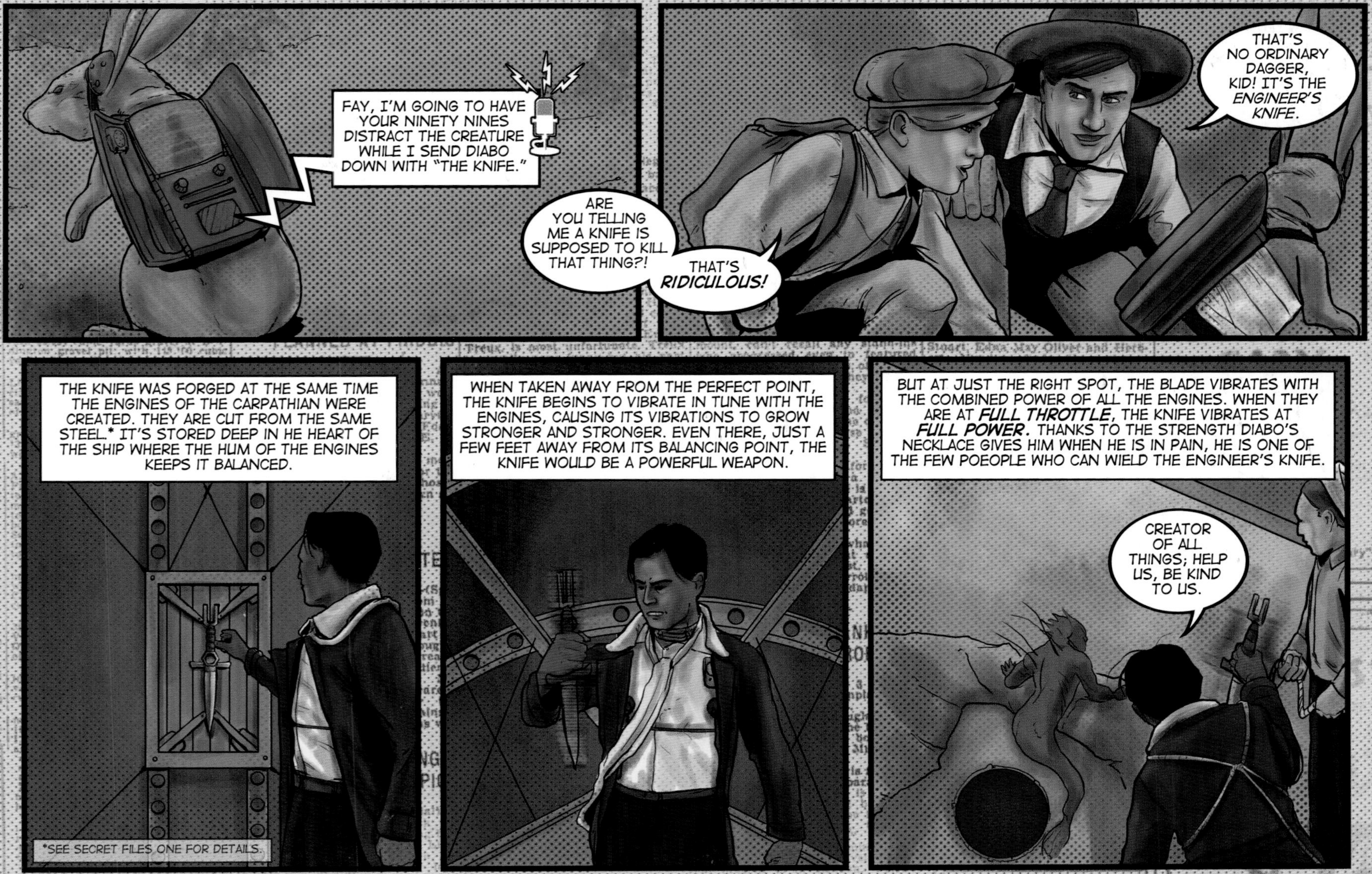

FAY, I'M GOING TO HAVE YOUR NINETY NINES DISTRACT THE CREATURE WHILE I SEND DIABO DOWN WITH "THE KNIFE."
ARE YOU TELLING ME A KNIFE IS SUPPOSED TO KILL THAT THING?!
THAT'S *RIDICULOUS!*
THAT'S NO ORDINARY DAGGER, KID! IT'S THE *ENGINEER'S* KNIFE.
THE KNIFE WAS FORGED AT THE SAME TIME THE ENGINES OF THE CARPATHIAN WERE CREATED. THEY ARE CUT FROM THE SAME STEEL.* IT'S STORED DEEP IN HE HEART OF THE SHIP WHERE THE HUM OF THE ENGINES KEEPS IT BALANCED.
*SEE SECRET FILES ONE FOR DETAILS.
WHEN TAKEN AWAY FROM THE PERFECT POINT, THE KNIFE BEGINS TO VIBRATE IN TUNE WITH THE ENGINES, CAUSING ITS VIBRATIONS TO GROW STRONGER AND STRONGER. EVEN THERE, JUST A FEW FEET AWAY FROM ITS BALANCING POINT, THE KNIFE WOULD BE A POWERFUL WEAPON.
BUT AT JUST THE RIGHT SPOT, THE BLADE VIBRATES WITH THE COMBINED POWER OF ALL THE ENGINES. WHEN THEY ARE AT ***FULL THROTTLE***, THE KNIFE VIBRATES AT ***FULL POWER***. THANKS TO THE STRENGTH DIABO'S NECKLACE GIVES HIM WHEN HE IS IN PAIN, HE IS ONE OF THE FEW POEOPLE WHO CAN WIELD THE ENGINEER'S KNIFE.
CREATOR OF ALL THINGS; HELP US, BE KIND TO US.

DIABO WILL HAVE TO STAB THE BEAST AS THE CAPTAIN TAKES THE ENGINES TO FULL POWER. THEN THE CAPTAIN WILL HAVE TO *KILL* THE ENGINES IMMEDIATELY OR EVEN DIABO MAY NOT SURVIVE.

LET US BE HAPPY ON EARTH; LET US LEAD OUR CHILDREN

TO A GOOD LIFE AND OLD AGE.*

*MOHAWK PRAYER

The 99s shot down any small flying creatures that made it through the gate. The Dagon began a shrieking scream that filled the valley and sent us all to our knees.

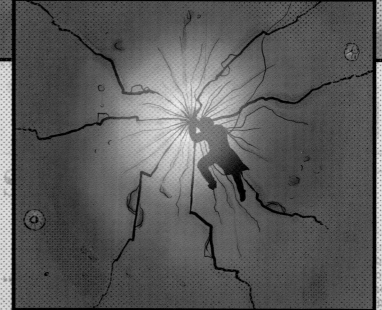

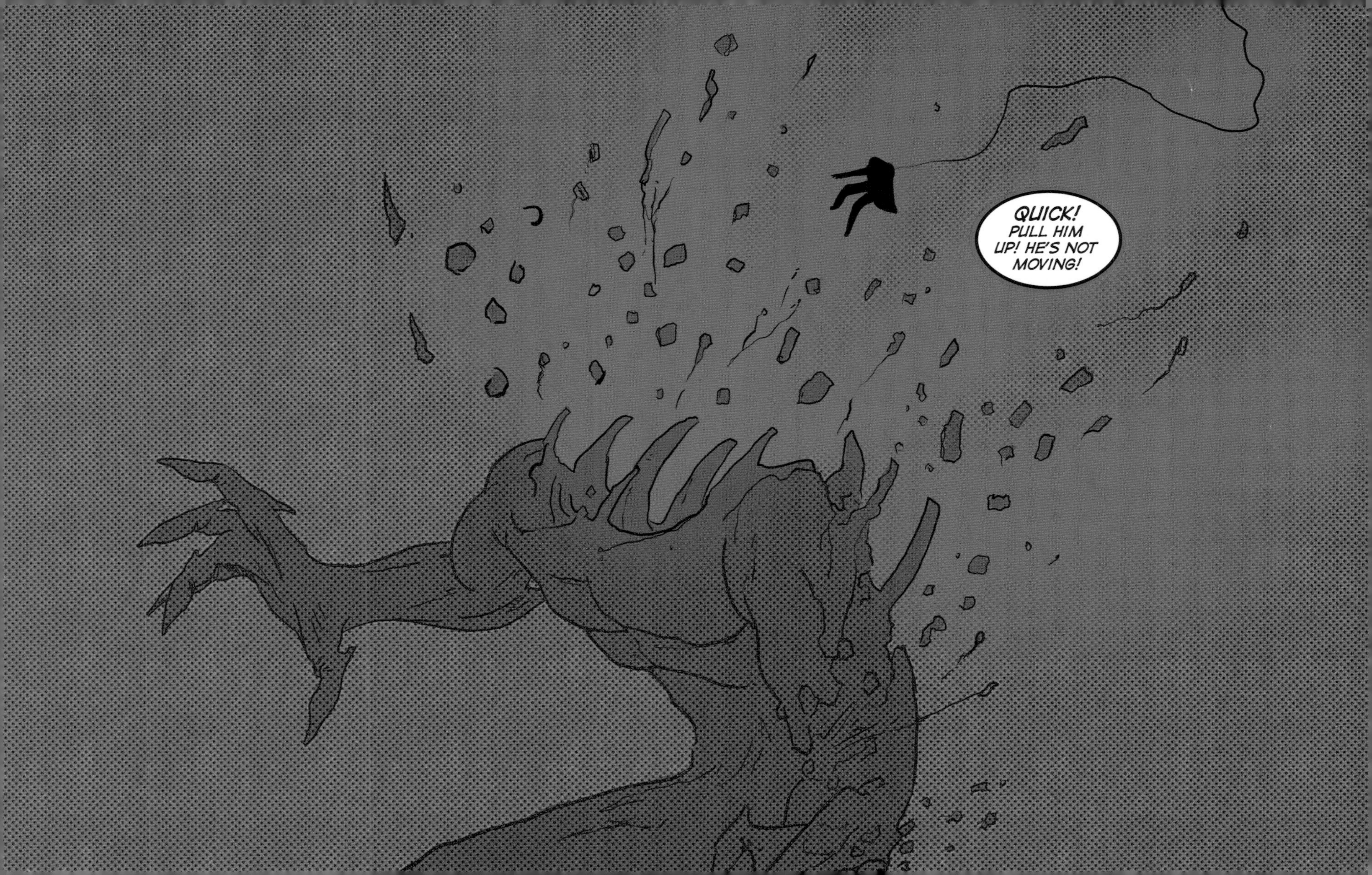
QUICK! PULL HIM UP! HE'S NOT MOVING!

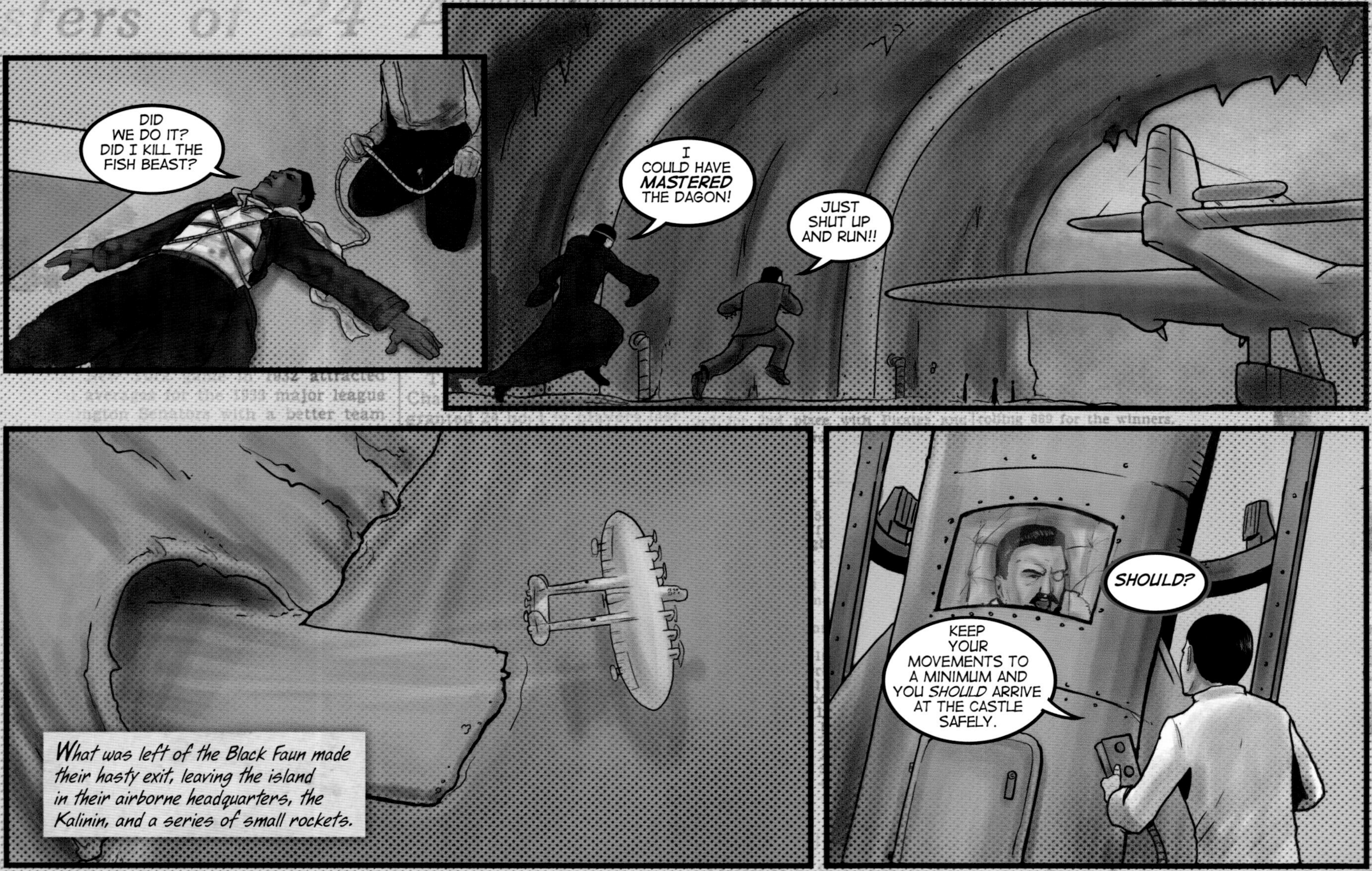
DID WE DO IT? DID I KILL THE FISH BEAST?
I COULD HAVE MASTERED THE DAGON!
JUST SHUT UP AND RUN!!
What was left of the Black Faun made their hasty exit, leaving the island in their airborne headquarters, the Kalinin, and a series of small rockets.
SHOULD?
KEEP YOUR MOVEMENTS TO A MINIMUM AND YOU SHOULD ARRIVE AT THE CASTLE SAFELY.

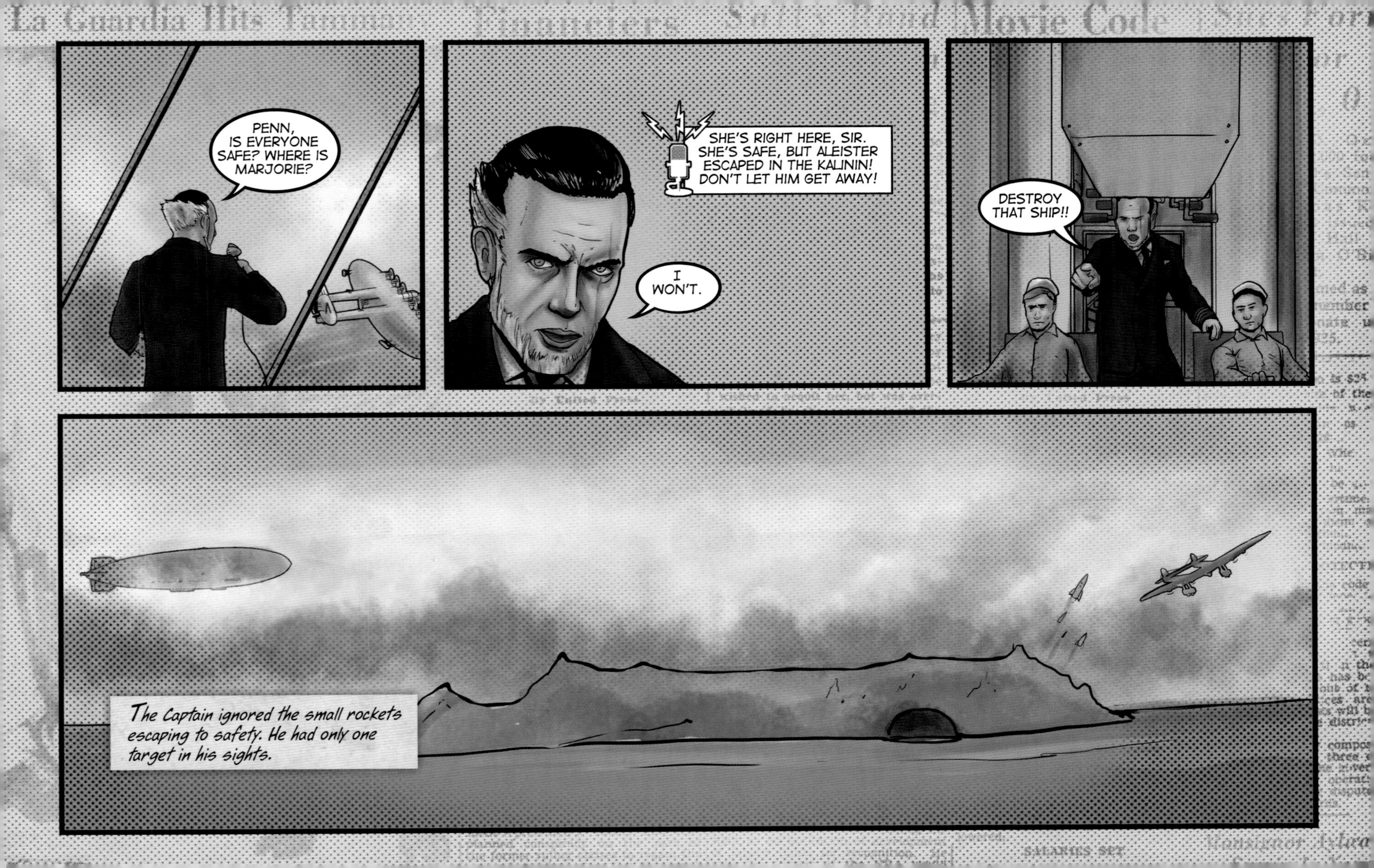
PENN, IS EVERYONE SAFE? WHERE IS MARJORIE?
SHE'S RIGHT HERE, SIR. SHE'S SAFE, BUT ALEISTER ESCAPED IN THE KALININ! DON'T LET HIM GET AWAY!
I WON'T.
DESTROY THAT SHIP!!
The Captain ignored the small rockets escaping to safety. He had only one target in his sights.

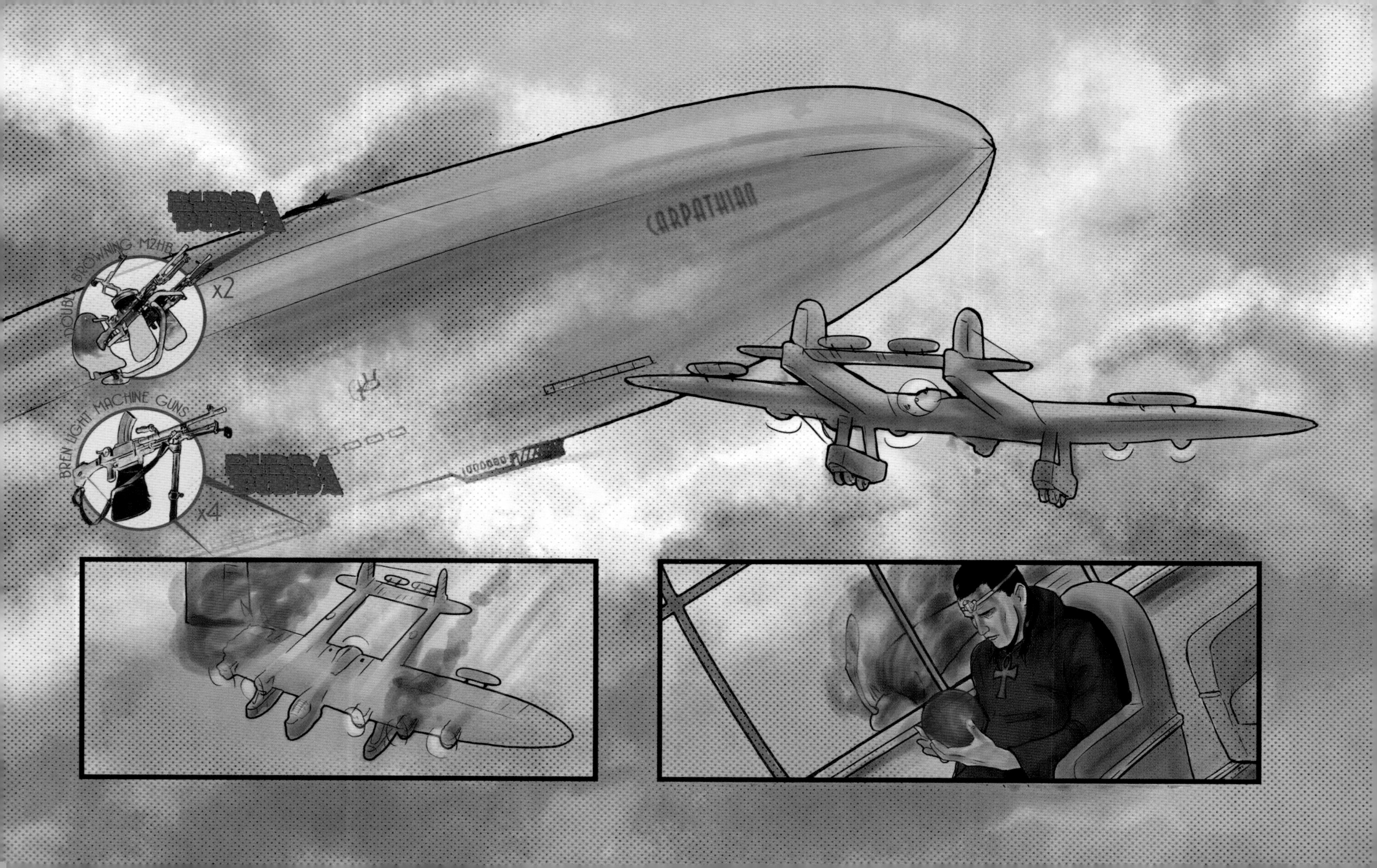

BUDDA BUDDA
CARPATHIAN
DOUBLE BROWNING M2HB
x2
BREN LIGHT MACHINE GUNS
x4
BUDDA BUDDA

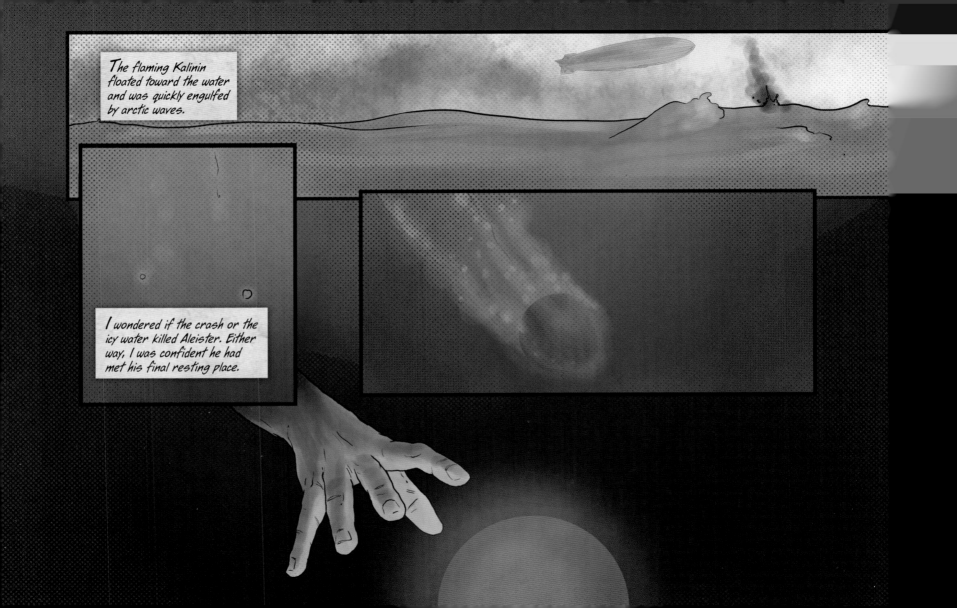

The flaming Kalinin floated toward the water and was quickly engulfed by arctic waves.

I wondered if the crash or the icy water killed Aleister. Either way, I was confident he had met his final resting place.

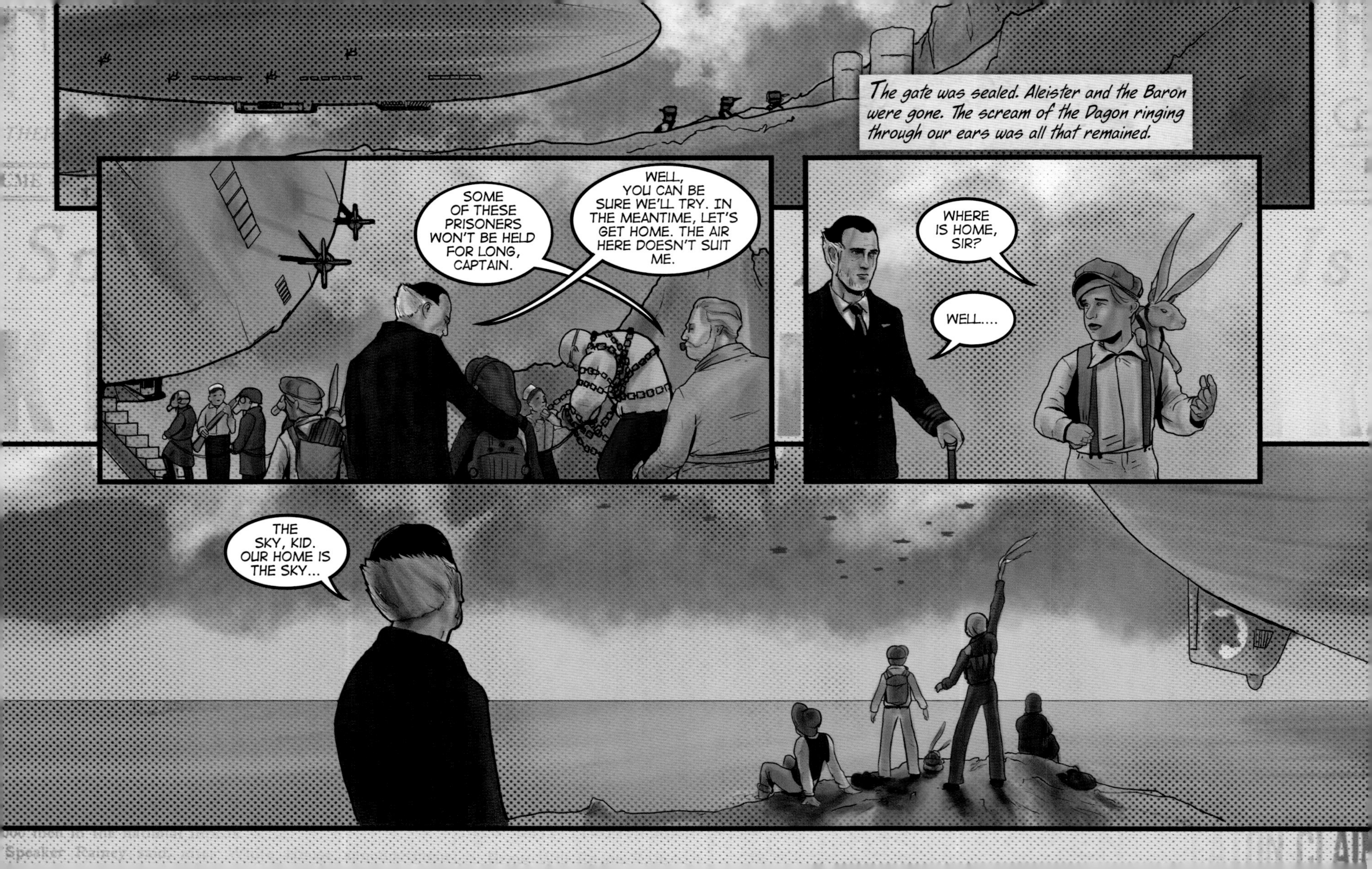
The gate was sealed. Aleister and the Baron were gone. The scream of the Dagon ringing through our ears was all that remained.
SOME OF THESE PRISONERS WON'T BE HELD FOR LONG, CAPTAIN.
WELL, YOU CAN BE SURE WE'LL TRY. IN THE MEANTIME, LET'S GET HOME. THE AIR HERE DOESN'T SUIT ME.
WHERE IS HOME, SIR?
WELL....
THE SKY, KID. OUR HOME IS THE SKY...

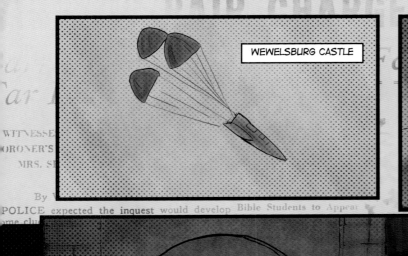

WEWELSBURG CASTLE

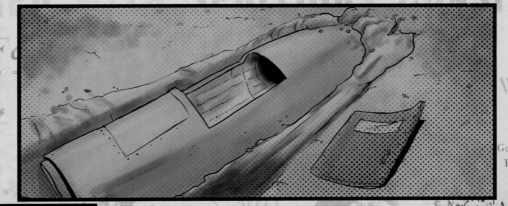

I WAS WONDERING WHEN THE *BLACK FAUN COUNCIL* WOULD SEND ITS THUGS.

THE WORLD IS CHANGING, *BARON*, AND THE ORDER OF THE BLACK FAUN HAS TO CHANGE ITS GOALS.

OUR FUTURE PLANS NO LONGER HAVE ROOM FOR YOU IN A LEADERSHIP POSITION.

AND PEOPLE LIKE ALEISTER FIT IN WITH YOUR FUTURE PLANS? YOU CAN IMPRISON ME, KILL ME, EXILE ME, BUT I PROMISE YOU...

YOU WON'T BE ABLE TO CONTROL THAT LEVEL OF *DESTRUCTION.*

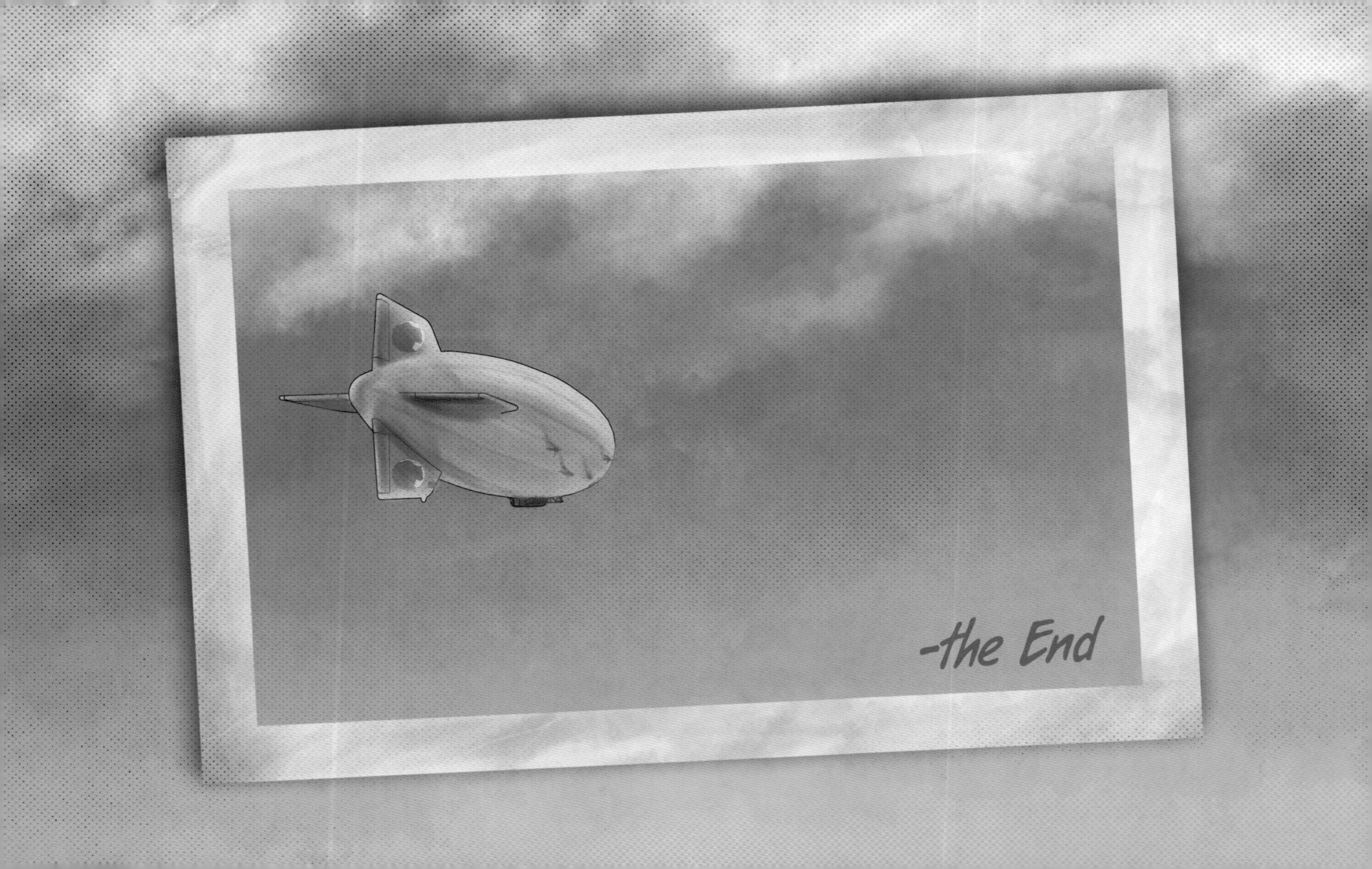
-the End

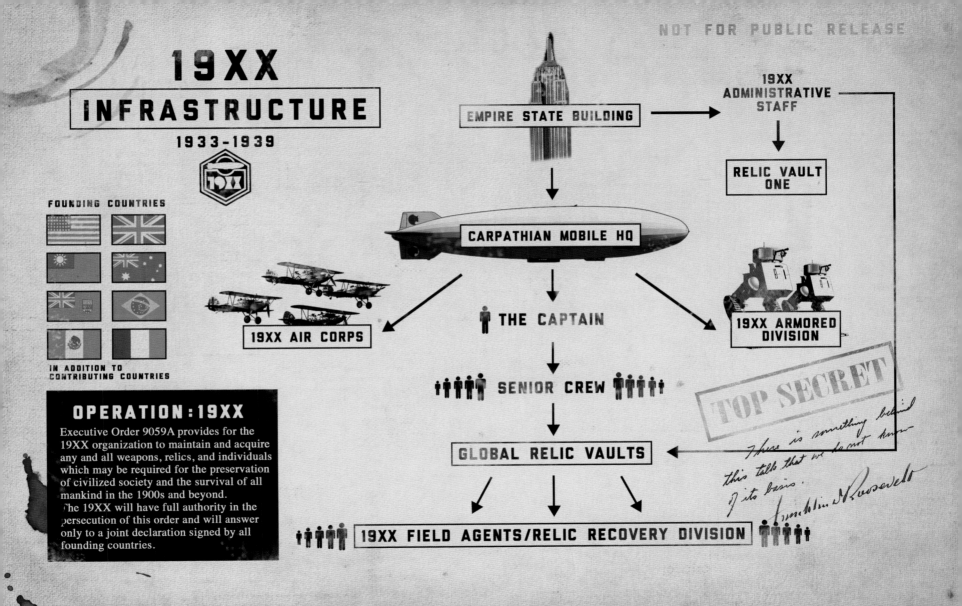

19XX

INFRASTRUCTURE

1933-1939

FOUNDING COUNTRIES

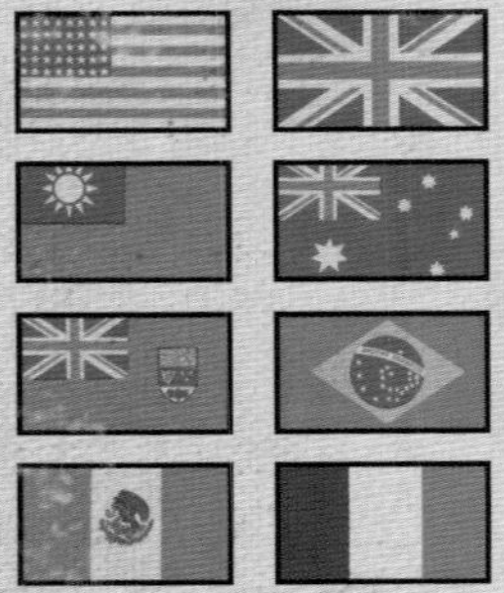

IN ADDITION TO
CONTRIBUTING COUNTRIES

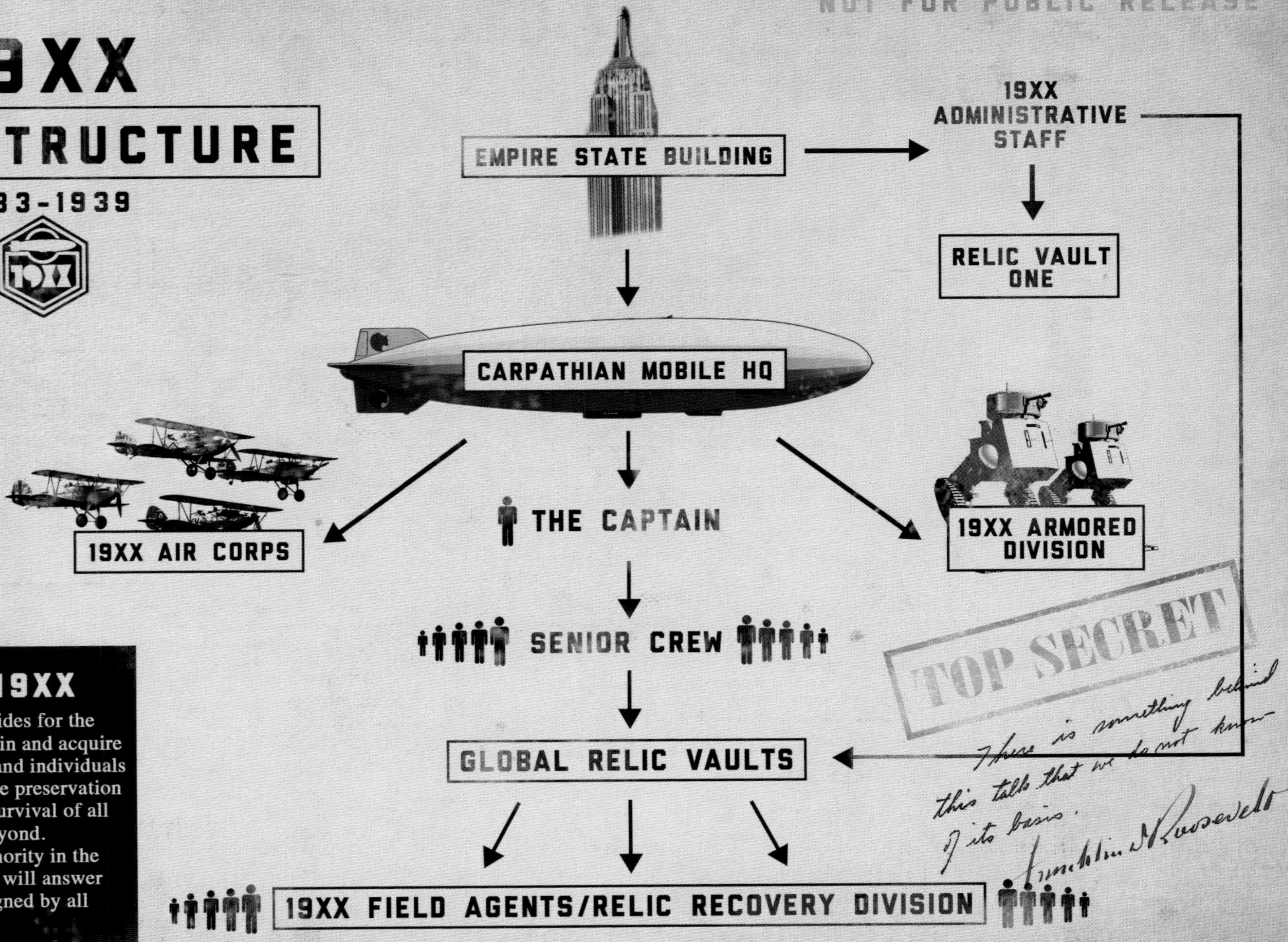
EMPIRE STATE BUILDING
19XX
ADMINISTRATIVE
STAFF
RELIC VAULT
ONE
CARPATHIAN MOBILE HQ
19XX AIR CORPS
THE CAPTAIN
19XX ARMORED
DIVISION
SENIOR CREW
GLOBAL RELIC VAULTS
19XX FIELD AGENTS/RELIC RECOVERY DIVISION
TOP SECRET
There is something behind
this talk that we do not know
of its basis.
Franklin D Roosevelt

OPERATION:19XX

Executive Order 9059A provides for the 19XX organization to maintain and acquire any and all weapons, relics, and individuals which may be required for the preservation of civilized society and the survival of all mankind in the 1900s and beyond.

The 19XX will have full authority in the persecution of this order and will answer only to a joint declaration signed by all founding countries.

Machines and magic

Soldiers
LOAN
for AMERICAN Civilians
CTORY LIBERTY LOAN

In writing this story, I wanted to create a work of fiction that was directly plugged in to historical reality. My goal was to take real events and real people and use them as a jumping-off point. Here are some of the real people who show up in Rise of the Black Faun and short descriptions of what made them interesting in real life.

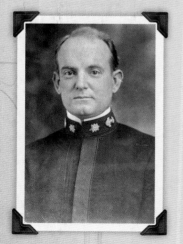

William A. Moffett
1869-1933

If you have a chance, be sure and visit the Moffett Field Air Museum in California. There, you will learn all about the man who was one of the most vocal advocates for the lighter-than-air airship program in the United States. Moffett earned his nickname the "Air Admiral" for his part in pioneering uses of aircraft in the Navy, including the use of aircraft carriers and the creation of the Navy Bureau of Aeronautics.

Nikola Tesla
1856-1943

An icon in the age of steam and diesel, not enough can be said about Tesla's influence on technology in the early part of the 20th century. His contributions to radio and electricity helped shape the modern world. Perhaps more valuable than his published works are the projects that no one ever saw. At least, that's what the U.S. government thought. When Tesla passed away in 1943, they seized all of his papers and analyzed them thoroughly for information on advanced weaponry.

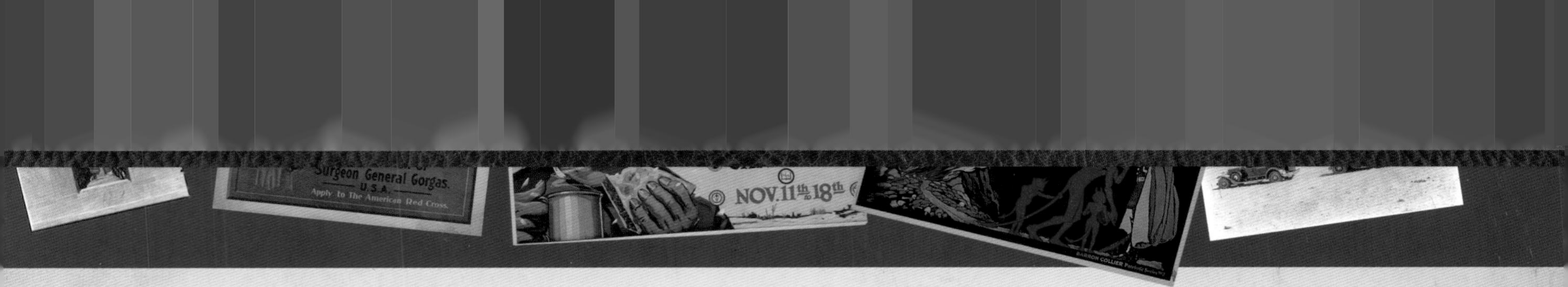
Surgeon General Gorgas.
U.S.A.
Apply to The American Red Cross.
NOV. 11th to 18th

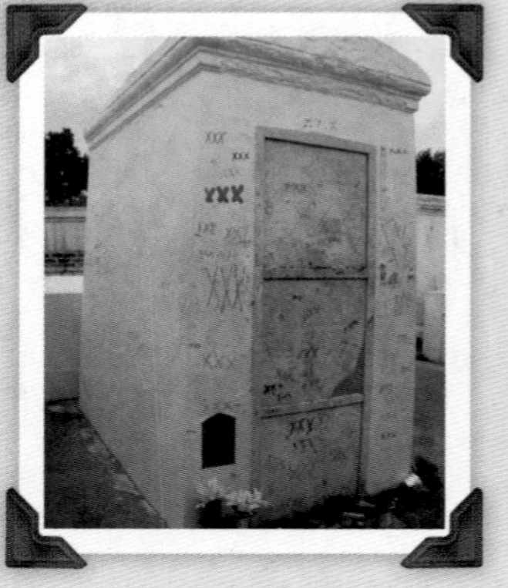

Marie Laveau
1794-1881

It's hard to take a step in New Orleans without seeing her name or picture in a shop window. Laveau used a combination of Black Magic and blackmail to wield influence in the French Quarter. She was said to have had a pet snake named Zombi, which added to her mystique as a Voodoo priestess.

Harry Houdini
1874-1926

The master of escape was also a skeptic, spending years trying to expose fake spiritualists. The interesting part about his career as a skeptic was the truth about his motives. Was he a man who had no belief in the after life and spent his last years trying to prove it? Or was he desperately trying to escape mortality, searching the globe for a shred of proof that the hereafter exists?

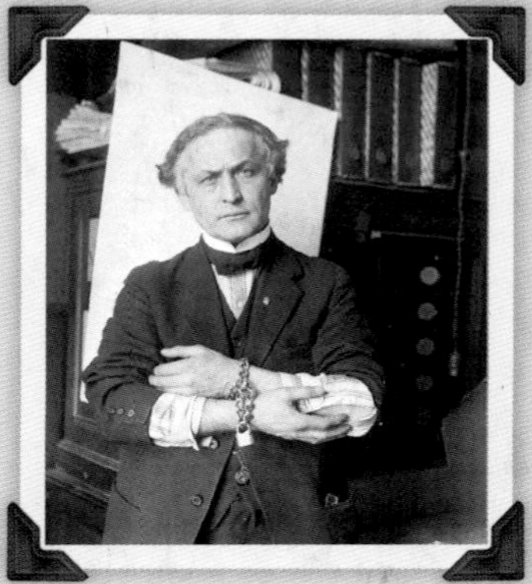

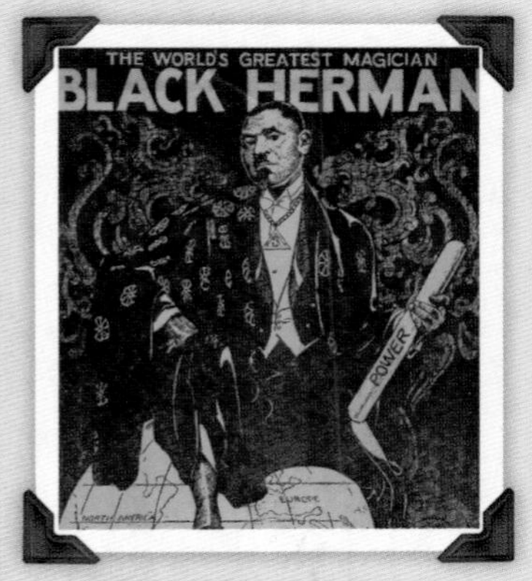
THE WORLD'S GREATEST MAGICIAN
BLACK HERMAN
POWER

Black Herman
1892-1934

Learning from Prince Herman, Black Herman eventually became the most popular African American magician of his time. He was one of the few black entertainers who played to a mixed audience of blacks and whites. After collapsing on stage and dying during a performance, Black Herman's assistant charged admission to view the body because no one in the audience actually believed he was dead.

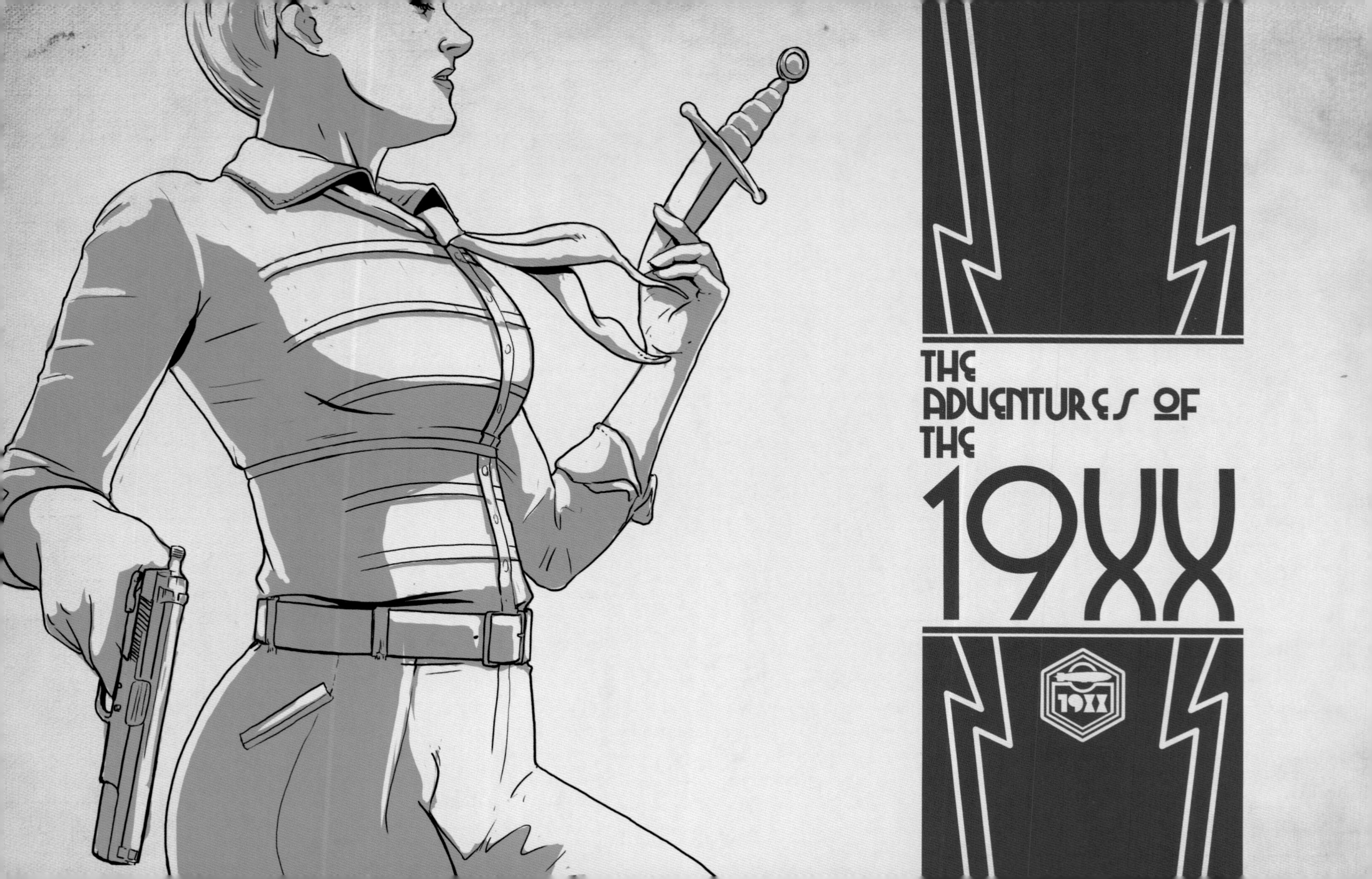

THE ADVENTURES OF THE 19XX

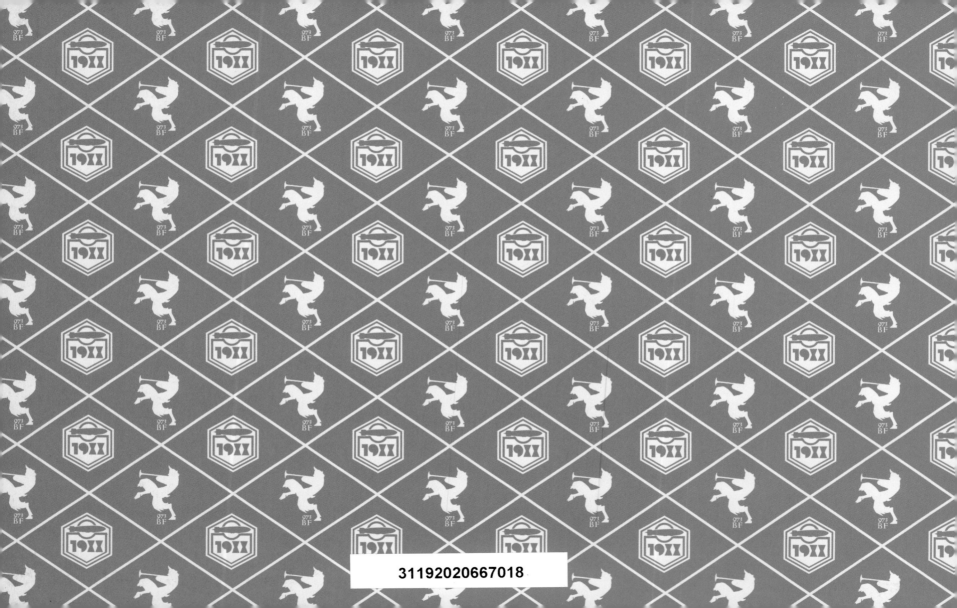

31192020667018